CELEBRATION

Books by Fern Michaels:

FERN MICHAELS

CELEBRATION

ZEBRA BOOKS
KENSINGTON PUBLISHING CORP.
http://www.kensingtonbooks.com

ZEBRA BOOKS are published by

Kensington Publishing Corp.
850 Third Avenue
New York, NY 10022

All Kensington titles, imprints, and distributed lines are available at special quantity discounts for bulk purchases for sales promotion, premiums, fund-raising, educational, or institutional use.

Special book excerpts or customized printings can also be created to fit specific needs. For details, write or phone the office of the Kensington Special Sales Manager: Attn. Special Sales Department. Kensington Publishing Corp., 850 Third Avenue, New York, NY 10022. Phone: 1-800-221-2647.

Zebra and the Z logo Reg. U.S. Pat. & TM Off.

ISBN-13: 978-1-4201-0842-2
ISBN-10: 1-4201-0842-5

First Kensington Hardcover Printing: March 1999
First Zebra Mass-Market Printing: January 2000

20   19   18

Printed in the United States of America

For Cher Hildebrand, Pat Walker,
and all those beautiful Goldenray Yorkshire terriers

Prologue

May, 1963

Kristine Summers gathered up her books the moment the school bus ground to a stop. She turned around to look at Logan Kelly to see if he was going to follow her. He was staring out the window. It was what she expected. Still it hurt. Sometimes Logan was so thoughtless, so inconsiderate.

She stood at the farm-road entrance waving until the big yellow bus was out of sight. Then her shoulders slumped. She wanted to cry so badly. For some reason she always wanted to cry when Logan was away from her. Once she'd asked him if he ever felt the same way. He'd said yes, but only after a very long pause.

Logan was still miffed that she wasn't going north to college in the fall. Like it was really her fault. Sometimes he just refused to understand. He wasn't going to understand that she couldn't go to the prom with him next week, either. She should have told him today but was unable to make her tongue say the words in the lunchroom. Or was it the fear that if she told him, he would take someone else? If she waited till the last minute, no other girl would go with him at the eleventh hour. It took weeks of planning, getting just the right dress, the right shoes, getting one's hair done professionally, and all the other stuff that went with going to the most important event of the year.

As Kristine trudged down the road, she wished, the way she wished every day of her life, that she lived in town instead of way out here where there was nothing to do and nowhere to go except another farm. If she wanted to, she could run across the fields and be at Logan's house before the bus got there. She'd done it before, the wind in her hair, her feet winged. Logan had never reciprocated. Oh, he'd come to the farm, but always on horseback. He never stayed, saying her parents didn't like him. She didn't know if it was true or not. They'd put obstacles in her path but had never come right out and said they didn't like Logan. Logan said you had to be deaf, dumb, and blind not to see their feelings. He made her feel stupid when she defended her parents. Logan made her feel stupid a lot of the time, especially in front of his friends. If she didn't love him so much, she wouldn't care. She never let him see how he hurt her, preferring to cry into her pillow at night.

"Pick up your feet, girl," Jason Summers bellowed. "I need you down at the barn."

"Okay, Daddy. I just have to change my clothes."

"Make it fast and don't be mooning over that prom dress hanging in your room either."

"Okay, Daddy." She knew better than to argue. Just once she wished her father would call her by her name or one that sounded endearing, like honey or sweetheart. He was like Logan's parents, cold and hard. Her mother wasn't much better.

In her room, Kristine shed her clothes and pulled on her coveralls. She tried not to look at the frothy dress hanging on the closet door. She'd bought the material herself in town and had taken it straight to her home economics class, where Evelyn Russell had agreed to help her make the dress so it would be ready for the prom. Miss Russell had even delivered it to the farm so Kristine wouldn't have to carry it home on the bus.

She'd fallen in love with the material, which was the color of the spring bluebells that dotted the fields. The yards and yards of tulle that Miss Russell helped her sew onto the waist made her feel like a fairy princess. Her mother had gasped, then smiled when she saw it. Not so her father. He'd frowned, wanting to know what she was going to wear under the skinny, lacy straps that exposed her neck and shoulders. Right then she'd told the first lie of her life to her father, saying a shawl went with the dress that tucked around the straps. Her mother had actually winked slyly at her, recognizing the lie. Even then her mother must have known she wouldn't be going to the prom with Logan. Sometimes she almost hated her parents.

Kristine took a moment to stare at the lovely gown. Evelyn Russell said it would be the prettiest dress at the prom and went on to say she might even be picked prom queen. It was a given that Logan would be king. King Logan Kelly. Queen Kristine Summers. Tears dripped down Kristine's cheeks.

"Kristine, your father's waiting!" her mother called from the bottom of the steps.

"I'm coming, Mom." With one last longing look at the gown she'd never get to wear, Kristine ran through the hall and down the steps.

"Is something wrong, Kristine?" her mother asked.

"Of course something is wrong, Mom. I can't go to the prom. I worked for months on that dress. I used up all my spending money on it. You know how important the prom is to me. Now Logan's probably going to take someone else. How do you think I feel knowing that? It was bad enough when you and Dad said I couldn't go to Cornell. I didn't think you'd forbid me the prom, too. I don't want to go to the community college. It's going to take me a long time to become a vet. I need to go to the right schools."

"Ladies in our family do not become veterinarians. Teaching is a suitable profession. Nursing is acceptable."

Kristine's shoulders slumped. She was never going to win this battle. Eventually, though, she'd win the war. She offered up a parting shot, "I have no intention of becoming a teacher or a nurse. I would be a failure at those professions. I'm going to marry Logan Kelly. I don't care if you like it or not."

"Don't you sass your mother, young lady. I won't tolerate it."

Kristine whirled around. "You don't tolerate anything, do you, Mom? You don't care about me at all. If you did, you'd help me. You know how bad I want to go to the prom. All you care about are those animals in the barn and Daddy. Why'd you ever have me in the first place? I'm never going to forgive you for this. You aren't a mother, you're . . . You're like some evil stepmother. I've been a good daughter, Mom, I really have. I've always been respectful, I get up at four-thirty to help in the barns, I clean house and cook and do laundry. I never, ever, gave you one moment of distress. You don't have to go to Roanoke. You could go the following week. Do you know how I know that, Mom? I called the Jetsons and asked them myself. You lied to me. My own mother lying to me. I'm never going to forgive you for that, either."

"That will be enough, young lady!"

"No, that's not enough. I'm not going down to the barn today."

Kristine ran then, her barn boots digging up the soft earth, the clumps flying behind her. She was breathless, falling to the ground when she finally reached the Kelly front yard. "Logan!" she screamed as loud as she could.

Logan raised the window on the second floor. "Kris! What are you doing here? I'll be right down!"

"Hide me," she cried as she threw herself into his arms. "My father's going to come after me. I had a row with my mother. Hurry, Logan, where can we go?"

"The woods, I guess. Is he going to come with a shotgun?"

"If he had one, he would. I don't think that old blunderbuss hanging in the living room works. We need to hurry, Logan. I'm scared."

"What the hell did you do, Kris?" Logan asked, looking over his shoulder.

"I sassed Mom and didn't go down to the barn to work the way I always do after school. Listen, Logan, I need to tell you something."

"We're still too close to the field. He'll spot us right away. Run, Kris."

"Logan, I can't run anymore. I ran all the way here. They know this is where I'll come. Did your parents see me?"

"Nah. They're in town. Mom goes to the beauty parlor on Fridays and today is Dad's week to get his haircut. No one's in the house. Okay, I think this is far enough. Now what do you want to tell me?"

"I can't go to the prom, Logan."

"What are you saying?" Logan hissed.

"I'm saying I can't go to the prom. My parents are going to Roanoke to the Jetsons. They lied to me. They don't want me going with you. I called the Jetsons and Mrs. Jetson said the following week would be better for their visit but that my parents insisted on next week. Oh, Logan, I worked so hard on my gown. It's so beautiful, and now I'm never going to get to wear it."

"Now what am I supposed to do, Kris? We had a good chance of being prom king and queen. This is shit for the birds. Can't you get around your parents? Did you cry and do all that girl stuff?"

"That doesn't work in our house. I have to do what I'm told. I'm not going back there. I mean it. If you bring me your sleeping bag and some food, I can camp out here. Let them think I ran away. Maybe they'll appreciate me then."

"Kristine, what about the prom?"

"What about it, Logan? I can't go. Are you still going to go?" Kristine felt her heart jump around in her chest as she waited for his reply.

"Just because you can't go doesn't mean I can't. My

parents are dreary, too, but they wouldn't stop me from going to the prom.''

"Are you saying you want to take someone else?''

"I don't *want* to take someone else. How's it going to look me going stag? Everyone knows you're my girl. Are you going to tell everyone your parents won't let you go? They'll laugh you right out of school. I'll say you're sick.''

"Who . . . who will you take?''

"Maybe Ellie Norris.''

Kristine started to cry. "You could stay home with me. You could come over to the farm and it will be just us. I'd like that. Your parents wouldn't even need to know.''

"Maybe I could do that after the prom. We could *fool around* if no one is going to be around.''

Kristine cried harder.

"You gotta do something, Kris,'' Logan said. "First they said you can't go to Cornell. You're Cornell material. All your teachers said so. Now this. I'm only going to see you summers.''

"We can write letters. I'll write every day.''

"It's not like your parents are poor, Kris. They make bundles of money breeding those show dogs.''

Kristine continued to cry. "I know. Are you really going to take Ellie Norris to the prom?''

"Well, sure. I'm going to go up to the house and call her. I'll bring the sleeping bag and some sandwiches. Do you want a soda?''

"Are you going to buy her a corsage and kiss her good night?'' Kris sobbed.

"Only if I have to. Stop crying, Kris. You don't look nice when you blubber like that. You need to blow your nose, too.''

"Sometimes you sound like my father,'' Kristine said as she stifled her tears.

"I won't be long. Don't go anywhere.''

The moment Kristine knew Logan was safely in the house, she got up and started the long walk home. Better to go home and take her punishment before her father sent the sheriff out to look for her. It didn't matter now. Her little act of defiance was already costing her dearly.

Kristine applied her makeup, curled her hair, and slipped into her prom dress. The dogs would love it. She tripped down to the barn, holding her skirts high so they wouldn't drag in the dirt. With the barn door closed tightly, Kristine let all the dogs and pups out of their little stalls. As they swirled around the barn, sniffing everything in sight, Kristine plugged in her record player. A dog cuddled in each arm, she danced to the strains of the music, tears rolling down her cheeks. Each dog had a turn around the floor to the mellow voice of Nat King Cole.

Exhausted, Kristine toppled to the pile of hay used for the kennels. The dogs frisked about, sniffing and tearing at the tulle on her gown. She laughed and cried. "I bet you think I'm good enough to be a queen, don't you?" The miniature Teacup Yorkies were everywhere, licking at her tears, nibbling at her ears, pulling at her hair. Finally, they settled down in the straw next to the sleeping girl.

It was late, after one in the morning, when Logan Kelly cracked the barn door slightly to look inside. The sudden uproar made him slam it shut. "It's me, Kris."

"You have to wait until I get the dogs back in their stalls, Logan." *Thank you, God, for letting him come. Thankyou, thankyou, thankyou.*

"It's okay, you can come in now. I'm so glad you came, Logan. How was the prom? Did you have a good time? Did Ellie look nice? Did you kiss her good night?"

"Is that your prom dress? You ruined it. Why'd you do that, Kris? There's dog poop all over the hem. Jeez," Logan said, a look of disgust on his face.

Please don't let me cry. Please, God, don't let me cry. "I think, Logan Kelly, you need to go home. The prom is over. I don't even care if you kissed Ellie Norris. I danced with my dogs all night. I don't care if there is dog poop on my dress. If you'd been a real boyfriend, you would have stayed here with me instead of taking Ellie Norris to the prom. Maybe my parents are right about you. Go home now so I can throw this gown in the trash and go to bed."

"Don't you want to hear about me being named prom king?"

"No, I do not want to hear about you being named prom king. Don't ever tell me about it."

"It's not my fault you missed the prom. Lay the blame on your parents where it belongs," Logan blustered.

"I will, but I'm laying it on you, too. You said you loved me. If you did, Logan, you would have stayed here with me. You go home and think about that."

"Okay, I will," Logan said, stomping out of the barn.

Kristine checked the dogs one last time, turned the lights low, locked the barn door, and walked up to the house, where she stripped off the prom gown in the kitchen, bundled it into a brown grocery bag, and tossed it in the trash can on the back porch.

Logan Kelly didn't love her.

It was all just one big, bad dream.

PART I

⌒

Bremen,
Germany
1987

1

Kristine Kelly propped her chin on her elbow to better observe her husband's slick, naked body. She felt a second burst of passion but knew she had to squelch it. Instead, she stared boldly at Logan's hard, wet body, aware that he was staring just as boldly at her. How was it, she wondered, that after twenty years of making love to the same man, she could feel exactly the same as she had felt on her wedding night? She was about to voice the question aloud when Logan said, "Was it as good for you as it was for me?" She squirmed closer, savoring the slickness of their two bodies meshed together. Was it her imagination or did Logan's words sound practiced, rehearsed, even flat? Where was the light teasing banter that was always present after one of their marathon lovemaking sessions? Why wasn't Logan lighting a cigarette the way he usually did? A cigarette they both puffed on. According to Logan, a cigarette was the ultimate conclusion to a satisfying session of lovemaking. She didn't know if she agreed or not. If the choice was hers, she would opt for serious pillow talk and a second round of lovemaking. The cigarette was always better the second time around. She waited.

"Well?"

"Of course," she said, offering up her standard response. "I feel like crying," she blurted.

"Are you going to cave in on me now, Kris? We've been over this a hundred times. You said you were okay with it. The kids said they were okay with it. Thirty days is not an eternity. You've been a model military wife, so don't go all wimpy on me now and screw it up. We've always gone by the book. It is not the end of the world. When you return to the States you will be so busy you won't have time to miss me. You need to register the kids for school, get the farmhouse ready, buy a car, get ready for the holidays. It's the way it is, Kris. What *is* your problem?''

Kristine picked up on the impatience in her husband's voice. So it wasn't her imagination after all. Logan was annoyed with her, and he wasn't bothering to hide his feelings. She felt the urge to cry again and didn't know why. No matter what she said or how she said it, her voice was going to be defensive-sounding. She struggled for a light tone. "I guess it has something to do with your long career coming to such an abrupt end. Twenty years is a long time, Logan. I think we handled it well. Like you said, we went by the book and never complained. We were a family of good little soldiers. I wish for your sake that you could have gone all the way and made general because I know it's what you wanted. I have to take issue with the medical board. Why does having just one kidney prevent you from getting promoted and staying in for thirty years? You never faltered, you did your job, you went by the book, and we all played by the rules. It's not fair. I know it's bothering you because it's bothering me. I don't like it when you pretend, Logan."

"I don't want to talk about it, Kris. It is what it is. I'll muster out in two weeks and two weeks later you'll see me driving up the road. Make sure you have a big, four-layer chocolate cake and a very large pan of your lasagna waiting for me. Two bottles of wine. Good stuff now. One for you and one for me. After that, if we're still standing, we'll make love all night long. How do you feel about that?"

"It sounds wonderful, Logan. I wish I could turn off my emotions the way you can, but I can't. The truth is, I'm going to miss you terribly because you're going to be half a world away. Figure it out, Logan, how many miles is it from Leesburg, Virginia, to Bremen, Germany?"

This time the impatience in her husband's voice was more noticeable. "The mileage isn't important. I'll call and write. I've never let you down, so where are these negative feelings coming from? Are you telling me now that you aren't capable of taking the kids back to the States and getting the house ready? I've always admired the fact that you were your own person. There isn't anything you can't do if you set your mind to it. It's just thirty days! We've been separated before, and you never acted like this. I need to know what it is, specifically, that's bothering you."

Kristine looked her husband in the eye. He was almost snarling now, and she hated it when he got like this. "It's the end of a chapter for us. The end of our lives in the military. The kids don't know anything else. Nor do I. I guess being a civilian again scares me. I try not to think about it, but most times I lose the battle. It's all going to be so *new*. The kids are scared, too, even though they've been managing to bluff their way through the days these past few weeks. Furthermore, I just don't understand why we can't stay and go home together. Why do we need to go first and you follow thirty days later? We should be here with you when you walk out those doors for the last time. I put in my twenty years, too, Logan."

"Kris, we settled this months ago. Our belongings are en route. Major Tattersol is ready to move in here the moment we move out. You said you could handle this." Logan swung his legs over the side of the bed and stomped to the bathroom. "You do realize you just ruined what was supposed to be a perfect evening, don't you?" Logan shot over his shoulder before he slammed the door shut. Kristine cringed when she heard the lock snick into place.

Kristine buried her face in the pillow. *Damn, I can't do anything right. Perfect evening, my foot. What is wrong with saying how I feel? Doesn't he understand how much I love him, how much I'm going to miss him? Thirty days could be an eternity when one has to cope with three teenagers who have a hate on for everything in the world, including their parents. Shit!* She hadn't even mentioned their finances. Her eyes filled. *I'm sick and tired of being a good little soldier. I never wanted to be a soldier. All I ever wanted was to be a good wife and a good mother.* She moved then to curl into a fetal position, at the same time noticing the two rolls of extra flesh that moved upward to press against her breasts. She yanked at the sheet as she wiped at her tears with the hem of the pillowcase. The evening was not going the way she had planned. In four short hours she would be herding the children out the door to a waiting car for the ride to the airport. She needed to do something, but had no idea what it was.

Kristine squeezed her eyes shut as she ran the scene over in her mind. The kids would be cranky, mouthy, and hateful because they were leaving their friends, enduring the long plane ride home, and taking up residence in a place they could barely remember. The worst thing of all for the three of them was the prospect of starting over in a new school. She'd spent whole days trying to reassure her children things would be wonderful if they would just open up to the move. Nothing had worked, probably because they sensed her own anxieties and fears, something a good soldier should never reveal.

Kristine jerked upright when the bathroom door opened. She stared at her husband, who was fully dressed. "Where . . . where are you going at this time of night, Logan?" she whispered. She hated the sound of fear in her voice.

"I'm going to take a walk. I need some fresh air. Look, Kris, I'm sorry. I guess I'm just as *antsy* as you are. Believe it or not, this whole thing is just as traumatic for me as it is for you."

"I love you," Kris whispered again.

"I know, Kris, I know. I won't be long. Why don't you try and get some sleep?"

"Is that what the book says, sleep? How can I sleep, Logan? Something is wrong here. I can sense it. It's not my imagination."

"Yes, Kris, it is your imagination. This separation is just

a little rocky bump. We've had rocky bumps before. Thirty days is just thirty days. I expected more from you, Kris."

Kristine sighed. She was about to throw off the sheet and swing her legs over the side of the bed until she remembered the two rolls of fat. "Go for your walk. When you get back, I'll make some coffee."

Logan blew his wife a kiss before he left the house. Kristine's heart fluttered in her chest when she heard the front door close.

She headed for the shower, her shoulders shaking with unhappiness. Under the tepid spray she allowed her mind to conjure up the early days of her marriage to Logan Kelly. They were so happy when they said their vows and walked under the crossed swords at West Point. The twins came first, then Tyler came along shortly afterward. Logan had been delirious with joy just the way she had been. It was wonderful living all over the world. Her children spoke four languages, as she did, thanks to their multifaceted education. She was one of the rare wives who loved life in the military, but she didn't love the stupid rule book Logan insisted they live by. He could recite chapter and verse at the drop of a hat. She also knew the book by heart, which was all the more reason to hate it, and her children hated it even more than she did. Logan lived by it, page by page, word by word. Would he discard it when he got back to the States or would they continue to live by it? Logan's rationale would be that the book had served them well for twenty years and to tamper with it in the private sector would be sacrilegious.

As Kris stepped from the shower, towel in hand, her thoughts stayed with her. She wrapped her body in one of the few remaining towels, then dabbed at eyes that were now red-rimmed. Early on, Logan had sworn he would make general, go all the way, maybe even become a five-star. They'd played a game in those early years about the things they would do, how they would act when the fifth star was pinned on his shoulder. How sad for Logan that it could never come to pass. He had said he accepted being felled by a rare kidney disease in his seventeenth year in the military, knowing he would get passed over because his medical condition would be a blight on his record. He'd slapped her once, shouting to be left alone when she'd tried to console him. She needed to give him space now to come to terms with what Logan considered betrayal on the army's part in giving him a medical discharge, something he fought against and lost. He had a right to be bitter, but he didn't have the right to take his bitterness out on her. She'd wanted tonight to be perfect so that Logan would remember their last night and look forward to the time when they'd all be together again back in the States. Now it was all spoiled. Here she was taking a shower in the middle of the night while her husband was out walking alone. She crossed her fingers and offered up a little prayer that Logan's attitude wasn't a harbinger of things to come.

Thirty minutes later, Kristine was in the kitchen, fully dressed and making coffee. She looked in dismay at the small amount of coffee left in the can. Logan liked his coffee black and strong, the way most of his colleagues liked it. There was barely enough left to make two full cups, and at best it was going to be weak. She'd cleaned out everything from the ancient refrigerator because Logan was going to stay at the barracks until it was time for him to leave. The new tenants would move in the moment their belongings were unloaded from the truck. The army did not sit around sucking its thumb when it came to the comfort of one of its officers.

When the coffee finished perking, Kris poured a small amount into a cup, leaving the rest for her husband. She sipped at the coffee, her eyes on the blackness outside the kitchen window. She shouldn't be sitting here alone. Her husband should be with her, holding her hand, telling her things would be okay. The kids hadn't wanted to stay home with her either, preferring to spend their last night with their friends. She'd begged them to stay home with her and Logan, but the three of them had kicked up a fuss.

In the end she'd given in rather than stare at their miserable faces all evening. She looked at the clock. Ten minutes past four. Tom Zepack would drive them. Logan would say his good-byes at the door because he had to report for duty at six o'clock. And she still didn't have the bankbooks from Virginia. Logan had said everything was in the glove compartment of the car.

Her coffee finished, Kris meandered out to the car parked at the side of the house. She withdrew the small packet with her name on it, carrying it back to the house. Relieved that she hadn't forgotten, she slipped the envelope into her purse. She wished she knew more about their finances, but Logan had always handled them. It would be nice, though, to know how much her husband's pension would be once they were home. She knew they would be more than comfortable, thanks to the check that came every month from her parents' estate. Logan was going to do some consulting work, and she'd given serious thought to starting up her parents' business again. She could breed the world-class dogs her parents had bred for decades prior to their deaths. She was actually excited about working at her own business. With the monthly check from her parents' estate, Logan's pension, and whatever she was able to bring in, the kids would be able to go to the best colleges in the country.

Life was going to be wonderful, she told herself, once they settled in and adjusted to farm life in Leesburg, Virginia. They could renew old friendships, join clubs, get involved in community affairs. When the twins went off to college next year, and Tyler the following year, they would have the house to themselves and a twenty-four-hour-a-day marriage, the way it had been before the kids came along. Yes, life would be good, very good, provided that Logan threw away the damn rule book. She poured another inch of coffee into her cup. It tasted like colored water. Logan would surely have something to say about it.

She heard her children before she saw them as they

bounded into the house, snapping and snarling at one another. It was obvious to Kris they hadn't slept.

Tom Zepack held the door for Logan, a frown on his face. Even from this distance, Kris could smell liquor on her husband's breath. For some strange reason it elated her, proving, she thought, that this parting was just as hard on him as it was on her. She smiled. She would be upbeat if it killed her. No tears, no clutching, no sobbing. Maybe she should just pat him on the cheek and say something flippant like, "I'll see you when I see you. Let's go, kids." Could she do that? Never in a million years. She could try, though.

"Time to go!" Tom Zepack said.

"Do you have everything, Kris?" Logan asked.

"Yes. You know me. I was packed two weeks ago. We're ready."

The kids barreled out to the car, Tom Zepack on their trail.

Kristine sucked in her breath. "I made some coffee, Logan. It's on the weak side because there wasn't enough left. I guess I cut it too close. Rinse the pot and throw it away or leave it for the new officer and his wife. Remember to take the wet towels with you."

"Yeah, sure. Ah, listen, Kris, I'm sorry. I acted like a real ass earlier."

"It's okay, Logan. We're all upset. We all knew this day was coming. Even though we thought we were prepared, we weren't. I guess I better get going. Tom is such a slow, careful driver. I don't want to miss the plane. Take care of yourself. Call me so I can meet you at the airport when you have your flight information."

"Kris?"

"Yes."

"We had a good life, didn't we?"

"The best. We've been happy. We have three wonderful kids. This move is hard on them because they know it's the last one. As Macala said, from here on in everything *counts*."

"You sound strange, Kris. You aren't going . . ."

"No, I'm not going to make a scene. Take care of yourself, and hopefully we'll all be together for Christmas. I know just where I'm going to put the tree, too. I do love you, Logan. I just want you to know I will always love you."

Logan nodded. "I feel the same way, Kris. Don't make this any harder than it is. Go on, Tom's waiting."

Go on, Tom's waiting. That was all she was going to get? "See you," she said in a choked voice.

"Bye, Dad," the kids shouted from the car.

"Bye," he shouted in return.

Kris climbed into the car, tears streaming down her cheeks. If nothing else, she had at least waited until her back was turned before she allowed the tears to flow. She looked out of the car window, expecting to see Logan outlined in the open doorway. The door was shut. She couldn't even wave good-bye.

"Relax, Mom, thirty days will go by just like this," Macala said, snapping her fingers.

"Thirty whole days without that damn book," Mike, her twin, said happily.

"I like the book. It's how things get done. Everyone needs structure in their life," sixteen-year-old Tyler said, slouching down in the corner of the car.

"That's a crock, and you know it," Mike said. "That stupid book stinks. You're just a suck-up. Get over it. The book is history."

"Hear! Hear!" his twin said.

Kris continued to cry.

Chaplain Tom Zepack stared at the road in front of him, wondering what lay in store for the Kelly family once they returned to the States. With God's help they would all survive and lead happy productive lives. He was almost sure of it.

"This is it! It looks . . . shabby, Mom. Do we *really* have to live here?"

Kristine took a deep breath. "It does look shabby, Cala, but you have to remember that no one has lived here for over twenty-two years. This dreary, rainy day isn't helping either. By this time next year your dad and I will have it all fixed up. Paint works wonders." It was hard to believe this strangled-sounding voice was coming from her own mouth.

"I don't think a bucket of paint is going to do it, Ma," Mike said. "Did that banker guy get someone to clean it up? Is there any furniture? Did our stuff get here? Are we going to be sleeping on beds that are full of dust? Jeez, why can't we stay in town. This place is in the middle of *nowhere.* Do we have a telephone?"

"Of course there's a telephone. Mr. Dunwoodie said everything was hooked up and turned on. It's going to be okay. We're always jittery when we move to a new place. It was a beautiful estate when I was little. It can be that way again."

"Ma, that was back in the Dark Ages. Look at it! Forget the way it looked *back then.* Are you seeing what we're seeing? Half the shutters are gone. The porch is sagging. Jeez, I bet it isn't safe; and take a gander at those steps—they're lopsided, too. It will cost a fortune to fix this baby up. Do you and Dad have a fortune?"

Did they? She had no clue. Logan had handled their finances from the day they got married.

"I think it's safe to say we have enough to get by. Repairs won't be done all at one time. We'll work on it. Now come on, let's exit this brand-new station wagon and open our front door. We're home. My old home, our home now. All those other places we lived were just buildings where your dad and I paid rent. This is home, like it or not."

"Add my name to the list of people who don't like it," Cala snapped. "God, I will never bring anyone here. That's assuming I meet some farmer who is interested in me, which is so laughable it's beyond belief."

"I second that," Mike said as he hefted his bags from the backseat to dump them on the ground.

"Did Dad know what this dump looked like when he decided to ship us here?" Tyler demanded.

Kristine dropped her overnight bag on the ground. "Listen to me. I'm only going to say this one more time. This is our new home. No, Tyler, your father hasn't seen this house in fifteen years. Time takes its toll on everything and everyone. We have no other options. The farm your father grew up on is probably in worse shape than this one. Instead of fighting me every step of the way, help me. The four of us can make a beginning. I know that if your father was standing here, none of you would have opened your mouth. Why are you taking this out on me? I'm trying to do the best I can."

"What page is that on in your book?" Cala snarled.

"Page sixty-two, and watch your mouth, young lady. End of discussion. Now move your asses and get in the house."

"Wow!" young Tyler said as he walked around the spacious rooms. "Was I ever here, Mom?"

"You were just a toddler when we came back here the last time. You were too little to remember. Cala and Mike spent the whole time sliding down the banister. It's a wonderful old house. All the beams and wainscoting are original, as are the wooden pegs they used for nails back in those days. The floors are solid oak. They could stand to be refinished at some point. The people Mr. Dunwoodie hired to clean everything up did a good job. It's more than livable."

"It's freezing in here," Cala grumbled.

"Guess that means you kids have to go outside to the woodshed and bring in some wood. Mr. Dunwoodie said he had two cords of cherry wood delivered. In the meantime I'll turn up the thermostat and hope it works. Take your gear upstairs, pick out a bedroom, and put on an extra sweater. This house was always drafty, and heat rises," Kristine said, pointing to the high ceilings. "I want to check out the kitchen to make sure the stove and water pump work."

"Are you saying we have to *pump* water too?" There was such disgust on Mike's face, Kristine cringed.

"If you want water, that's exactly what you do," Kristine said, her patience wearing thin. She wondered what her children would say and do when they saw the archaic contraption that heated the water in the upstairs bathroom.

Kristine was priming the pump in the kitchen when she heard her daughter's screech. "One bathroom! There's only one bathroom up here! What am I supposed to do? There's no vanity either. What the hell is this . . . thing?"

Kristine knuckled her burning eyes. She would not cry. She absolutely would not cry. "You should be here, Logan. We should be doing this together. They wouldn't be acting this way if you were here," she muttered under her breath as a steady stream of rusty water shot from the pump spout. She continued to pump water because it was something to do. She didn't want to think about what Cala would say when she washed her hair for the first time in the hard well water. She wished she could lie down and go to sleep and not wake up until Logan walked through the door.

"It's sleeting out, Mom. The temperature is dropping," Tyler said, coming up behind her. "How much wood do you want us to bring in? I counted ten fireplaces in this house. Which ones do you want to light?"

"I guess you better light the ones in the bedrooms and the one here in the kitchen and the one in the living room. The heater doesn't seem to be working. The propane tank could be empty. I'll look into it tomorrow. I don't think we'll freeze. My mother had wonderful quilts and down comforters on all the beds. A lot of wood, Tyler. There's a wood carrier in the shed that holds a lot of wood. Off the top of my head I'd say you need four loads. Bring it to the kitchen door. If the three of you work at it, you should be able to drag it up the kitchen staircase. My father used to do it on his own, so I think you three robust children should be able to handle it. It's called, work, Tyler."

"There's no television set, Mom."

"So there isn't. I guess you'll just have to miss the tube for one day until our belongings get here tomorrow. Read a book."

"This is like one of those houses you see in horror movies," Mike said as he slammed through the kitchen door behind Tyler. "What do you mean there's no television set?"

Kristine clenched her teeth so hard she thought her jaw would crack when she opened the refrigerator. Eggs, a can of coffee, bread, butter, jam, bacon, juice, and milk. "This certainly takes the guess-work out of what to cook for dinner," she muttered. *Tomorrow things will be better,* she thought.

Since the preparation time for dinner would be ten minutes or so, Kristine gathered up her baggage to carry upstairs. She shivered as she walked through the old house, drafts swirling about her legs. She took a minute to marvel at the old furniture, antiques really, and the fact that everything was in such good condition. Her own comfortable, worn furniture wasn't going to fit in anywhere in this barn of a house. Still, she would have to spread it out for the children's sake and gradually get rid of it. There was a lot to be said for antiques.

Cala swept by her on her way down the stairs. "I can't believe you're making me carry in firewood. That's a man's job."

Kristine turned. "Cala?"

"Yeah."

"Don't say yeah. I need to know why the three of you are so . . . belligerent today. Why are you fighting me over every little thing? We belong in the United States. We're citizens of this country. This is where we belong. Daddy's tour is over, and this is what we decided to do. I grant you it's an adjustment, but if we all pull together, we can make it work. In September you and Mike will be going off to college, so what's the big deal. It's nine months out of your life."

"Daddy said it was your idea to come back here. He said since you never squawked about moving all over the world every couple of years, it was your turn now. Daddy didn't care. He would have been happy staying in Germany. We didn't want to come back here. You're the one who wanted this move."

"Of course I wanted it. Your father did, too. He was upset, Cala, about being passed over. He had no other choice. What kind of work would he have done over there? Nothing that paid any kind of money, that's for certain. I would never renounce my citizenship to live in a foreign country. There's too much unrest in Europe. I wanted us to be safe on our own soil."

"Skip it, Mom. We're here, so what difference does it make. Don't think I'm joining one of those farmer 4-H clubs, either. I'm not going to have one thing in common with anyone around here. I know it, and so do Tyler and Mike. Right now Mike and I could go right into our second year of college. Tyler could be a freshman. Instead, we're going to be going to some rinky-dink high school where we have to take classes we took two years ago. It's not fair. There's no stimulation in doing something like that. You didn't think about that, did you?"

"No, I didn't. I will now, though. Perhaps something can be worked out. I've been away so long I don't know what the requirements or procedures are these days. Tomorrow when I take you to school I'll find out. In the meantime, will you cut me some slack and help your brothers."

"Sure, Mom. When I finish doing that, do you want me to plow the south forty?" Cala shot over her shoulder as she continued to stomp down the steps.

Kristine made her way to her old bedroom at the end of the long hallway. Her hand trembled as she turned the flowered white-ceramic knob. She found it amazing that everything was as she remembered it. The double four-poster was polished, as were the two oak dressers. Years ago there had been dresser scarves on them, along with all the junk young girls needed or thought they needed. The cushions on the old Boston rocker were faded but fluffed up by one of the cleaning crew who had gone through the house. The windows sparkled behind the Venetian blinds. She wondered what had happened to the Priscilla curtains her mother favored for the dormer windows. Rotted, she supposed. The seat cushion on the window seat matched the one on the old rocker. It, too, was faded but fluffed up. Old toys that were probably antiques by now marched across the white shelving that covered all four walls. How strange that her mother had kept things the way Kristine left them when she went off to college. She wondered if her mother ever came into this room when she was at school just to sit in the rocker and remember happy days when she was little. Reminiscing about past birthday parties, Christmases, and, of course, all those times when she was sick in bed with a cold.

Kristine sat down on the rocker, amazed that the dry old wood didn't squeak on the shiny hardwood floor. She'd had a big old tiger cat named Solomon back then who sat on the rocker or on the window seat to wait for her to come home from school. He'd died when she was in her second year of college. Logan had never understood why she had to rush home because a stupid cat died. That was probably the only time in her life when she'd stood up to Logan and told him she didn't give a good rat's ass if he understood or not. She'd done nothing but cry for a solid week. Her first experience with death. She was back at school less than two weeks when she was summoned home a second time. Nothing in the world could have prepared her for the deaths of her parents. According to Dunwoodie, her parents' banker and trusted advisor, the barn had caught fire and her parents had rushed in to save the dogs and been overcome with smoke.

She hadn't gone back to school that semester. Instead

she'd sat in her rocker for months trying to figure out where her life was going. Logan had been so supportive during that awful time. It was Logan who put the dust covers on all the furniture, Logan who did all the things necessary to closing up a house, Logan who locked the door for the last time, and Logan who drove her away and held her hand when she looked back over her shoulder, tears streaming down her cheeks.

They'd come back to Virginia fifteen years ago when Logan's elderly father passed away. Even then she was barely able to open the door and walk through her old home. Logan held her hand that time, too, while she struggled with the key.

Kristine rubbed at the tears in her eyes. It was all so long ago. Another time, another life.

As she unpacked her bag, Kristine wondered if living here with her family would be as good as the life they had led in all the foreign countries they'd lived in.

Logan's picture was the first thing that came out of her bag. She set it on the night table next to a small onyx clock that no longer told time. It would be the first thing she saw when she opened her eyes in the morning and the last thing she saw before she closed her eyes at night. "I wish you were here, Logan," she whispered. "We should be here together." She was jolted to awareness when she heard a loud thump and squabbling coming from the hallway.

"Now look what you did. I'm not picking it up. You were supposed to hold up your end, Tyler. God, I hate it when you act like a *priss.*"

"Stuff it, Cala. I'm soaking wet, and I'm freezing. Mike should be on the bottom and I should be on the top with you."

"Guess what, you jerk, we're cold and wet, too. We still have three more loads to go, so get moving."

"Do it yourself. I'll make my own fire with my own wood. I'm sick and tired of getting dumped on by the two of you. I don't give a shit if you're twins or not. So there.''

"That's enough,'' Kris shouted from the hallway. "The quicker you get those fires going, the sooner you'll be warm. You won't be able to take a hot bath because there's no propane.''

"Are you saying there's no *shower*? I hate taking a bath because you just sit in your own dirty water. I hate this stinking place. I really hate it!'' Cala said tearfully.

"That's exactly what I'm saying. Now, get moving, and someone has to clean up all the splinters from the steps. I'll start dinner.''

"I'm not hungry,'' Mike muttered.

"Me either,'' Tyler grumbled.

"What could there possibly be to eat in this dump?'' Cala said, blowing her nose.

Kristine threw her hands in the air. "Fine, don't eat. Starve. I've had it with the three of you.'' She stared at the phone that suddenly pealed to life. A phone call! She picked up the receiver to hear her husband's cheerful voice.

"Logan! Oh, Logan, it's so good to hear from you. Is everything okay?''

"More to the point, is everything okay with you?''

"No. The kids hate it. There's no heat. They're giving me such a hard time. I guess we're all just tired. The house is fine inside. It's clean and there's some food. Tomorrow I'll get the propane. It's sleeting out, and this house is drafty. At least the phone is working. I picked up our new station wagon.'' Kristine lowered her voice to a hushed whisper so the children wouldn't hear her. "This is the right thing, isn't it, Logan. Moving here, I mean.''

"Kristine, what's going on?''

"It's the kids. They're mouthy, disrespectful, and they hate it. Maybe it's first-day jitters and tomorrow will be the first day of school in what they refer to as a rinky-dink farm school. Look. You didn't call me to hear me complain. Do you miss us?''

"Of course I miss you. That's why I called. Did the furniture get there?"

"Dunwoodie said it would arrive tomorrow afternoon. Do you think I should call a plumber to install a shower? No one likes to take a bath."

"Sure. Make sure it's all done before I get there. I hate a messy bathroom." Logan chuckled. "Make sure you position my chair just right."

"Yes, sir, Colonel Kelly, sir."

"I'll say good-bye then. I'll try to call again next week. Take care of things, Kris. Love you, old girl. Let me talk to the kids now."

Kristine crooked her finger at her oldest son. "Your father wants to talk to you."

"Ah shit," she heard Mike mutter. Cala sat down on the top step, her eyes murderous. Tyler leaned against the wall, shivering.

Kristine stepped over the fallen logs on the steps as she made her way to the kitchen. Her shoulders straightened imperceptibly as she slid strips of bacon into an old cast-iron skillet. Suddenly she felt better than she had in weeks. Logan would straighten the kids out in two seconds. Her husband loved her, but then she'd known that. Still, it was nice to hear the words occasionally. Now if she could just get the kids back on track, maybe things would fall into place.

What seemed like a long time later she heard movement behind her. She turned to see her three bedraggled-looking children. She smiled. "Dinner's almost ready. Change your clothes. By the time you get down here the kitchen will be warm and toasty."

"We're sorry, Mom," the three of them said in unison.

They were just mouthing words. Their eyes said they weren't sorry at all. "Me too. Hurry now before you catch cold."

"I'm starved," Mike said.

"I could eat a horse," Tyler said.

"I'll settle for three eggs, four pieces of toast, and six slices of bacon," Cala said.

"Coming right up," Kristine said cheerfully as she struck a match to light the logs in the cavernous kitchen fireplace.

2

Kristine stared at the less-than-perfect Christmas decoration on her kitchen table, her eyes watering with the intensity of her gaze. The bright red holly berries were withered, the spiky green leaves were turning yellow and looked dry, their edges curling under. She wished she'd been more creative and taken more time with it. Last year she'd decorated the house in Germany from top to bottom. She'd started the day after Thanksgiving, finishing late in the afternoon on December 10, the day Logan chose for their annual Christmas party. Everything had been so festive and fragrant. She'd done it all and when each guest left at the end of the night, she'd handed them a gaily wrapped gift of homemade Christmas cookies.

She'd been so happy that day. Logan and the children had been in exceptional spirits, and it had been contagious. She'd even gotten a new red-velvet gown trimmed in faux ermine, an extravagance she winced over from time to time, and a new hairdo and a cosmetic makeover. Logan had leered at her all night long. Like a silly schoolgirl, her heart had fluttered and pounded all night long at the thought of what would happen after the last guest left. Logan had always been an exceptional lover, but that night he'd performed like a master.

Kristine shivered as she drew her sweater tighter across her chest. The fire was blazing in the kitchen, the heat was on full blast, and she was still cold. She looked down at the cold tea in her cup. Should she make a fresh cup?

Did she even *want* more tea? Her movements were robotic as she filled the teakettle. The gas jet *swooshed* to life.

She paced from one end of the kitchen to the other, her shoes making clicking sounds on the old Virginia brick, careful to avert her eyes from the calendar hanging next to the refrigerator. She knew every printed word on the calendar issued by the Reynolds Propane Company. She'd stared at it a hundred times a day, her eyes watering as she ticked off the days until Logan's arrival. Somewhere, somehow, something had gone awry. There were three too many Xs on the calendar, which meant Logan was four days overdue. Christmas was five short days away. One letter and one phone call in thirty-four days had to mean there was a snafu somewhere along the chain of command. She tried not to look at the red X with the big red circle she'd drawn around December 16. Maybe there would be a letter in today's mail. Her gaze swept to the kitchen clock. Thirty more minutes until the mailman tooted his horn out by the road. One toot meant no mail. Two toots of the foggy-sounding horn meant mail. She kept the house purposely quiet around this time of day, turning off the kitchen radio and the new television set in the living room to make sure she heard the horn.

"Logan, I am going to strangle you when you get here for causing me all this worry. How much trouble is it to make one phone call, send one scribbled postcard? This is so unfair of you." *Damn, if I don't watch it, I'll be blubbering all over the place.*

Kristine continued to pace as she waited for the water to boil. She really needed to make a new one and this time put some creative effort into it. In a rush of something she couldn't define, she picked up the dried-out Christmas centerpiece and tossed it in the trash can under the sink. Now, all she had to contend with was the calendar. She wished she could ignore it, but the propane advertisement drew her like a magnet. She turned away as she tried to focus on the old-fashioned kitchen. Everything now looked halfhearted. The red-checkered curtains were too short and too faded. The braided rugs were skimpy and looked out of place on the expanse of brick floor. The place mats that matched the curtains were wrinkled and tacky-looking on the claw-footed monster table. Now that the centerpiece was gone, the table looked forlorn. There was no life in this kitchen the way there always had been life and energy in her other kitchens around the world. The kids always did their homework at the kitchen table with hot cups of cocoa. Now they huddled in their rooms with the doors shut.

Nothing was working out the way it was supposed to. A chill ran up Kristine's arm just as the kettle whistled. At the same moment the kettle shot off its plume of steam, the phone rang and the mailman tooted twice. Kris burst into tears while she struggled with the gas burner. She managed to pick up the phone and to say hello in a garbled voice she didn't recognize as her own.

"Kristine, it's Aaron Dunwoodie. You sound strange. Is everything all right?"

"Everything is fine, Aaron," she lied. "I think I might be coming down with a cold. What can I do for you today?"

"I'd like you to come into the bank tomorrow if possible. I'll be free all morning."

"Is something wrong?"

"I believe so. I don't like to discuss business over the phone. How does ten o'clock sound?"

"It's fine, Aaron. I'll be there. Do I need to bring anything?"

"Bring whatever Logan sent home with you. All the account information and your bankbooks."

"All right. I'll see you at ten."

"Perhaps we should make it nine instead. There's a snow advisory tomorrow for midday. These weather people never get it right. Yes, nine is good."

"Then nine it is."

Kristine hung up the phone, a frown building on her face. What exactly did Aaron mean when he said bring everything Logan gave her? Logan hadn't given her anything. She shrugged. Right now she had more important things on her mind. She beelined for the door, shrugging into her jacket as she raced out to the mailbox. She wanted to howl her misery as she withdrew two catalogs and a bill from Reynolds Propane. She slammed the door of the mailbox so hard it flopped open again. She gave the post a kick as she clicked the metal door to the fastener. "Well, I've had enough of this!" she stormed as she raced to the house to get out of the cold. Aaron was right about the snow. It felt like snow right now. She looked upward at the gray scudding clouds. She didn't need a weatherman to tell her it would snow before the day was over. If she was going to go into town tomorrow, she had to find her father's old set of chains in case the roads weren't plowed. She also needed to gather some evergreen branches to make a new centerpiece. Later. Everything these days was always later. She also needed to think about making something for dinner, something that didn't come out of a box.

Back in the kitchen, Kristine sat down on the raised hearth, the searing heat warming her back and neck. She hated crying like this, but she couldn't seem to help herself. Something was wrong. Logan should have been here by now. Morbid thoughts ricocheted inside her head as she sought for reasons why her husband was four days late in returning to the States. Did he have an accident? Was there one last mission? The thought was so stupid she bit down on her lower lip. Logan had never gone on a mission in his entire military career. Amnesia was a possibility. A plane crash. There had been nothing on the news. He stayed longer than intended to party with some of his fellow officers, most of whom he would never see again. That must be it. Maybe he simply lost track of time, missed his flight, and had to wait for a reservation to open up. He would pop in anytime now shouting, "Surprise!" at the top of his lungs.

It wasn't going to happen. She didn't know how she knew, she just knew. Woman's intuition along with good old gut instinct.

"I've had enough of this," she muttered. Within minutes she had what she called her global address book in hand. Upstairs she had three more just like it, each page filled with names, addresses, and little notes about the people she'd met during twenty years in the military. She flipped the pages to the section marked Germany, running her fingers down the list until she located the names she wanted. As she dialed the country code, she calculated the time difference in her mind. Not that she cared one way or the other.

The chaplain's voice was somber-sounding to her ears. Did she interrupt his prayers? "Tom, it's Kristine Kelly. How are you? Shivering! It's very cold here in Virginia, too. It is December. I understand the weatherman has predicted snow for tomorrow. *Get on with it, Kristine, ask him. Stop with the small talk.* Tom, Logan is three days late. Do you happen to know if he was detained for some reason? Mail is so slow at this time of year and our phone system is not the best way out here in the country."

"As far as I know Logan left on schedule, Kristine. There was the usual round of parties, gag gifts, hoots, and hollers. It was my understanding that Captain Dellwood drove him to the airport. Logan did come by the night before he left to say good-bye. We had a beer and talked for about an hour. It was my impression he was flying straight into Dulles. I wish I could be of more help. I can call around to see if there was a change in plans and call you if I find out anything."

"I would appreciate it, Tom. I'm worried. This is not like Logan. He's only called once and sent one letter. The kids are as jittery as I am. Logan is not a thoughtless, inconsiderate person. I think you know that, Tom."

"Yes, I do know that. Like I said, I'll check around and get back to you. I'm sure there was a glitch along the way. It's possible he's stranded somewhere. The weather here has not been good."

Kristine's voice was tortured when she said, "Tom, you don't think anything happened to him, do you?"

"Kristine, you would have heard by now if something had happened. I'm sure it's nothing more than a mixup somewhere along the line. I'll call when I know something. Say hello to the children for me."

"I will. Thanks, Tom. You've been a wonderful friend to this family. Don't eat too much plum pudding this year. Merry Christmas."

"I need to do something with this kitchen before Logan gets home," Kristine muttered. Somewhere in the storage room there were boxes and boxes of fabric she'd purchased over the years in all the foreign ports they'd stopped at. If she hauled out her sewing machine, she could whip up a new set of curtains, make cushion covers for the chairs and the rocker that sat by the fire, and even make some new holiday place mats. If she really wanted to be creative, she could glue some fabric on the pull-down shades on both kitchen doors. If she wanted to, she could go outside and gather armfuls of evergreens to put in clay pots. A colorful ribbon around the crock would add a festive touch. If she hurried, she could have it all done by the time the kids got home from school at four o'clock. If she wanted to. The only problem was, she didn't want to. She wanted to sit here at the table sucking her thumb while she pretended nothing was wrong.

Dellwood. Kristine squeezed her eyes shut to try and get a mental picture of the captain. When the captain's likeness failed to materialize, she opened her eyes. Maybe the captain was new to the base. Was he in the directory?

Stapled to the last page of her address book was the latest list of new as well as old officers living on base. Her friend Sadie Meyers had handed her the list the day before she left, saying, "In case you want to get in touch with any of us." A smile tugged at the corners of Kristine's mouth. Trust Sadie to put the list in alphabetical order. She ran her finger down the list and there he was, Captain Laurence Dellwood.

Kristine didn't stop to think. She dialed the number opposite the captain's name. The words hurtled from her mouth, the moment the captain identified himself. She ended with a rush saying, "I'm sure you understand how worried we are. Can you tell me anything, Captain? Was there a mixup? Did Logan's flight get canceled?"

"Ma'am, as far as I know, Colonel Kelly boarded his flight with ten minutes to spare. I saw him checking his ticket en route to the airport, and he said he had a straight through flight to Dulles. He said he couldn't wait to get home, and this was going to be the best Christmas ever. Did you check with Dulles, Mrs. Kelly?"

"No. No, I didn't, but I will when I hang up. I don't suppose you know his flight number."

"The colonel said he was flying Lufthansa, with one stop somewhere, but I can't remember where it was, ma'am. I'm sorry. The colonel's flight left at 0600 hours December 15. He said he would probably be drinking coffee while he stared at his Christmas tree on December 16, all the while marveling at the fact that he was a civilian again. He wished me luck with my tour, shook my hand, said 'Merry Christmas, Captain,' and then he was gone. That's all I know, ma'am."

Kristine felt a wave of dizziness wash over her. "What about his luggage, Captain?"

"Luggage?"

"Yes, what happened to it?"

"The colonel didn't have any luggage, ma'am, just a small flight bag. I assumed everything else had been shipped."

"I see." Damn, she didn't see at all. "Thank you, Captain. Have a nice holiday."

In a near trance, Kristine paced the kitchen. Logan had left Germany on schedule. Where in the name of God was he? Something was wrong? "My God!" she cried, Logan could be buried in a ditch somewhere, and I'll never know. *Oh, God, Oh, God!* She was going to do something. What? Make coffee? Tea? A centerpiece for the kitchen table? Even a new wreath for the front door? She was going to do some sewing. The middle of the huge bare table made her flinch. No, no, no, she wasn't going to do any of those things. She was going to call Dulles Airport.

Fifteen minutes later, Kristine slammed the phone down in disgust. Civilian passenger information was sacrosanct. Maybe she could call the airline in Germany. She placed the call and switched to German when she spoke. The result was the same. Lufthansa did not divulge passenger information. Now what was she supposed to do? Make coffee, create a new centerpiece for the kitchen table like a good little wife, write another letter she would never get to mail.

All of the above if she wanted to keep her sanity. Like hell! The phone found its way back to her hand. Her first call was to her friend Sadie in Germany. When she heard her friend's cheerful voice on the other end of the phone the tenseness between her shoulder blades lessened. The moment she wound down from her spiel, she asked, "Do you know anything, Sadie? Did you and Jim go to Logan's going-away party?"

"It was one of those guy only things. Don't get riled up now. It was held in the Officers' Club and aside from some risqué entertainment, everyone left alone. Logan stayed here that night in the spare bedroom. I think you're overreacting, Kris. He could have missed his stopover flight.

"Just wait, he'll waltz in like nothing happened, his arms full of presents. That's Logan, Mr. Showman himself. Stop worrying. When did you become so neurotic and paranoid?"

"Four days ago, that's when. I'm going to call the American Consulate and have them check it out. Maybe the airline will give them the information. Four days is a long time, Sadie."

"I think you're worrying needlessly. And you're running up your phone bill at the same time. Kick back, relax, and get the house ready for the holidays. You are Mrs. Christmas herself. You need to go by the book, Kristine.

Military wives do not buckle under pressure. We measure up!''

"I'm not in the military anymore, Sadie. My measuring-up days are long gone. I did decorate," she said, her voice sounding defensive.

"An old Virginia farmhouse. It must have tons of character. Did you bake cookies and streusel?''

"Of course," Kristine fibbed. She didn't even have any flour. How could she bake?

"How are the kids?''

"Testy. They don't like it here. They haven't made really good friends yet. Their educations are too advanced for the school system here. The twins could really have skipped this last year and gone straight to their sophomore year at college. The paperwork was mind-boggling. Logan did some of it back in August, but I can't find it. The kids are upset over that, too. I think they all sleep through their classes. There is a possibility Logan can get them registered for the next semester if he can come up with the paperwork.''

Sadie asked, her voice sharp and blunt, "Why are you waiting for Logan? That's a mother's job.''

"Goddamn it, Sadie, I've been waiting for Logan. I unpacked everything, and there is no box with college papers or anything else. I can't pull it out of thin air, can I?''

"You always said your family was your top priority, Kris. I'm trying to figure out what's wrong here. You sound to me like you're teetering on the edge. The Kristine Kelly I've known for fifteen years is not an insecure twit. The kids must know what Logan did on their behalf. You said Mike was going to VMI and Cala was going to Georgetown. Start there. Call the damn schools, for God's sake.''

"It's Christmas recess right now. I'll do it the first of the year.'' It wasn't an admission that Logan wasn't coming back. It truly wasn't.

"I've never heard you like this," Sadie said. "What's *really* bothering you?''

Kristine sighed. "The not knowing. If Logan called and said he couldn't make it home until Easter, that would be fine. I could handle that. It's the not knowing, the worry. What if something *did* happen, Sadie?"

"If something happened, you would have heard by now. When he does get home, I'd kick his butt all the way to the state line. That's if he was my husband. My suggestion to you is shift into neutral, have some intense dialogue with the kids, call the colleges. At least leave your name. I'm sure there's a skeleton staff in Admissions to take down your information. Then go Christmas shopping. You need to be a good little soldier and . . ."

"I'm going to hang up now, Sadie, before I say something I'll regret later on. It was nice talking to you. Say hello to Jim. Have a wonderful holiday."

Kristine broke the connection so she wouldn't have to hear her friend's reply. What did Sadie know? Everyone in the whole world knew Sadie Meyers never had a serious thought in her entire life.

Kick back, shift into neutral, relax. Easy to say. Not easy to do. It was just that she loved Logan so much. Sometimes in her secret thoughts she realized her love was sickly obsessive. If something happened to Logan, she wouldn't be able to go on. She would want to die, too. Life without Logan was unthinkable.

She needed to do something, and she needed to do it now before she fell apart. She was a whirlwind then as she raced about the old farmhouse, dragging out her sewing machine, rummaging in the packing boxes for material. The old treadle almost smoking, she whipped up new curtains, seat cushions, and place mats. She used up another thirty minutes ironing everything and hanging the curtains, then carried bundles of evergreens into the house to make arrangements, wreaths, and, finally, the centerpiece for the kitchen table. Her hands covered with the pungent resin, Kris stood back to survey her efforts. Next she carried the huge clay pots with their bright red bows and fragrant evergreens all over the house. In a matter of minutes the scent from the greens filled the house. She inhaled deeply. Two jobs down. Energy seemed to ooze from her pores as she nestled a fat red bayberry candle in the middle of the new centerpiece she'd created.

Kris turned on the oven. A pie was in order. The kids wouldn't care if it was a Mrs. Smith's deep dish apple pie or not. She slapped a rump roast into a baking pan, seasoned it, peeled potatoes and carrots. The house was going to smell heavenly when the kids came in from school. She dusted her hands dramatically as she walked from room to room. The corner of the living room had been cleared earlier to allow for the Christmas tree. The boxes of decorations waited next to the tree stand. There would be an hour of daylight when the kids got home, just enough time to cut down a tree from the back of the property. Tomorrow after her meeting with Aaron Dunwoodie, she would go Christmas shopping and do some extensive grocery shopping. She also needed to plan a Christmas dinner and do some baking. She'd bring home Chinese and it would be almost like old times. The key to everything was keeping busy.

Now it was time for a cup of coffee, coffee she would actually drink while it was hot. She needed to think about Aaron Dunwoodie and what it was he expected her to bring to the bank. Later this evening, after the tree was up and decorated and the kids were settled, she would go to the storage room and look through the boxes again to make sure she hadn't missed whatever it was Dunwoodie wanted.

Plump, lacy snowflakes dotted the windshield of the Chevy station wagon as Kristine pulled into a wide parking space outside the Virginia National Bank. It didn't look the way it had when she was a child going to the bank with her parents on Friday mornings. The huge columns were now pristine white, complementing the pale pink of the brick building. She decided she liked the crisscross-paned doors with the huge evergreen wreath. Long ago the build-ing was smaller, dingier, and the columns were a dirty beige color. "Progress," she murmured as she opened the door that led into a luxurious lobby. She had an immediate impression of wealth with all the polished brass, thick car-peting, and elegant window treatments. The furniture was heavy but comfortable-looking, the desks polished cherry wood. Even the staff looked affluent. A floor-to-ceiling Douglas fir sat in the center of the lobby, silver gift-wrapped packages with huge red bows underneath. Everywhere she looked there were bright red poinsettias in silver and gold pots. It all looked and smelled wonderful. She untied the thick wool scarf around her neck as she made her way to the first desk across from the elegant-looking Christmas tree. "I have an appointment with Aaron Dunwoodie at nine o'clock," she said to the woman behind the desk.

"Mr. Dunwoodie is expecting you, Mrs. Kelly. Go around the corner, and he's the last office on the right side."

He was a pleasant, good-looking man, Kristine decided as she shook hands with the banker before slipping out of her coat. She didn't remember him at all. *He must be two or three years older than I,* she thought. Obviously, he'd stepped into the banking business when his parents retired. She suspected he looked older than his age. Possibly because of the stress of taking care of other people's money.

"Did you bring your records, Kristine?"

"I didn't have any records to bring, Mr. Dunwoodie. Logan always kept everything in a big brown accordion-pleated envelope. I remember seeing it at one point, but moving was so hectic. I just assumed Logan had it because it wasn't sent with our belongings. The only thing I can think of is he's bringing it with him because he didn't trust it with the movers."

The banker leaned back in his burgundy chair, a frown on his face. "When do you expect your husband, Kristine?"

"He's four days late, five if you count today. Something

must have gone awry with his plane reservation. You look . . . you look like something is wrong."

"Something *is* wrong. Your account here is carrying a debit balance. How do you plan to clear that up?" While his tone was conversational, it scared Kristine.

"I don't understand. Logan opened a checking account here months ago, back in the summer if I remember correctly. I signed the papers in July to the best of my recollection. Logan sent enough money to cover the cost of the car and enough to carry us for six months. He said it would take a while to transfer everything back to the States and to do all the paperwork for his pension. Are you telling me the monies never arrived?"

"Some monies arrived, but you've used them all up. It was my understanding the trust monies from your parents would be relayed back here. I had a long conversation with your husband in the early part of October. He said that in November a portion of the trust would be wired here. He even gave me the routing numbers. The remainder of the trust would then automatically go into that new account in December. The November amount was never wired. I checked with the Swiss bank, and no wire transfer was ever executed. There are no monies in that account nor have there been since February of last year. Your husband led me to believe the trust account was quite robust."

Kristine's heart thumped in her chest. "Mr. Dunwoodie, at last count, Logan told me we had close to eight million dollars in the trust account. Where is it?" The panic in her voice was palpable.

"I don't know, Mrs. Kelly. I was hoping you could shed some light on the matter. It is never wise to have just one name on an account." *Mrs. Kelly. First it was Kristine and now it's Mrs. Kelly.* Kristine's heart continued to thump.

"My name was on the account, Mr. Dunwoodie. I've seen the statements. Perhaps Logan changed banks for better interest rates. I suppose it's possible, but unlikely, that he would have put it in a Swiss numbered account. I don't even know why I'm saying that."

"Did you see any bank statements since last February?"

"The last one I saw was in January, when we filed our taxes. Logan commented on how nicely the account had grown over the years. We rarely touched it. I was frugal, and we lived on Logan's pay and my monthly checks. I was even able to save from my budget. It was a small account, seven or eight thousand dollars. It was in a separate account that we called our excess money. So you see, I don't understand why you're telling me I'm carrying a debit, or are you saying that account didn't make it to this bank either?"

"That's what I'm saying, Mrs. Kelly."

Mrs. Kelly again. Kristine thought she would black out any second. "Is it lost?" Any minute now she was going to burst into tears.

"Banks do not lose money, Mrs. Kelly. In order to lose something, you have to have it in hand first. We never had it in hand. Therefore, we did not lose it. Do you understand what I'm saying?"

"No, Mr. Dunwoodie, I do not understand. What I do understand is that you are implying something here that isn't sitting well with me. When is the next trust payment due?"

"The first of January."

"And where will that go?"

"Right here, into an account at this bank. I have a form for you to sign. However, you cannot write any more checks on the account until that time."

Kristine took a deep breath. "If I'm overdrawn, how can I get through the holidays? I need to do some Christmas shopping and buy some groceries. Can't the bank lend me some money until January first? Ten or eleven days isn't much time if you know you can debit the account on the first day of January. Logan will be home any day now and will straighten things out. I know my husband, Mr. Dunwoodie. He's going to be very angry when he hears about this. He won't want to bank here any longer if you don't help me."

"I didn't say I wouldn't help you, Mrs. Kelly. I'm more than willing to give you an advance to get you through the holidays. I am simply looking at the broad picture here. I want to know, as you should want to know, where the eight million dollars in your trust account is. If I didn't ask these questions, I would not be respecting your parents' last wishes. That money was entrusted to you, Kristine. Which brings up another point. Why did you give your husband your power of attorney?"

"I gave my husband my power of attorney because he is my husband. He managed the account very well. The money almost doubled."

"What good is that going to do you if you don't have it?"

Kristine threw her hands up in the air. "I can't tell you something I don't know. All I can do is go through the unpacked boxes again and wait for Logan to get home. Do you . . . do you think . . . think Logan ran away with the money? My God! That *is* what you think, isn't it?"

"I said no such thing, Mrs. Kelly. Put yourself in my place. Your parents placed their trust in this bank and in my father, who, when he retired, placed that same trust in my hands. I have obeyed the letter of the banking laws we are forced to live by. How well do you know your husband?" he asked coolly.

"God in heaven! We've been married for twenty years! I know him as well as I know myself. I hope that satisfies you. I do not like your tone or what you're trying to imply. Now, I'd like five hundred dollars, please."

"I'll call out to the head teller. I assume you want cash."

"Cash will be just fine."

"Mrs. Kelly, what will you do if the eight million dollars never arrives?"

She was starting to hate the sound of her own name. "I don't have one damn clue as to what I'll do. And from here on in you would be wise to keep your insinuations to yourself, or I'll be banking somewhere else."

"Your father told my father he didn't like Logan Kelly.

My father thought I should know that when he passed your account over to me.''

"That's a bald-faced lie if I ever heard one," Kristine said, her voice rising dangerously. "Both my parents adored Logan. How dare you say something like that to me! How dare you!''

"It's not a lie. Here, read this. It's a letter your father gave to my father at the time the trust was set up twenty-five years ago. You can apologize to me later. I have a meeting, and I'm late. Good-bye, Mrs. Kelly. Have a nice holiday.''

Kristine recognized her father's handwriting. She also recognized both parents' signatures at the bottom of the letter. It was a photocopy, but readable. No doubt the original was locked up in the bank vault somewhere. She read the letter twice before she crumpled it into a ball to toss across the room. Tears streaming down her cheeks, she fled the office. It wasn't until she was in the car with the engine running that she remembered she hadn't gone to the teller for the five hundred dollars. She blew her nose lustily as she cursed under her breath. Ten minutes later she was back in the car. Until that moment she hadn't noticed how much snow was on the ground. Damn. Now what was she supposed to do? If she spent a few more hours in town shopping, would she be able to make it home without chains or should she make a stop at the first gas station she came to and buy new ones? She opted for new chains. She was back on the road in thirty minutes. Her second stop was at a shoe store, where she bought a pair of rubber boots. There was no way she was going to give any credence to what Aaron Dunwoodie said or implied. She was never, ever, going to think about the letter her parents wrote either. She had groceries and Christmas presents to buy, and that's what she was going to do. When she got home, she was going to make a big pot of stew and bake an angel food cake. One-pot meals were perfect for eating off trays in front of the television. The extra plus would be the twinkling lights on the Christmas tree. The kids would love it. Then again, maybe they wouldn't. Lately it seemed like she knew nothing about her three children.

"I hate your guts, Aaron Dunwoodie," Kristine snarled as she parked the car outside the department store. "I will never forgive you for your ugly thoughts about my husband."

Kristine continued to mutter to herself as she walked up and down the aisles of the department store until she saw people staring at her. She clamped her lips shut as she squared her shoulders. She was here to buy Christmas presents, and that was exactly what she was going to do.

3

Her arms loaded with packages, Kristine climbed from the station wagon and stepped into four inches of snow. Even with the chains on her car, she'd been scared out of her wits that she would have an accident on the slick, icy roads. She sighed her relief, stinging sleet spitting in her face, as she struggled with her bundles. *Thank God I'm home.* The lights twinkling from the upstairs windows meant the kids made it home safely, too. *Damn, how are we going to cut down a Christmas tree in this weather?*

Don't think about anything, Kristine. Go in the house and check the Crock-Pot. Get dinner ready. You can worry about the Christmas tree later. Don't think about Aaron Dunwoodie. Don't even think about Logan. Do what you have to do. That's how you get through the days. That's what the book says. Go by the book now. The book is all you have going for you right now.

"Mom! We were worried," the three Kelly children shouted in relief as Kristine entered the warm, fragrant kitchen.

"We cut down the tree when we got home from school," Mike said.

"It's a monster," Tyler volunteered.

"We even got it up in the stand. There are pine needles everywhere, but it smells great. It looks like we might have a white Christmas. We wanted to wait for you to decorate the tree. I set the table and made some eggnog. Any mail from Dad?" Cala asked.

She doesn't sound like she cares one way or the other, Kristine thought.

"Where did you get the saw to cut down the tree?" Kristine asked.

"Buried under a ton of junk in the barn. It was rusty, but it did the job," Mike said. "It's a great-looking tree, Mom. Your eye was good yesterday when you picked it out even though it was dark. Did you buy a saw?"

"Yes, but I can take it back. I'm just glad we got the tree. It looks like it might snow through the night. Right now it's sleeting. Thanks for pitching in. No mail from Dad. I made some calls yesterday. The consulate is checking on things. I'm starved. Can we eat?" *Don't think. You have all night to think when the kids are in bed. Forget about the ugly insinuations Aaron Dunwoodie made.*

"The house looks really great, Mom. It smelled so good when we came in from school. It's almost Christmas, and there's no more school until January," Cala said, unpacking groceries. "Tyler, pour Mom some coffee and then the two of you help me put away these groceries. Dad is going to be so surprised when he walks in. I bet he waits till Christmas Eve!" she continued to babble.

Kris could hear the doubt in her daughter's voice. *Play the game; go by the book.*

"Yeah, he'll show up Christmas Eve like nothing happened. His grand entrance," Mike groused.

"Today was the last day of school before Christmas break, right? For some reason I thought tomorrow was the last day," Kristine said as she sipped at the coffee Tyler handed her.

"Yep, we're off till January tenth. What are we going to do, Mom?"

"I don't know about you guys but I'm going to go through my parents' records and see what I have to do to get their old business up and running. I think this Crock-Pot was one of the best things I ever bought," Kristine said, hoping to ward off any questions about Logan and the future.

"Dig in!" Mike said happily as he loaded his plate to the brim. Kristine smiled at the way his freckles danced across the bridge of his nose. He looked so much like Logan it was scary. Cala looked like her, and Tyler had both Logan's and her features. She looked away.

"Mom, we need to talk about Dad. You said you made some calls yesterday. I think you need to share information with us," Cala said, an edge to her voice.

"I agree about the sharing part, but there's nothing to share. The airlines don't give out passenger information. I spoke to Captain Dellwood. He's new to the base, and he's the one who drove your father to the airport. I called Tom, and he knew nothing. I even called Sadie, who said I was neurotic and paranoid. After that, I called the American Consulate and asked them to check on your dad. I'm hoping the airline will tell them something. Nobody was the least bit interested."

"He'll show up Christmas Eve, make a grand entrance, look at us all in wide-eyed wonder, and say something titillating like, 'Now why would you worry about your old man?' He would be right, too. Why the hell are we worried? So he's late, so what. I for one do not miss him at all. I personally don't care if he ever shows up. Don't any of you notice how quiet and peaceful it is without him ragging on us twenty-four hours a day," Mike said, bitterness ringing in his voice.

Kristine watched and listened in dismay as her son filled his plate a second time. She should say something, anything that would lighten the moment. Even if she could think of something to say, it wouldn't matter to Mike. Undercurrents of something she could never understand were always present when father and son were in the same room. As near as she could tell, Logan wanted his son to conform, and Mike wasn't about to follow any order given by his father. Cala had at times stood by her twin and at other times bowed to parental pressure. Tyler, on the other hand, was a dutiful son and the apple of his father's eye, and Logan made sure the twins knew he was his favorite.

Sometimes Logan could be unnecessarily cruel. She felt disloyal at the thought.

"That's enough, Michael," Kristine said, using her son's full name, a sign that enough was enough. Out of the corner of her eye she saw Tyler smirk. "Wipe that smirk off your face, Tyler," she said, getting up from the table.

"We'll clean up, Mom. You get the stuff ready in the living room."

"All right. I'm going to change my clothes first. Do we have a ladder?"

"I brought it in earlier," Mike said.

Tears welled in Kristine's eyes when her son hugged her. He whispered in her ear, "I probably didn't mean half of what I said. I hate what this is doing to you, Mom. He always does it, and you don't do anything. You just swallow it up and wait for the next time. He beats on you, and you don't seem to care. We're all doing fine, can't you see that?"

"Maybe you are, but I'm not. I don't want to talk about this, Mike."

"You need to open your eyes, Mom. We don't care. Tyler pretends and Cala feels like I do. You're the only one who cares. I hope the three of us are around when you finally realize what a son of a bitch your husband really is. Don't say it, Mom, because *I* don't want to hear it."

Tears blurred her vision as Kristine made her way to the second floor. She was losing control, if she ever had any control to lose. It was all getting away from her, and there was nothing she could do about it.

She sat down on the bed and cried.

"Mom, it's nine o'clock. If we don't eat now, everything is going to be dried out," Cala said. She struggled for a light tone. "The table looks so . . . festive, but the candles are at the halfway mark. I think we should eat now. I wish

I knew why we're having lasagna for Christmas Eve. We always have turkey, ham, and plum pudding.''

"I . . . I know. Your father requested lasagna and a chocolate cake. He said he wanted it to be waiting when he walked through the door. I thought . . . you're right, we should eat. There's some extra sauce in case it dried out too much. Is the salad wilted?''

"It's okay, Mom. Who says grace?''

As Tyler said grace, Kristine stared at the four-layer chocolate cake she'd made from scratch. It looked like a giant evil eye sitting in the center of the table. She wished she had the guts to throw it at the kitchen wall. Where did one get guts like that?

Logan wasn't coming home. Not tonight, not tomorrow, or the day after. She knew that now. Hot tears pricked her lids as she glanced around at the pitying looks on her children's faces. "Listen. I was never overly fond of lasagna. I say we toss it and throw out that cake for the birds. We have some hot dogs in the freezer, and I can make up some french fries in a few minutes. I made a Jell-O mold yesterday we didn't eat. Everyone in favor say aye.''

"Aye," the three Kelly children said in unison.

"Then let's do it!''

If it wasn't the happiest Christmas Eve dinner ever, it was the next happiest. At least that's what her children said over and over.

Kristine was on her fourth glass of wine when they ushered her into the living room. "We'll clean up out here, Mom. I'll bring in the eggnog when we're done. We'll sing some carols and make our wish on the North Star. And then we'll open our presents. You guys are just gonna love what I got you.''

Kristine nodded as she reached for the half gallon wine bottle to take with her into the living room. She smiled. They'd tried so hard for her sake. They'd gotten dressed in their best. Cala had spent hours on her makeup and Mike and Tyler had moussed their unruly curls. It was their jackets and ties that made her realize how hard they were trying.

She herself had spent hours on her makeup, hoping to cover the circles under her eyes. Her hair was lusterless and looked dry and stiff. Frustrated with her looks, she'd pulled it back into a tight bun. Until this evening she really hadn't paid much attention to her weight loss. When she saw how her burgundy-velvet dress just hung on her lanky frame, she'd tied a sash around the A-line dress. Logan would not approve of her looks.

She knew they were standing in the doorway. She could hear them whispering.

"She looks tired," Tyler said.

"Wrong word, little brother. She looks *haggard.*"

"I think we all know he isn't coming back now or ever," Mike hissed. "Why in the hell are we pretending and tiptoeing around it?"

"To make it easier for her. He was her world. That world is falling down around her. Look at her, for God's sake," Cala said. "Do you have any idea how much pleasure I got throwing out that damn chocolate cake into the snow? Well, do you?"

"About as much pleasure as I got tossing the lasagna," Mike said.

"What should we do?" Tyler asked fretfully.

"I have no clue. What do other people do when their families fall apart?" Cala asked.

"I can hear you," Kristine said. "Come in here and sit down. I want to tell you something, and for heaven's sake, take off those jackets and ties. Cala, pour the eggnog. Did you put *anything* in it?"

"I followed your recipe, Mom."

"Good, we're all going to need something. I want you to know I do not approve of children drinking, but this is Christmas Eve and an exception. I might be just a little bit . . ."

"Sloshed," Mike said.

"Sloshed is a good word," Kristine said, enunciating

each word carefully. "I want to tell you what Mr. Dunwoodie at the bank told me. Among the four of us we might be able to figure it out." She accepted the cup of eggnog Cala handed her.

"Spit it out, Mom," Mike said gently.

Kristine told them about the money and the banker's implied words.

The children stared at her with stunned expressions. "You should have told us, Mom," Tyler said.

"I didn't want you to worry. I knew you all had your own adjustments to make with this last move. None of you were exactly warm and friendly at the time. Besides, I was worrying enough for all of us. Now, tell me, do you remember when was the last time you saw those two brown, accordion-pleated envelopes we kept our bank records in? The one with your birth certificates, insurance policies, and stuff like that."

"Years," Cala said.

"Back in the summer. I saw Dad working in his office. He had piles of stuff everywhere," Mike said. "Eight million dollars, and it's gone!"

"A long time ago, more than a year," Tyler said. "That's a lot of money."

"I don't know if it's gone or not. The only thing I really remember was how elated your father was when he locked the money into a certificate of deposit for five years that was paying twenty-four and a half percent interest. That's how the account became so robust. It didn't get here the way your father said it was supposed to. I need the three of you to go into the storage room and look through the boxes that were not unpacked. I did look through them, but I was far too jittery. It's possible I missed them."

"Why would you ship personal stuff like that? I would have thought you would have packed it in your suitcases. Did Dad say anything about bringing it?"

"No; he said he was packing it with his office things. I thought he did. It's just records. He thought it was safe to send them. The boxes were sealed and stamped."

"What you're saying is we're broke unless we can find the records. What good are the records if the money isn't there? Is that it?" Mike said, an angry, bitter look on his face.

"That's what I'm saying. I had to get an advance on next month's check. My own personal checking funds didn't get here either. I had a little over eight thousand dollars in that account."

"What exactly does power of attorney mean?" Cala asked.

"It means Mom turned over her inheritance to Dad and let him handle it any damn way he saw fit. Eight million smackeroos, and it's gone just the way he's gone. Does anyone around here need a blueprint?" Mike demanded.

"You have to stop saying things like that, Mike. You don't know any more than I know about what happened to your father. We have to give him the benefit of the doubt. He could be hurt or injured somewhere. He could have amnesia. You're implying the same thing Mr. Dunwoodie implied, that your father deserted us and absconded with the money."

"My theory makes sense. Your theory doesn't, Mom. Besides, none of us could understand why we came here first and Dad was to follow. Most families travel together. You should have stood up to him, Mom."

"That's not fair, Mike," Kris said. "There was a lot to do to get this house ready. It's going to be an ongoing project. Your father's time wasn't up. It was a bad time for him, being passed over and having to leave the military. He truly believed he could go all the way and make general. He always said he was a thirty-year man, not a twenty-year man. He didn't want us to see how traumatic it was for him. I understood. I thought you did, too."

"See, Mom, you're sticking up for him again. To a point I can understand it. This is the result. Other families, and we've all seen hundreds of them, stick together and tough it out. We were prepared to do that until he chopped us off at the knees. This is not by the book, by the way."

"Boy, what I could do with eight million dollars," Cala said.

"South Sea islands, here I come," Tyler said dreamily.

Exasperated, Kristine said, "Is that all you're thinking about, the money? Don't you care about your father?"

"From where I'm sitting it doesn't look like Dad cares much about me, Mike, or Tyler, so to answer your question, no, Mom, I do not care at this particular moment. I saw this coming; so did Mike and Tyler. I guess the big question is, why didn't you see it?"

"See what? You're making your father out to be some sort of . . . I don't know, a horrible person. Why is it so hard to believe something terrible happened to him? It's an ugly world out there. We were sheltered, protected, while under the umbrella of the military. Your father did not desert us, and he did not steal my money. Excuse me, *our* money. Why are you saying all these ugly things *now?*"

"We never had the chance to say them before. We thought about it every day of our lives, and I think I'm speaking for Cala and Tyler when I say this. Dad was never shy about whipping our asses when we said something out of line or did something wrong. You never took our side, so why all the interest now? We were the good little soldiers. It was always 'yes, sir, no, sir, yes, sir, whip my ass, sir' for looking at you crossways. We were never allowed to go anywhere or do anything. He picked our friends, told us what to eat and when to eat it. We had to do calisthenics by the hour, we needed to be tough so we would grow into good *big* soldiers. We hated it, but we did it because we didn't have any other choice. It was how we survived. You had eight million dollars, and you wouldn't let Cala and me go on the class trip to France because Dad said it was too expensive. We were the only two who didn't go. We even said we'd pay him back. I didn't see you intervening. We did not have a good life, Mom, so stop deluding yourself," Mike said. The bitterness in his voice wafted across the room.

"Tyler, Cala?" Kristine said tearfully. "Do you two feel the same way?"

"Mom, where were you all those years we were growing up and moving around? You're our mother; you were supposed to see all those things. Good little soldiers that we were, we were not allowed to whine or cry. Stiff upper lip and all that stuff, and then, of course, there was that stupid book you and Dad went by. In case you haven't noticed, this is our rebellion stage. I can't wait to leave for college. I suppose we won't be able to go now. Is that the next thing you're going to tell us? Guess what, I'm going, and so is Mike, even if we have to work our way through. Aw, Mom, don't cry. Look, we're going to go to the storage room and look for those folders. Three sets of eyes are better than one."

"In cases like this you always follow the money trail. I saw that in a movie once. It makes sense," Mike said soberly.

"Merry Christmas to all of us," Tyler blurted. "Trust Dad to pick a holiday to screw things up. This is one of those things we'll remember all our lives."

"You need to stop this kind of talk right now. Your father is a good, kind man. A stern man. There have to be rules; otherwise, things . . . what happens is . . . things go . . . awry. I admit that at times your father got . . . carried away, but he meant well. He wanted the three of you to grow up independent with a strong sense of . . . of . . . the way life really is outside the military. In civilian life no one seems to care. In the military we took care of our own. You know that."

Mike dropped to his knees and reached for his mother's hands. Cala and Tyler did the same thing. "Mom, Dad was a tyrant. He abused his parental authority. He was not kind; nor was he good. And he was never gentle. He wasn't stern, either. He was hateful. If I had to find a word that suited him, I'd choose dictator. He was none of those things you said he was. He wasn't even a good husband to you. He was the talk of every base we ever lived on. He came on to every woman that even looked at him. If we knew that, why didn't you?''

Kristine blinked at her son's ugly words. She felt like she'd been slapped across the face with an ice-cold rag. "I refuse to listen to any more of this kind of talk. I'm going to bed. We'll have to open our presents in the morning, or you can open yours now. I don't care one way or the other.''

Kristine turned once on the stairway to look back at her children, who were huddled together at the foot of her chair, crying. She knew she should go back to comfort them, but if she did that, it would be admitting she was giving credence to everything they had said.

Her legs felt like they had fifty-pound weights tied to them as she climbed the steps. She felt woozy from all the wine she'd consumed. Tomorrow was another day. Tomorrow she would think about everything that had been said during the past hour. Tomorrow she would think about the chocolate cake and the tray of lasagna. Tomorrow she would think about and read the last letter Logan had sent to see if there were hidden messages she might have missed.

Tomorrow.

"You're sure you'll be all right here alone?" Kristine asked.

"Mom, we aren't babies. We know how to cook, we know how to carry in wood and make a fire. We'll look out for each other. We'll take down the tree and pack up everything and, yes, we'll be careful of your grandma's ornaments. We'll unpack all the stuff in the storage room, too.''

"We'll shovel the driveway if it snows. Don't worry about us, Mom. We have tons of college catalogs to go through and phone calls to make. Just go and do whatever you have to do. Your taxi is waiting. Don't worry about the car.

We aren't planning on going anywhere, but it will be nice to know it's there if we need it."

"I hate leaving you. I left money in the kitchen in case you want to go to town to a movie or get a pizza. I should be back in a week. As much as I don't want to do this, I have to. I need to know. I don't want you worrying about me. I'll call every day."

"You better not call. Overseas calls are expensive. When you get there, ring once and hang up so we know you're okay," Mike said.

"Mom, the driver is honking his horn. Go already."

"I'm going. You take . . . I'm going."

The three children rushed to the window in time to see their mother close the taxi door. They waved.

"I feel like crying," Cala said.

"For Mom or *him?*" Mike snapped.

"For me. For you and Tyler. Our lives are changing. We said we wanted change, but I don't think any of us meant this kind of change. Where do you think he is?"

"Some place nice and warm with some bimbo half his age spending our mother's money."

"How long do you think he was planning this?" Tyler asked with a catch in his voice.

"I'm certainly no authority on stuff like this, but if I had to take a guess, I'd say for some time. I think the first clue was last summer when he kept going away for weekends. He never did tell any of us why. Mom said it was secret business, but even I don't think she believed that. Mom just took his word for everything and believed everything he said. I bet he started planning this two years ago, when he had that kidney operation."

"Are you saying our father, Colonel Logan Kelly, had a mid-life crisis?" Cala asked in awe.

"Yep. That's what I'm saying," Mike said. "Listen. I have an idea. Let's drag our mattresses down here and sleep in the living room. If we do that, we won't have to lug firewood upstairs every day. We can all use the bathroom down here because it's the warmest one in the house.

We can eat junk food until it comes out of our ears. We won't do dishes for the whole week until we know for sure when Mom is coming home. No beds to make, either. We can live like slobs for a whole week. What do you say?''

"I say that's the best idea you ever had," Cala said.

"I made up my mind to go to Georgia Tech," Mike said.

"Great school. I might consider it myself. I haven't crossed off Tulane or Georgetown, though," Cala said.

"He's never coming back, is he?" Tyler asked, a sob building in his throat.

"In my opinion, no, Ty," Mike said.

"I agree with Mike, Tyler. He's got eight million dollars; why does he need us? He always liked you the best if you need consolation. Mike and I are okay with that."

"Nah. You don't know the half of it. He was harder on me than you because, as he put it, I was just like him. I'm not like him, am I?"

"No way," Mike said.

"Absolutely not," Cala said.

"Let's go get those mattresses," Tyler said, knuckling his eyes.

"We need to look into student loans, aid, and all that stuff. Come August, one way or another, I'm outta here," Mike said.

"What about Mom? If Dad doesn't come back, she'll be alone," Cala said.

"Look, let's all understand something right now. I love Mom, so do you. She's all grown-up. Maybe this will give her some incentive to take some courses or better yet, get the degree she's always talked about. If she starts up the business again, she doesn't need a college degree. It's her decision to make, not ours. She's not old. I'm sorry to say I am not feeling too charitable where Mom is concerned. When was she there for us? If she was, why did we spill our guts to Sadie on a regular basis? Well?"

"What if she has a breakdown or worse? She's drinking a lot," Cala said miserably.

"That's by her choice. Not ours. That's her weakness, not ours. We're tough, remember. Why didn't all that bullshit rub off on her?"

"Because Dad kept her under his thumb. He liked her submissive. She lived for those little pats on her head and the few kind words he doled out when he was in the mood. She bought into it. Let's not forget she was the rich one, not him. I hope he goes fucking *bald*." Mike's words had the desired effect on his siblings, and they burst into laughter.

"Sadie, how nice of you to meet me. Thanks. Lord, it's freezing. Are you sure you don't mind me staying with you for a few days?"

"Not at all. I'm worried about you. Do you have any idea how ghastly you look? I'm saying this because I'm your friend. Friends are allowed to say things and worry about their friends. I guess I do and don't understand why you're here. What is it you hope to accomplish? If Logan is gone, then he's gone."

"Just like that. If he's gone, he's gone. If he is gone, that means everything was a lie. How do you expect me to live with that?" Kristine said as she settled into the passenger seat of the Volvo. "The kids . . . God, I don't even know where to begin. The things they said, the way they feel . . . I can't handle it. Mike is . . . so belligerent. Cala is mouthy, and Tyler, his eyes fill up constantly. I don't know how to make it right for them."

"The time to make it right was a long time ago. You didn't do it, and this is the result. I'm going to tell you the way it is, Kris, and I'm not going to sugarcoat it."

"Tell me what, for heaven's sake?"

"Your children detested their father with a passion. They weren't wild about you, either, because, according to them, you'd prostitute yourself to Logan for a smile or a pat on the head. That's pretty strong stuff coming from kids. All I did was listen. So did Jim. They never wanted or expected anything from us. They just wanted to unload. They needed someone, and we were there. End of story."

"Dear God! They said . . . implied . . . they believe that Logan was a womanizer. Do you know anything about that? If you did know, I wonder why you didn't tell me, Sadie. Well?"

Sadie fumbled in the console for a cigarette. "Rumors like that are always around. Every day I hear a new one. You were his wife, Kris. Did you ever suspect Logan was anything but the White Knight you believed him to be?"

"No. The kids sounded so sure. Other kids hear their parents talking, and they repeat what they hear. So, what you're saying is, you did hear the rumors."

"I did hear them, Kris. I didn't want to believe them because you were so happy. Men slip when they're having affairs. You would have picked up on something. Wouldn't you?"

"Obviously I didn't. He took all our money. It wasn't transferred the way it was supposed to be. My personal checking monies were never transferred, either. I don't know a thing about Logan's pension. He took care of everything. I simply signed papers when my signature was required. He's had my power of attorney for twenty years. He never abused it."

"That was pretty damn stupid of you, Kris."

"Yes, I guess it was. I loved him so much, Sadie. He was my life. Waking up next to him every morning was a thrill not to be believed. I worshiped him. There was nothing I wouldn't have done for him. He said he felt the same way. We were good together. We were in love. Twenty years later we were as much in love as we were the day we got married. I refuse to believe I was so stupid I didn't see . . . things."

"You were obsessive, Kris. You saw and heard what you wanted to see and hear. You made excuses and believed those excuses. Your kids saw through it. Look. That's past. You can't unring the bell. In case you haven't noticed, you've been talking in the past tense, so I guess that means in your heart of hearts you know something is very wrong. Is it possible you're beginning to believe your kids?"

Kristine shrugged. "Has Jim said anything?"

"No. It's a guy thing, Kris. These guys have their own cockamamie code when it comes to stuff like this. I did hear him talking to Joe Evans one day last summer. He made a comment that ol' Logan was off again for fun and games. It was the weekend of Sandy Richards's birthday party. You came alone."

"I remember. That far back, huh?"

Sadie steered the Volvo to the curb and cut the engine. There was concern in her dark brown eyes when she stared at her friend. "I'll wait here for you. How much money are we talking about, Kris?"

Kristine felt the snow crunch beneath her boots as she leaned down to respond. "Eight million dollars," she said in a strangled voice before she slammed the car door shut.

It was a good twenty minutes before Kristine was ushered into Steven Owens's office at the American Consulate. She held out her hand. "I'm Kristine Kelly, Mr. Owens. I called you last week about my husband Logan. Do you have any news?"

He was a tall man, thin, with ginger-colored hair that stood on end. Dressed in a heavy wool sweater and thick corduroy trousers, he motioned for Kris to sit down. "Our heat isn't too good today. Can I get you some coffee?"

"No thank you. What were you able to find out?"

"Colonel Kelly never had a reservation on Lufthansa. I checked the military flights as well as the other airlines. There was never a reservation. Your own and the children's showed up, though. When Captain Dellwood dropped him off, Logan must have waited and then left. No ticket was ever issued in his name. I had two of my aides go to all the airports to show his picture around. No one remembers seeing him. That's it, Mrs. Kelly."

"He couldn't have just dropped off the face of the earth. He has to be somewhere."

"He could be anywhere. Someone could have driven

him someplace. He could have taken a train. There were thousands of travelers at that particular time. During the holidays everyone is busy, and no one pays attention. Did he have much money on him?''

"I don't know if he had it on him or not, but he had access to eight million dollars.''

"I see.''

"What do you see, Mr. Owens?'' Kristine asked coldly.

Steven Owens looked away. "It's just an expression.''

"You aren't a very good liar, Mr. Owens. You think the same thing everyone else thinks. You think Logan took all our money and lit out. Whether he did it with another woman is optional. That is what you were thinking, isn't it?''

"Well, I . . . it is one explanation. I'm sorry to say I have no others.''

"What about his passport? Is there any way we can check to see if he entered another country?''

"Not really. He could be anywhere, Mrs. Kelly. If he is in fact eluding you and doesn't want to be found, then you won't find him. I'm sorry to be telling you this. It's the way it is.''

Kristine struggled to find her voice. It was rusty-sounding to her ears when she finally managed to get the words out. "Did you check the hospitals and clinics?''

"Of course, Mrs. Kelly. There was nothing to find. Is there anything else I can help you with?''

"What about an assumed name with new papers?''

"I don't know. It's possible. I would need a name, something more to go on. Unfortunately, real life is nothing like the movies, Mrs. Kelly.''

"Thank you for your time, Mr. Owens.''

Kristine felt a thousand years old as she made her way down the long corridor and the hundred or so steps that led to the ground level. She wanted to cry. She needed to cry. Her eyes felt dry and hot, but there were no tears.

Inside the warm car, Sadie reached out to her friend. "What did they say?''

Kristine stared at her friend, seeing things she'd never noticed before. The light spattering of freckles under her eyes and how compassionate those brown eyes were. Her hairdo was new and lighter or was it always that way and she just never noticed? She appeared to have lost weight, too. And her children adored her, confided in her. "They said Logan never had a reservation on Lufthansa or any other airline. I wanted to make it for him, but Logan said I had enough to do with the packing and he would handle it. I said okay. He was to leave on the fifteenth and arrive home on the sixteenth. They checked the hospitals and the clinics and came up dry. He did ask how much money Logan had, and when I told him, he said, 'I see.' That was the end of that. I rather imagine you're thinking the same thing right now."

"That kind of money is way over my head. I guess you want to go to the bank now."

"If it's not too much trouble. If you'd rather go home, I can rent a car and do all the chasing around on my own. I hate to impose, Sadie."

"You aren't imposing. We're friends. I just wish there was more I could do."

"There is. You can take me to Winklers for something to eat after I finish at the bank."

Sadie steered the Volvo into traffic. *She's so capable, so efficient,* Kristine thought. She loved Sadie, loved the bright auburn curls with the tinge of gray at the temples, the light dusting of freckles across her cheekbones, loved her ready smile. Childless, she was godmother to so many children she had to keep a book with the birth dates listed in alphabetical order. She was Kristine's one true friend.

"I'd love to go to Winklers. Do you think the bank will tell you anything?"

"They have to tell me. My name is on the account. They can't refuse to tell me what I want to know."

But they did refuse to tell her, citing banking laws.

"No, no, you don't understand. Get out the file card. My signature is on it."

"Madam, your account was closed out three years ago. There is no account at this bank that has your name on it. Colonel Logan himself had an account with only his name on file. I cannot divulge any more information."

"That money is mine! I can prove it!" Kristine all but screamed.

"Madam, you must lower your voice. This is a bank."

"Then you better get someone here to talk to me who knows what the hell is going on. Where is my money?"

"Please, come with me, Madam."

Kristine scurried after the pompous, fussy little man into a tiny office where an obese man sat behind a desk that was much too small for his girth. "I speak German fluently so don't think you can talk and I won't understand. Where is my money, Mr. Hoffstetler?" Kristine asked, looking at the name plate on the man's desk.

"Your money isn't here, Mrs. Kelly, and it hasn't been here for three years. Your husband transferred large sums of money into another account bearing only his name. This was legal since the account was a joint account. When those transactions were completed, he then closed out the joint account. That is all I can tell you. I must contend with privacy and banking laws. Your husband had your power of attorney, Madam."

Kristine felt her shoulders sag. "I can't find my husband, Mr. Hoffstetler. He was supposed to return to the United States on December sixteenth. He never arrived. The money he was supposed to wire to our Virginia bank never arrived, either. Eight million dollars is a lot of money, Mr. Hoffstetler. I have three children. Tell me what to do."

"I cannot help you, Mrs. Kelly. The answers you seek lie with your husband."

"Goddamn it, I can't find my husband. If I could, do you think I'd be sitting here talking to you? Can you tell me when my husband closed out his own account?"

"No, Mrs. Kelly, I cannot tell you that."

"Go to hell!" Kristine snarled as she gathered up her purse and gloves.

"It didn't go so good, eh?" Sadie said as she shifted gears. "What happened?"

Kristine told her. "My God, Sadie, he must have been planning this for a long time. How could I have been so stupid?"

"You loved him. Love makes one blind at times."

"Blind, dumb, *and* stupid. Me of all people. The saddest part is I did not have a clue that something wasn't right. That certainly doesn't say much for me, does it?"

"The circumstances might be a little different, but you and I have both seen this happen to hundreds of families over the years. Somehow, they all managed to survive and get on with their lives. You will, too, Kristine."

"Sadie, I didn't say I was buying this whole package. I admit that things look black right now. I am not about to rule out the possibility that something happened to my husband. Foul play is not out of the question either as far as I'm concerned."

"I don't believe what I'm hearing," Sadie said. "Do you need to be run over by a truck first? It's in your face, Kristine. Look at it and deal with it."

"Not until I'm sure. In his letter Logan said he loved me. He said we'd had a good life, which is true. He loves the kids. He really does, Sadie. Yes he was strict, yes he made them toe the line, but they're better people for it."

"They don't think so. Speaking four languages and living all over the world doesn't make them better people. You and I both know that. Now that Logan isn't on the scene, you are the one who has to take responsibility for the loss of their childhood. They didn't ask to be good little soldiers; they didn't ask to live their lives by Logan's book. If you don't face up to what is right under your nose, then you are going to lose it all—and that includes your children. I've never been a mother, but my heart tells me there can be nothing worse than one's own child turning on you. In your case, three children. You will have no reserve to draw on. This is not a good situation, Kristine."

"Let's skip Winklers. I need to get some sleep. I've never been good with jet lag."

"I guess that's your way of telling me you aren't interested in my opinions. Sometimes, life isn't fair, Kris. You do look kind of ragged. A few hours' sleep will work wonders. Jim is working this evening, so we can do dinner at Winklers if you want."

"That sounds good. I promised the kids I would call to let them know I arrived safely. Did you have a nice holiday, Sadie?"

"Hectic. It was one party after the other. Same old same old. I just put away all the decorations yesterday. Now I'm concentrating on spring and the colorful flowers I'm going to plant in my small garden. And how was your holiday?"

"Lousy. We had hot dogs, french fries, and Jell-O. The tree was nice. The kids tried. I guess I didn't try hard enough. I also drank too much. I've been doing that a lot lately. It helps me to sleep."

"You better watch it, my friend, or you'll end up like Miriam Laskey. Liquor is not your answer. Dealing with the problem at hand is your answer. Now, tell me, what are you going to do?"

"I'm going to do what I came here to do, check out everything personally. Then I'm going to go back to Virginia to wait for my husband. It's all I can do, Sadie. If I do anything else, that means my whole life has been one big lie. I absolutely refuse to believe that."

"Okay, Kristine, I won't believe it either."

Kristine smiled wanly. "You're a good friend, Sadie."

Sadie shrugged, a chill running up her arms. "You, too, Kris."

4

"Have a safe trip, Kristine. Call me so I know you got home safely. Kiss the kids for me." Sadie shouted to be heard over the airport noise.

Kristine nodded, her eyes on the military police that had escorted her to the plane. Sadie winked at her. "Someday you will appreciate the humor of this, Kristine. You of all people being arrested for causing a disturbance with your husband's commanding officer. Jim is going to have a fit when he finds out. The worst part is we didn't find out a damn thing." It was all said in one long shouting breath.

"It's not over, Sadie," Kristine hissed. "It won't be over until my husband comes home. With my . . . *our* money. No one gives a damn. They didn't even try to help me. They all believe Logan went off with another woman. I will never, ever believe that."

"At least you got his pension. That's a plus. Threatening to go on national television and writing to the president sure got things moving. I'm still having a hard time figuring out why Logan didn't change that over. I guess it would have left a paper trail of some kind. You got it, that's the important thing. I'll talk to you soon, Kristine."

Kristine stared disdainfully at the MP, who was returning her stare. "I hate the whole goddamn, fucking military system. I gave you twenty fucking years of my life and when I need you, what do you do, you fucking arrest me and put me on a plane to get rid of me," Kristine snarled.

"Yes, ma'am," the MP said.

"Kristine, shhh, people are staring," Sadie whispered.

"Like Logan says, who gives a good rat's ass if they stare or not. I'm going, I'm going," she said to the MP, who motioned her to move forward with the announcement of the last boarding call.

Aware that people were staring at her, Kristine felt herself cringe. In her entire life she'd never acted the way she'd just acted. She'd never mouthed four-letter words in public, either. Lack of sleep, too much alcohol, jet lag, and very little food were probably the cause, along with not knowing what had happened to her husband. She'd just faced the proverbial brick wall and crashed into it.

Kristine reached into the overhead bin for a pillow and blanket. She buckled her seat belt and was asleep within minutes. She woke twenty minutes before the plane set down at Dulles International Airport.

Haggard, disheveled, and out of sorts, Kristine managed to get through customs with her bags and was standing outside the terminal when Cala and Mike pulled to the curb.

"I guess it didn't go very well, huh, Mom."

"Well, I managed to get myself arrested by the MPs and thrown out of the Officers' Club all within an hour. The MPs escorted me to the plane. The consulate as much as told me not to call them again. Everyone, even Sadie and Jim, are convinced your father absconded with the money and another woman. I slept the entire flight, but I am so very tired. I just want to go home and go to bed."

"Are you sorry you went, Mom?" Cala asked hesitantly.

"I never knew so many people detested your father. I thought he was respected and well liked. People I thought were my friends didn't seem to like me, either."

Mike snorted but said nothing.

"Now what?" Cala asked, getting into the backseat so her mother could sit next to her brother.

"Well, we at least get your father's pension. Something went awry there. It's a decent amount of money. Jim seems to think your father didn't really screw that up. He thinks if he had taken it, there would have been a paper trail. It's your father's way of taking care of us. That's how I have to think about it.''

"Twenty-five grand in place of eight million. Yeah, that's a pretty fair swap. Wise up, Mom. Take off those blinders. He screwed us over, and you're still defending him. I hate this damn bullshit,'' Mike said through clenched teeth.

"I do, too. We went up to the attic while you were gone. We had a few really bad snow days, so it seemed like a good thing to do. We found Grandma and Grandpa's old trunks. We found their wills. The will said . . . what it said was . . . the money Dad stole was to be put in trust for their grandchildren, if any. The remainder, the money which your parents inherited, was put in trust for you until you reached the age of fifty. The income was to be paid to you monthly. Did you know that, Mom?''

Kristine jerked to full wakefulness. "No. No, I didn't know that.''

"Why is that, Mom?'' Mike bellowed. "Just tell us why that is.''

"I . . . I was distraught . . . first it was Solomon, then my parents, all the animals in the barn. It was a terrible time. Your father handled it all, even though we weren't married until two years later. I couldn't get a grip on things. All I did was cry. I signed whatever he told me to sign.''

"Like now. You can't get a grip now either. Why are Cala, Tyler, and I supposed to be so tough, so grown-up, so responsible, and you're this . . . person who can't get a grip? Well, guess what, Mom. Your children are going to file a lawsuit against your husband to reclaim the portion of our grandparents' estate, that was supposed to come to us when we reached our majority. It's not the money. It's that the son of a bitch stole it right out from under us. With your help. You should have been aware. You should have protected our inheritance. *You* were the trustee, not him. Instead you gave that bastard the license to steal from all of us. Don't forget he stole the eight thousand dollars you saved out of your housekeeping money," Mike bellowed in his mother's ear.

"Stop it! Stop it right this second! You will not sue your father. I forbid it. You can't sue someone you can't find. How are you going to have papers served on your father if you don't know where he is? I don't want to hear any more talk like this. Not now, not tomorrow, not next week, not ever again. It's over."

"No, it's not, Mom. One of these days he's going to surface. I don't know why or when, but it will happen. That's when the lawyers will pounce on him. Don't you get it, Mom, he stole from us? Tell me, is that little ditty in the rule book?"

"We're leaving, Mom. Mike and I got accepted into Georgia Tech. Sadie got all our transcripts and had them faxed to the school. We go in as sophomores. Tyler goes in as a freshman. We'll be leaving next week. Sadie did it all for us. She said she called in some favors and made it work. She did what you should have done. We called Mr. Dunwoodie at the bank, took in Grandpa's will, showed him how we were supposed to inherit, and a portion of your monthly check is going to the school for our tuition. We're getting jobs, so that won't be too much of a drain on you. You'll have Dad's pension, and there's still money each month from your inheritance."

Kristine felt the silent scream building deep in her throat. "You went behind my back and did all that. Sadie helped you! I will never forgive her for this betrayal. How dare you do this! How dare you! You aren't going anywhere. Let's make sure we understand that fact. You're underage. You only leave if I say you leave, and I say you aren't leaving."

"Yes, Mom, we're going. If Dad had followed through, we'd be leaving anyway. If he was here, you wouldn't be able to wait to get rid of us. You know it, and we know it. There's no point in dancing around this. It's the way it is," Mike said.

It was true, every word her son said. Kristine started to cry. "What will I do without you?"

"What did you do before?" Cala shot back. "You were never there for us. You were always busy with dear old Dad. You were never too busy for him. Sadie was more a mother to us than you were. I'm sorry, Mom. I wish it was different. We'll look after Tyler. We'll call to let you know how we're doing."

"When . . . when are you leaving?" Dear God, she'd caved in.

"Next week. We have to settle in, get jobs, get the lay of the land. Mr. Dunwoodie offered to drive us to Georgia. He's a really nice man. I think he felt sorry for us. He went to Georgia Tech, too. He pulled as many strings as Sadie did."

Kristine curled into the corner and stared out the window. She wished she could lie down and die. She didn't mean to say the words aloud, but they tumbled from her lips like a runaway train. "Your father was a stern man and had definite ideas about child rearing. I don't want you to hate him."

Kristine was jolted from her nest in the corner of the car and flung forward when Mike slammed on the brakes on the old country road. "Our father and your husband was a sadistic son of a bitch. My back and ass are full of scars from the beatings. So are Cala's. Tyler has psychological problems. We're going to get him fixed up. They have counselors at school who will help him. We're just damn lucky Dad's mind games didn't screw up our heads. Cala and I fought him. Sadie and Jim helped us. Sadie wanted to go to the CO, but Jim said it would be worse on us if he did. It was our decision to endure. Just so you know, we couldn't have done it without them. That's why Dad hated Jim so much and why he used to make fun of Sadie all the time. Tyler wouldn't open up, though. He was afraid of Dad. That was okay; Cala and I had enough hate in us for him, too. You let it happen, Mom."

"Every child gets a whipping once in a while," Kristine

said lamely. "My father used to spank me all the time."
Her voice was lamer still when she said, "I never hated
him for the spankings."

Mike groaned. "We aren't talking about a spanking
here. Cala, pull up your sweater. Show Mom your back. Is
that what you call a spanking, Mom?"

Kristine gasped, her hand going to her mouth.

"End of discussion!" Mike roared as he slipped the car
into gear and barreled down the road.

Kristine ignored her son's words. "Your father would
never . . ."

"Where were you, Mom?"

"You never cried . . . you never said . . ."

"The goddamn book, Mom. Good little soldiers didn't
cry and whine. We were good little soldiers. Where were
you, Mom?"

"I was there. Your father . . . didn't like interference. He
said his way was best. You should have come to me. I swear,
I didn't know. Dammit, you didn't cry. I didn't see . . . I
stopped giving you a bath when you were five. You wanted
to do it yourself. What . . . what did he use?"

"His army belt," Cala said quietly. "I'm adding child
abuse to the charges when we file our suit."

"Dear God." It was all she could think of to say. This
had to be some kind of black nightmare. All she had to
do was wait it out, and she would wake up. It wasn't going
to happen. Deep in her gut she knew what her children
said was true. They had absolutely no reason to lie. Mike
was right. Where in the name of God *was* she when all this
was going on? Doing all the things the book said she was
supposed to do so her husband could move up in rank.
Luncheons, committees, driving pools, dinner parties. Call
Kristine. She'll be glad to do it. And she had. Because it
pleased Logan. Everything in her life was about pleasing
Logan. Merciful God, what had she done to her children
and herself? How was she ever going to make this right?
She gave voice to the question in her mind.

"We're home," Cala said tightly.

"So we are." Kristine wondered if the deep weariness she felt showed in her voice.

"I'll put the car in the barn. It's supposed to snow tonight," Mike said.

"I made dinner," Cala said.

"That was nice of you, Cala, but I'm not hungry. I think I'll go upstairs and . . . and think about things."

"Mom?"

"What is it, Cala?"

"I'm sorry. We're all sorry. This way is best. Time and space between us is probably what we all need. Mom, he isn't coming back."

Kristine turned to face her daughter. "If you believe that, then why are you leaving?"

"Because we know you, Mom. You are going to sit here and wait for him to walk through the door. It isn't going to happen. We don't want to watch you destroy yourself, and that's what you're going to do. In your mind you're already trying to find an excuse for what he did to us, so you can live with it. We aren't going to be that far away. There are telephones. We all need to heal. We aren't the brightest people in the world, but from where we stand this seems to be our only option. If it doesn't work for us, we'd like to know we can come back to this place and, by the same token, if you need us, you only have to call."

"This *place?*" Kristine said in a strangled voice.

"Yes. This place. *Your* home. We never had a real home. All of us wanted that. You know, a room of our own like the one upstairs that was yours when you were little. It's still your room, with all your old things. We never had things to keep. Each move stuff got lost or thrown out. The beds were the same. The rooms were always different. We're going to get an apartment off campus. Tyler will be able to visit and eat with us. The first year he has to stay in the dorm. He needs friends. It's going to be good for him, and for Mike and me, too."

Kristine felt such a sense of loss she didn't know what to do. "You grew up right under my eyes, and I didn't even notice. My God, what does that say for me?" she muttered to herself as she made her way to the second floor.

It was Cala's turn to sit down on the steps and cry. Her sense of loss was so overwhelming, Mike had to put his arms around her.

"Guess she didn't take it too well, huh?"

"About as well as we're taking it. I hope we're doing the right thing."

"Sadie said it was the right thing. Jim agreed. Mom will have to snap out of it with us gone. Look, if it doesn't work, we can come back and go to Virginia State or some other local college. This is for now. Later will take care of itself. It's dinnertime, so I suggest we eat and talk in the kitchen. Where the hell is Tyler?" Mike demanded.

"Mashing the potatoes. Go easy on him, Mike. He's never been away from home before. This is a big step for him."

"All of a sudden I feel like I'm fifty years old," Mike grumbled as he headed for the kitchen. "Phone's ringing!"

"I got it," Tyler said. "It's Sadie."

Cala reached for the phone. "Everything is fine, Sadie. We just got back, and Mom went to bed. We told her in the car. She didn't take it too well. Yes, she's upset with you, but she'll come around. She still has hope. I could see it in her eyes. I don't think she's ever going to give up. Thanks for everything, Sadie. Give Jim a big hug from all of us. Of course we'll write. I have to warn you, we won't be making any overseas phone calls. If you hear anything, will you let us know? Bye, Sadie."

Their plates loaded, grace said, Tyler held up his hand. "I just want to know one thing. Do we love Mom or not?"

Cala and Mike looked at one another. "Of course we love Mom. Now, let's eat and talk about something pleasant for a change," Cala said.

Upstairs in her old childhood room, Kristine paced. How was it possible to be so stupid and blind? She'd failed her children, and Sadie and Jim had been there to pick up the pieces. Mike was right. Where in the hell was she when all this was going on? Was she deaf, dumb, blind, *and* stupid as well? Did cooking meals for her children, washing their clothes, and asking if their homework was done make a good mother? The answer was obvious. Somehow she'd convinced herself, or Logan had convinced her, that her family was a tight little family. Doing things together, the children home all the time. She racked her brain to think of things they had done together as a family. Where were those memories?

Damn, she needed to think, to plan. Maybe a warm bath, a nice glass of wine, maybe two, and then bed. Tomorrow would be time enough to think about the past week and today's events. Yes, tomorrow would be soon enough.

Kristine wished the earth would open up and swallow her as she watched her children load their bags and trunks into the back of Aaron Dunwoodie's minibus, which had the bank's name emblazoned on the side in bright red letters.

"It's not too late, Kristine, to change your mind. There's plenty of room. Are you sure you don't want to come along?"

If she had any doubts about changing her mind, they evaporated with the looks on her children's faces. "No, I haven't changed my mind. It's nice of you to drive them all the way to Georgia."

"I have business there, so it's no problem. I guess that's it. Now, if you youngsters will just say good-bye to your mother, we can be on our way."

They look like they're rooted to the ground, Kristine thought. *They don't know what to do.* She solved their problem by running down the steps to gather them all close. "I know you don't believe this, but I am going to miss you." Tears sprang to her eyes when she felt Tyler's trembling body. She stroked his hair, and whispered, "I love you," in his ear. "I swear, you two are the best-looking set of twins I've ever seen," she said lightly before she kissed them soundly. "Please come home soon," she whispered.

"Bye, Mom," they chorused before Kristine ran into the house.

In the kitchen, she broke down completely. How was she going to manage alone? How was she going to get through her days in this old barn of a house? Where would the noise come from? How did you cook for just one person? How did you walk past a child's empty bedroom and not cry?

Kristine raced up the steps and down the long hall to enter Mike's bedroom first. It was so tidy and clean she swallowed hard. She knew she could bounce a quarter off his bed and catch it in her hand. Where were the pictures, the trophies, the ball and glove? Mike had those things. She was sure of it. In a frenzy she opened dresser drawers, then moved on to the closet. Nothing. Everything was gone. It was as though he'd never been here. Maybe he stored his things in the storage closet downstairs. He should have left something behind, a paper clip, a pencil, a rubber band. A second search yielded nothing.

Cala's room was the same, barren and empty, clean and tidy.

Tyler's room surprised her. He was the sloppy one of the three, yet his room looked exactly like Mike and Cala's. There was no stray sock, no pencils or rubber bands. She knew then, in that one instant, that her children were sending her a message. What exactly the message was, she wasn't sure. What she did know for certain was they were gone, and she was alone. And all because of Logan.

A quick glance at her watch told her it was only nine o'clock. What was she going to do for the rest of the day? Make something for dinner so that she could eat it for the rest of the week? Write a letter to Logan she would never mail? Wait for it to snow so she could shovel the walk in case she wanted to go someplace? She looked around, a helpless look on her face before she reached for the wine bottle on the kitchen counter.

Kristine tugged and pulled the heavy footlocker from the front porch into the house—Logan's personal belongings, which had arrived by Lucas Freight. Her heart took on an extra beat. If Logan's locker was here, he must be close behind. Finally, she was going to get some answers.

Using all her strength, Kristine pushed and shoved the heavy trunk across the wood floors. She knew the metal corners were gouging and nicking the old oak floors, but she didn't care. Logan's belongings meant more to her than some three-hundred-year-old floors. This had to mean Logan was on his way. Finally. A month and a half overdue, but he was coming. She was sure of it. It would be just like Logan to show up on Groundhog Day and laugh himself silly.

How was she going to open the trunk? Where was the key? Logan had the key, of course. All the bank records must be inside. Did she dare break the lock? Should she wait for Logan to arrive? Maybe she should call the kids. Maybe she should have a drink. Brandy in coffee would be good. Ten o'clock in the morning wasn't too early if you were going by the time in Germany or England or even Spain or Italy. Besides, she needed something to shore up her nerves.

Kristine was on her third cup of coffee before she got the courage to go to the storage closet for a hammer. On the way back to the kitchen her gaze drifted to the coffeepot. She'd made four cups, and the pot looked like it was still more than half-full. She purposely avoided eye contact with the brandy bottle on the counter.

When she told Logan about the trauma she'd been through these past weeks, he would forgive her for breaking into his trunk. The hammer rose and fell, twice, three times, then, on the fourth try, the metal flange flew to the side.

Breathing like a racehorse, Kristine squatted down to pull and tug at the heavy lid. A wave of dizziness swept over her at the scent emanating from the trunk. Logan's scent. Her touch was reverent when she removed each item to place it carefully on the floor next to her. She loved the feel of her husband's things, loved the smell, loved touching the toothpaste tube. It wasn't until the trunk was completely empty that she realized there were no brown, accordion-pleated envelopes. However, there was a stack of letters that had never been opened. Letters she'd written. His wallet and car keys were the only other items in the manila envelope. Logan hadn't touched the trunk once she packed it. Fanatic that she was where her husband was concerned, she knew the toothpaste tube was exactly the way she'd packed it. There were no messy clothes. Everything was ironed to perfection and stacked neatly.

Kristine pawed through the contents, her breathing ragged and raspy. If Logan's wallet and car keys were in the trunk, that had to mean something happened to him. Logan never went anywhere without his wallet and keys. *Who put the letters, keys, and wallet in the trunk? Logan? Some stranger? Who?* She looked around, her eyes wild. *What does all of this mean?*

She needed more coffee. More brandy. Lots and lots of brandy to figure this out.

Rage, unlike anything she'd ever experienced, rivered through her. She kicked at her husband's belongings, scattering them in every direction. That was when she saw the scribbled words on the back of the manila envelope. She squinted to read the words.

Colonel Kelly was in such a hurry to return to the States, he asked me to ship his belongings January 1. Enjoy your new life.

It was signed by Corporal John McElveen.

Kristine peered at the date. January 1. It was now February 1. She'd been in Germany on the first of January. She'd tried to locate Corporal McElveen but was told he'd been reassigned to a post in the States. No other information was given her.

It was all too much for her. With one of Logan's tee shirts in her hand, Kristine curled into a ball on the braided rug by the fireplace, the tee shirt next to her cheek.

She slept, tears running down her cheeks even in sleep.

5

Kristine sat on the sagging front steps leading up to the wide front porch. In her hand was the coffee cup she was never without. Only she knew the cup held more liquor than coffee.

She heard the car before she saw it. Were the children finally coming home? They'd said maybe in June, but then June passed, and now it was July. Maybe it was better if they didn't come home. Maybe it would be better if she just drank herself to death. Would they come home then? She didn't know. An hour from now she wouldn't even remember having these thoughts. She slurped from the heavy mug.

There was dust on the road. The dust meant the car was coming to the house. She never had guests or company of any kind. For one crazy second she wondered if it was Logan. She rejected the idea the moment she saw the red lettering on the bank's minibus. Aaron Dunwoodie. He was dressed impeccably, the way all bankers dressed, but he had an extra plus; he was fit, trim, and very good-looking. She felt like calling him Judas.

"Get off my property. I didn't ask you here. Go away. I don't want to talk to you. You're a Judas is what you are."

"I need to talk to you, Mrs. Kelly."

"Why? I have nothing to say to you. I am not overdrawn at the bank. Take your bus and go back to the bank. I'm never going to forgive you for helping my children leave me. You had no right to do that. No right at all. Why are you still here? I told you to leave."

"I'm concerned about you, Mrs. Kelly. Your account has been inactive for six months. How are you living? What's happened to you?"

"I hit rock bottom is what happened. You took away the only thing I had left—my children. If you don't leave, I'm going to call the police."

"How are you going to do that, Mrs. Kelly? Your phone was disconnected last month. You have no electricity, either. That's what happens when you don't pay your bills."

"So what! It's none of your business. I have plenty of candles." Maybe that's why she hadn't heard from the children.

"There's a rumor in town that a deranged person is walking the highway and the fields. They say the woman has hair like a wild bush and ragged clothing. I came to see for myself. They're talking about you, Mrs. Kelly."

"It's a free country. I didn't do anything wrong. Go away. I was born here, and I'm going to die here."

"When was the last time you ate decent food, had a bath, washed your hair?"

"That's none of your business. I told you to go away."

"How long have you been drinking? You're drunk, Mrs. Kelly. It's nine o'clock in the morning."

"Yes-I-am-drunk! That's none of your business either. Don't you need to open your vault or something?"

"I did that already. The bank opens at eight. I brought you a present. I want to help you, Mrs. Kelly."

"I don't *need* your help. I don't *want* your help. I'm doing just fine. At least I was until you showed up. What kind of present?"

"Come over to the bus, and I'll show you."

"You're trying to trick me."

"No. The present is in the bus. I'm not going to give it to you until I make up my mind that you're worthy of it. This particular present requires a great deal of responsibility."

"That's something Logan would say. Take your present and go back to your bank."

"If you insist. First, though, do me the favor of at least looking at the present."

"If I do, will you leave?"

"Yes."

"All right."

Dunwoodie watched in horror as Kristine teetered on the sagging steps before gaining her footing. He was appalled at her condition, and she reeked of alcohol. He reached for her arm, but she shook it off. "I can manage."

"Let me help you, Kristine. I don't mean at this precise moment. I mean really let me help you."

"Do you feel guilty about something, *Mister* Dun-woodie?"

"People in town are talking about you. Your parents and their parents lived here all their lives, just the way mine have. I hate to see you tarnish their names and your own as well. You came back here because your roots are here. That's commendable. Things went awry, and this is the result. You can't wallow forever. Other women's husbands have left them, absconded with their money, and they didn't fall apart. It isn't too late for you, but you have to commit to yourself that you're going to rise above all this."

"What is *all this?*" Kristine sneered.

Dunwoodie sucked in his breath. "Your drinking. You're slovenly. You reek of alcohol and body odor. I would imagine the house looks the same way inside. You need to think about your children. It isn't too late."

"Just show me the damn present and leave."

"Open the door. It's on the front seat."

"Oohh, oohh. Are they yours?"

"No. I bought them for you. Gracie is the smaller one. Slick is the boy. They look just like the first dog I ever had. Your parents gave him to me when I was seven. He lived till he was eighteen. God, I loved that little dog. I didn't think I would ever get over his death. I guess I didn't, because I never got another dog."

"Can I pick them up?"

"In case you haven't noticed, that's what they're waiting for. Ahhh, they seem to like you even though you smell to high heaven."

"Shut up, Dunwoodie."

"Why should I?" Dunwoodie quipped. "They're my present. I have a say here. Can you handle it, Kristine?"

"I don't know, Dunwoodie. Probably not. They're beautiful."

"Blue ribbon dogs, Kristine. Listen. I have an idea. I have six weeks' vacation time coming to me. How about if I move out here and help you get straightened out. I'm a fair handyman, and I can get you off the sauce if you don't fight me. No strings. Just your word that you will work with me. I can have you back on your feet inside of six weeks. There are more dogs where those two came from. Right now you have a tidy little bank balance we can work with. The bank will not be averse to lending you money to start up your own business. As long as you're clean and dry."

A headache started to hammer behind Kristine's eyes. Join the living. Could she handle that? A pink tongue licked at her chin. She smiled as she cupped the tiny head in the palm of her hand. "Are they true Teacups?"

"Yes. Three pounds tops."

"I don't know if I have the stamina . . . what I mean is . . ."

"I know what you mean. Will you at least try?"

Kristine looked at the two balls of fur in her hands. She didn't trust herself to speak. She nodded.

"Then I say let's get this show on the road. I came prepared in case you agreed."

Kristine watched in amazement as he hefted two large canvas bags from the back of the small bus. "I'm yours for six weeks. The first thing we're going to do is eat some breakfast."

Kristine made a strangled sound that could have passed for laughter. "I don't think there's any food in the house."

"As I said, I came prepared. Groceries are in the back along with dog food, gear, and anything else we might need. You are going to scrub up, and I do mean scrub, while I make us some breakfast. Any messes the dogs make, you clean up. The only word you need to concern yourself with is *responsibility*. Know this. I'm throwing out all the liquor in the house."

Kristine sighed, tears welling in her eyes. She nodded, the pups clutched close to her breast. "Just tell me why."

Dunwoodie waited so long to reply Kristine was about to prod him a second time. "Because your children asked me to watch over you. I promised I would." Kristine nodded again.

"I like my bacon extra crisp and the butter on my toast melted."

"Duly noted."

Kristine smiled.

In the old-fashioned bathroom, Kristine made a nest in the middle of the floor by using two fluffy yellow towels. The pups closed their eyes and were asleep in an instant.

Kristine stared at herself in the mirror. Who was this ugly hag with the dark circles under her eyes and wild bush of hair? Who was this bony caricature staring back at her? How had she come to this? Dunwoodie was right, she looked like hell and smelled awful. She scrubbed, rubbed, and brushed until she thought her skin would come off in one long piece.

Once more she looked at her naked body before she got dressed. The two rolls of fat under her breasts were gone, and her breast size had diminished along with all the extra padding on her hips and thighs. The word emaciated came to mind. A lightweight sweat suit would help a little. There was not much she could do with her wild bush of hair except to pull it back and tie it into a bun. The last thing she did was brush her teeth not once, not twice, but three times. Then she gargled and rinsed, using a great quantity of mouthwash.

She still looked like she'd been struck down by the wrath of God, plus she wanted a drink so bad she found herself shaking with the thought. Just one drink. A little one. Maybe just a swallow. She'd squirreled bottles everywhere in the house. Surely there was one in her bedroom. A nip. Then her eyes fell on the sleeping puppies. How contented they looked. By bringing them up here to the second floor she had accepted the responsibility of ownership and caring for them. They'd trusted her to bring them up here, to fix a bed for them, then they fell asleep because they felt safe and content.

Kristine jammed her hands into the pockets of her sweatpants. *I can do this. I will do this. I have to do this. All my options are gone. I will do this.* "I will do this," she murmured over and over as she picked up the carpet with the sleeping pups to carry downstairs.

She felt self-conscious, vulnerable as well as ashamed with someone else in her house who knew about her drinking problem and how low she'd managed to allow herself to sink.

Kristine's jaw dropped as she approached the kitchen doorway. She saw the mess on the kitchen floor that she'd never cleaned up. For months she'd walked around Logan's footlocker and his belongings. Dunwoodie was sitting at the table sipping coffee. He nodded approvingly.

"I would have cleaned up but I wasn't sure you would want anyone touching your husband's belongings. Those are Logan's things, aren't they?"

"You went to school with Logan for a few years, didn't you. They called you Woodie. Logan said you were a hell of a football player. He said you were good enough for the big leagues."

"I never got to find out. I blew out my knee my second year at Georgia Tech. The upside to that is I can always tell when the weather is going to change. What do you think we should do with all this?"

"Right this minute I would love to burn it, but Logan might return one day and want it, so I guess I'll just pack it up and put it in the storage room. His wallet and car keys are here. Logan never went anywhere without his wallet and keys. There is forty-five dollars in the wallet and all his identification. You're a man, what do you think it means?"

"I think it means he's left everything behind and gone off somewhere with a brand-new identity. With eight million dollars he could buy top-notch identification that would pass muster anywhere. You don't need keys if you're going on to a new place with a new identity. The fact that they're in the trunk is just to throw you off. Obviously Logan knew you better than you knew him. It's up to you if you buy into it or not."

"Are you trying to make me angry?"

"No. I just want you to recognize what's in front of you and not deny it. False hope is a terrible thing."

Kristine slammed the lid of the footlocker shut. Her hands were still shaking, and her knees felt rubbery. "You don't like Logan, do you?"

"I didn't care for him as a boy. I thought he was arrogant and an opportunist. I don't know the man he is today. However, from what I do know now, I would say my earlier assessment of him is on target." He clapped his hands together and stood up. "Are you ready for the Dunwoodie Breakfast Special?"

"Sure. He's coming back. I just don't know when that will be. He would never do this to me without a reason."

"He already did it, Kristine. If he comes back, it will be because he wants something else. Let's call a truce here. You believe what you want to believe, and I will believe what I want to believe. Right now we have three primary goals. One is to get you back on your feet, two is to make things right with your children, and three is to take care of these two sleeping dogs. Agreed?"

"Agreed. I want a drink."

"Here you go. Drink as much as you want. It's all you're

going to get," Dunwoodie said, pouring coffee into a large, heavy mug.

"What should I call you?"

"Aaron, Woodie, whatever you feel comfortable with."

"I like Woodie. I thought you were pretty stuffy when I first met you."

"I thought you were pretty stupid the first time I met you."

"Touché," Kristine said. "Is there a Mrs. Dunwoodie?"

"There was, but it didn't work out. She thought the bank's money was hers to spend as she saw fit. Our customers thought otherwise. It was a big scandal at the time. I survived. I like your kids. They have their heads on straight."

"I thought they would be home by now."

"I guess you wouldn't know, since your phone was turned off. They aren't coming home for the summer. All three of them got good jobs on St. Simons Island. They wanted to get some money ahead for next semester. The twins finished the semester with a 4.0 GPA. Tyler was a little behind with a 3.8. You should be very proud of them."

"Right now I don't think I have the right to feel anything where they're concerned. Perhaps someday we can all make it right. I'm willing to take all the blame. Good God, I can't eat all that!"

"Then you don't get up from the table. Two eggs, three slices of bacon, two pieces of toast is not a lot of food. The orange is optional. The vitamins are a necessity, and you take them after you eat. Eat!"

Kristine ate. From time to time she risked a glance at her breakfast companion. When he was satisfied that she would indeed clean her plate, he excused himself. "Tell me which bedroom is mine. I want to change, so we can get on with the program."

Kristine laid down her fork, her eyes full of questions. "First room on the right. It was Mike's room. What program?"

"You know, hard work. Exercise, work, more exercise,

then more work. A good dinner and it's bedtime at nine o'clock because we get up at four. It pays to start early before the heat takes over. We're lucky today, no humidity.''

"Just tell me one thing. Do you have a book you go by?''

"No. Just good old common sense. I work with youngsters at the YWCA three days a week. If it's good enough for them, then it's good enough for you. The idea is to keep you so busy you won't have time to think about drinking. I just need fifteen minutes. That will give you time to clean up, since I cooked.''

"I can't believe I'm listening to you, much less following your orders. What about the dogs?''

"We'll barricade the kitchen. They'll be fine. Give some thought to what you're going to do with that trunk.''

The minute Kristine heard the banker's footsteps on the second floor, she was off her chair to drag the footlocker into the storage room off the kitchen. Huffing and puffing with the exertion, she then filled the sink with soapy water. She was drying her hands when Woodie walked into the kitchen. Neither of them mentioned the footlocker. "Egg plates need to soak," Kristine said.

"Now we're going to walk five miles.''

"Five miles!''

"Unless you feel you can go for six or seven. In a few days, when you build up some stamina, we'll run three and walk two. Twice a day.''

"Twice a day! Are you trying to kill me?''

"No, I'm trying to get rid of the toxins in your body. Alcohol does terrible things to your body.''

"How do you know all this?'' Kristine asked sourly.

"My mother was an alcoholic. No one knew but Dad and me. The doctor, too, but he's dead now. It was a dirty little secret we shared. Dad referred to it as Mom's spells. We had to keep it a secret. How would it look if the town's leading banker had a lush for a wife? I had to learn how to cook and clean and take care of her when the other kids were out playing. She died in her sleep with a whiskey bottle in her hand. Try growing up with that one.''

Kristine blinked. "I'm sorry. I guess I'm ready.''

"Then let's do it!''

Two hours later, Kristine limped up the steps to the front porch. "I'm never, ever going to do that again. Do you hear me? I have charley horses that have charley horses. I also have blisters that have blisters. And a corn.''

"It's not a problem. We'll cut holes in your sneakers so the canvas won't rub on the sore spots. It's twelve-thirty. We'll have some lunch and then we're going to tackle the barn to get it ready for your new business.''

"You do all that. I'm going to sit here and rub my legs.''

"No, no, that's not what you're going to do. You're going to fix us a nice sandwich and some ice tea. Then you're going to do the dishes, after which we will tackle the barn. We'll do our three miles before dinner, which I will cook. Eight miles is good. Really good.''

"Go to hell!''

"I've been there a time or two, and it isn't a nice place. C'mon, let's get crackin' here. Time waits for no man.''

"Bullshit!'' Kristine muttered as she stomped her way up the steps and onto the porch. "You are a sadist! What do my kids see in you?'' she continued to mutter.

Woodie grinned as he followed Kristine into the dim, cool house.

Out of the corner of her eye, Kristine observed the banker as she made lunch. *Cala probably thought him handsome. Mike would think of him as a good athlete with a trim, hard body. Tyler would like his openness and his tell-it-like-it-is attitude. Is he handsome? Kind of. Too tall? No, just right. The jeans and jersey look perfect on his lean body. On his best day, Logan never looked as good as the banker.* She squelched her thoughts immediately, her cheeks flaming.

"How's lunch coming? I'm starved. Kick off your sneakers. I'll cut holes in them for you.''

"What part of I'm-not-doing-any-more-walking didn't you understand?'' Kristine yelled as she slapped cold cuts between slices of bread. "Where did these groceries come from?"

"They were delivered while we were walking. I called for them this morning after the phone was connected. You owe me $23 for the bill."

Kristine sat down on one of the kitchen chairs. "Listen, I appreciate your help here, but I am not athletically inclined. I can't . . . won't . . . I don't want to exercise. There, I said it. You can pack up and go home now."

"It doesn't work that way. You might be a quitter, but I'm not. We're doing it!"

"Kiss my ass, Aaron Dunwoodie. Don't you listen? I'm a sedentary person."

"Do all you army people talk like that? It certainly isn't becoming, any more than a drunk for a mother is becoming."

"Yes. No. I never talk like this. You're bringing out the worst in me. I'm not going to drink anymore, okay?"

"All drunks say that. Right now you're probably wondering where you stashed some bottles. You think a little sip, a nip, just a swallow will get you over the hurdle. Hey, I've been there, remember? I've seen it all. Don't try to con me, okay? Where's lunch?"

Kristine, her eyes murderous, slid a plate across the table.

"This sandwich requires pickles. We need some carrot sticks, a banana, and an orange. You need to start eating right."

Kristine bit back the sharp retort she was about to utter. Instead she scraped the carrots, cut them, and peeled the oranges. To her dismay she ate it all and probably could have eaten more. She dumped the dishes into the sink with the other ones, muttering, "I'll do them later."

"Let's head for the barn. What shape is it in?"

"About as bad as this house. It's doable if that's your next question."

"Then let's go."

"Yes, sir!" Kristine said, snapping off a sloppy salute.

At three-thirty, Woodie called a halt. "The pups like it out here. Look at them. They're full of straw. You're going to have to give them a bath at some point today. We did remarkably well. Most of this stuff is still good. I thought this place burned down."

"That was the other barn. Logan had them clear everything out so when we came back it wouldn't be a constant reminder. It was in a lot better shape than this one. Look, I'm never going to get enough money to patch this place up. It needs major work."

"Not as much as you think. This is one sturdy building. We can get someone to come in and clean out the wood rot. There's not that much. I know just the man to do it, too. Two or three weeks, and it will be in top shape. You do a little at a time. How do those sneakers feel now?"

"Okay. I know I can't walk three more miles. Maybe you have a death wish, but I don't. I'm not walking one mile, two miles, or three miles. Get that through your head."

"Yes, you are. You said you weren't a quitter."

"I never said I wasn't a quitter. I am a quitter. I want to take a bath and go to bed. I don't care about dinner. Please."

"Ready? Fall in."

"I hate you. I hate your guts. No one in her right mind goes through torture like this. I don't even know you. You moved into my house and took over. You have no right. Do you hear me? You have no right to make me do this."

"Shut up and walk."

Kristine clamped her lips shut and followed the banker out to the front of the house. Later she would think about why she was such a blind fool.

"Try to keep up this time. No lagging behind. I want to see some spirit in your movements. I want some enthusiasm."

"When I kill you, I will be full of enthusiasm. Don't talk to me. I'm plotting your death. While you sleep. You'll never know what hit you."

Woodie grinned. "I sleep with one eye open. C'mon, lift those feet. Put some muscle into those legs. You're shuffling. Old people shuffle. People your age are supposed to be full of vim and vigor. Of course most people aren't drunks. Move, move!"

"If you open your mouth one more time, I swear to God I will put my foot in it. Shut up. I don't want to hear any more of your little ditties. I don't want to hear your voice. Period."

Seventy minutes later, Woodie said, "Good time. We actually did better this time than we did this morning. I guess that means you're getting the hang of it. I'm going to make dinner, but first you have to wash the dishes. While you're doing that I'll make up a solution for you to soak your feet. You can watch me cook."

In spite of herself, Kristine asked, "What are you cooking?"

"Chicken, salad, baked potato, fruit, and maybe some carrots. Why?"

"Because I'm hungry, that's why."

"I thought you said you were too tired to eat."

"That was then, this is now. I like my potatoes twice baked with cheese and sour cream. Bacon bits are good."

"I know a restaurant that serves them that way. Ours are going to be plain. Wash the dishes."

It was simpler to wash the dishes than it was to argue. When Kristine finished, she sat down to lower her feet into a dishpan full of bubbling salts. Nothing in the world had ever felt so good. She sighed her relief, tears filling her eyes.

"Tell me something, Kristine. In the past four hours how many times did you wish for a drink and how many times did you think about where you might have hidden bottles of liquor?"

Kristine jerked to full wakefulness. Her eyes wide with shock, she said, "I didn't."

"Good for you. Maybe I'll let you have some butter on your potato."

A moment later, Kristine was asleep at the kitchen table, her head resting on her arms.

"You just might make it after all, Kristine Kelly. What do you guys think?" Woodie asked as he cuddled the dogs.

"They think you're as crazy as a bedbug," Kristine muttered. "Don't get attached to those dogs, they're mine."

"Yes, ma'am," Woodie said smartly.

Kristine's eyes widened in awe. "I didn't think it was possible to restore this old barn to the way it was when my parents were in business. Everything is older, worn, but it's good enough to get me started. I thought for sure when you suggested pressure-washing everything, the whole building would collapse. I love the smell of whitewash. Mom was always funny about that. She wouldn't let Dad paint anything. She did all the whitewashing herself, on a ladder with a long-handled kind of squeegee thing. She said it was important for customers to see how clean and sanitary it was when they were paying top dollar for a pup. Sometimes I'd just come in here and lie in the sweet-smelling hay to cuddle with the pups and sniff to my heart's content. Pretty silly, huh?"

"I like the idea that you aren't going to keep the dogs in cages. There's something in me that revolts at seeing anything in a cage," Woodie said, looking around.

"Me too. Mom said they used the kennels in the beginning but got rid of them as soon as they could. The dogs that were caged weren't well adjusted. She's the one who came up with the bins with the straw. Yorkshire terriers are small, and the Teacups only weigh in at between three and seven pounds. They can't get out, but they can see what's going on. It makes them people-friendly, which is what this is all about. You did a good job constructing those little havens. The hay smells sweet, doesn't it?"

"I think we're farm people. We like the same things. To me this is a slice of heaven. Are you going to hire a vet?"

"If I can get this all up and running, I am. And a handler, too, in case I decide to show some of the dogs. I always wanted to be a vet, but my parents said that was an unseemly profession for a woman. Back then I didn't have any backbone. My parents said I had to go to the community college, so I did one year there and I was so miserable, they relented and allowed me to go to Old Dominion. I did one semester, and then they died. I always regretted not finishing and pursuing my dream. I guess it wasn't meant to be. Do you really think I can pull this off, Woodie?"

"Yes, Kristine, I do. The day we started work in here, you committed one hundred percent. I guess the real question is, where are you going to get your dogs?"

"From a lady named Cher Hildebrand in Dayton, Ohio. She's agreed to handle the dogs for the shows if I decide to go that route. It's a bit intimidating at first. When you show dogs you earn points toward a championship and have to win over the other Yorkies by the judge of the day. You breed for perfection in the Yorkie, trying to create that perfect dog. It's called a Standard for each breed, and as show people you are breeding toward that Standard to show. You show to make sure you are on target with the breeding program and producing an excellent dog that is good enough to become a champion. Sometimes you show two or three weekends a month. Our operative words here are going to be socializing our pups. The first pups arrive next month. Ms. Hildebrand is driving them here personally. I have a feeling she and I are going to become very good friends. She thinks like I do.

"My parents were considered ethical breeders. Their reputations were known all over the country. I want the same kind of reputation, and I know I'm going to have to earn it. Ms. Hildebrand is known for her ethical reputation and her Goldenray Yorkshire terriers. She's the one I'll be doing most of my business with, but I am getting two other pups from a breeder in Kansas. I'm starting small. I'm just so thankful my parents' old records didn't burn along with the barn. I've forgotten so many things, but I'm good to go, as they say. Let me give you the guided tour, Mr. Dunwoodie. That's the first thing my mother always said when a customer came through the doors. She allowed me to do it a few times. I always felt important.

"These, Mr. Dunwoodie, are the bins or stalls where we keep the pups. The straw keeps them warm even though the barn is heated. Note the soft flannel sheets. New pups need warmth. No one is permitted to pick up or handle the dogs except me. We have twelve of these bins. At some point, Mr. Dunwoodie, I hope to have them all filled with gorgeous, beautiful dogs that will make each new owner very happy. As you can see, everything is whitewashed and clean. It's always like this. Our dogs are healthy and happy. You will never notice an odor in here. We have fans overhead and cross-ventilation. We have outside runs for the dogs. Pups are kept separate during the first month. Everyone gets plenty of exercise. Our dog food is nutritionally balanced. At some point, I'll sell the food along with a line of collars, leashes, and dog treats, but not just yet.

"This is our kitchen. As you can see, everything is stainless steel, the bathing tubs as well as the refrigerator. The washer and dryer are probably on their last legs but will serve the purpose for now. We use old towels, sheets, and blankets and wash them daily. Each pup gets his or her own blanket and toy when they're a month old. It makes it easier when they go off with a new owner and have to leave siblings and Mom behind. I used to cry my eyes out when it was time for one of them to leave. You get a feel for people when they arrive. My mother was like a hawk when it came to the owners. If she had the least suspicion that someone wasn't up to her standards, she said no. Over the years I saw her turn away dozens of people. I want to match the right owner with the right dog. I want each dog to be loved, and I want the dog to love his new owner. It's that simple. In later years, Mom started to breed Maltese and, before the accident, she and Dad were considering Jack Russells. Sometime down the road, I might do that, but Yorkies are my passion now.

"This is the office. It's kind of spartan, with just a desk, chair, and file cabinets. I'll bring in some green plants, a coffeemaker, and some stuff to make it a little homier.

"This last room is what Mom always called the clinic room. Examining table, stainless-steel sink, cabinet, chair. Lots and lots of disinfectant in the cabinets. That's your tour, Woodie."

"I'm impressed. I brought you something, Kristine."

"A present? What is it?"

"It's in the car. Do you have a ladder?"

"Silly question. You spent the past three weeks on it. It's on the back porch."

"I need a screwdriver and some pliers? I'll put the ladder in the car and we'll drive out to the main road. What do you think?" Woodie asked, lifting a sign out of the backseat of his car.

Kristine's vision blurred. "Woodie, this is wonderful. I thought about getting a new sign but decided to wait. Who painted it? We need a celebration of some kind. But, not now."

"I love celebrations. Aren't we backlogged on our celebrations? One of these days we're really going to have a big one and combine everything in one. Actually, one of the girls at the bank painted the sign. Her father cut the sign into the pattern of a Yorkie, and she did the painting and the lettering. I think it looks professional."

Kristine's index finger traced the raised lettering: SUMMERS KENNELS. Owned and operated by Kristine Summers. "Oh, Woodie, this is just perfect. Thank you so much."

"What do you want to do with the old one?" Woodie asked as he tightened the last screw on the cheerful-looking sign.

"Throw it away."

"Do you think your parents would approve of this one or is it too . . . *cutesy?*"

Kristine's lips tightened. "They probably wouldn't approve. They rarely approved of anything I did. My mother was a master at finding fault. I think I tried all my life to win their approval. There was never a pat on the head or a smile or words of encouragement. I never knew why that was. I was dutiful. All I wanted was a smile or a word of praise. Sometimes, now, when I think back, I think I turned myself inside out trying to please them. I did the same thing with Logan. Then when the fire happened, I wigged out. All this guilt came crashing down on me. Maybe I should have tried harder, done more. Sometimes I still have nightmares over that.''

"It doesn't pay to think about the past. It's gone. Tomorrow isn't here yet, so all you have is today. And today, Kristine, is, in a manner of speaking, the first day of your new business life. Congratulations!''

Kristine could feel her throat start to tighten up. Hot tears pricked her eyelids. "I couldn't have done it without you, Woodie. I will be forever grateful. If you hadn't come along when you did, my snoot would still be in the bottle. How do I thank you for that?''

"You just did. I think you would have done it for me if the situation were reversed.''

"Not the old Kristine. Maybe this new improved model.''

"I'd like a cup of coffee before I head back home. I might even be able to eat a ham and cheese sandwich,'' Woodie said as he tossed the old sign into the backseat of his car.

"Mr. Dunwoodie, it will be my pleasure to offer you lunch." Kristine offered up a snappy salute in the general direction of the sign as Woodie turned the car around in the middle of the road.

Things were definitely looking up.

"I think we should go out on the town and celebrate,'' Woodie said.

"Six weeks of torture and you want to celebrate. No thanks. I have to admit, I think it's going to be a little strange around here with you gone. The dogs are used to

you. I guess I need to thank you for getting me the loan."
Kristine wondered why her voice was so stiff and defensive-
sounding.

"You qualified for the loan. This house and acreage
are great collateral. I'd like to come out to visit from time
to time if that's all right with you. You know, keeping tabs
on the dogs and our business investment. The bank likes
its officers to do things like that. It's nothing personal."

"To check on me?"

"Yes. Promise me that if you have the urge to drink,
you'll call me. AA has a chapter in town you can go to any
time of the day or night."

"I know, Woodie. Don't worry about me. I'm sorry I
put you through so much misery. It was such a bad time
for me. My head's on straight now. I have a few fences to
mend, then I'll get on with the business of living. Don't
be a stranger."

"See you around."

"Yeah. See you around," Kristine said. "Hey, wait a
minute." She ran down the steps Woodie had repaired to
wrap her arms around him. She kissed him soundly, her
eyes widening in shock at the electricity running through
her body. "Ah, I didn't mean to do that. It was . . . you
know, spur of the moment, serendipity, that kind of thing.
Thanks, Woodie, for everything."

A strange look on his face, the banker tried for a smile.
"It was my pleasure. Call me if you have any problems."

"I'll do that."

"Even with the dogs."

"Okay."

"Day or night."

"I'll remember that."

"Bye, Kristine."

"Bye, Woodie."

"Kristine?"

Kristine whirled around. "Yes."

"Georgia isn't that far away. You could drive it in a day.
Or you could fly. The weekend is coming up. I bet the

kids would love to see you. If you don't want to go to Georgia, mark your calendar to go see them when the fall semester starts."

"I'll think about it."

"You could take a few more days and stop at that vet hospital in Atlanta. You said you wanted to look into taking some courses. It's just a thought."

"It's a good thought, though. I'll think about it."

Kristine stood on the porch with both dogs in her arms until Woodie's minibus was out of sight. She felt like crying and didn't know why.

"I think Aaron Dunwoodie is going to be a good friend to us. I miss him already. And, what are you guys going to do when you find out he took all his shoes with him?"

Gracie stared up at her mistress with adoring eyes. Slick wiggled in the crook of her arm to get more comfortable.

"You know something. He is a nice man. A very nice man. I thought he was a stuffed shirt, you know, one of those nerds the kids always talk about. I liked him. The kids liked him. Kids, like you guys, are very good judges of character. I wish I had paid more attention to their opinions. C'mon, let's go out to the barn and do some paperwork. You guys can play in the straw."

The puppies were like greased lightning as they streaked through the house and out to the kitchen, where they waited patiently for Kristine to open the door.

"I miss him already," she murmured.

PART II

❧

Leesburg, Virginia 1991

6

"You're sure now, Pete, that you can handle things while I'm gone. I'll check in at least twice a day. I don't foresee any problems, but you never know."

The young vet grimaced. "I might be young, but I think I can handle things. And, I've been here working side by side with you for two years. Like you said, there don't appear to be any problems. Two days is not an eternity. Go to Georgia, be proud of your children, take them all out to a nice dinner and celebrate. If there's any time left over, shower Woodie with affection. He's in love with you. You do know that, don't you, Kristine?"

"I don't know any such thing, Pete. He's a good friend. Do I need to remind you, I am still married. I would never be unfaithful to my husband. You also need to mind your own business."

Two years of working side by side allowed Pete Calloway to speak openly. Normally, Kristine didn't take offense, but today was different. He wished now he had kept quiet, but as long as his foot was in his mouth he might as well run with his thoughts. "You can only be unfaithful when you have a husband. You don't seem to have one, Kristine. You haven't had one for years. You're too young to wither on the vine."

Kristine forced a laugh. "What do you know about women withering on the vine? Never mind. I don't want to know. For your information, I have a very full, active life. For me, it's more than satisfactory. I work hard, I'm actually turning a profit, and I love the animals. Not to mention the fact that I am able to pay you a decent salary. I go out one night a week for dinner. I sleep well. I haven't had a drink in three years. I'd say I'm doing okay. And before you can say it, I am not being testy. I am a little anxious. I haven't seen the kids in over three years. By their choice, not mine. Talking to them isn't the same as seeing them. They don't like me, Pete, and I don't think they are ever going to forgive me. I understand that, and, while I may not like it, I have to respect their feelings. When Logan didn't come back, I couldn't clutch at them. I tried, but they were smarter than me. They didn't let it happen. I had to learn to stand on my own two feet. I'm getting there. I'll be the proud mother tomorrow. I won't weep or grope at them. They're young adults now. I still can't believe all three of them are graduating from the same school on the same day. The twins took a semester off to work full-time, but I think it was so they could graduate with Tyler. They certainly don't get their brains from me. Woodie helped a lot. Georgia Tech was his alma mater. I think he privately and publicly donates handsomely to the school. He never said he did. It's an assumption on my part. The kids like and respect him. He's the one they call when they have a problem. They might be calling Sadie, too, but I'm not sure of that. What I am sure of is they only call me to let me know they're alive and well."

"And you want more?" Pete asked.

Kristine frowned. "Someday more would be nice. Right now I don't deserve more. The children don't think I deserve more. Their opinion is the only one that counts."

"I hear Woodie's horn. You better get cracking, Kristine. Drive carefully and don't worry about anything."

"Okay, Pete. You're in charge. I'll see you when I see you."

The young vet watched his boss sprint out to the road. She was too nice a person to have so many problems. He hated the unseen Logan Kelly, hated him with a passion. He wasn't sure, but he didn't think he liked the Kelly children either. "Good luck, Kristine," he murmured as he started his preparations for the new day. "Okay, ladies and gentlemen," he said, addressing the sixteen new pups, "listen up. This is the way it's going to be for the next two days . . ."

"I hope you don't mind that the top is down. Are you one of those women who worries her hair will blow all over?" Woodie asked. His tone said he didn't care if she was one of those women.

Kristine laughed. "I have it pinned up pretty tight. If it gets too bad, I can always cut it off." Logan had always loved her hair. "A crowning glory of hair isn't all that it's cracked up to be. I've been thinking of getting one of those wash-and-wear dos. You're a man; what's your feeling on women's hair?"

Woodie grinned. "Is this one of those trick questions?"

"No."

"Good. I like hair. Period."

Kristine giggled. "I want to thank you for making the trip with me. You'll be good moral support when the kids stare through me."

"That isn't going to happen, Kristine."

"Of course it is, and I'm okay with it. This is the way it has to be for now. Things . . . the situation might change someday, and then again, maybe it won't. I just had this same conversation with Pete a little while ago. I want to leave right after dinner if that's okay with you. I don't want the kids to feel uncomfortable."

"That's fine with me. For today, I thought we'd just kind of mosey along. My housekeeper packed us a picnic lunch. It's a beautiful day, and we're in no hurry. It would be nice if you'd smile."

Kristine grimaced. "Is this where you give me pep talk number forty-three? You know the one, life is wonderful, life is good, life should be lived?"

Woodie guffawed. "Yeah, that's the one. Life is whatever you make it. Life will go on, with or without you. I'm very fond of you, Kristine. I think you know that."

"You've been a very good friend, Woodie. I truly don't know what I would have done without you. I literally owe you my life."

"I don't want you to owe me your life. I want you to share your life with me. It's time."

Kristine's heart started to pound in her chest. "Are you saying . . . do you want . . . I'm married. I can't . . . do you expect . . . ?"

"What I would like, Kristine, is for you and me to have a relationship. I'm in love with you. I knew you never wanted me to say the words aloud. I know you have feelings for me. Feelings you stifle. If I wasn't in your life, if I left, moved away, how would you feel?"

Kristine didn't have to ponder her response. "I would be devastated, Woodie." A knot formed in the pit of her stomach. "Are you trying to tell me something?"

"I'm retiring from the bank at the end of the year. The way I look at it, twenty-five years in any job is long enough. I've made some wise investments over the years that will allow me to retire with the lifestyle I want. I just want to enjoy my life and do all the things I never got to do with a nine-to-five job. I want to do all those things while I'm still young enough to enjoy doing them. I guess I'm trying to say I'm going to start planning for my future. I'd like to know if I can include you in my plans."

Kristine loosened her seat belt so she could turn to face Woodie. He was such a dear, sweet person. And she did care for him. What would life without him be like? She depended on him in so many ways, as did her children. Right now his shoulders were tense. She wished she could see his eyes, but the dark glasses and baseball cap were shielding the upper portion of his face. However, the grim set of his jaw told her this particular discussion was one that needed to be resolved. She'd often fantasized about him, then felt so disloyal with her thoughts she would run to take a cold shower. Life without Woodie. Unthinkable. No one had ever encouraged her the way Woodie had. No one ever smiled at her the way Woodie did. He was always there, in the daytime, in the middle of the night, holidays. And he loved her. He was probably the only person in the whole world who loved her.

"What are you thinking, Kristine?"

Kristine gave voice to all her thoughts and added more. "I don't know if I'm ready, Woodie. I have thought about . . . us. Lately I've been thinking about . . . a lot of things. I've never been with another man. That's a king-size fear right there. Then there is the disloyalty aspect of it. I know you don't understand that. When I got married I really did believe in 'till death do us part.' I had all these hopes and dreams. I thought Logan and I would grow old in rocking chairs on that big old front porch. I still have trouble with that. I'm not sure what I feel for Logan. I still have feelings. I know the way things look. There wasn't a page in the book about how I should deal with this. I need some kind of closure. There has to be closure before you can move on. Mentally, I think I'm in a pretty stable place, thanks to you. I have thought about a divorce. I've thought about it a lot lately, but somehow I can't make myself go to an attorney. It's that loyalty thing, I guess."

Woodie took his eyes off the road for a moment to stare at Kristine. His voice was sad and gentle when he said, "Where does that leave us?"

"With me afraid to take off my clothes in front of you. I'm forty-five, Woodie. I've never been with any man but my husband. We're talking fear and trepidation here."

Woodie took his eyes off the road a second time. "I could rip your clothes off. How about that?"

"Yeah, how about that? That strategy might work. I thought about it, too."

"Me too. We could sort of have a dry run when we stop for our picnic."

Kristine licked at her dry lips. She thought about all the strange places she'd made love with Logan. If they'd ever made love on a picnic, she couldn't remember it. "What does dry run mean exactly?" she asked breathlessly.

"It means we go for it. If it works, it works. If it doesn't work, we'll try again later. Dry runs are something to think about."

Kristine looked at her watch. Lunch was three hours away. Thinking about something as wonderful as making love for three hours would be hell. "What's your feeling on an early lunch?" She imagined her friend Sadie saying, "Go for it, girl!"

"I'm starved. Hold on."

Kristine reached for the strap over the door and held on as Woodie careened off to the side of the road, where he waited for a break in traffic on the secondary road. The moment traffic cleared, he crossed the road and barreled along until he came to a dirt road. "I have no idea where this road goes. It's a kidney crusher, that's for sure," he said as they bounced along. Five minutes later he pulled into a small clearing. The moment he cut the engine, Kristine undid her seat belt.

"Should I bring the picnic basket or is that just window dressing?"

"Yeah. No. There's food in it but . . . I think we just need the blanket."

"The blanket. Yes, yes, the blanket. The food . . . The hell with the food," Kristine said.

The moment Woodie spread the blanket, Kristine said, "You said something about tearing off my clothes."

"I thought the word was rip."

"Rip, tear, same difference. I'll rip yours, and you tear mine."

"Sounds good."

"I haven't done this in a long time," Kristine said.

"Me either," Woodie said. "It's like riding a bike or swimming. It will come back to us. I read that somewhere."

"My God, you talk a lot," Kristine said, sliding her slacks down over her hips.

They were like two first-time teenagers as they groped and prodded one another before they toppled to the blanket.

A long time later, Woodie rolled over. Kristine thought his eyes were glassy. She said so. "Yours look like mirrors." He laughed.

"That was a hell of a dry run." Kristine laughed. "Aren't you supposed to whip out the potato salad and hard-boiled eggs about now?"

"Wait till you see the real thing tonight. Are you saying you're hungry?"

"I'm starved. You said this was a picnic. So, feed me. I think we should sit here, buck-ass naked, and eat all that food in the basket. It will make for a delicious memory."

Woodie tossed Kristine a hard-boiled egg and a chicken leg. He watched as she munched contentedly. "You okay with this, Kristine?"

"I'm okay with this, Woodie." She was, she realized. She really was. *Oh, Sadie, if you could only see me now.*

"Good. Me too."

"We should probably get dressed and get going," Kristine said.

"Yeah, we probably should."

Kristine crooked her index finger under Woodie's nose. Her voice dropped to a husky purr. "On the other hand, one can never have too much practice." Out of the corner of her eye she saw a hard-boiled egg sail over Woodie's shoulder as he pounced on her. "I'm expecting *big* things tonight with all this practice," she managed to gurgle before Woodie's lips clamped down on hers. When she managed to come up for air she gasped, *"Really* big things."

"And you say I talk too much! Shut up so we can practice."

"My mother didn't raise any fools," Kristine said as she clamped her lips shut.

"Aahhhh."

* * *

"I feel like crying. They look so, I don't know, grown-up. Don't they look grown-up, Woodie?"

"Very much so. You promised not to cry."

"I lied. How can I help but cry? My three children are graduating from college at the same time, at the same college, ahead of schedule. And they did it on their own. I feel such a loss. I can never get those years back. I love them so much I ache with the hurt."

"Time heals all wounds, Kristine," Woodie said gently.

"It might heal, but the scars will always be there. Look. Here they come. Oh, God, my babies are graduating!" Kristine clutched at Woodie's arm as her children, eyes straight ahead, followed their classmates down the long aisle.

Ninety minutes later, Kristine stood with Woodie in the warm, spring rain as they waited for the children to find them.

"Mom! Woodie!" the three said in unison.

Kristine turned, her eyes filling. She held out her arms, and her three children stepped into them. "Congratulations to the three of you! I bet you set some kind of precedent at this university. I'm very proud of you."

Mike's hug was robust. Cala squeezed her mother's shoulders, her own eyes wet. Tyler grinned and clapped his mother on the back. "This means we're adults now! Guess what, Mom! Mike and Cala already have jobs. I don't want you boo-hooing now, but I joined the Marines."

"Tyler!" Whatever she was about to say, Kristine changed her mind when Woodie's fingers dug into the fleshy part of her arm. "Congratulations, honey. Aren't they the ones who are always looking for a few good men?" she managed to quip.

"You got it! They saw me and snapped me right up. You aren't upset?"

"No. If it's what you want and it makes you happy, then it makes me happy."

"That's a relief. I thought . . . never mind."

Kristine turned her attention to the twins. Her eyes questioned them.

"We're off to Sacramento, California. Some guy at the job fair snapped up the two of us. We leave tonight on the redeye," Mike said.

"So soon. I was hoping you'd come back . . . to"—she was about to say *home* but changed her mind—"Virginia for a week or so. I'd love to show you the pups and the barns." She would not cry. She absolutely would not cry.

Tyler took the sting out of the bad moment by saying, "Yeah, they're leaving me to clean up the apartment, turn off the utilities and do all that stuff because I have two extra days before I report to Camp Lejeune."

A lump formed in Kristine's throat. Woodie pinched her arm again.

"I think a big guy like you can handle it," Kristine said lightly. She thought she heard a collective sigh of relief.

"Now that we've settled all that, I suggest we get on with our celebration. Your mother and I want to hear everything. She has a lot to share, too. Do you want to change and meet us at the restaurant or do you want us to wait?"

"I think it will be better if we meet you there, in say, two hours," Mike said. "We have to load our bags and stuff we're taking with us into the car. Cala hasn't finished packing and I have a few friends I need to say good-bye to. One in particular."

"He has a girlfriend, Mom," Tyler said. "Cala has a boyfriend, too."

Kristine blinked. "Would you like to ask them to join us?" Woodie pinched her arm as much as to say, good girl. She wondered if her arm was black-and-blue.

"Would you mind?" the twins asked in unison.

"Of course not. The more the merrier. This is your night, and we need to celebrate."

Mike reached for her, crushing her against his chest.

"Thanks, Mom. She's special. You're going to like her. By the way, you're lookin' good."

Kristine's heart leaped in her chest. Was this the first step in forgiveness? She smiled shakily. "You're looking pretty good yourself. Go ahead. Woodie and I are going to walk around the campus."

"In the rain?" Tyler said, shock in his voice.

"Yes, in the rain. It's a warm rain, and we have an umbrella. Don't worry about us. Do what you have to do. We'll meet you at six." Kristine looked longingly at her daughter, waiting.

"I'm glad you came, Mom. I can't wait for you to meet Tom. He's my fella," she said, suddenly shy.

"If he had the good sense to pick you, then I know I'm going to like him. You look so pretty, Cala. I like the way you're doing your hair."

"Is all the bad stuff behind you, Mom? I'm asking because I care about you. I want you to be happy."

"I am, Cala. The bad stuff is . . . on a shelf somewhere. If I'm lucky, maybe someday it will go away completely. For now, everything is fine."

Cala stood back to look at her mother. "You have a *glow*. I've never seen you look like this. Is it that you came to terms with things, or is it Woodie?"

Kristine flushed as she met her daughter's intense gaze. "Both," she said honestly.

"Good for you, Mom. See you later."

Kristine watched as her three children ran through the rain to the parking lot. A small smile tugged at the corners of her mouth.

"That wasn't so bad, was it?"

"No, not at all. The three of them were kinder than they had to be. I don't think it was strained, do you?"

"Not at all. I don't think it gets any more genuine than that. Are we really going to slop around in the rain?"

"Yes, we are. I love walking in the rain. I want to walk every inch of this place that my children walked for the past three years. Besides, I never walked in the rain with a . . . fella."

"Really," Woodie drawled. "Then, lady, I am your man. My arm, Madam."

Kristine linked her arm with Woodie's. "My daughter said I *glowed.*"

"You have a very astute daughter, Kristine."

"I know."

It was ten o'clock when the Kelly clan exited the restaurant. "I hate good-byes," Kristine murmured to no one in particular.

"We do too, Mom," Tyler said as he got in line to kiss his mother good-bye.

"I like your girl, Mike."

"I knew you would. I'll write and call, Mom. I promise. I do love you, you know that, don't you?"

Kristine's tongue felt thick in her mouth. "I wasn't sure . . . I hoped. Be happy, Mike."

"You too, Mom. Woodie's a great guy. I don't think they come any better," he whispered in her ear. "Hey, I'm a college man, I know how to interpret things." In spite of herself, Kristine burst into laughter.

"You should do that more often, Mom. Laugh, I mean."

"I will."

"Mom, thanks for coming," Cala said. "We weren't sure if you would want to see us. Let's face it, we were a bunch of shits. We needed to grow up. I think we turned out okay. You need to know something, though. We have the papers ready to go if your husband ever comes back. Okay?"

"Each of us has to do what we have to do. I'm okay with it. I like Tom."

"I like him, too. A lot. I'm glad you like him. I wish Tyler would find someone."

"Don't rush him. When it's his time, the right girl will find him. Trust me."

"So Woodie is the man of the hour, huh? I knew that glow had something to do with him. He's a great guy. Don't blow it. I love you, Mom. If it seemed at times like I didn't, I'm sorry."

Kristine burst into laughter a second time. "I'll try not to."

It was Tyler's turn. "Give me a really big hug, Mom. I love you. Sometimes I didn't like you, but I never stopped loving you. I just want you to know that. I missed you so much."

Kristine's throat closed up as she hugged her youngest son. "Not half as much as I missed you. I just want you to be happy, Tyler."

"I'll be home when I get my first leave."

"I'll be waiting, honey. You be careful now."

Kristine stepped back as her children embraced Woodie. And then it was her turn again. Tears rolled down her cheeks. She was almost delirious with joy when she saw her children's wet eyes. Maybe something good would come of this after all.

Woodie put his arm around her shoulder. "There go three great kids. I'm so damn proud of them, and they aren't even mine. I don't know how to figure that one out."

"They said they loved me. I didn't think I'd ever hear them say that. I had myself prepared for the worst. God, Woodie, I am so happy. Can we go home now? I have sixteen pups I want to cuddle."

"When I'm here you want puppies!" Woodie said in mock horror.

"They're the next best thing to babies and children. It was a great weekend, Woodie. I loved every minute of it."

"Are you going to start to cry?"

"So what if I do. Don't you have a broad shoulder?"

"It's yours anytime you want it, Kristine."

"I want it."

"Then it's yours."

They drove in comfortable silence until Kristine spoke.

"Woodie, what do you think about me selling the old Kelly farm? I know it's in ramshackle condition, but it has to be worth something. The acreage has to be valuable. I don't want the money for myself. I'd give it to the kids. Do you know if I can sell it legally?"

"I don't know. I can look into it for you. Is this the first step in . . . whatever it is you see down the road?"

"The kids could use a nice nest egg. They might want to buy a house, put down some roots. It will probably take a while to sell it. The house and barns are beyond fixing up. Actually, the whole place is a disaster. The thousand acres it sits on have to be worth money to the right buyer. We might get lucky and net enough profit so the kids can buy houses and not have to carry mortgages. That's the least Logan can do for them."

"You might have to declare him legally dead, Kristine."

Kristine's jaw dropped. "Dead? I don't think I could . . . how can you declare someone dead if you aren't sure? Doesn't desertion count? If what was mine was his, why isn't what was his mine?"

"I'm not a lawyer, Kristine. I will look into it, though. You are also going to have to look into finding a good investment counselor. When you turn fifty, you take control of the money in trust for you. I know you don't want to hear this, but you need to listen, Kristine. According to my father, your parents didn't care for Logan, and were afraid that you would marry him. That's the reason they set things up the way they did. It's a very complicated business when you inherit this kind of money. You'll need to set up new trusts, make a new will, hire an estate planner, get a good tax man. You should go to New York soon to start all the paperwork. It's going to take time. I also suggest you put your house into a trust for the kids, with the proviso that you can live out your life there if you want. You need to clear everything up in case Logan does show up at some point. Does Logan know that you stand to take control of the trust at age fifty? Did he ever see the will?"

"I don't think so. I never had a copy of it. To tell you the truth, after my parents' death, I didn't ask any questions. Your father said there would be a check every month. If he said anything else, I don't remember. I really wasn't interested in the money, Woodie. Hard as it is to believe, it's the truth. I was in love, I was young, and I was grieving. All I wanted to do was run as far away as I could. Even if Logan knows, so what? He can't do anything about it. We opened all new accounts with just my name on everything."

"You're still married, Kristine. If your husband is alive, that gives him certain rights."

"Beyond stealing my eight million and my eight thousand dollars? I don't think so, Woodie."

"When can you get away to go to New York? I'll do some checking and put you in touch with some good people. Two days at the most."

Kristine felt her stomach start to knot up. "Will next week be soon enough?"

"Next week will be just fine. You can't afford to be sloppy now. The last time you were lax, you got taken. Keep thinking about those three wonderful kids of yours."

"I understand, Woodie. You never told me how much money I'm going to come into."

"I can't tell you because I don't know. Your grandparents socked all their assets in New York banks. Your parents followed suit at some point along the way. My father was a little perturbed over that. I guess he got over it. I've asked for an accounting on your behalf. While you're in New York, you can go to the banks yourself as long as you have the proper ID. I'll also write you a letter on bank stationery."

"I don't want to talk about this anymore. Let's talk about the kids. Do you ever regret not having children?"

"Yes. I guess it wasn't meant to be."

"I'm hungry," Kristine said.

"Have you ever been on a moonlight picnic?"

Kristine rolled down the car window. "Do you mean the kind with no food and no moonlight and wet grass?"

"Yeah, that's the kind."

"No, I can't say that I have. I'm one of those people who likes to try new things."

"Yeah, me too."

Kristine started to laugh and couldn't stop. In between choking fits of laughter she managed to say, "Then let's go for it."

"My mother didn't raise any fools either, Kristine Kelly."

Kristine continued to laugh. She couldn't remember the last time she felt this good. Hadn't her son said she should laugh more often? Oh, yeah. She cuddled as close to Woodie as the console in the middle of the two seats would allow. Woodie's arm moved to cover her shoulder. It felt right, good, and so very wonderful.

There was a spring in Kristine's steps as she bounded through the house, out to the kitchen, then to the barn.

"Whoa" Pete said, holding up his hand. He had three pups in his arms who were trying to lick at his chin. "Is this the same Kristine Kelly who left here two days ago? You're lookin' good, Kristine. How was the trip?"

Kristine beamed. "The trip was, in a word, wonderful."

"That good, huh?"

"Better than good, my friend."

"Tell me about it," Pete said, transferring the pups to Kristine's waiting arms.

"The sky was bluer, the air sweeter, the sun more golden. The warm summer rain was delicious," she said, nuzzling the pups.

"I don't think I ever heard a graduation summed up quite like that. Or, are we talking about Woodie?"

Kristine flushed. "Both. Don't be nosy."

"I deserve to be nosy. How was the graduation?"

"It was wonderful. I was so fearful but the kids . . . they

said they loved me, Pete. I never expected to hear that from any of them. Mike has a girlfriend and a job in California. Cala has a boyfriend, and she's going to work in California, too. Tyler enlisted in the Marines. That shook me up a little, but I'm okay with it. He's going to come here when he gets his first leave. They're so grown-up. I had to fight not to cry, but then I did and so did they. It's a start, a kind of new beginning. God, it was so wonderful. Listen, do you think you can handle things here? We drove all night, and I'd like to get a few hours' sleep."

"No problem, Kristine. Now, what about Woodie?"

"He's wonderful, too. Everything is wonderful. Isn't *wonderful* a wonderful word?"

"I guess that means you got laid."

"Pete!"

"It's written all over your face. Listen, I'm happy for you. Woodie is a great guy. In fact, I don't think they come any better than him with the exception of myself. I'm for anything that puts a smile on your face. Don't look at me like that. You and I have shared a lot of secrets these past two years while we waited for the dogs to give birth. I just want you to know I'm happy for you, and I don't want any details. Go on, take your nap, and I'll take care of things."

"I might have to go to New York next week for a few days. Woodie thinks I need all these people to, you know, set up trusts and stuff. He wants to make sure I'm protected. Do you mind? I'll be glad to pay you overtime."

"Woodie's right. I don't mind, and overtime is not necessary. The free room and board takes care of everything. Do what you have to do."

Kristine handed over the three small balls of fur. "I'll see you later, Pete."

"Yeah, later," Pete said as he tried to get a firmer grip on the wiggling dogs.

Upstairs in her room, with the door closed, Kristine's shoulders slumped when she looked at the room she'd slept in for the past three years. Her body started to shake the moment she made eye contact with the picture of Logan on her night table.

Anyone seeing the room for the first time would have thought it was a shrine to Logan Kelly. There were pictures and mementos everywhere.

Kristine felt a lump form in her throat at the same moment her stomach gave birth to a huge knot. For one brief moment she thought she was going to black out. She steadied herself, then reached for the photograph, her fingers tracing the outline of her husband's face. "I'm sorry, Logan, but I can't wait forever. I'm human. I deserve a life too. Woodie is ... Woodie is ... someone I care about. Just so you know, I didn't tell him I loved him. I wanted to, but the words stuck in my throat. He loves me, cares about me, and he hates your fucking guts. I should hate you, too. I want to, but part of me will always belong to you. That was a terrible legacy for you to leave me, Logan. If I'm going to get on with my life then I have to cut you out of that life. I'm not going to be a good little soldier any longer. That book is going in the trash as soon as I can lay my hands on it."

Kristine walked over to the built-in window seat and propped open the lid. She dumped all her mementos and pictures on the bottom, not caring if the glass frames broke or not. She looked around to see if she had forgotten anything. She hadn't. The lid snapped shut.

Gone but not forgotten.

Kristine's gaze swept to the mantel, where only one picture remained, of her three children, taken in Sadie's backyard. She smiled.

"Your loss, Logan. Your loss," she murmured as she drifted into sleep.

7

Her heart pounding in her chest, Kristine followed the receptionist down a long hallway. The meeting with her advisors, which had to be put back a month because Kristine had come down with a bad cold, was about to take place. The meeting Woodie had gone out of his way to arrange. She wished she knew more about finances. She'd been a fool to trust Logan with everything. These men were going to see how stupid she really was. Was. *Was is my keyword,* she thought as the door opened.

They stared at her, polite looks on their faces. She wanted to smile, but her facial muscles felt like they were stretched tight on an embroidery hoop. She inclined her head slightly, and said, "Gentlemen," by way of acknowledgment. Like Woodie said, *Don't let them intimidate you. You're paying them. They're going to work for you.*

One of the men rose to hold her chair. She sank down gratefully and waited expectantly as coffee was poured, cigarettes lighted. Then the introductions. Edwin Leavitt-Gruberger, estate and pension planner; Martin Friedman, attorney; Peter Rubolotta, broker; Michael and Audrey Bernstein, CPAs. She nodded again, and the meeting was under way.

Six hours later, with a thirty-minute break for lunch, the meeting was over. Kristine heaved a sigh of relief as she made her way to the rest room with Audrey Bernstein. "I think you're in good hands, Mrs. Kelly."

Kristine smiled. "I think so, too."

"It will take a little while before everything is formalized. Papers will arrive by the pound. Read everything carefully, and if you have any questions, we're only a phone call away. I'm sorry your life didn't turn out the way you had every right to expect it to. I have two little girls, and my husband and I both feel that nothing is more important than family. You're on the right track now. The important thing is, are you comfortable with everything that was said and done in that room today. If not, we can go back in there and start over."

"No, everything is fine. I understand everything we talked about. On the plane today, coming here, I felt an awful sense of disloyalty. I felt like I was trying to cheat my husband when I don't even have a husband. I don't know if he's alive or dead. All I know is he stole eight million dollars from me along with my eight-thousand-dollar household savings. I turned into a drunk, lost my children, and I feel disloyal. In a million years I will never understand that person I once was."

"Just think about who you are now. Think about what you accomplished and what you will continue to accomplish. If there are any losers here, you aren't among them. Believe it or not, you came out the winner. In time, you'll come to realize that. My husband is waiting for me. We have to drive to New Jersey, and this is rush hour. We promised Jessica and Corinne we'd take them to Chili's. We try never to break a promise. It was nice meeting you, Mrs. Kelly. We'll talk again."

"I'm sure we will. Thank you very much."

Kristine was the last one to leave the office, her head swimming with everything that had been said during the previous hours. Her shoulders straightened imperceptibly as she stepped into the elevator. "So there, Logan Kelly, so there," she murmured over and over as she rode to the main lobby.

* * *

She knew he would be waiting for her. What she didn't know or expect was the rush of adrenaline she would feel as he held out his arms. She stepped into them as though she'd been doing it all her life. It felt right. It felt good and oh so wonderful. She smiled to herself. There was that word wonderful again.

"How about coming to my house for a sleepover?" Woodie grinned.

"Now that's the best idea I've heard all day. Aren't you going to ask me how it went?"

"No. That's your private business, Kristine. I have been assured that all the professionals you finally got to meet with today are tops in their fields. You're going to be nurtured, Kristine."

"I know. I'm glad it's done, and I'm glad it's out of the way. I have to call Pete to tell him I won't be home tonight. Do you mind waiting a few minutes?"

"I took care of that. He said to stay as long as you like."

"Is that what he said?" Kristine drawled.

"Yep. Word for word."

"In that case, I might stay the weekend. I'm all wired up as my son Mike would say."

"I know something that will help to alleviate that particular condition."

"Are you going to tell me or show me?"

"What do you think?"

"I always did like show-and-tell and in that order."

"Me too."

Kristine stepped from Woodie's car, a stunned look on her face. "This is a modern house," she said in surprise. "Why did I think you lived in a house like mine? This is gorgeous. I love redwood and all that glass. Good Lord, who cleans all those windows? Do you have shades? Do you have a gardener?"

"Slow down. I had this house built because I personally hate old, moldy things, and my parents' house was old and moldy. It would have cost more to restore it and it would still have been an old house with antique plumbing and electricity. I think of myself as a modern kind of guy, you know the kind, push buttons everywhere, Jacuzzis on every floor, a satellite dish, wide-screen TV for sports events. I have a cleaning crew who cleans the windows twice a year. There are no shades because I like to look outdoors winter or summer. The views from every window are spectacular. Since there are no immediate neighbors, I have no worries about privacy. This house sits on six acres, all of them wooded except for my lawn. I even have a bubbling or is that babbling brook in the back. There's also a wraparound deck off the family room with a hot tub. I have a lady who comes in daily to clean and cook dinner for me. Her husband does the gardening. It all works for me. Trust me when I tell you there will be a dinner warming in the oven. There will be wine in a chilled bucket along with some sparkling cider for you. Betsy probably used one of the good tablecloths and real napkins. She likes to fuss. Come inside, and I'll give you the tour.'' Woodie reached for her hand. Kristine clutched his tightly, an electric current shooting through her body. She wondered if she gave off sparks.

"Oh, this is gorgeous! I love these vaulted ceilings. I bet you have a magnificent Christmas tree. Do you polish the woodwork?''

Woodie blinked. "I have no idea. I don't do it. Maybe Betsy or Frank does it. I wanted everything natural so I wouldn't have to paint every couple of years. Do you think this looks like a man's . . . you know, a bachelor's house?''

"Kind of. Obviously you like leather furniture. I would have picked something in pale gray, a nubby kind of material. A center rug would be nice. It would close in the room a little more and make it cozy. I like cozy. I guess I'm just a nester by instinct. The floors are beautiful, though. The fica trees and all those green plants help a lot. I would imagine your daylight lighting is perfect for growing any-'hing. Did you live here with your first wife?'' Kristine sucked in her breath as she waited for his response. She could feel a streak of jealousy start to consume her.

"God, no. We lived in a condo, all glass and chrome. It was black and white. Not one bit of color. Maureen was a black-and-white person. She hates this place. One time I bought her red roses, and she sent them back and asked for white ones. That was a long time ago. You wouldn't have liked her. Hell, I didn't like her, and I was married to her. I was lucky I came out of it in one piece."

"How long have you been divorced, Woodie?"

"Five years."

"Where is she now?"

"Why do you want to know, Kristine?"

"Just curious. You don't have to answer the question."

"She lives in town. I see her once in a while. I suppose you could say we're friends now that we're no longer married. She calls from time to time."

"I see."

"What do you see, Kristine?"

"I see that she hasn't let go. I think that happens in divorce a lot. One or the other never seems to want the divorce. It's a process you have to go through. Show me the second floor, then I want you to feed me. All I had was a liverwurst sandwich with pickles for lunch.

"What do you do with five bedrooms, and did you say seven bathrooms?" she asked as she started the long climb up the circular staircase.

"Guests. Friends. The architect said a house like this needed all those things along with a formal dining room for resale value. Someday I might want to sell it to a family with four kids and two dogs. I'm glad you like my house. Can you see yourself living here, Kristine?"

Kristine whirled around. She held up her hands to ward off anything else he was about to say. "It doesn't matter what I think at the moment. I don't want to open up a can of worms I'm not ready to deal with. Didn't we agree . . . ?"

"We didn't agree to anything, Kristine. We need to talk. Seriously talk. You know how I feel about you. I haven't kept my feelings a secret. I suspect you feel something for me besides fondness. We've known each other for over three years. The fact that our friendship has turned into something more serious makes this talk necessary."

"Woodie, it's too soon. Let's not spoil things. I have a lot of baggage I'm not prepared to deal with just yet. I need time."

"How much time, Kristine? Are we talking weeks, months, years?"

"I don't know, Woodie. If I could give you an answer, I would. Right now I can't. If you can't accept that, maybe I should go home. I can call Pete to come and pick me up."

"You've had over three years to come to terms with what Logan has done to you. Three years, Kristine. Three years is a very long time from where I'm sitting. I need some assurances before we let things get out of control."

"I think you need to explain that statement to me, Woodie."

"It's simple, Kristine. We aren't kids anymore. I'm going to be forty-seven on my next birthday. You're not far behind me in age. These last three years went by in the blink of an eye. As we get older, the time seems to go faster. I don't know why that is, it just is. I've worked hard all my life and I want to enjoy what's left of it. I want to enjoy it with you. I will not wait around while you wait around for Logan to come back. You aren't being fair to yourself or to me. Logan doesn't even factor into this. If what we have is just fun and games, rolls in the sack, something to take the edge off while you wait for Logan, it won't work with me. That's not what I want."

"You're setting conditions here, Woodie. I don't like ultimatums."

"That's a strange statement coming from you. You lived with ultimatums all your married life."

Kristine's stomach grew queasy. "Where did you hear a thing like that? Oh, I see, that's the kids' version. Well, that was then, this is now. I don't live by that damn book any longer. One of these days I'm going to write a final chapter to that stupid book and get it published. If I can't get it published, I'll have it printed myself. Then, by God, I'm going to send it to every military wife and child I know. Don't push me, Woodie."

"I'm not pushing you, I'm telling you what I think and what I feel. You, on the other hand, are not telling me anything. Do you still love Logan? Do you still believe he's going to return? Are you just playing a waiting game? I need to know, Kristine, and I don't think I'm being unfair in asking you since I love you and want to marry you. This isn't exactly the way I planned on proposing, but for now it will have to do."

Kristine wished the floor would open up and swallow her whole. This was not what she expected or wanted to hear right now. How could she explain her life and what she was feeling and thinking when she didn't understand it herself? She longed for a drink but forced the thought out of her head as soon as it entered. Her nails dug into the palms of her hands as she fought the tears that were burning her eyelids. Her voice was husky, tortured-sounding. "All I can say, Woodie, is I am trying to come to terms with everything. It's not something I can do because you say I need to do it. I don't know what I feel for Logan. I don't know if in my heart of hearts I'm waiting for him or not. I packed up all the mementos and pictures just last month. That was a tremendous trauma for me, but I did it. I did it because I didn't want you to see all those things when you spent the night at my house. I know it was only one small step. I'll take other small steps along the way. I can't tell you how, why, or when that will happen. I know you deserve more. Unfortunately, right now, I cannot give you more. I think I should go home, Woodie. Will you drive me, or shall I call Pete? Better yet, lend me one of your cars and I'll return it tomorrow. That will be best. I need to think. For some reason, I can't think around you."

"I'm sorry," Woodie said.

"I know. I'm sorry, too."

Woodie fished in his pocket for his keys, tossing them to her.

Kristine clutched at the keys. She struggled to find her voice as she licked at her dry lips. "Where . . . where does this leave us, Woodie?"

"You're the only one who knows the answer to that question. I won't be hard to find. Don't hit any jackrabbits on your way home," he said lightly.

"I . . . I'll try not to. I'll call you." Woodie nodded.

Woodie stood by the bedroom window, his hands jammed into his pockets as he watched the only woman he had ever truly loved drive away. He watched until the taillights were pin pricks of red in the dark night. "I hate your fucking guts, Logan Kelly," he seethed.

"If you don't mind my asking, Kristine, what got your panties in a wad these past three weeks?"

"I do mind, Pete," Kristine snapped. "What time are the Olsens coming for their dog?"

"They should have been here by now. I gave them good directions, but they might have gotten lost. I think I hear a car. That must be them."

Kristine turned. *Please let it be Woodie,* she thought. Three long weeks and she hadn't heard a word from him. Twenty-one days. Five hundred and four hours. Thirty thousand two hundred and forty minutes. Almost a lifetime if you were counting, and she was counting. Every single day. She wished she knew how many times she'd walked to the phone, picked it up, only to replace it. Woodie was the one who had given her the ultimatum. God how she missed him.

"It's not the Olsens. It's some guy," Pete said. "Doesn't look like a dog man to me. He's probably selling something. Do you want me to get rid of him?"

"Yes, but be polite. I'm going to give Victoria one last brushing for her new owners. Where's Gracie?"

"Sleeping under your desk. Slick is in his crate with his

baby." It brought the desired smile to Kristine's face. She loved the two little dogs, and he knew for a fact that both of them slept on the empty pillow on her bed. He also knew she fed them white-meat chicken when she thought he wasn't looking.

The man at the door was young, perhaps a little older than the twins, with a head of curly black hair and incredible blue eyes. "I'd like to see Mrs. Kelly please."

"Why," Pete asked briskly.

"Jackson Valarian. I'm a reporter for the *Washington Post.* I'm doing a series of articles on old Civil War houses and the families that aided runaway slaves. My research led me here." He handed over a business card, which Pete in turn handed to Kristine.

"How exactly can I help you?" Kristine asked.

"By talking to me. By letting me poke around. If you have any journals or books in your attic, I'd like to look at them. I'd like to try and find the underground tunnels that led from this house to the Kelly farm."

Kristine stared at the card in her hand. "I didn't know there were any tunnels. My parents never talked about them. I don't know if we have any books in the attic or not. I really don't have the time to help you."

"You don't have to help me. I'll do everything myself. Would you mind if I started with the Kelly farm? I was out there yesterday. It was wide-open, and there weren't any NO TRESPASSING signs anywhere. I didn't go inside the house or anything. I just walked around trying to figure out where the tunnels were."

Kristine eyed the dust on the road as a car made its way to the barn. *Please let it be Woodie.* "You'll have to wait a few minutes. You can go up to the house and wait for me in the kitchen. There's some lemonade in the refrigerator. I'll be up as soon as I finish with Mrs. Olsen."

"Thanks, Mrs. Kelly. I'll wait all day if I have to."

"Mrs. Olsen, hello. Here she is. Isn't she gorgeous? I hate to part with her. Pete has all the papers and your starter bag. Victoria loves to be held as you can see. She's

a good little eater, and she does like to snuggle. She's big
on kisses, too. This little toy is what she sleeps with."

"Oh, I love her already. You won't have to worry about
me holding her. Her feet will probably never touch the
floor. My husband is going to love her to death. How much
notice do I need to give you if we want to get a boy for
her to play with?"

"At least six months. Don't be in too big a hurry. Bond
with her, enjoy her together before you bring another dog
into the house. If you do decide to get another dog, you
may want to do it before she turns a year old. She'll take
to it then and have enough mother instinct to coddle it.
If there are any problems, call us, day or night. She's had
all her shots, and she's been wormed. Bring her back in
a month.

"God, I hate to part with them," Kristine said, dabbing
at the corners of her eyes.

"Kristine, that little dog is going to get so much love
from the Olsens it would be a shame to deny them the
pleasure of Miss Victoria's company. Victoria is the winner
here." Pete waved the generous check under her nose.

"I know, I know. It's still hard to see them leave. C'mon,
Gracie. Slick, let's go to the house."

The two fur balls yipped and raced to Kristine. She
scooped them up, aware of Pete's speculative gaze. "Let's
get some Fig Newtons. Let's also not tell Pete." Both dogs
yipped at the words *Fig Newtons,* their special treat.

In the kitchen, Kristine introduced the young reporter
to the dogs, who immediately hopped onto his lap. He
reminded her of Tyler when he threw back his head and
laughed.

A glass of lemonade in her hand, Kristine sat down
opposite the young man. "Now tell me what exactly it is
you hope to accomplish by searching my house and the
tunnels. Like I told you, I am not aware of any tunnels. I
think my parents would have said something."

Kristine listened as the reporter droned on and on
about his career and the hundreds of people who had

helped him. Her eyes grew thoughtful. "You must have an incredible network to rely on."

"Oh, we do. So, will you help me?"

"This network, how extensive is it? I realize you're young, but do you have sources like the reporters do on television?"

Jackson's eyes as well as his voice grew suspicious. "Why are you asking, Mrs. Kelly?"

"You know that old saying. One hand washes the other. You help me, and I'll help you. Just how important to you is this series of articles?"

"It could make me in the newspaper business. I like doing human-interest things. One day I hope to be an investigative reporter, but for now I have to pay my dues. I like what I'm doing, so I don't mind. People around here love to read stuff like that. It might even get picked up by the AP. Stranger things have happened, but I'm not going to count on it. My editor is very encouraging. I need your help, though."

Kristine pretended to think. "You *were* trespassing on private land. The Kelly farm is posted. I saw the signs myself. The truth is, I have no personal interest in the tunnels, if there are any, and I have no interest in reading about the Civil War. I find the past to be very depressing. One needs to live in the present and look toward the future."

"But it was your . . . I don't know how many 'greats' it goes back, but it was your grandparents, some of your ancestors who helped the slaves to freedom. Don't you want to know about that?"

"No."

"Is it because you think I might find out something that wouldn't be favorable to your family?"

"If you did, I hardly think it would matter to me at this point in time. That was then, this is now." Kristine leaned back into the soft cushion of the kitchen chair. She fired up one of the few cigarettes she smoked during the day. She watched the desperation build in the reporter's eyes.

For one brief moment, she felt ashamed of herself for what she was about to do. "Unless . . ."

The desperation on the young reporter's face was suddenly replaced with hope. "Unless what, Mrs. Kelly?"

"Unless you help me."

"How can I help you? I don't know anything about the dog business. The truth is I don't much care for dogs. I'm a cat person. We always had cats in our house growing up. I hope that doesn't offend you."

"I'm not offended. To each his own. I'm interested in your network and your sources. Are they local, state, nationwide, or global?"

"Mine are pretty much statewide. Some of the older reporters are global. Why?"

"I'd like to avail myself of those sources and, of course, your network. Perhaps we could strike a bargain here."

Jackson followed Kristine's lead and leaned back in his chair but not before he reached for one of her cigarettes. "Tell me what you want."

"I want to find someone. Someone who dropped off the face of the earth. In Germany. That was the last place he was seen."

"I don't want to commit to anything. Personally, I do not have those kinds of sources. I can, however, talk to some of the others to see if they can help. Why don't you meet me tomorrow for lunch? I'll bring along two of our seasoned guys. Maybe even our editor. How does that sound?"

"It sounds good."

"If they won't help you, will you still let me do the search?"

"No."

"I guess I better get going then. I might have a lot of arm-twisting to do. By the way, who is it you want to find?"

"My husband."

"Oh."

"Where shall I meet you tomorrow?"

"I'm staying in town at the Fairmont. How about the

Golden Dragon? Your other choice is fast food. My expense account is limited. I can't even promise the other guys will drive down here. If they don't, I'll at least have answers for you. Is it a deal?''

"It's a deal, Mr. Valarian. I'll meet you at say twelve o'clock.''

"Noon is fine. You can call me Jack. What shall I call you?''

"Mrs. Kelly will do nicely.'' She held out her hand. His handshake was so firm, Kristine fought the urge to squeal. "Tonight I'll go up to the attic to see if there are any books or journals. If there are, they're probably rotted by now.''

"Not if they're packed in trunks. You'd be surprised at some of the stuff I've found. If I find something that isn't too flattering to your ancestors, assuming we work together, I'll come to you with it first. That doesn't mean I won't print it. Is that understood?''

"Perfectly. I expect the same thing from your sources and that global network of yours.''

"Understood. I hope this works out, Mrs. Kelly. I can see myself out.''

Kristine sat at the table for a long time sipping her lemonade and smoking. More than once she ran the conversation with the reporter over and over in her mind. She squeezed her eyes shut with pain as she recalled her words. *One needs to live in the present and look toward the future.* Too bad she didn't practice what she preached.

Kristine opened her eyes and closed them again so she could conjure up Woodie's face behind her closed lids. Her heart thumped in her chest. Why hadn't he called her? Why hadn't she called him? "This is so stupid, it's ridiculous,'' she mumbled as she bent down to pick up both little dogs. "You two are the best thing that ever happened to me. You wouldn't like Logan at all, and, you know something, he wouldn't like you. He doesn't like animals in the house.'' Slick growled at her strange tone as he nipped her lightly on the ear. Gracie swatted him with one little paw. "Guess that tells us who is the boss.

Right, Slick? Maybe I'll call him after dinner. Then again, maybe I won't. I think I'll go up to the attic now to see what I can find. You know, sweeten the pot for Mr. Valarian. You have to stay down here, though. It's probably three hundred degrees up there right now."

She was right about the heat in the old attic. Sweat dripped down Kristine's face as she went through the trunks and boxes that were neatly labeled. She finally found what she was looking for at the far end of the attic of the rambling old house. Each generation seemed to have its own corner of the attic. Obviously, her mother hadn't disturbed anything. She had a bad moment when she saw her old sled and first tricycle. Her roller skates and ice skates hung from nails hammered into the ceiling. Her skis leaned drunkenly against a stack of boxes that said, KRISTINE'S BOOKS. She rubbed at the sweat dripping down her face. She had none of these things for her own children. When you moved around the world, you traveled light. Logan had seen to that. "Guess what, Logan, some-day I'm going to have grandchildren, and their things are going to be put up here. So there, Logan, so there."

Kristine pushed a wicker doll buggy out of the way in her scramble to get to the alcove where the last boxes and trunks were stored. She didn't know if it was the heat or thoughts of Logan, but she thought if she didn't get out of the attic she was going to pass out. She clawed at one of the trunks and finally managed to lift the lid. Books and journals were stacked to the brim. She reached for one and ran to the steps, taking great gulps of the cooler air as she raced down the steps. She ran to the bathroom, where she stepped into the tub to douse herself, clothes and all, with cool water. It was a full hour later before she felt able to step from the tub to change her clothes.

Another hour passed before Kristine padded over to the window seat. She moved the stuffed cushions to the floor before propping open the top of the seat. Staring up at her was her favorite picture of Logan in his dress uniform. *One needs to live in the present and look toward the future, Logan.* The words seemed seared into her brain. She repeated them over and over in her mind. She continued with her low-voiced monologue. "Woodie's right, I need to lay you to rest. I can't see into the future. The reason I can't see into the future, Logan, is because there is no future for us. I feel like such a fool. Woodie loves me, and I walked away from him. Because of you. I allowed you to do all this to me. I wish I could put all the blame on you, but I can't. All I can do now is live in the present and look toward the future with Woodie. If it isn't too late."

Kristine galloped down the hall and then down the steps in her rush to get to the storage room to search for an empty carton. Logan Kelly was not going to take up one more inch of space in her house if she could help it. She picked the first box from a pile and galloped back up the steps. She dumped the contents of the window seat any old way into the cardboard carton. *This is the end of it,* she thought. *Once this part of my life is put into storage, I can start fresh. Is that before or after you write your final chapter?* A niggling voice queried. *Before, after, now, what difference does it make? I'll do it when the time is right. The bottom line is I'm going to do it. I won't look back either, because the past is prologue. So there, Logan.*

Forty minutes later, after moving the heavy carton, one step at a time, down the long, steep staircase, she dragged and pushed it to the farthest corner of the old storage room. She didn't label it, but she did pile other boxes on top of it so she wouldn't have to see it every time she came into the room to search for something. She had just done what she never thought she would be able to do, and it was over. She felt so light-headed she had to reach for the doorjamb to steady herself.

In the kitchen, Kristine washed the coffeepot. Unlike people who drank tea when things went awry, she drank coffee. Pots and pots of coffee. The coffee would help her get through the mountain of paperwork on her desk.

Pete opened the screen door and poked his head inside.

"I could use some coffee about now. I saw that, Kristine. Fig Newtons are not good for dogs. They probably aren't good for humans, either."

"You eat them by the bagful, Pete. It's a treat. They're my dogs and my Fig Newtons. The coffee is perking."

"Do you want me to go to the bank this afternoon to deposit the Olsens' check? We didn't deposit Carter or Wainwright's checks last week either."

Should she pass up the perfect excuse to go to the bank tomorrow when she went into town to meet Jack Valarian? She'd just march into Woodie's office and say . . . what? *I was a fool. I'm sorry. I really do care for you. I want to share that life you were talking about.* Then she could tell him she had moved Logan to the storage room where he belonged. She eyeballed the vet. "I have to go into town tomorrow morning. I'll do it then."

"So are you going to help that guy or what?" Pete demanded.

"I think so. I went up to the attic, and there's a trunk full of books and journals. It was too hot to go through it. He can come out some evening when it's cooler and do it. Let him pass out from the heat."

"And what do you get out of this? I know you, Kristine. Your brain is whirling. Let me guess. It's a trade-off. You want him to help you find your husband. He's a reporter, so that means he has access to all kinds of stuff. How am I doing so far?"

Kristine turned her back on Pete. "Were you eaves-dropping?"

"As a matter of fact I was. The window was open. I came up for coffee but decided to turn around and go back. As a friend who cares about you, Kristine, I'm telling you to let it go. You're just opening yourself up to more heartache. If Woodie finds out, he won't take it well. He will find out. Stuff like this always gets out."

"Come with me, Pete. I want to show you something."

Gracie and Slick raced ahead, their tiny paws barely skimming the slick wooden floor.

"You want to show me the storeroom. Jeez, Kristine, what do you want me to look for this time? We need to get you some kind of system, you know—stuff you use, stuff you don't use, etc. etc."

"See that huge box in the corner with all the other stuff piled on top of it."

"Yeah. What's in it?"

"Logan. That box is all that is left of Logan Kelly. I cleared out everything. I brought it down the steps one at a time and dragged it in here. I cleared him out of my house."

"What good is that, Kristine, if he's still in your heart?" Pete asked gently.

"I can't carve him out of my heart, Pete. Asking Mr. Valarian's people to help is the very last thing I'm going to do. I couldn't live with myself if I let the opportunity pass. I want to be able to say I did everything I could. I need closure, Pete."

"Of course you do," Pete said, putting his arms around Kristine's shoulders. "Let's hope it works. Are you going to tell Woodie?"

"I haven't heard from Woodie for three weeks. He wants . . . he expects . . . he doesn't understand," Kristine said, her face miserable.

"He's a stand-up guy, Kristine."

"I know that. I have to be able to live with myself, Pete. If it means losing Woodie, then I will have to live with that, too."

"For God's sake, call the guy already."

"The guy is supposed to call the girl. You know that, Pete."

"Each situation is different. Girls call me all the time. I love it. It makes me feel important. Is that why you're taking the checks to the bank tomorrow?"

"I felt . . . feel like it will give me a . . . reason. A bona fide reason. I have some pride left, Pete."

"Do you love Woodie, Kristine?"

Kristine nodded, her face more miserable than before.

"I never told him I did. I wanted to, but I couldn't get the words past my lips. He gave me an ultimatum. I hate ultimatums. Most women I know do not do well with ultimatums, and I am no exception. That's why I haven't called him. I recognize the fact that I literally owe him my life, but that doesn't mean he can dictate to me. Logan did that to me. I cannot and will not let that happen to me again."

"So, just bumping into him at the bank, maybe, will make things all right?" Pete asked skeptically.

"Probably not, but it's all I have going for me at the moment. If it doesn't work, then I'll switch to Plan B."

"Which is?"

"I have no clue. When I do, you will be the first to know. Coffee's ready. Let's drop it for now, okay?"

"Sure."

"What shall we toast here? It seems kind of appropriate, don't you think?"

"To Gracie and Slick and may you run out of Fig Newtons!" Pete said, an evil grin spreading over his features.

At the sound of the magic words, both Gracie and Slick sat up on their haunches, panting and waiting, their eyes on Pete.

"Okay, okay, just this once," Pete said.

"Yeah, that's what I said, too." Kristine laughed. "Now they are Fig Newton addicts."

It was good to hear her laugh, Pete thought as he broke one of the Newtons in two. Really good.

It didn't seem right, Kristine thought, that a man could be so ugly, have such suspicious eyes, and yet have a gentle voice.

"Jack filled me in, Mrs. Kelly. It's almost four years. If there ever was a trail, it's cold by now. I'll put out some feelers, do a little calling around on my own, but I don't hold out much hope. In cases like this we usually follow the money, but Swiss banks are so buttoned up it's mostly a waste of time. I'll do what I can, but I want you to know I think it's going to be fruitless. The deal is, if I understand Jack, I help you, regardless of the results, and you give him access to your property and any books and journals. The Kelly farm, too. Is that right?" Andrew Pomeroy said.

Kristine nodded.

"It's going to take some time."

"How much time?" Kristine asked.

"We're calling in favors here. No one moves fast on favors. Now if money was being paid out, it would be different. People react to money when it comes at the end of a job."

"Are you saying you want money?" Kristine demanded.

"No. I said it was going to be slow because no money is changing hands. I'll be the one calling you. I don't want you pestering me, is that understood?"

"Fine," Kristine snapped.

"It's settled then," Jack said. "When can I come out to the house?"

"I'd suggest going through the attic at night after the sun goes down. It's hot as hell up there. I almost passed out. I can show you exactly where the trunks are, then you might want to carry the books down to the first floor. The steamer trunks probably weigh more than the contents. The attic steps are narrow and steep. You can start tonight, if you like. I don't know if there are any blueprints of the house or not. I also do not know if there's anything in the Kelly attic. I've never been on the second floor, much less the attic."

Kristine finished her wonton soup. She watched in amazement as a giant sizzling platter was set in the middle of the table. "If you gentlemen don't mind, I have some errands to run. Enjoy your lunch. It was nice meeting you, Mr. Pomeroy."

"Likewise, Mrs. Kelly." The moment the words were out of his mouth, Kristine knew she was forgotten. She watched a moment as the senior reporter loaded his luncheon plate with the crisp vegetables and rice.

"I'll be out tonight around seven, Mrs. Kelly," Jackson said.

"I'll see you then."

Her heart hammering in her chest, Kristine drove to the bank. Instead of going in the front entrance, she drove around to the back to park in the shade. She couldn't remember the last time she felt this jittery. Probably when she was a teenager and dating Logan, who was always late for dates. She was checking her makeup in the rearview mirror when she saw Woodie and a beautiful young woman walk toward his car. They were both laughing, his arm around her shoulder. Her heart thudding in her chest, she continued to watch as Woodie held the door for the striking blond woman. Fashionable. Chic. Pricey outfit. Sun-glitzed hair. Gorgeous tan. Then the man she thought she would spend the rest of her days with walked around to the driver's side of the car, the wide smile still on his face.

Kristine threw herself across the wide front seat of the station wagon when it appeared Woodie was going to exit the parking lot the way she had driven in.

Kristine cried her misery all the way back to the farm.

8

~

"Whoa. What have we here, guys?" Pete said as he pushed the baseball cap that was always on his head farther back to observe Kristine barreling down the driveway. When she skidded to a stop, dust spiraled upward in decorative designs. He continued to watch as she slammed the door of the station wagon and ran to the house, taking the steps on the front porch two at a time. "I don't know this for a fact, Gracie, but I'd say off the top of my head, something ain't right. What say we check it out," Pete said to the little dog nestling in the pocket of his plastic apron.

Pete loped up the long path from the barn to the back porch, where he watched Kristine reach for a wine bottle that always sat on the kitchen counter. *Don't do it, Kristine. Please, don't do it.* He continued to watch as a gambit of emotions registered on his employer's face. When her shoulders slumped and she reached for the coffeepot, he knew she wasn't going to give in to the temptation to take a drink. Kristine was one tough lady. He silently applauded her.

"Wanna talk about it?" he asked through the screen door.

"No. Yes. There's nothing to talk about."

"If there's nothing to talk about, then why do you look like you lost your best friend? Why were you tempted to take a drink? Why are you shaking like that? Sit down. I'll make the coffee. Two heads are better than one."

"I hate men," Kristine said bitterly. "You can't trust them any farther than you can throw them. They lie, they cheat, they steal from you. I hate them."

"Consider me an overgrown boy," Pete said flippantly. "Are we talking about Logan here or Woodie or that guy from the newspaper?"

"What's the difference?" Kristine snapped. "Put them in a bag, shake them up, and they come out the same. I swear to God, I will never trust another man as long as I live."

"I think you need to explain that statement, Kristine. If it's your intention to lump me in with the gruesome threesome, I'm outta here."

"Not you, Pete. It probably isn't even them. It's me. I'm dumb, I'm stupid, and I can't get a handle on things. Just when I think I'm making some kind of progress, bam, I'm back to square one. Do you see some kind of invisible sign on my forehead, Pete, that says, Kristine deserves to be made miserable?"

Pete dropped to his haunches to take Kristine's hands in his own. Behind him he could hear the cheerful plop, plop of the water dripping into the pot. "Let's take it from the top, Kristine. It's entirely possible you are overreacting. Taking the step to finally move Logan's things into the storage room has left you feeling vulnerable. Now, tell me what happened."

Kristine told him. "She was beautiful, Pete. Drop-dead gorgeous. Younger than me. It was the way Woodie had his arm around her shoulders. He was smiling from ear to ear. He looked happy, like he didn't have a care in the world. I've been so damn miserable. I haven't slept through the night since I returned from New York."

"Kristine, the woman was probably a bank customer and Woodie was taking her to lunch. Bankers do that when they want your money. It's all part of the game. It's called business."

"No. They were too familiar with each other. I saw how they looked at each other. It's not my imagination. I was there, Pete."

"All it will take is one phone call to clear it up. What

happened to innocent until proven guilty? Woodie is too nice a guy to do what you think he's doing."

"I thought Logan was a nice guy, too. Woodie's another one who sees dollar signs where I'm concerned."

"Kristine, Woodie is loaded. He doesn't need your money. You're off the track here."

"Yeah, right. He told me his wife took just about every-thing he had. That doesn't sound to me like he's loaded. Money does awful things to people. How could I be so wrong? Not just once but *twice*. I'm going to make a phone call all right. I'm moving my trust and my accounts to Anchor Savings. That's the phone call I'm going to make."

"Don't do it today, Kristine. Wait till tomorrow when you've calmed down. It never pays to do things recklessly. I know there is an explanation for all this. You aren't being fair if you don't give Woodie a chance to explain."

"Do you see him calling me, Pete? Well, do you?"

"You said you would call him. You can't switch up now. You were holding the ball, and you know it. In three weeks you have not called him the way you said you would. What the hell do you think he's been thinking? Maybe the woman was a cousin or a sister."

"He doesn't have any cousins or sisters," Kristine snapped.

Pete's voice turned stubborn. "I know there's an expla-nation. It also occurs to me to wonder if you aren't taking this as a way out now that you committed to the reporter and his buddy. Are you secretly hoping the guy can find Logan? Let's just assume for the sake of argument that they find him. Do you want him back after what he did to you? Hope springs eternal, Kristine. You're off the hook now where Woodie is concerned. Now you can go back to pining away for your husband."

"That's bullshit, Pete."

"And she has a temper," Pete said as he poured coffee into two mugs. "Call Woodie, tell him you saw him and the woman. Ream him out and wait for his response. Then make a decision. For some reason, I don't see him lying to you. Do it, Kristine."

"Whose side are you on, Pete?"

"I'm on yours. That's why I want you to call him. Just do it, Kristine. If you don't, you could ruin something wonderful. It's one phone call."

Kristine reached behind her for the telephone. She dialed the number of the bank. "Mr. Dunwoodie, please. This is Kristine Kelly," she said, her voice shaking. She listened for a moment before she replaced the phone. "Mr. Dunwoodie won't be back until tomorrow morning. He decided to take the afternoon off. Is there anything else you want me to do, Pete?"

Pete grappled for a reply. "He might have gone to the dentist. Maybe he had a doctor's appointment. Hell, maybe he went fishing. It's not the end of the world. Don't read something into this that isn't there, Kristine."

"Pete, if Mr. Dunwoodie decides to return my phone call, tell him I'm out of town. I won't view you favorably if you try to play matchmaker. I will consider it betrayal on your part, and then I'll have to fire you. Do we understand each other?"

"Yes, ma'am. What if he shows up?"

"Close the gate out front. It's that simple. I'm going upstairs. I have some paperwork to take care of. Why don't you take the rest of the day off? Go riding or go into town and take some nice girl out to dinner. I'll be fine. There's nothing pressing going on. The dogs are okay. I'll take care of the feeding this evening. If you're worrying that I'll take a drink, don't. I'm not that weak-willed person I used to be."

"Are you sure?"

"I'm sure. Take her some flowers."

"Okay, I will."

Kristine smiled. "Thanks for listening, Pete."

"Are you keeping Gracie and Slick up here?"

"Yes. Make sure you lower the gate when you leave."

"Then I guess I'll see you in the morning."

"Take your time. I'll be here."

Kristine watched as Pete hopped into his Ford Bronco. He tooted the horn, two snappy blasts of sound as he careened down the road to the highway.

The old house was tomb-quiet as Kristine cuddled the two small dogs in her arms. Then it erupted with sound as hard, driving sobs tore at her body. Tears rolled down her cheeks. Gracie tried valiantly to lick at the salty tears as Slick tried to burrow deeper into the crook of her arm. She knew she was frightening the little animals, but it was the only way she knew to release the misery engulfing her.

A long time later, when there were no more tears to shed, Kristine crooned to the tiny dogs in her lap as she stroked their silky fur. They slept, having weathered their mistress's storm.

Woodie suffered through the obligatory kiss on the cheek. How well he remembered the heady scent of his ex-wife's perfume. If he remembered correctly, he was the one who gave her the sinful fragrance.

"You look happy, Aaron."

"That's because I am happy. It's been a long road, Maureen. Are you sure now that you're doing the right thing? You've only known the man a little less than two months. Is that enough time to get to know him and accept his proposal? On top of that, he's *old*. Seventy-two is old, Maureen."

"I know," Maureen said sweetly. "I rather thought you would be glad. No more alimony. I'll be moving away. You won't have to pretend you like me for other people's benefit. Besides, he's filthy rich."

"It always comes down to money with you, doesn't it?"

"You know what they say, darlin', you can never be too thin or too rich. I love money. Actually, I adore money. He doesn't even want a prenup. He's my kind of guy. Did I tell you he has some serious ailments? He does. I promised to take care of him. By that I mean, I'll oversee the help, you know, nurses, aides, that sort of thing. I'll read to him, go for drives with him, we'll have breakfast and dinner together. He doesn't have high expectations where I'm concerned. In short, he can't get it up, Aaron.''

In spite of himself, Woodie laughed. ''I guess you really did step into it. When are you leaving?''

''Day after tomorrow. I just came by to close out my savings account. At the last minute I decided to leave twenty dollars in it. Who knows, I might come back here someday and need an active account. This way I won't have to go through all that paperwork you insist on when someone opens a new account. If I don't come back, the bank is twenty dollars richer.''

''It was nice of you to suggest lunch. Do you believe it? We're actually being civil to one another. I'll always have a soft spot in my heart for you, sweetie.''

''Exactly where are you going to be living?'' Woodie asked.

''For starters we're going to Paris. Health permitting, we'll travel all over the world. When you have unlimited wealth you can do things like that. Stedman has homes all over the world. I cannot believe how lucky I am. Just yesterday we were in New York shopping. I bought out the stores. Stedman has his own private jet. It was loaded when we came back last night. I bought six Chanel bags, and he didn't blink an eye. It is mind-boggling, darlin'. Will you listen to me go on and on. Tell me what's going on with you.''

''I'm leaving the bank at the end of the year.''

''Are you going to live in that ghastly wooden house with all those windows?''

''For the time being. I happen to love that ghastly wooden house with all those windows. I might even get married next year. Who knows, I might take the plunge over the holidays.''

''Tell me all about her,'' Maureen cooed.

''Are those fingernails your own?'' Woodie asked as he

stared at the scarlet tips of his wife's fingers. Kristine's nails were short, clear and shiny.

"Absolutely not. These eyelashes aren't mine, either. Sweetie, Stedman paid through the nose for this costly makeover. I know you don't know much about women, but once you hit forty, you start to *droop*. In all the wrong places. I've been nipped and tucked, sliced and diced from one end to the other. I could pass for twenty-nine instead of forty-one. Everyone says so. I don't know why I'm bothering to tell you all this. What do you think, Aaron?"

"Actually, Maureen, you look the same to me."

"You're trying to sidetrack me. Tell me about your girlfriend. You must need glasses," she sniffed.

"Kristine is not a girl. She's a woman. She moved back here three years ago and started to breed show dogs the way her parents did."

"Is she the one whose husband disappeared with all her money? Don't look at me like that, Aaron. Everyone in town has heard that story. I also heard she was on the sauce for a while and that she bounced checks all over the place. It's a small town, Aaron, where nothing happens. They love to chitter in the beauty shops. Is she the one?"

"Don't believe what you hear, Maureen. Those same people who chitter in the beauty shop chittered about you when you helped yourself to their money at the bank."

"Oh, phooey, Aaron. You made that all come out right. You never should have trusted me with the bank account. You know I have no head for numbers."

Woodie laughed again. "Does Stedman know how bad you are with money?"

"Absolutely. He thought that bank business was hysterical. Be sure to send me a wedding invitation. Stedman loves it when I send presents to people and sign both our names. I really have to be going, Aaron. Thanks for lunch and, you know what, it's nice to see you smile again. The first couple of weeks we were married were good, weren't they?"

"That's because we never came out of the bedroom.

Once we opened the door it was all over. Be happy, Maureen."

"You too, Aaron. What does she call you?"

"Woodie."

"That's such a *bubba* name. Oh, well, to each his own. Don't forget to send me a wedding invitation. Who knows, we might even show up for the wedding."

"Please don't. Kristine would never understand someone like you."

Maureen laughed, a musical sound that sent chills up and down Woodie's arms as it wafted upward in the light summer breeze. He shivered even though the temperature was in the high eighties. He couldn't help but wonder if what he was feeling was a harbinger of things to come.

Finally, finally, after all this time, Maureen was out of his life. It was definitely a cause for celebration. He was going home to call Kristine to invite her to the house for a romantic dinner. What difference did it make who called whom? That was teenage thinking, and he was a far cry from being a teenager. When you loved someone the way he loved Kristine, little things like who was supposed to call who, didn't matter.

Kristine sat in the office behind the old, scarred desk that had belonged to her parents and probably their parents, the dogs napping at her feet. She was sipping coffee as she stared at the road. Did Woodie's secretary call him to tell him she'd called? Would Woodie call in to check his messages? Who was the gorgeous blond woman in the designer suit? Chanel bags were expensive. While she might not own one, she knew what they cost. Of course there was the possibility it was a knockoff. The cut of the suit said it was pricey, so the bag had to be real. Like she cared. What she cared about was the ear-to-ear smile on Woodie's face and the way he draped his arm around the woman's shoulder. She sniffed again. Thirty if she was a day. Maybe twenty-eight. Young enough to be his daughter.

The phone chose that moment to ring. Answer it or not? She was running a business; of course she had to answer it. On the other hand she could let the machine take the message. She debated so long the answering machine clicked on. She sucked her breath in one long *swoosh* when she heard Woodie's voice.

"Kristine, it's Woodie." Like she wouldn't recognize his voice from miles away. "I'm calling to invite you for dinner. I guess you're busy with the dogs. Give me a call. This is so silly. Does it really matter who calls whom? What really matters is, I miss you. As an added incentive, I've given my housekeeper the day off, so I'll be the one doing the cooking. Everything will be ready by seven. I'll see you then. I love you, Kristine."

"Sure you do," Kristine muttered, her eyes filling with tears. What was it Cala would say? *Did the blonde blow you off, and I'm your second choice?* An empty house meant she was to stay the night. By now he probably knew she'd been to the bank. Like most men, he was simply covering his tracks. Maybe his afternoon tryst with the ravishing blonde didn't work out. Well it wasn't going to work out at seven o'clock, either.

Kristine looked pointedly at the answering machine until her eyes started to water. Would Woodie come out to the farm? The guardrail fence that rose and lowered automatically was certainly no deterrent to anyone wanting to come to the house or barn. All one had to do was get out of the car and walk around the long mechanical bar. Woodie would do that and not care if his car blocked the road.

How long could she avoid a confrontation with Woodie? A few days? Her nostrils quivered. She wanted a drink so bad she thought she could smell the earthy scent of grapes all about her. She clutched her hands into tight fists, banging them on top of the old desk. When the feeling stayed with her, she bent down to scoop up the two tiny dogs into her arms. She buried her face between the two of them, a long, tortured sigh escaping her lips. How strange that these two little animals could calm her better than a drink or a tranquilizer. "Let's go up to the house and make something wonderful and decadent for dinner. Something that will make us feel guilty and take the edge off this pain I feel." The tiny dogs yipped their delight at the word dinner. Kristine set them down and watched them streak toward the house. Her own steps were slow, her shoulders slumped. She thought she heard a car off in the distance. Three zippy notes of the horn made her pick up her feet and run the rest of the way to the house, where she slammed the kitchen door shut and locked it. She almost tripped over the dogs in her mad race to the front door to shove the bolt home.

Safe.

From what?

From Woodie? Her own emotions? Her own fear?

The two dogs, confused with the mad dash to the front door, proceeded to chase each other in circles, nipping Kristine's shoelaces at each frontal whirl. "Shhh," she said, placing her finger against her lips. Slick growled. Gracie nipped his ear, then waited, her tiny pink tongue flapping in the air. "Shhh," Kristine said a second time. This time, Slick obeyed and sat down next to Gracie. Both little dogs wore an expectant look as they waited for their next order.

Kristine peeked out the front window. "It's Pete and the reporter! There goes our wonderful, decadent dinner."

Kristine unlocked the kitchen door. "What are you doing back here?"

Pete shrugged. "I was worried about you, so I came back. Besides, every girl I called turned me down. One does not call a girl at the last minute to ask her to dinner. It seems they have to do their hair, their nails, and a bunch of other stuff. What's for dinner? I thought I might keep you company. Jack here was right behind me."

"Dinner was going to be something wonderful and decadent, but now it's going to be tomato soup and grilled cheese. Would you like to join us, Jack?"

"No thanks. I'd like to get to it if you don't mind."

"You can use the kitchen stairway over there," Kristine said, pointing to the far corner of the kitchen. "The attic steps are at the end of the long hall. The trunks you want are over this section of the house. There's a wicker doll buggy by the alcove. The sun might be going down, but it's still going to be hot up there. My advice would be to carry the things you need down here. Understand, Jack, nothing leaves this house. You can make all the notes you want. We have a copy machine in the office in the barn you can use. Are we clear on this?"

"Crystal."

A moment later he was gone.

"I don't think I ever had that much energy. How does one get excited about all those musty old books?" Pete groused.

"To each his own. There must have been *one* girl who was interested in dinner."

"Kristine, I do not have a little black book. I know three girls, young women, two of whom are sort of, kind of, you know, seeing someone. For some reason being a vet is not a turn-on for women. In case you haven't noticed, I am not exactly Robert Redford. Everyone wants someone who looks like him."

"Do you *ever* get dressed up?" Kristine demanded.

"For funerals and weddings. How about you?"

"I used to. Logan always . . . never mind. Clothes are not my top priority. Woodie called and left a message."

"And . . ."

"And nothing. I listened to it. He invited me for dinner. Guess his little afternoon lark didn't pan out."

"You are jaded, Kristine. I'm telling you, it was business, and now you've boxed yourself into a corner. Go pick some of those daisies by the front door and go over there for dinner. Put some perfume on so you don't smell like the dogs."

"I'm not doing any such thing. I know what I saw. I know a little bit about men."

"Get off it, Kristine. You know as much about men as

I know about women. That's as in zip, nada, nothing. If either one of us knew anything about the opposite sex, we wouldn't be sitting here with two dogs eating tomato soup and grilled cheese.''

"You would be perfect for my daughter Cala.''

"I think so myself," Pete said, slapping a slice of cheese between two pieces of bread. "So when do I get to meet her?''

Kristine shrugged. "She's dating some guy named Tom. That's all I know. I'm hoping they come home for Christmas. She loves animals. All the kids love animals. Logan would never allow us to have a dog or a cat.''

"I can't imagine a life without animals in it," Pete said. "Do you want milk or water in the tomato soup? Milk is better.''

"Then go with the milk.''

"Didn't you invite me for dinner? Why am I making it?''

"Because you were hungry and couldn't wait for me to start.''

"Kristine, did I ever thank you for allowing me to stay in the apartment over the garage?''

Kristine smiled. "At least a hundred times.''

"By not having to pay rent, I saved almost enough for a new car. I'm glad we became such good friends.''

"You're a good vet, Pete. I'm lucky you stuck with me that first year. If things keep going as well as they're going now, I was thinking of asking you if you would be interested in a partnership.''

"Are you serious?''

"I'm serious. The business is growing. We're actually making money. That mass mailing we sent out last year to my parents' old client list paid off. Children and grandchildren are calling for our dogs. This business had a wonderful reputation when my parents were alive. I think between the two of us we can bring it up to speed.''

"I don't know what to say, Kristine. Of course I accept. Jeez, I burned the sandwiches.''

"So make new ones. There's lots of cheese."

"I have a better idea. Let's get dressed and go out dining and dancing. My treat. Have you ever been to Jezebel's?"

"No, but I heard about it. Isn't it kind of pricey?"

"Yeah. I heard the food is decadent. Their dance floor is big enough for two couples. C'mon, Kristine, let's do it!"

Never spontaneous by nature, Kristine said, "Yes, let's do it. I have to change. Do we need reservations?"

"Probably. I'll call from the barn. Is it okay to leave that guy here? You said you didn't want him taking stuff away from the house."

"We'll simply take the distributor cap off his car. He won't be able to go anywhere. We'll replace it when we get home. He'll never know the difference. If you don't know how to do it, I do. Tyler was showing Mike how to do it one time, and I watched."

"You never cease to amaze me, Kristine Kelly."

"I'm thinking of taking my maiden name back. Moving forward, not looking back, that sort of thing."

"If that's what you need to do, then you should do it. What about Gracie and Slick?"

"I'll put them in my bedroom. They'll be fine. I'll be ready in half an hour."

"I'll be ready in ten minutes. I'll be the guy in the suit."

"I think I'll recognize you."

Kristine almost jumped out of her skin when the phone rang behind her. "Don't answer that, Pete. I'm not expecting any calls. The machine will pick up."

"Whatever you say," Pete said, closing the door behind him.

Kristine stared into her closet. What should she wear? It had been so long since she bought any clothes. Everything she had was out of style. Still, European fashions were light-years ahead of the United States in her opinion. Maybe she could squeak by with her tangerine-silk dress. If she piled her hair on top of her head and wore her mother's pearls, she would be okay. She'd only worn the outfit once in Paris when Logan had taken her there for a birthday celebration. Her birthdays usually went unnoticed. Somewhere in one of her drawers there were matching shoes wrapped in tissue along with a small clutch bag with a seeded-pearl clasp. Woodie would appreciate the outfit. She wasn't sure about Pete. Sweet, wonderful Pete with the ear-to-ear grin. He really cared about her the way a good friend was supposed to care about a friend. The same way she cared about him.

The tangerine silk slithered over her body. Her summer tan, while not dark, made the pearls at her throat glow. At the last second, she added a pearl comb to her upswept hairdo. Two quick spritzes of her favorite perfume and she was ready to dine and dance the night away. Her eyes filled. She blinked away the tears.

Kristine walked to the foot of the attic stairs. "Jack, can you come here a minute."

Overhead, the boards creaked as the reporter made his way to the top of the steps. "I'm going out for a while. Are you all right? Aren't you going to carry the books downstairs?"

"Yes, but first I have to go through them. No sense in making double work. I've found some amazing things. Listen, would you mind if I slept in your barn this evening?"

"You can sleep in the house if you like. Take the first door on the left. The bed is made up. The bathroom is right next door. Don't answer the phone if it rings. The machine will pick up."

"If you're sure you don't mind, I'll take you up on the offer on the room. It will save me the trip back and forth to town. I really appreciate this. You look really nice, Mrs. Kelly," he said almost as an afterthought.

Kristine nodded as she closed the door. Back in her room she rattled off a list of instructions for the dogs, who watched her with unblinking eyes. "Don't mess on the carpet. I put paper in the bathroom. Gracie, do not bite Slick's ears. Slick, do not take Gracie's chews. Leave my shoes alone and take a nap. Here's a chew for each of you. Be good now," she said, wagging her finger in front of them. Gracie yawned while Slick scratched at his ears.

Downstairs, Kristine gasped at the sight of Pete in his khaki suit with pristine white shirt and designer tie. "I keep telling you. I clean up good. May I say you look worthy of a night at Jezebel's? You look great, Kristine. I mean that."

"So do you, Pete."

"Our own mutual admiration society. My arm, Madam."

In spite of herself, Kristine giggled.

Two hours later, Kristine said, "I can truthfully say that was one of the best meals I've ever eaten. I can feel the pounds settling over my hips as we speak. My arteries snapped shut an hour ago. I can't even begin to imagine what the bill will be. It was a great dinner, Pete. Thanks for inviting me."

"I promised dancing. Cheek-to-cheek. One dance, and we can go home. Is it a deal?"

"It's a deal. First I want my coffee and dessert."

"Let's get that thing they set on fire by your table," Pete said.

"Let's get *two* of those things they set on fire by your table," Kristine said.

Across the room in a cozy alcove, Maureen Dunwoodie stared at Kristine and the young man seated across from her. "Excuse me, Stedman," she said to the man in the wheelchair. "I want to powder my nose. I'll be right back."

In the ladies' room, Maureen searched for a quarter in her new Chanel handbag. She dialed her ex-husband's number from memory. "My, my, we sound grouchy this evening, Aaron Sweetie, something you said at lunchtime bothers me. Did I understand you correctly when you said you were seeing and thinking of marrying that dog-breeding person? What's her name, ah, yes, Kristine? I guess my question to you would be, does she know about your feelings? The only reason I'm asking is Stedman and I are having dinner at Jezebel's, and your lady friend is here with a very nice-looking *young* man. He's definitely *half* your age. She looks your age, however. What does it mean, sweetie?" Maureen stretched the wire from the phone so she could open the door to peek out. "They're dancing cheek-to-cheek. I believe the song is 'I'll Always Love You.' Their waiter is setting fire to one of those flaming desserts, you know, the big fire where everyone claps their hands and everyone else wishes they'd ordered the same thing. I hope I didn't upset you, Aaron. I told you I'll always have a soft spot in my heart for you. Gotta go, sweetie. Stedman gets nervous when I'm out of his sight for too long. Don't forget to invite us to the wedding. If there is a wedding," she muttered as she traced her lip line with a crimson stick. "Life is just one big bowl of cherries, Aaron. Yours is full of pits, and mine is full of fruit." She tossed herself a kiss in the mirror before she left the luxurious rest room that was full of fresh flowers and deep, comfortable chairs. At the last second she pinched off a yellow rose for Stedman. What the hell, it was free, and if it made the old man happy, so be it.

"Bitch!" Woodie seethed as he turned off the stove and removed his apron. Maureen was a bitch, yes, but as a rule she didn't lie. It would take him less than ten minutes to drive to Jezebel's to check out her story. He knew the restaurant well, having dined there many times with business associates. He could park on one of the side streets and watch, or he could brazenly drive through the parking lot to check the cars. *Should I do it or shouldn't I do it? Why the hell not! Kristine didn't return my phone call. I have a right to know what is going on. Dammit, I'm going to do it. And if I get caught, what will I say? The truth. What else.*

Woodie drove into the lot just as a sleek limousine was crawling toward the exit. He groaned when he saw the darkened window slide down. Maureen poked her head out the window. "They were paying the check as we were leaving. Unless you want to make a fool of yourself, sweetie, I'd head for cover.'' His ex-wife's tinkling laughter set Woodie's teeth on edge as he slammed his foot on the accelerator. He pulled into a parking spot at the far end of the lot just as Kristine and Pete walked out the door. He felt like a lovesick teenager *and* a Peeping Tom. He watched through the rearview mirror as Pete handed a claim check to the valet-parking attendant. Both of them wore the look of a couple celebrating something. He'd never seen Kristine look so lovely, and he had no idea Pete could look so handsome and so very *young*. He could pass for a Washington power broker in his well-cut suit and pristine white shirt and tie. Was thirty-three really that young? How much difference did twelve years make to a woman? How in the goddamn hell was he supposed to compete with a young stud fourteen years his junior?

Woodie felt like he'd been kicked in the gut by an elephant.

9

Woodie stared at the mess that was supposed to be a wonderful dinner. He was a cat with its tail on fire as he poured and dumped everything down the garbage disposal. He slammed the dishes and pots any old way into the dishwasher before he turned it on. Fourteen years. Twelve years. Pete of all people! Pete was a goddamn vet. He ran around in torn coveralls with a baseball cap jammed on his head; *backwards* no less. He and Kristine had a lot in common. They both loved animals. He was good at his job, and he fucking lived in the small apartment over the garage. They even ate together. Kristine extolled his virtues every time they were together, saying the dogs loved him and he had such a gentle way with animals and the most soothing voice she'd ever heard when they were about to deliver their pups. Once, she'd even said she *adored* the young man. He remembered the pang of jealousy that shot through him at her words, but then she'd smiled and kissed him until his teeth rattled.

He knew exactly what he should do. He should march his ass out to the farm and demand an explanation. That's what he *should* do, all right. Instead, he reached into the cabinet over the sink for a bottle of hundred-proof Kentucky bourbon. He took a long slug from the bottle, his eyes watering as the fiery liquid roared down his throat. Maybe it wasn't such a good idea to go out to the farm. He'd want to punch the young vet smack in the nose and maybe hurt him. On the other hand, the feisty jock might knock him on his forty-seven-year-old ass and damage the pricey porcelain caps he'd had to get his senior year in high school because of a football mishap. He took another long pull from the bottle as he made his way to the kitchen table. He plopped the bottle square in the middle of the table and squinted at it, trying to remember the last time he'd gotten drunk. The day of his divorce from Maureen. Actually it was a two-day drunk and a four-day hangover. On the fifth day he'd sworn to God, the banking industry, his dead parents, and anyone else he could name, that he would never, ever, get drunk again.

That was then. This was now.

Woodie eyed the bottle, wondering how much he could take in one swallow. He reached behind him to one of the kitchen drawers and withdrew a black magic marker. He drew a line on the bottle and gulped. He thought for a minute smoke was coming out of his ears. He actually craned his neck to see his reflection in the glass on the oven door. No smoke. He marked the bottle again and swigged. He gurgled his approval as the bourbon swished to the black line.

Forty-seven wasn't old. Fifty wasn't old either. Fifty was prime if you didn't count the droop to one's ass, the slight loss of hair, the extra thickness around the waist, and the beginnings of jowls. He tried to remember what he was doing the year he turned thirty-three. No memories surfaced.

Thirty-three meant you were full of piss and vinegar, and you could get it up three or four times a night. Not to mention all that instant gratification at other times. When you were thirty-three, you had the world by the tail because you were lean and hard, a man's man. Curly hair, freckles, incredible blue eyes, and a charming grin be damned. Women loved you when you were thirty-three because they liked lean, suntanned, hard bodies. They loved mesmerizing blue eyes and running their hands through curly locks.

Woodie craned his neck to stare at his reflection in the

oven glass a second time. He still looked good for forty-seven. Reasonably good. Hair plugs weren't out of the question. Grecian Formula was a possibility. He could get rid of his boxers and wear those shit-kicking jockeys all the young studs wore. The Calvin Klein colored ones. He could start wearing deck shoes instead of his Brooks Brothers wing tips.

He took another long slurp from the bottle, marveling at how close he came to the black marks. He was precise. He'd always been precise. He had to be precise because he handled money all day long. Bankers were as boring as Certified Public Accountants. He wondered what kind of underwear CPAs wore. If he was a betting man, which he wasn't, because bankers couldn't bet, he'd bet the vet wore yellow Calvins. Yellow, for Christ's sake. What was wrong with white or gray? Oh, no, that guy had to wear yellow. Yellow was bright and cheery. Summery. He could just picture him in one of the fields, stripping off his ragged coveralls and standing there like Tarzan in his yellow Calvins while Kristine voiced her approval. The stud probably had an electric-blue Speedo, too.

His head buzzing, Woodie clutched at the bourbon bottle before he brought it to his lips.

What were *they* doing right now? Were they in the barn rolling around in the hay? Were they upstairs in Kristine's bedroom, or were they in the little apartment over the garage on the narrow bed that was only big enough for one person?

Woodie continued to torture himself with thoughts of Pete, wondering if he was one of those rub-a-dub men who liked to run their hands over women's bodies and then suck their toes. Pete would be up on all the latest techniques. All young guys were. Spontaneous, serendipitous. That was Pete. What the hell was he? A forty-seven-year-old fart who didn't know his ass from his elbow. "I've managed to do all right," he muttered, "without yellow Calvins and a blue Speedo."

Woodie blinked as he peered at the bottle. Empty.
"Shit!"

His gait unsteady, Woodie staggered to the cabinet over
the kitchen sink. Cooking sherry, olive oil, Balsamic vinegar. No liquor. Well, he could fix that. He had a liquor
cabinet that was *stuffed* with the good stuff. All he had to
do was find the damn thing. Maybe he should take a nap
first, or maybe he should go with his original thought and
go out to the farm.

In the living room, Woodie eyeballed the liquor cabinet
and the couch.

It looked, to his bleary eyes, like an either-or situation.
"Like hell!" he mumbled as he staggered back to the
kitchen to look for his car keys.

As drunk as he was, he knew he couldn't go on the
highway. He could, however, drive through the fields to
arrive within walking distance of Kristine's barn. All he
had to do was remember the way. Maybe he needed a map.

A brown grocery bag from under the sink found its way
to the kitchen table. With the black magic marker, Woodie
started to draw lines on the grocery sack. He made stars
alongside what he thought were the various fields that
would lead him to Kristine's farm.

Smacking his hands together in satisfaction, Woodie
reached for his glasses on the kitchen counter. One had
to be careful when driving while inebriated.

Outside in the warm, humid air, Woodie headed for
the garage, where he was overtaken by indecision. He felt
woozy; his knees were rubbery, and his head felt like a
million bees were buzzing inside his skull. Should he take
his racy Jaguar or the bank's minibus? The shocks were
probably better on the bus, and it had four-wheel drive.
In addition, it lit up like a Christmas tree in the dark with
red-and-blue flashing lights on the roof.

Woodie turned on the ignition. It took three tries
before he was able to shift into reverse and another two
tries before he could shift into first at the end of his long
circular driveway. He flicked on all the knobs, all the dials,

and all the buttons as he sailed across the field in a crazy zigzag pattern in search of his true love.

"I still can't get over the fact that Jack cleaned up the kitchen," Kristine said.

"In case you haven't noticed, Kristine, Jack has taken over your kitchen. He's got those moldy books and journals spread all over. Gracie already peed on one of them, and Slick is about to lift his leg as we speak. I suggest we sit outside and have one last cup of coffee. Thanks for having dinner with me."

"I enjoyed it, Pete. Next time it's my treat."

"How many times did Woodie call?"

"Just once. I didn't listen to the message. I just erased it. I think we should invite Jack to join us. I'd kind of like to know what he's found so far. After all, he's going to be writing about my ancestors," she whispered.

"Sure. I'll bring the coffee. It's hot, isn't it?"

"It sure is. I like to sit out on the porch and listen to the frogs and crickets. It's so peaceful watching the fireflies."

"What are you going to do about Woodie, Kristine?"

"Nothing."

"I don't think you're being fair. You owe it to him to listen to his explanation. I'm sure he has one. He's a stand-up guy, boss."

"*Was* a stand-up guy. I saw what I saw."

"You're making him pay for things Logan did to you. That's not fair."

"Whose side are you on, Pete?"

"I'm on the side of what's right. I know you're my boss, and I know you're my friend. I wouldn't think much of myself if I didn't try to point out to you when you're doing something wrong. By the same token, I'd want you to tell me if the situation were reversed."

"Can we just drop it, Pete? The evening is too beautiful to spoil, and I really don't want Jack knowing my business."

"Okay. We're picking up tomorrow, though, right where we're leaving off now. Deal, Kristine?"

"Sure." She heard the screen door slam and turned to see Jack appear on the porch, a big smile on his face.

"So, Jack, what have you found out?" Kristine asked brightly.

"I'm still trying to organize the books and journals according to dates. The ink is faded and blurred in a lot of them. So far, I haven't found even a clue as to where the opening to the tunnel is. I'll have your kitchen back to normal before morning."

"Aren't you going to sleep?"

"Are you kidding? I'm too excited to sleep. Being a reporter is rather like being a doctor—you learn to go without sleeping. I take catnaps when I'm on a find like this. What are all those lights over there?"

"I bet it's a UFO," Pete said, standing up to peer into the darkness. "They're all over the place. Wow!"

"Whatever it is, it's getting closer. Do you have a gun, Mrs. Kelly?" Jack asked.

"No, I do not have a gun. The Department of Defense says there are no such things as UFOs. What do you think it is, Pete?" Kristine asked as she cuddled Gracie and Slick in her arms.

"A police car. An ambulance. What else has flashing lights?"

"In my fields?"

"It's almost here, whatever it is. I think we need to check this out. You wait here, Kristine. Jack, you come with me." The reporter tripped along behind Pete, his steps hesitant.

"Move, move!" Kristine hissed. "I thought all reporters had a nose for news. Yours isn't even twitching. You might have a real scoop here. A Pulitzer!"

"God!" the reporter said.

"It's a bus," Pete said in disgust! "The bank bus. It's your friend, Kristine. And from the looks of things, he's three sheets to the wind."

"Woodie! Jack, go back to the house."

"You told me to stay here."

"Now I'm telling you to leave. Go!"

"Get out of my way, you ... you ... stud," Woodie said, trying to push Pete out of the way.

Kristine watched as Woodie swayed back and forth in the evening breeze. "I saw you! And I saw you, too!" Woodie said.

"Guess what, Woodie, I saw you, too. What are you doing here? You're drunk."

"Yes-I-am," Woodie singsonged. "That's why I drove through the fields. I didn't want to have an accident."

"We thought you were a UFO," Pete said, just to have something to say.

"I don't want to talk to you. You think because you're thirty-three you know everything. Just because I'm forty-seven doesn't mean I don't know anything. So what if you have curly hair and big blue eyes. So what? I had a lot of hair. Once. So what?"

"Pete, get him some coffee."

"This is just a wild guess on my part, Kristine, but I think this guy saw us at Jezebel's this evening," Pete said, moving closer to Kristine.

"I saw you. All dressed up. Dancing, eating desserts on fire. I trusted you, Kristine."

"What I do is none of your business. Now that you're making it my business, Aaron Dunwoodie, who was the woman I saw *you* with in the parking lot this afternoon?"

"Her! That was Maureen. My ex-wife. She came by to tell me she was getting married. No more alimony. She snagged herself a rich husband. I was so happy to be finally rid of her I took her to lunch." He paused, staggered, regained his balance. "You were dancing cheek-to-cheek while they fired up your dessert. I know all about that. So there, Kristine."

Kristine's heart soared. "Pete took me out to dinner to get my mind off *you*."

"Who's that other guy?"

"That's none of your business, Woodie. You're drunk. Go up on the porch and drink some coffee."

"Are you going to marry me, Kristine?"

"I don't know."

"Damn it, when are you going to know?"

"I don't know. When I do know, I'll tell you."

"That's not good enough." Woodie hiccuped.

"It's all you're going to get," Kristine said.

"Then I accept."

"Drink your coffee. You can sleep on the couch tonight. Pete, you better shut the lights off on the bus or his battery will die."

"I called you," Woodie said.

"I called you, too, Woodie. We're both too old to play games like this."

"You're telling me we're old. You don't know the half of it. I thought . . ."

"I know what you thought. You were wrong. Just the way I was wrong. How did you know I was at Jezebel's?"

"Maureen called and told me. I went there to spy on you. I'm not sorry."

Kristine smiled in the darkness. "Tomorrow you will be. Finish the coffee and sleep it off."

"Are we still friends?"

"We're still friends, Woodie. Come with me. You can sleep on the sofa. There's no way I'm going to try to get you upstairs."

"I'm drunk, Kristine. The last time I got drunk was the day my divorce from Maureen was final. Bankers have to be pillars of society. We're a boring lot, kind of like those number crunchers. I'm going to get some deck shoes."

"Deck shoes are good," Kristine said, "if they still call them that."

"Some yellow Calvin Klein underwear."

"I like yellow. Yellow's good."

"Maybe a bright blue Speedo."

"Uh-huh." Kristine turned so Woodie wouldn't see her wide grin.

"Maybe some hair plugs and that Grecian Formula they advertise on television."

"I don't know how you've managed to get this far without either one of them. We'll talk about it tomorrow, Woodie. Go to sleep now."

"Will you park the bus?"

"Pete did. I'll see you in the morning."

"Okay."

"I heard but I don't think I understand," Pete said after Woodie lurched inside.

"He's jealous of you. I think I understand everything except the Speedo and the yellow Calvin Kleins."

"Jeez, do they come in colors? I'm a boxer man myself."

Kristine giggled as she scooped up the dogs. "You were right, Pete. One should never assume or presume."

"What are you going to do come morning?" Pete asked.

"Wing it. Talk it out. Woodie wants things from me I'm not ready to give. I don't know if I'll ever be ready. I truly care for him. It's me, not him. I just need more time."

"Time isn't always the great healer we all think it is, Kristine. Sometimes you need to run with the ball when it's in your court. If you don't, you lose it."

"I'll remember that. Life isn't easy, is it?"

"I don't think we'd be happy if it was. We need to get shaken up from time to time to make us realize how wonderful life really is. And, on that note, I'm off to bed."

"Thanks for a great evening. Thanks for your concern, and thanks for being my friend."

"Sleep tight, boss," Pete said, hugging her.

Both dogs in her arms, Kristine stood next to the sofa where Woodie was already sleeping. She watched his chest rise and fall with his deep breathing. "Shhh," she said to the dogs when both of them whimpered in her arms. "He's fine. He's just sleeping. Everything is okay now. It's kind of nice to have a man in the house again, even if he is drunk and sleeping on our couch," she whispered as she made her way up the long flight of steps to the second floor.

* * *

Kristine rolled over before she cracked one eye open to see warm, glorious sunshine shooting into the room. Gracie and Slick danced on the bed. Clearly it was time to let the little dogs out for their morning race to the barn. She sniffed. Was that bacon and coffee she smelled?

"Five minutes. I have to brush my teeth. Don't you pee now. All I need is five minutes with my toothbrush and a comb."

The heady aroma of frying bacon and brewing coffee cut Kristine's five-minute morning ritual to three before she raced down the steps, her slippers slapping on the stair treads, her robe flapping in her own breeze, the dogs in hot pursuit.

She skidded to a stop at the kitchen doorway. Slightly disheveled and definitely bleary-eyed, Woodie was instructing Jackson Valarian on the fine art of omelet making as they tiptoed about the mess on the floor. "We're dining on the back porch this morning," he said.

"Oh," was all Kristine could think of to say as she held the door for the dogs.

"Both of you look awful," she added brightly as she poured herself a cup of coffee. "I'll be on the porch. I like my toast light with soft butter, and I'm partial to blackberry jam."

Woodie winced. "Looking is one thing. Feeling is something else. In my case, I feel like I look. Jackson here is just tired. He claims to have worked all night. Pete will be up in a few minutes. I'll apologize to you both at the same time."

Kristine nodded. "Tomato juice with Tabasco and a shot of lemon will help. I used to be a drunk, remember?" Woodie winced again. Jackson stared at his hostess, bug-eyed. Kristine didn't feel the need to explain her words.

"Morning, Pete," Kristine said as she sat down at the table. "I could get used to someone making me breakfast every morning. How about you?"

"It sure beats those Pop-Tarts you toss me every morning." Pete grinned. "He looks like shit!"

"Yes, he does. I think it's safe to say he feels the same way. We need to be charitable. He said he's going to apologize to both of us. It seems like forever since there were four people at my breakfast table," Kristine said, a wistful look on her face.

"Kristine, your son Mike called. He wants you to call him back. I offered to wake you, but he said not to. I guess he forgot the time difference."

"What time did he call?"

"Six-thirty on the button."

"But that would make it three-thirty in the morning California time. Did he say anything was wrong?"

"No. He just said to call him. Here's the number."

Her heart in her throat, Kristine managed to weave her way through the piles of books and journals that were scattered all over the kitchen floor. At the expression on her face, Woodie turned off the stove and waited expectantly as Kristine dialed her son's telephone number.

"Mike, what's wrong? I know something is wrong or you wouldn't have called here at three-thirty in the morning."

"Listen, Mom, don't get excited now. Sit down, and I'll tell you what happened. Cala had a date this evening. I met the guy. He seemed okay. Nothing like Tom. That fell by the wayside a few weeks ago. Anyway, they were driving home and the guy put the moves on Cala, and one thing led to another. It got physical, and she got banged up pretty bad. The guy is in the hospital. She broke his collarbone and he's pressing assault charges on her. I can take care of police matters here. I want to send her home to you, Mom. The company we work for has a private jet, and some of the officers are heading for Washington today. They offered to take Cala. Is it okay?"

"Of course it's okay. Are you sure she should be traveling? Did she see a doctor? Are you sure she's okay? Don't spare my feelings so I won't worry. I'll drive to Washington to pick her up. Just tell me where."

"I'll have to get back to you on that. At first Cala didn't want you to know. She looks pretty bad, Mom. She needs some mothering. Can you handle it, Mom?"

"How bad is bad, Mike?"

"She has a couple of cracked ribs. They treated her at the hospital. She's black-and-blue all over. She's got some stitches in her forehead. I think she's more angry than anything else for allowing herself to get into that kind of position."

"I can take a plane and be there in a few hours, Mike. Pete can take care of things here."

"Mom! Didn't you hear what I said? Cala wants to go home. She *needs* you."

Kristine felt herself start to shrivel as she listened to the disgust in her son's voice. "I was thinking she might not want anyone to see her in that condition."

"Cala doesn't care about that, Mom. You worry about the damnedest things sometimes."

"Yes, I guess I do. I'll do everything I can. When will you know the flight arrangements?"

"An hour or so. She's okay, Mom. She isn't going to die or anything like that. I'm going to go to the hospital to check on that bastard that did this to her. I'll call you when I know something."

"That's good, Mike. I'll wait for your call. Please, don't do anything foolish where that person is concerned."

"Yeah, sure, Mom. I gotta go now."

Kristine turned away from the phone to see the three men staring at her. "I guess you heard. That was my son Mike. It seems Cala's date attacked her, and she ended up sending him to the hospital."

"What a gal!" Pete chortled.

"She . . . she has a few cracked ribs. Some stitches and, according to Mike, is black-and-blue. The people she works for are coming East on their private plane and she's going to be with them. Cala is okay, she isn't going to die or anything," Kristine said, repeating her son's words.

"I can have someone from my paper pick up your daughter," Jack said.

"I'll be glad to go, Kristine," Pete said. "You're too emotional to drive."

"I can go with Pete," Woodie said.

"This is something I have to do. Me. Myself. Besides, I want to do it. I want my face to be the first one she sees when she gets off the plane. I appreciate your offers, though. Now, I believe someone said something about breakfast," Kristine said, walking out to the back porch.

Following Kristine's cue, the others made small talk, mostly about the mess on the kitchen floor.

"Would you mind, Mrs. Kelly, if I moved the books and journals to the dining room? I realize I'm in your way in the kitchen, and I'm sorry for the mess. I need to lay out the books and label them so I can make a chronological calendar, if that's all right with you." Kristine nodded. "It was a good breakfast, Mr. Dunwoodie. Would you like me to clean up?"

"Yeah, that sounds good," Pete said. Woodie seconded Pete's statement. Kristine stared off into space.

"Why is it nothing ever goes right?" she said, breaking her silence.

"It's called life," Woodie said.

"I wouldn't know what to do or how to act if things went right every day. I kind of think life would be boring. It's not knowing what's coming next that makes you want to keep on going. Since I'm not needed here, I'll go to the barn. Come on Gracie. Slick, hop on," Pete said, stooping down so both little dogs could perch on his shoulders.

"I don't remember ever having that much energy," Kristine said.

"Me either," Woodie volunteered. "Kristine, I know this isn't the time or the place, but we do need to talk. I've never been as miserable as I've been these last three weeks. I love you, and I want us to be together. If I can't have that, then I'm willing to settle for whatever you feel comfortable giving me. Plain and simple. I don't want to lose you. That said, I'm going to go home and clean up. I apologize for last night. If there's anything I can do or help you with in regard to Cala, call, okay?"

"Woodie, I'm sorry, too. The mind is a dangerous thing. I thought the worst of you, and you felt the same way about me. I was jealous when I saw you with Maureen. I started to think you were like Logan. I'm so glad you had the good sense to come here last night, or we might still be at odds and never know it was all a big mistake. I still can't believe you drove through the fields in your condition."

"I guess I was feeling desperate. Under normal circumstances, I would never drink and get behind the wheel of a car. Or, I was out of my mind."

Kristine smiled. "All's well that ends well. God, Woodie, you don't think Mike was lying to me, do you?"

"Your son would never lie about his twin sister. I'll call you tonight; is that okay?"

"That's very okay. You better make it late to be sure I'm back from Washington."

"Are you sure you don't want me to go with you?"

"I have to do this myself. I'm getting a second chance at motherhood, and I don't want to mess that up. You need to go to the gym and work off that hangover."

"Drive carefully."

"I will."

Kristine waited until Woodie backed up the bank's bus before she motioned for him to stop. "Just for the record," she called out, "he wears boxers." Woodie's laughter warmed her heart and stayed with her as she finished her coffee, her thoughts centering on her children and Cala in particular.

Nothing in the world could have prepared Kristine for the first sight of her daughter's bruised and battered face. For one brief instant she thought her heart was going to leap out of her chest. Rage, unlike anything she'd ever experienced, coursed through her as her daughter stepped into her waiting arms. She knew in that one moment of time she was capable of killing the person who had done this despicable thing to her daughter.

"Mom, this is Mr. Ulyesses, Mike's boss."

"Thank you so much for bringing my daughter with you, Mr. Ulyesses," Kristine said, extending her hand.

"I wish it was under more favorable circumstances, Mrs. Kelly. Our staff will follow through and advise you of all details. And you, young lady, listen to your mother and take it easy. Your job will wait as long as need be. I hate to run, but I'm already late for a meeting. I'll be staying at the Hyatt on Capitol Hill if you need to reach me for any reason."

"Thank you again."

"Do you have any luggage, Cala?"

"No, Mom. Mike rushed me to the airport too quickly. Are you mad or upset, Mom?"

"Well yes, Cala, but not with you, honey. What did the doctors say? What are your limitations?"

"Only do what feels comfortable. Eat, sleep, rest. If you think I look bad, you should see that jerk. I knocked his front teeth out, yanked a glob of hair out of the side of his head, and cracked his collarbone. When I managed to open the car door and we tumbled out, I kicked him in the groin. The cops told Mike the guy is going to file charges against me. Mr. Ulyesses said I shouldn't worry about it. They took pictures of me at the hospital, and he said that's all the firm's lawyers will need. Mom, don't look so devastated. I look worse than I feel. Honest. I'm not going to cramp your style or anything, am I?"

"Not in the least. Gracie and Slick are going to love you." Her eyes wet, Kristine hugged her daughter, who winced but tried to smile for her mother's benefit.

"Mom?"

"Yes, Cala."

"Thanks for letting me come home. This is so strange, but I need to tell you that when all this happened, I wanted you right then. When Mike came to the hospital to pick me up, all I could think of was, I wanted you to come and get me. I wanted my mother. I guess coming from me that's kind of strange, huh?"

"A little, but it's nice to know you thought about me. I didn't want to be pushy and keep calling you. I think about all of you every day. I have so many regrets, Cala. I hope we can rectify that during your stay, and, by the way, you can stay as long as you like. It's home. Mine and yours. Mike and Tyler's, too. After all of you left, I made a real effort to make the house more homey. I think, all things considered, it came out okay. We have good central heat now. I wallpapered your rooms and had two bathrooms put in. I know it's after the fact, but it was like a starting point for me. It didn't last long, and then I started drinking. It's been a learning experience. I've learned a lot about myself in the process. I can't go back and make things right, but I can make it better for the future, for all of us. I think we can work together, don't you?"

When there was no response, Kristine glanced at her daughter; she was sound asleep. "I guess we can talk about this another day," she said as she settled herself more comfortably for the ride home.

Her daughter had said she wanted her at one of the most critical moments in her young life. She'd actually said she needed her. Kristine smiled. Maybe things would right themselves after all.

"We're home, Cala," Kristine said, shaking her daughter's shoulder gently.

"Already?" Cala said sleepily. "You know what I want more than anything, Mom?"

"What, Cala?"

"A nice hot shower and one of your egg salad sandwiches. The kind you make with those little seeds in it."

Kristine smiled. "I think I can arrange that. Even the shower. Are you sure you can manage?"

"I'm kind of stiff from sleeping curled up in the car.

The shower will help. I just have to walk slowly. Oooh, is this Gracie or Slick? Can I hold them? I can't bend over to pick them up, though."

Kristine bent down to scoop up the two small dogs and handed them to Cala. "Oh, Mom, I just love them. They like me."

"And well they should. Woodie gave them to me during . . . probably the darkest hours of my life. I will be forever grateful to him and to these two little guys. Gracie is the boss, and she kind of thinks of herself as a guard dog. She sits by the bathroom door when I shower. Slick is Slick. He does his own thing. They'd be lost without one another. If you like, they can sleep with you."

"Won't you mind?" Cala said, fondling the dog's tiny ears.

Kristine lied. "Not at all. Come along, let's get you settled for that nice hot shower. I'll make some egg salad while you're cleaning up. I can lend you some clothes. Tomorrow, I'll go into town and get you some new things. By the way, I more or less have a guest. He's a reporter for the *Post*. He's doing an article on slavery and the people who aided the runaways through the tunnels. It seems the tunnels run under our property and all the way to the Kelly farm. His name is Jack Valarian, and he has his stuff spread out all over the dining room. I'll introduce you later."

"Gosh, Mom, you really did do a makeover. This doesn't seem like the same house anymore," Cala said as she walked through the downstairs.

"Does it feel comfortable and *homey*?" Kristine asked anxiously.

Cala squinted through her one good eye. "I'd say so. Wow, what a difference," she said as she passed the open door to her mother's room. "When . . . why . . ."

"It was time," Kristine said.

"Do you regret moving all *his* stuff out?"

"I don't know if regret is the right word or not. It was painful. I've come to terms with it. Tell me the truth, how do you like your room?" Kristine said, guiding Cala down the hallway.

"At first I tried to make it into the kind of room you would have loved when you were twelve or so. Then I decided that wouldn't work. I moved on to a sixteen-year-old theme, and that didn't work either. Those years are lost to both of us. I finally opted for what I thought was simply feminine. Do you like it, Cala? I made everything myself."

"Oh, Mom, it's so pretty. Did you cover this old chair, too?"

"Yes, but my upholstery skills leave a little to be desired. The chair was too comfortable to throw away. I know how you like to read, so I made this little nook for you with an ottoman and a good reading lamp. The best-selling books are a few years old now. I hooked the rugs during the winter. The rags were from all your outgrown clothing. The tulip appliqués on the coverlet were the hardest. I know they're your favorite flowers."

"I didn't know you knew that, Mom."

Kristine bobbed her head up and down, her eyes filling.

"You did all this for me, Mom? How did you know . . . you didn't know if I would ever . . ."

"I hoped. Please don't tell me it's one of those too much, too little, too late things."

"No, I won't say that. I think I'm overwhelmed that you went to so much trouble. It's wonderful. Does the bath connect to another room?"

"I'm afraid Mike won't appreciate the feminine touches. I thought powder blue and white was so clean and fresh. The seashell pictures are kind of neutral, as are the blue towels and carpets. The shower is wonderful. Unlimited hot water."

"I'm going to take a shower, then I'm going to curl up in that delicious-looking chair and either read or take another snooze. It feels like home, Mom. It really does. Thanks."

"I'll bring you up some lemonade and your egg salad.

Stay up here and don't try those stairs again until your legs are less wobbly. Is there anything in particular you'd like for dinner?''

"Spaghetti. Lots of garlic bread. Mom, when did you, you know, do all this?"

"I did it between drinking bouts. I wasn't drunk *all* the time. I did it for myself as much as I did it for you. I needed to do something constructive, but, as I said, there are glitches in all this work. Take your time in the shower. Do you need any help?"

"I think I can manage. Can the dogs stay up here with me?"

"Of course. That little keypad by the door is an intercom. Call me when you're ready for your egg salad."

Kristine's heart soared as she heard her daughter speak to the dogs. "This is all so perfect. And, she did it for me. For me. Do you believe that? Of course you do, you've lived here longer than I have. A pink carpet and tulips on my bedspread and on my walls! Who could ask for more?"

10

She nestled against him, burrowing as close as she could. She loved the way the hollow of his neck felt against her cheek as the silky strands of her hair fell over his shoulder like a veil. She breathed the scent of him. Only the rustling of their bodies against the sheets and the soft sounds of their whispers broke the silence of the night. Her fingers traced through the light furring of his chest hair; her leg, thrown intimately over his, felt the lean, sinewy muscles of his thigh.

They were like light and shadow—she silvered, the color of moonlight, and he dark like the night. He held her, gentle hands soothing her, bringing her back down from erotic heights.

It was the best of all times, this moment after lovemaking, when all the barriers were down and satiny skin melted into masculine hardness.

Kristine snuggled deeper into the nest of Woodie's embrace. He drew her closer, bringing a smile to her lips. He was the best thing that ever happened to her.

"Want to talk about it?"

Did she? "Maybe later. I want you to make love to me again."

"Do you now?" Woodie drawled.

"I absolutely do."

"I need time to think about it."

"I'll give you thirty seconds," Kristine said, her hands hot and demanding, covering his flesh with eager deliberation. His lips were pressed against her throat, his husky voice sending tremors through her body. "Make love to me, Kristine," he croaked hoarsely, the fire in his belly shooting upward to his head, making him feel light-headed, as a deep, aching longing for her surged through him.

Her body was ready for him, arching, needing, eager for his touch and for his ultimate possession of her. Her head swimming with anticipation, she felt words she never thought she would utter again slip from her lips. Their mouths touched, teasing little tastes of his tongue while he held her so tightly that each breath was a labor. He anchored his body to hers while her senses took flight, soaring high overhead until her thinking became disjointed, and her world was focused on those places which were covered by his hands, by his lips.

Taking his dark head in her hands, she cradled his face, kissing his mouth, his chin, the creases between his brows.

"Love me, Kristine, love me," he groaned, his voice deep, husky, almost a primal cry of desire. Those few words in the silent room made his passions flare. He covered her with his body, holding her fast with his muscular thighs, while he skillfully caressed her heated flesh. She drew his head down to her breasts, offering them. His lips closed over one crest, then the other, nibbling, teasing, drawing tight, loving circles with his tongue. His excursion traveled downward to the flatness of her belly and the soft, darker recesses between her legs.

Kristine felt herself arch instinctively against his mouth, her head rolling back and forth on the pillow as though to deny the exquisite demand of her sensuality. Her fingers curled in his thick, dark hair, her body moved of its own volition against the caress he excited against her. Release, when it came, was the ebbing of the flood tide, seeping from her limbs and the sudden exhaling of her breath. She was floating, drifting on a cloud, the whole of her world consisting of his lips and her flesh and the contact between them.

Still, his movements were slow, deliberate and unhurried, although there was a roaring in his ears that was echoed in the pulses of his loins. His hands grasped her hips, lifting her, drawing her against him, filling her with his bigness, knowing his own needs now and demanding they be met. His breathing was ragged, his chest heaving as though he had run a mile. Lips met, lingered, tasted, and met again. He moved within her imprisoning flesh, insistently, rhythmically, bringing her with him to another plateau so different from the first yet just as exciting. He rocked against her, feeling the resistance she offered, knowing that as she tightened around him as though to expel him from her, she was coming ever nearer to that climaxing sunburst where he would find his own consolation.

Panting, Woodie's body covered hers, calming her shudders and comforting her until their spasms passed. It was with reluctance that he withdrew from her and silently pulled the covers up, taking her in his arms to cradle her lovingly. Contentedly, Kristine rested against him, sweeping her hand down the length of his body and finding him moist from her own wetness. Curled together in a dream of their own, they murmured love words until at last they slept.

A long time later, Woodie, said, "Now that was something to put in the old memory book."

"Really," Kristine drawled. "Would you care to be more explicit?"

"There's sex and then there's sex. What we just had was *SEX!*" Woodie drawled in return.

"Is this where I'm supposed to say, 'Was it as good for you as it was for me,' or are you the one who is supposed to say that?" Kristine teased.

"Does it matter? It was heart-stopping, that's for sure."

"That it was. I've got to go home, Woodie. I don't want to, but I have to. I didn't mean to stay this long."

"It's only ten-thirty," Woodie said.

"I know, but Cala and I always have a cup of tea together

before we go to bed. I enjoy it and look forward to my daughter's company. I may be premature, but I think we're becoming friends. She's almost healed now, and it will be time for her to leave soon."

"I thought she might be attracted to Pete. Isn't that working out?"

"She doesn't mind Jack or me seeing her, but she's been shying away from Pete. I take that to mean she could be interested. They talk on the back porch every night after dark. We're at the point where makeup will cover the worst of the bruises. I think the next few days will be interesting."

"I take that to mean you would approve," Woodie said.

"It doesn't matter what I think or if I approve or not," Kristine said, zipping up her jeans. "It's what Cala and Pete think. You know what they say about long-distance relationships. They rarely work."

"This might be the exception to that rule. I miss you already, and you haven't even left. Now what am I going to do for the rest of the evening?"

"Snuggle under the covers and go back to sleep and dream about me."

"Kristine, I don't want to end this evening on a sour note but have you heard anything from Jack's reporter friend?"

"Not a word. It's not your problem, Woodie, it's mine." Kristine kissed the tip of his nose before she danced away from his outstretched hands. "Call me tomorrow, okay?"

"Will you dream about me, Kristine?"

"I dream about you every night, Woodie. I'll lock the door on my way out."

"If you moved in, you wouldn't have to go out in the middle of the night or lock the door," Woodie said good-naturedly.

"I know, and I'm thinking about that, too. Night."

"Drive carefully. Ring the phone once when you get home so I know you're safe."

"Yesss, Mother."

* * *

Kristine parked the car and walked around to the backyard. Gracie and Slick woofed their pleasure as they pretended to nip at her ankles. "What are you guys doing out here at this time of night?" She scooped them up just as her daughter's voice spiraled down from the back porch.

"I brought them out, Mom. Pete and I are up here having coffee. Want some?"

Coffee with Pete. Guess that means the mother/daughter evening cup of tea is out. "No thanks. I've had my share of caffeine for today. I'm going to check on Jack, then it's bedtime for me. Shall I take the dogs up with me?"

"I'll keep them if you don't mind, Mom. Do you miss them?"

"A little. It's okay, though. I want them to get to know you. I'll say good night."

"Night, Mom."

"Night, Kristine," Pete said.

Kristine smiled to herself as she entered the house to find Jackson waiting for her. "You look awful, Jack. What in the world is wrong?"

"Mrs. Kelly, did you know your ancestors and the Kellys were *slave traders?*"

"That's ridiculous. Where did you get an idea like that? Long ago they had slaves, but my family freed them. So did the Kellys."

"Where do you think all the family money came from?"

"What money are you talking about, Jackson? My ancestors made their money from tobacco and cotton. Way back when, before the family moved to Virginia, there were rice plantations in the Carolinas. I think that's where the bulk of the money came from. My mother always told me her great-grandparents paid the workers a wage. Another point I want to make is they never called them slaves. They were workers. They were given land for their families and my great-great-grandmother taught the children to read and write. I don't want to hear you say anything different, Jack.''

"It's here in black-and-white, Mrs. Kelly."

"What is?"

"Your ancestors, as well as your husband's, sold slaves to rich Northerners. The payment book is right here. They separated families, sold off children. They made a fortune selling human beings. Yes, they farmed, but the fields were fallow for a long time, the crops were stunted. That was when the Carolina plantations were sold. The bottom line is there was more money in selling slaves than there was in farming.''

"You better be able to prove what you're saying, or I'm running you off my property. I don't want to hear this. My parents were proud of the way their families took care of their workers. My mother always told me stories about how her great-great-grandma took care of the sick children, made sure a doctor came by once a month. I told you. They gave them land to build their houses. They had a church and a schoolhouse, good food and decent clothes. Make sure you write that down, too. I don't want to hear any cockamamie story you're making up. Do you hear me, Jackson Valarian?''

"Mrs. Kelly, the tunnels weren't to aid the runaways, they were for selling the slaves to the Northerners, the ones they smuggled here from the Carolinas. It's here in black-and-white. You can't refute it. Your family's fortune, your fortune now, was from selling slaves. Like my colleague said, all you have to do is follow the money trail.''

"This is preposterous."

"It's not preposterous, Mrs. Kelly. It's fact. I'm really sorry.''

"You aren't printing this *crap*," Kristine said, her voice rising hysterically.

"We had a deal. It's not ethical to renege. My colleague is working on your behalf. You agreed to this. You can't blame me for what I've found out.''

Kristine sat down with a thump on the dining room

chair. Her voice was strangled-sounding when she said, "If what you say is true, everything is a lie. All our lives were lies, my parents, my grandparents. Just the way my life with my husband was a lie. What will my children think? I can't allow you to print . . . no, no, no, I forbid it."

"We had a deal, Mrs. Kelly. My colleague witnessed it. Let me show you the proof. Think about all those families whose children were ripped away from them and sold to rich people who weren't as good and kind as some of your ancestors were."

Kristine wished the floor would open up and swallow her whole. "It's horrible. It's despicable. I can't change it if it truly happened."

"Nor can I, Mrs. Kelly. If I print the story, if we're lucky, some family member might remember another family member and perhaps in time be reunited. Think about *that.*"

Kristine squared her shoulders. "How many families can you account for, Jack?" she asked.

"Possibly two hundred. It could be more or less."

"How many people in total?"

"I don't know that yet."

"When will you know?"

"Another week or so."

"We can talk about this tomorrow. I need to think. I'm going to want to see everything. Everything, Jack. Put it all in order. I'm going to want to go down into the tunnels with you, too. What about the Kellys?"

"They did the same thing your family did. It was a whole network. You need to understand that part of it. It's stated here."

A headache found its way to the base of Kristine's skull, moved upward to hammer away behind her eyes. This couldn't be happening. It was probably all a very bad dream, and she would wake any moment. How could she be responsible for something that happened hundreds of years ago? Jack acted like she would be held accountable.

Kristine moved like a robot to the window seat when

she finally managed to make her legs work and climb the stairs that led to her room. She sat down, drawing her legs up to her chest, and rocked back and forth, little mewling sounds escaping her lips. The word reparation came out of nowhere and rocketed through her brain. She thought about Logan and the eight million dollars he'd absconded with. How much of that money could be traced back to the trust fund from her parents? True, Logan had made some very wise investments, but what portion of her parents' estate came from their parents and her grandparents' parents?

Jack's somber words ripped through her brain as visions of wide-eyed, frightened children being ripped from their parents' arms surfaced behind her closed eyelids. The vision was so horrendous that she bolted to the bathroom, where the violent churning in her stomach fought with the hammer inside her head.

When it was over, Kristine perched on the side of the bathtub. *What did I ever do to deserve this? What am I supposed to do now? How am I supposed to separate the slave money from the farm money or my family's kennels? Am I supposed to give it all back? What about the money Logan made off with? How can I ever make it right? How in the name of God can I ever earn back eight million dollars? Do I have any options? Moral versus legal. Hundreds of years later there can't be any legal ramifications, can there? Slavery is an ugly thing, but back then it was legal.*

The headache continued to pound inside Kristine's head. She wanted a drink so bad her hands started to shake.

"Mom? Mom, what's wrong? You look terrible. What is it?" Cala asked from the doorway. "Why are you sitting on the edge of the bathtub like that? You're shaking like a leaf. Mom, what the hell is wrong?" Cala ran to her mother, dropping to her knees.

"I need a drink. Listen to me, Cala, I really need a drink."

"No, you don't. There's no liquor in the house. You

told me that yourself. I'll make you some tea, but first you have to tell me what's wrong. You're scaring me, Mom."

Kristine started to cry as she blubbered out the story. When the last words tumbled out, she said, "It's not that I want the money. If it isn't mine, I don't want it. How can I make this right?"

"Who says you have to make it right, Mom? Where is that written? You had nothing to do with what happened hundreds of years ago. Who says you have to take responsibility for what happened?"

"I say so. It was my family. How can I live with myself if I don't do something about it? I made a deal with Jackson Valarian. It's only right that I abide by that deal. I suppose I thought he might find out things, like some of our family were horse thieves or something like that. I never for one minute thought about anything like this."

"What can you do, Mom?"

"Tomorrow, he is going to show me everything. This is something I need to see in black-and-white with my own eyes. I don't have a clear picture in my head of all the things he said. I'll take that tea now, Cala, if you don't mind. Thanks for stopping in."

"I'll get the tea. Why don't you get into bed and, if you don't mind, I'd like to sleep with you tonight. Do you remember that time in Italy when I had tonsillitis really bad and you slept in my bed with me? Dad was working that night, so you said it was all right. He would have said tough little soldiers didn't need their mommies for a little thing like a sore throat. I felt so much better with you there."

"Was it only one night, Cala?" Kristine whispered.

"Yeah, but that's okay."

Kristine wanted to cry at the sadness in her daughter's voice. "I'm so sorry, Cala."

"I know, Mom. I am, too. I'll be right back. Gracie and Slick are on the bed waiting for you."

Kristine stripped down and slipped into a sleep shirt.

She was cuddling with the dogs when Cala returned with two cups of tea on a tray.

"Mom," Cala finally said, breaking the silence, "I can stay on here if you need me. I have this feeling you want to dive into the records and bring this to some kind of conclusion. I'm no vet, but I can certainly learn how to take care of the pups. Pete can show me what has to be done."

Kristine's eyes sparked. "What about your job, honey?"

"I like the job, but there are other jobs. I don't like California the way Mike does. He more or less talked me into it. It was easier to go than it was to argue with him. I'd really like to stay on, but only if you need me. I'm kind of getting used to this old house. It must have been wonderful growing up here."

"I'd like very much for you to stay on, but only if you're sure. Pete does most of the veterinary work. I deal with the prospective owners and the paperwork when I'm not playing with the pups. It's so hard to give them up. I do an exhaustive background check on all clients. You are going to get attached to the pups and cry when they leave. Can you handle that?"

"Probably not, but I will try my best. Knowing they're going to good homes will make it right for me. I think I'll like working with Pete. He's nice. Really nice. I like him, Mom."

"I won't be able to pay you much, Cala."

"As long as the room and board is free, I can handle it. Is it a deal then?"

"It's a deal."

Cala whooped her pleasure as she hugged her mother.

Kristine closed her eyes. Nothing ever felt as good as this hug from her daughter. Her heart soared.

Cala must have felt it, too, for she nestled against her mother, sighing happily.

"Mom, Mike called while you were out. He said the guy I had the hassle with dropped the charges against me."

"Oh, honey, that's wonderful. That must be a worry off your mind."

"It is. California is just too fast-track for me. Mike loves it, though. This is going to work for both of us."

"Tell me," Kristine teased, "what does really, really like mean in regard to Pete?"

Cala giggled. Kristine couldn't ever remember hearing her daughter giggle. *Thank you, God, thank you.*

"It means he asked me out Saturday night. He said he'll come up, pick some flowers on the way, knock on the door, and take my arm and walk me to the car. If, and this is the big *if,* you say it's okay. He's a little nervous about taking me out. Something about mixing business with pleasure. You like him, don't you, Mom?"

"What's not to like? I offered to make him a partner. That alone should tell you something."

"We just hit it off right away. I think he likes me."

"I think he does, too."

"Mom, do you want to talk about Dad?"

"Not really. I'm getting on with my life. Sometimes I dream about him. Those dreams aren't pleasant. I have to start thinking about filing for a divorce. I thought about having your father declared legally dead, but I don't think I can do that. I keep telling myself I'm going to do it, then something stops me. I guess a part of my heart will always belong to your dad. I know that isn't something you wanted to hear."

"No, but I understand. I do, Mom. I wonder where he is and what he's doing. Do you think he ever wonders about us?"

The word *no* exploded from Kristine's mouth like a gunshot.

Cala giggled again. "That's kind of my thinking, too. His loss, Mom."

It was Kristine's turn to hug her daughter. "You got that right, honey. I think we should go to sleep now.

Tomorrow is going to be . . . I don't know what it's going to be, but it's going to either make or break me."

"Want to share about Woodie?"

"Yes, but not tonight."

"How is he in the sack, Mom?"

Kristine was about to pretend outrage. Instead she laughed. This was, after all, the nineties. "Best I ever had."

Cala bounced on the bed, laughing her head off. "I always wondered if there was life after forty. Now I have my answer. My money is on you, Mom," Cala said. "I'll take Slick on my side, and you take Gracie on your side. We're finally sharing, Mom."

"Good night, Cala."

"Night, Mom."

Gracie and Slick barked at the same moment.

"Good night, Gracie and Slick." Kristine smiled in the darkness.

"Woof."

"Woof."

Kristine swung her legs over the side of the bed, careful not to wake her sleeping daughter. "Shhh," she said to the rambunctious dogs as she set them on the floor. She smiled as they raced for the hallway and stairs to their doggy door and the barn. Pete would bring them up for breakfast.

She looked so young, so vulnerable, this sleeping daughter of hers. A fierce protectiveness she'd never felt before washed through Kristine as she watched her daughter's even breathing. "Someday, you're going to pay for this, Logan Kelly, just the way I'm paying. Neither one of us deserves our kids. I'm going to try and make my end of it right. It might take me the rest of my life, but I'm going to do it. Cala was right. You're the loser, not us. Never us," she whispered.

* * *

The breakfast dishes soaking, Kristine cleaned off the kitchen table, her thoughts in a turmoil as Cala and Pete, the two Yorkies on their heels, made their way to the barn.

Jackson Valarian, his hair on end, his eyes red-rimmed and full of grit, stared at her as he tried to figure out what he wanted to say. Finally, he blurted, "You aren't going to let me do the story, are you?"

"That's not true, Jack. I will let you do it, but I can't give you a definite time frame. I didn't expect . . . what I mean is . . . I can't just sweep this under the rug. If my family and Logan's did all those things you say they did, then I have to make an attempt to set it right. I don't even know where to start. How do you go back two hundred years and try to right a wrong? I don't know the answer. I can tell you one thing, Jack. In my heart and soul, I believe my parents were ignorant of all this. I don't think those trunks we found in the attic were ever opened. I don't know about what you found in the Kellys' attic. It's possible there was a mistake somewhere along the way."

"It's in black-and-white, Mrs. Kelly."

"My parents didn't like my husband. I didn't know that until a few years ago. If both our ancestors were involved in this ugly thing, don't you think one set of parents would have said something?"

"People don't talk about ugly things like that. It was and probably still is the mentality of 'that was then, this is now.' Saying 'what can I do about it' is taking the easy way out. Obviously, that's not what you have in mind. I'd like to help you. You're going to need another set of legs and more eyes than you can come up with. I'm willing to put my life on hold to help you with this as long as I get the story. We could be looking at a Pulitzer or a Nobel Peace Prize."

"I'm not interested in awards or prizes," Kristine said.

"No, but I am. Listen, I might be young, but this is burning in my gut. I want to do it. If you let me stay here,

I'll do all the legwork. I have a small amount of savings. I'll contribute to the food bill. I'll shovel snow in the winter and carry in firewood. I'll do whatever you want. I have a computer in my apartment. I'll bring it here, and we can start to track the financials together. We'll be writing hundreds, maybe thousands of letters. This is not something you can do alone, Mrs. Kelly."

"I regret the day I met you, Jack."

Jack sat down on one of the dining room chairs. He finger-combed his hair, his eyes tired and weary as he stared at Kristine. "I understand how you feel. I can't walk away from this. That's not the kind of person I am. I don't think you're that kind of person, either. If we're lucky, together, we might be able to make some of this come out right. I'll give a hundred percent, Mrs. Kelly. Are you prepared to do the same?"

"Yes, I guess I am. How old did you say you are?"

"Twenty-six. Right now I feel like I'm a hundred and six. Is it a deal?"

Kristine held out her hand. "It's a deal, Jack. I think you can call me Kristine from here on in."

Jack pumped Kristine's hand vigorously. "You won't regret this, Kristine. My mother always taught me that if you do the right things in life, God will smile on you when you get to heaven."

"You're going to take your turn doing dishes and cooking. You have to do your own laundry and change your bed yourself. You can sleep in Mike's room. If he comes home, you sleep in Tyler's room. If they both come home, you either sleep on the floor or the couch. Keep your savings. You're going to need gas money. What about your job?"

"This is more important than my job right now."

"One other thing, Jack. We're going to keep regular hours here. That means we go to bed around eleven or twelve. We eat three times a day and walk to the Kelly farm for our exercise."

"That's five miles! Each way!"

"Invest in a good pair of running shoes," Kristine snapped. "Now, let's get to it! Just out of curiosity, how long do you think this will take us?"

Jack mumbled something indistinguishable.

"What was that again?"

"Years."

"*YEARS!*"

He found his voice. "This isn't going to be one of those Mickey Mouse productions. We're going to be dealing with people's lives. When it's time for you to come into your major inheritance, we should be wrapping this up."

"Over four years! Are you saying this is going to take us more than four years? I'll be fifty years old! You'll be thirty-one!" Kristine's voice was so strangled-sounding, she ran to the kitchen for a drink of water.

Light-headed with Jackson's words, Kristine leaned against the kitchen sink. More than four years! Woodie would never wait that long for her. Woodie wanted to get on with his life. A life that was set to include her. A life where they both would live happily ever after. Where was she going to get the time to file for a divorce, carve Logan Kelly out of her heart once and for all, if she committed to this project with Jack? Not to mention the brand-new relationship she was experiencing with her daughter. "What about my business?" she wailed loud enough for Jack to hear. "Dammit, Jackson Valarian, I'm going to need the business to live."

"I know, Kristine. I'll help in any way I can. This is the right thing to do, Mrs. . . . Kristine."

Kristine closed her eyes. A vision of a child being torn from its mother's arms flashed behind her lids. "I know," she whispered. "I know."

PART III

Nairobi, Kenya 1995

11

He was a twelve-year-old kid again, hiding in the alcove near the attic stairs. A place where no one ever looked for him, especially his mother, who had crippling arthritis and never ventured to the second or third floors. He'd played here since he was a wobbly toddler and allowed to use the stairs. It was his own personal hideout, where he could play with things he wasn't supposed to, and then later a place where he could avoid doing homework and chores. A special place where he kept the piles of *National Geographics* he snitched from the school library, a place where he could dream his special dream and gaze at pictures of bare-breasted African women.

The books were old, tattered, and they smelled, but he didn't care. Someday when he was rich and famous he was going to go to Africa, the land of the sun. He would travel every inch of the land, ride on elephants, and make friends with all the wild animals the way his idol Tarzan did in the movies. Maybe he would be a tour guide for rich people. They would be so grateful for his expertise and knowledge they would reward him handsomely with rare gems and stacks and stacks of money. That's how he would get rich. He'd wear one of those hats with the little holes in it and a safari suit with pockets all over the place. Maybe he'd learn to smoke a pipe and pretend he looked like Dr. Livingstone. The natives would love and respect him. All the women and girls would be bare-breasted, their titties bouncing as they wiggled their rear ends for his benefit just so he would smile at them. Maybe he would marry one of them. Maybe he would marry a girl for every day of the week. Maybe they would walk around naked all day. He'd get brown as a berry.

If he saved his money from now until he was twenty-one, he wondered if he would have enough to go to Kenya's Utalii College, where he would learn to speak Swahili or Kikuyu.

It was 1957. Logan leaned back against the pile of blankets that covered his little nest. He pawed through the pile of *National Geographic*s until he found the one he wanted. His two favorite places in the whole world; Kenya and Tanganyika. He closed his eyes as he started on his safari. He took a deep breath as he envisioned the snowcapped mountains, the cavernous valleys, the vast deserts, and the lush forests with sparkling lakes and vibrant waterfalls. He stepped aside as a parade of sleek cats—lions, leopards, cheetahs—and elephants headed toward a water hole. When he had his fill, he opened his eyes and sniffed, imagining he could smell the pungent jungle and the overpowering scent of luscious blooms of every color of the rainbow. Life was full of warm, golden sunshine, and the air carried the scent of a thousand bottles of perfume.

He would be a king.

Logan rummaged beneath the blankets and pillows to find the ceremonial robe his mother had made for him two years ago for a Halloween party. It was beautiful burgundy velvet with faux ermine down the front and around the collar. It felt regal as did the papier-mâché crown and scepter at his side.

Logan squeezed his eyes shut a second time. Where to visit this time, the Serengeti or Mount Kilimanjaro? He leaned back, his crown askew as he watched a family of cheetahs cross the road to get away from an elephant charge. The trees in the distance moved as a group of giraffe raced after the cheetahs to get away from the stampeding elephants. He stepped backwards only to realize what he thought was a clump of bushes was a pride of lions. Moving farther back, his eyes on the thundering elephants, he leaned against a rock and was jolted forward for his effort by a rhino scrambling to move deeper into the bush. And all about him was the overpowering scent of jasmine.

His heart racing, Logan's eyes snapped open when he heard his mother calling his name from the front porch. Didn't she care that he was in Africa, the place of his dreams? Kings shouldn't have to take out trash, mow the lawn, and shovel snow. When you were a king, your loyal subjects did all those things. He leaned back into his nest. He wanted to see the peacocks and the native dance that were next on his agenda. He didn't want to go to the barn for the milk, didn't want to carry in firewood for the wood-burning stove his mother preferred to cook on. Nor did he want to set the table or do his homework.

"Logannnn!"

The boy sighed as he removed his crown and robe. He piled his magazines neatly in the corner, the scepter on top of them.

Angry that his dream had been interrupted, Logan stomped his way down the stairs and out to the front porch.

"Where were you, Logan? I've been calling you for the past ten minutes."

"Africa," he muttered as he made his way to the barn. "I'm going to go there someday, you just wait and see. I'm going to be rich and famous and the animals will love me and all the people will bow their heads when I walk by. They're going to be afraid of me, but they will respect me too. You just wait and see," he continued to mutter.

Kathleen Kelly stared after her son. Logan was such a strange child. On more than one occasion she wondered if there had been a mixup at the hospital.

Why in the name of all that was holy would a child of twelve want to go to Africa, where all those savages lived?

Today was one of the days when she totally believed there had been a mixup at the hospital the day her son was born. How, why, where, when did Logan become so obsessed with that faraway land? She should know the answer, but she didn't. Neither did his father or his teachers. Maybe he was a *spawn* of . . . of . . . *something*. She shivered in the late-afternoon sunshine.

The offices were plush, elegant, stopping just short of being embarrassing to those walking through the doors for the first time. No expense had been spared on the rich furnishings. The man seated behind the ornate desk looked just as plush, just as elegant as the elaborate furnishings.

The suite of offices was empty of clients, the phones silent, the fax machine just as quiet. The silence meant a death knell for Eberhart Safaris, and Logan Kelly knew it.

The stacks of bills, the blank registration forms, and the month's payroll vouchers caused Logan Kelly, aka Justin Eberhart, to suck in his breath. For all intents and purposes, he was going to go belly up, and there wasn't a damn thing he wanted to do about it. It was all part of his plan. Eight million dollars shot to hell. Actually, if you counted Danela's five million, it was thirteen million shot to hell. He refused even to think about all the money Eberhart Safaris owed the banks. All he had left in the world was Kristine's eight thousand dollars, plus the interest it had earned and a few hundred dollars in his personal checking account. Danela had less than a hundred dollars in her own account. Again, it was all going according to plan.

Even if a well-heeled tourist scheduled a safari, he wouldn't be able to accommodate him. Oh, he could talk it up, make wild promises, take his money and skip out, but that was as far as he could go. One lone tourist simply wasn't going to do it this time. He owed a fucking fortune to his guides, his directors, the hotels, the airlines, his personal servants, and the bank. If the heavens and the roof didn't open up to deposit millions in the middle of his desk within the next forty-eight hours, he was down for the count.

The palatial home he had lived in with Danela these past years would just be a memory. The two Mercedes Benz, along with the land cruisers, would be reclaimed; these offices would be emptied, the furnishings sold, and he would be the laughingstock of East Africa. Like he really cared. He was set for life. It was time to move on.

It had been a grand venture in the beginning. But it was nothing like the dreams he'd had when he was that twelve-year-old kid. That was a dream, reality was something else. Instead of starting small, he'd shot for the moon and gone whole hog, hoping to put a dent in the competition's business. He'd succeeded for the first year, with a profit margin unlike anything he'd expected. The second and third years were good too, even though he'd secretly funneled millions into his Swiss bank account. He'd gotten cocky, arrogant the fourth and fifth years, believing his own PR machine run by Danela. Even so, he'd still managed to funnel money out of the business during the worst of it. Workers, unused to his military style of doing things, quit in droves, often forcing him to cancel safaris. Travel agencies, afraid of his reputation, stopped booking tours during the sixth and seventh years. His head remained above water until three months ago, when his reputation got so bad, word went out on the wires that Eberhart Safaris was a joke run by a clown who didn't care about his customers.

His lifelong dream was coming to an end. Eight fucking years down the drain. Thirteen million dollars pissed away on a dream that was now a nightmare. A smug look settled on his face. He was actually beginning to believe all this crap.

Then there was Danela.

The silence finally broke when a stunning redhead opened the door to the office. "I'm going shopping, Logan. There's nothing to do here except stare at the telephone that isn't ringing. Do you want me to bring you some lunch?"

"We don't have any money for you to go shopping, Danela. Bring me some lunch from home." Never in a million years did he believe he would ever hear himself say these words. Never, ever. A game was a game. There were always winners and losers if you knew how to play. He knew. Danela didn't.

"Don't tell me what to do, Logan. I said I was going shopping. You need to go to the bank to borrow money. You need to pay the creditors. Then you need to sit down and figure where it all went wrong and try to make it right. We've been at this for eight long years and there isn't one thing we own outright. Are you listening to me, Logan? We spent thirteen million dollars plus what we borrowed from the banks, and we're still in the red. You're thinking about bailing out, aren't you?"

"I'm thinking, but not about bailing out. I have some ideas," he said vaguely.

"Maybe it's time you shared some of those ideas with me."

"Tonight over dinner. Go shopping but bring me some lunch."

"Are you just going to sit here all day and think about the past? This is not what I signed on for, Logan. My five-million-dollar settlement is gone. I need to know what's going to happen to *us.*"

Logan wanted to tell her there was no "us." There was just him. In life, only the fittest survived. "Tonight over dinner," he repeated. "Wear something sexy."

"I'm not in a sexy mood, Logan. I'm in a bad mood. The kind of bad mood shopping isn't going to help. By the way, the head of the motor pool just quit this morning. Before he quit, he let me know your safari cruisers were minus their distributor caps until you pay him and his men. He was rather ugly. You can deal with him from here on out."

"I will," Logan said shortly. He wished she would just leave. "Lock the door on your way out."

"Lock it yourself," Danela said smartly. "I don't know

what I ever saw in you. Your wife was the lucky one; she's rid of you, and I'm stuck with you. I have a good mind to call her up and tell her what a lucky woman she is."

Logan fought the urge to laugh in Danela's face. "Go ahead. All she'll do is profess undying love. Kristine will love me until the day she dies." *She'll even forgive me for taking her money.* "That's the difference between you two. She's a lady. You were a tramp with a good body who managed to snooker an old man's family into buying you off to save themselves from scandal. Don't make the mistake of threatening me again, Danela."

"What are you going to do, Logan, whip out that shitty book you go by and read me Rule Twelve or is it Rule Twenty-one? Kiss my ass."

"In case you've forgotten, I've already done that, and it wasn't the enjoyable experience you said it would be. I thought you said you were leaving."

"Go to hell, Logan."

Logan opened his desk drawer. An open-ended Lufthansa first-class airline ticket to Washington, DC stared up at him. He'd bought it his first year in Africa, the same day he'd started funneling money into his Swiss bank account. Each year he was careful to renew it. Just in case. In the bottom drawer he always kept locked, was a small flight bag with a change of clothes and his shaving gear, along with the bankbook in the amount of eight thousand dollars and a passport in the name of Justin Eberhart and one in the name of Logan Kelly. When he was ready, he could walk out of here in a heartbeat.

He'd always known things would come to this. It was okay. He had his ace in the hole named Kristine. Six weeks from now, Kristine would reach the half century mark and come into the bulk of her inheritance. If he wanted to, he could be on hand for that momentous occasion. Eight years wasn't long enough for her to get over him, he told himself. Plus, Kristine was a one-man woman, something she always boasted about. Kristine would welcome him with open arms. *If* he returned to the United States. The possibility of that happening was getting stronger with each passing day.

If he played his cards right, he could return to the States just in time for Kristine's fiftieth birthday. Just in time to inherit all that beautiful green money. Kristine was always a sharing person and when he showed her he hadn't touched her eight thousand dollars, she would weep with joy.

Logan shifted his mental gears. He wondered if he was a grandfather yet. Where were the kids and what were they doing? They'd be less happy to see him than Kristine would, and no doubt they hated his guts. That was okay. Growing up they'd been a constant source of disappointment. They were probably off on their own and wouldn't interfere with him or their mother, leaving him a wide-open field to work his magic.

When the phone rang fifteen minutes later, he almost didn't answer it, thinking it was Danela asking what he wanted for lunch. His voice was gruff when he barked, "Eberhart Tours."

Logan listened, his eyebrows shooting up to his hairline when the voice on the other end of the line asked if he could handle a tour of twenty-four people in four days' time. His mind raced as he calculated the money in his head. Talk about Divine Providence. Christ, he must be the luckiest guy in the world "Only if your people are prepared to rough it. All our tours have been booked solid for months," he said urbanely. "Our deluxe tours are booked a year in advance." He rifled through his desk to find the single sheet of paper with the list of travel agencies he'd dealt with in the past. Nowhere on the list was the name Alpine Travel. Hot damn. "Such short notice requires payment in full. You'll need to wire the money to our bank here in Nairobi within twenty-four hours. Remember, we're eight hours ahead of you. I'll fax the registration forms for all your clients to sign. I'm assuming they have visas."

The voice on the other end of the phone assured him

that all the passports were in order, and she had personally walked them to the proper offices to get them stamped with the Kenyan and Tanzanian visas. "They're middle-aged CPAs, all men, city dwellers," she went on to say. Hesitantly, she asked, "What exactly does roughing it mean? There's nothing in your brochure that mentions that kind of tour."

"That's because we rarely do it. Rough means tents, lots of riding, lots of walking, nourishing fresh food but nothing elaborate. We'll provide the tents and sleeping bags. There won't be any hot showers. I'll need the flight information at the time you wire the monies to our bank. All the forms are in back of the brochure. Are your clients a package tour?"

"Yes, they are. They all seem to be amateur photographers."

"There's no way I can send out our travel bags for them to arrive in time. They'll be handed out on arrival if that meets with your approval. One of our people will meet your clients at the airport. He'll be carrying a placard and wearing a green Eberhart uniform."

"Mr. Eberhart, could we briefly touch on the schedule?"

"Why don't I have my secretary type it up and fax it to you, in say, ninety minutes or so. Phone calls are very expensive from here to the States. Will you still be in your office?"

"My office is in my home. That will be fine, Mr. Eberhart. I appreciate you accommodating my group. Let me give you my phone number as well as the fax number."

Logan scribbled on a pad. "It's been nice talking with you, Miss Joclyn."

"Take good care of my people. I probably shouldn't be telling you this, but I just started the business, and this is my first major tour. I want everything to go perfectly."

Logan looked down at the travel-agent list. That certainly explained everything. "I'm sure your group will have the time of their lives. I'll be in touch if need be."

Logan's next call was to Danela. "Get back here as soon as you can and bring some lunch. We have a tour of twenty-four people arriving in three days, four if you go by State-side time. We need to fax some things to the States as soon as possible. Of course they have visas. That was one of the first things I asked. They'll be wiring the money into our account first thing in the morning. I explained it would be roughing it, and Miss Joclyn said that was okay with her group, who, by the way, are all male CPAs and everyone knows CPAs are the most boring professionals there are. Plus, they're city people. I want you on this safari, Danela."

"Oh, no. I did that once. You go. I don't like the bush, and I'm not sleeping in a tent."

"Then I'll cancel. It's that simple. Twenty-four people. Calculate the money in your head. It's seventeen days out of your life. So you won't be able to shop for a while. Think of what you can buy when you get back. You're going!"

Logan squared his shoulders. Twenty-four times twelve grand a pop was a tidy little sum of money. Tomorrow he would pay two of the guides and give them a bonus. The head of the motor pool would replace the distributor caps on three of the land cruisers, and he was off to the races. The household staff could clean and air the sleeping bags and tents and lay in provisions. He could make it work if he put his mind to it. He could do anything if he put his mind to it.

It was midafternoon when Danela turned off the computer. "Okay, Logan, it's done."

"Read it to me, Danela."

"The whole thing?"

"I want to make sure this goes right. First impressions are important. These people are plunking out twelve grand each for this safari. We'll put them up the first night at the Nairobi Safari Club. I'll go there personally tomorrow morning to pay for the night's lodging. I'll do the same thing and pay cash for the flight to Masai Mara National

Reserve. From that point on, you're roughing it. Now let's hear it."

Danela gritted her teeth. It never paid to argue with Logan because she always lost. "We go through customs. I tell them what a bustling city Nairobi is. I tell them Nairobi is in the heart of the Kenyan Highlands and mention that it is at an elevation of fifty-five hundred feet with warm sunny days and cool nights. I'll point out the riotous colors of the plants along the street. This is a mistake. I feel it in every bone of my body. There's no way you can pull this off. You're up to something. What are you planning?"

Logan stared unblinkingly at the woman he'd spent the last eight years with. Once she'd been ravishingly beautiful. When he first met her, she looked like a young Rita Hayworth. Unfortunately for Danela, the African sun had not been kind to her. She still had the same voluptuous body he'd lusted after in the beginning of their relationship, but even that was losing its appeal. He hated the way her leathery skin felt next to his, hated the heavy, greasy makeup she wore. She still turned men's heads, so that was a plus. She'd always been a quick study, and she knew the safari business as well as he did. What she did not have was a head for numbers of any kind. And at the moment, he didn't much care for the calculating look in her eye. He didn't trust her any farther than he could throw her. He had to tread carefully where she was concerned.

"As a matter of fact, I am up to something, as you put it. My mind has been racing since that call came through. It's safe to say we've both learned from our mistakes. Sometimes God in His infinite wisdom gives us a second chance. Alpine Travel is our second chance. If we pull this off and if things go smoothly, I want us to get married when you get back."

Danela sniffed, and her eyes lost a little of their wariness. "How can we get married? You aren't divorced. Don't think I'm going to go through one of those tribal weddings."

"Kristine had me declared legally dead after seven

years. I know that for a fact," he lied smoothly. "She's married again."

"How do you know that, Logan? You never said a thing about any of that to me."

"That's because it was my private business. I have never invaded your privacy. I never asked you for details of your life. I expected the same from you. We had a deal, Danela, in case you forgot."

"How do I know you aren't lying?" Danela asked, suspicion ringing in her voice.

"I guess you'll just have to trust me. If you like, we can apply for a marriage license before you leave on safari. It will give you something to look forward to while you're out there with the group. It's time for us to get married. I don't like living in sin," Logan said virtuously.

"I don't have a wedding dress. Where in the hell am I going to get a wedding dress?"

Logan forced patience into his voice. "There are any number of places where you can get a wedding dress. However, knowing your shopping history, how does this sound? When you get back, you go to England, to Harrods. I want you to be happy. You can shop to your heart's content. We'll be rolling in money. I've been running all of this over and over in my mind. I'm going to stay in touch with Alpine Travel, by phone because that's more personal. I'm sure the lady knows others who are just starting out with their own businesses. I'll offer some cut rates, make a few deals, and if things work out, we'll climb back to the top. I can do it, Danela, but I need your help. I want you on that safari, and I want you to charm those number crunchers right out of their jockeys. Wear those skintight flight suits you have. I want every one of those guys to come back with a hard-on. I want them to remember you first, Africa second. Tell me we're in this together, Danela."

"Swear on my life, Logan, that I can go to England and Harrods? If you swear, I'll do it. I also want to see the ticket before we leave."

"Not a problem. I'll pick it up first thing in the morning. How much money do you think you'll need?"

Danela's mind raced. "At least twenty-five thousand," she said smartly.

"You got it."

"All right. We have a deal. Do you still want me to wear something sexy tonight?"

"Damn right. Let's have two ceremonies. One here in town and one in the Serengeti."

"Okay. It's getting late. You better fax this itinerary off now."

"Are you sure you covered everything?"

"Game viewing, bird-watching, the salt-lick watering holes, and hopefully sightings of the elusive bongo and leopard. I did say that might not happen. I covered our asses on that one. They'll love Amboseli. Seeing Mount Kilimanjaro will take the sting away if we can't see any bongo or leopards. Two game runs while we're there. I think they will be stunned at the Masai tribesmen. I have to wonder though how they'll react to the tribe when they see them draw blood from a cow's jugular vein and mix it with milk. We might lose a few for a day or so. Not to mention the huts constructed of cow dung. I hate that part, Logan, I really do. I'm always sick for two days afterward."

"You'll get over it. The name of the game here is seeing everything with an expert such as yourself explaining the customs. They want to take home memories. You are going to give them those memories to take home. We can do this, Danela, if we work together. Think about it, honey, this morning we were down for the count. In a few hours' time our lives have turned around. We've booked a safari, you're going to London to shop, and we're finally getting married."

"It is rather wonderful. It isn't a dream, is it, Logan?"

"We'll know by morning when the money hits our bank account. Two hundred and eighty-eight thousand dollars minus the immediate expenses of the rough-cut safari will allow me to settle up with all our creditors, send you on your shopping trip, plan a decent wedding, and still leave us a modest balance. We'll be golden as of tomorrow morning. There is one little problem I want to run by you."

"A hitch! I knew it!" Danela squealed, her eyes sparking.

"As usual, you're off and running and you aren't listening. The moment that money hits the bank, it has to be transferred or the bank will snatch it. You know that as well as I do. I'll be on the computer within seconds. I want you to know and understand this right up front. I'm going to wire it to the Swiss bank account. If I don't do that, Danela, the bank will seize it. Are you okay with this? If not, we have to call the whole deal off. There's no other way to handle it."

Danela's brow furrowed. Logan was right. She wasn't about to give up a shopping trip to London and marriage to Logan over a bank wire. "I'm okay with it, Logan. I'm going home now. Send your fax."

At the door, Danela turned. "This is going to work, isn't it, Logan?"

"It's going to work, Danela. Trust me."

"If you fuck me over, Logan, I'll cut your heart out. Trust me on that one."

Logan's voice turned virtuous again. "Just because your old lover tried to screw you over doesn't mean I'm like he was. I've shared everything, and I resent your attitude. It's sick," he said, picking up the itinerary and heading for the fax machine. "I'll be home as soon as I finish up and take care of a few phone calls. Use that gardenia perfume I gave you for Christmas. This is going to be a night to remember."

Two hours later, Logan leaned back in his swivel chair, his booted foot hooked on one of the open desk drawers. In his hand was a glass with three fingers of hundred-proof bourbon. He sucked at it greedily, his mind racing.

A smug look settled on Logan's face. He was one of those rare people, in his opinion, who had the even rarer ability to take a situation and play it through in his mind, accepting and rejecting even the smallest nuance to a problem. His face grew more smug. His army training was something he practiced almost every day of his life. In one way or another.

Africa had been a disappointment, falling way short of his expectations. His childhood fantasies were just that, fantasies. Yes, he'd been successful for a short while. But this land was not the place of his dreams. He'd known that after the first six months, but he was in too deep to give up. Besides, he'd never been a quitter. What a stupid kid he must have been back then. The word *stupid* brought pain to his face. Dumb perhaps, never stupid.

He could get out of this intact. He could make it all work for him again. Two weeks in one of those pricey spas in Switzerland would give him back his waistline. Some custom-made clothes, a new hairstyle instead of his bush cut, along with a few facials would turn him into the man Kristine had kissed good-bye. It was time to check into a clinic to get a physical. What better place than Switzerland? Besides, he was going to need some medical forms. Some letterheads for his plan. He also had to buy some gifts. Nothing elaborate. Definitely thoughtful. Oh yeah. It was all going to be a piece of cake. Logan swallowed the last of his drink, then poured another.

There wasn't one single person in this whole country who knew he was Logan Kelly. Danela knew his name was Logan, but he'd told her his last name was Kilpatrick. Everyone else knew him as Justin Eberhart. He wouldn't have one bit of trouble getting out of the country. When you played your cards close to your chest and kept your mouth shut, there was little doubt you would succeed.

He would leave Danela the money he promised. If she chose to blow it in England, that was her problem. There would be no regrets where she was concerned. The upside to that was he'd fabricated an involved story about Kristine she could never keep straight in her mind. For all her threats about tracking down his wife, he knew she would never follow through. How could she? His tale about Kristine's whereabouts had been so convoluted, she'd need an army of investigators to prowl the Midwest, and in the end they'd only come up dry.

Satisfied with his thoughts, Logan lowered his feet to the floor and closed his desk drawer. He splashed bourbon into his glass and took it neat. Now, all he had to do was go home, eat dinner, screw Danela for a few hours, and return to the office to wait for the banks to open.

Life was looking good again.

They tore at each other, each seeking that which the other could give. There in the shadows of the exquisitely draped bedroom, away from the bright moonlight, they devoured each other with searching lips and hungry fingers.

When at last sensibility returned, they touched mouths with lips swollen by passion and tasting of salt. The salt of blood, the salt of tears. They lay together with the gentle breeze from the open windows wafting over their slick, naked bodies, feeling warmth where their nakedness touched, and when they sought each other again, it was with gentleness. Their mouths were tender and their fingers caressed.

They were two lovers, rapturous with each other, reveling in that private world known only to lovers.

Gently he embraced her, cradling her head in one of his hands while the other supported her haunches. Backward, backward, he dipped her. Into her line of vision through the open windows she could see the treetops swaying, the star-spangled sky and the shadows growing lighter by the moment. Slowly, deliberately, he bent his head, perspiration dotting his forehead. Closer and closer his mouth came to hers. Tighter and tighter became his hold on her, as if he were clinging to her, desperately cleaving to this moment of time, cherishing it, remembering it, burning it into his memory.

Later, when the lavender shadows lightened the room,

Logan slipped from the bed. He stared down at Danela. She was almost pretty in sleep. He needed to remember this moment, for he would think of her in the weeks and months ahead. Then she would fade from his memory the way the memory of Kristine had faded.

Logan felt exhausted. He wasn't a kid anymore. Three go-rounds a night were a little more than he had bargained for. Danela could go all night long, one orgasm after another, and sneer at him when he couldn't satisfy her. Tonight, though, he'd given it his all, and she was sleeping contentedly. From long habit he knew she wouldn't wake before noon, if then.

At precisely thirty seconds past eight o'clock in the morning, Logan hit the key that would transfer all of Alpine Travel's monies into his numbered Swiss account. A blizzard of numbers appeared on the small screen. Five seconds later the confirmation numbers lit up the same screen. His sigh was mighty as he punched in more numbers and again waited. Good. There was now fifty thousand dollars sitting in his Swiss checking account. Just enough to pay off Danela and pay the more pressing bills that would allow the safari to get under way.

The army of gods that looked after him in time of crisis marched alongside him to the tune of his own personal drummer.

Life was good.

Very, very good.

12

Kristine stared at the neat stacks of paper covering the dining room table as well as the overflow on the long buffet against the wall. Almost the end of the road. Daylight at the end of the tunnel. Four years of paperwork. Four years of conscientious obsessiveness. If there was such a thing as conscientious obsessiveness.

Kristine leaned back in her chair to stare at Mima Posy and Lela Mae Brown's folders. She closed her eyes to savor the memory of the day she and Jack had gone, as Jack put it, on the road to find closure to what lay in front of her.

"I hope we're doing the right thing, Jack. What if Mrs. Brown thinks we're invading her privacy or doesn't want to talk to us. I wouldn't blame her if she told us to get lost and to get off her property."

"I can't say I would blame her if she did. We sent her nine different letters. She didn't respond to any of them. Maybe she isn't one of the descendants from the *slave list* and thought it was all a bunch of bullshit. Christ, I hate those words."

"No more than I do," Kristine said through clenched teeth. "I think this is the turnoff, Jack. Those trees are gorgeous. I wonder how old they are."

"Probably as old as Miss Lela Mae Brown."

"Mrs. Lela Mae Brown."

"Do you see a fence anywhere? The postmaster said there was a wire fence with a mailbox. I wonder if he sent us to the right place. Everyone gets mail. Why doesn't Mrs. Brown get mail?''

"He said she got a 'flurry' of legal-looking letters a while back. I guess those were the ones we sent. Supermarket flyers hardly count as mail," Jack said fretfully.

"Look, there's a fence, and the mailbox is right where he said it was. The house must be just up the road. I don't see any neighboring houses. Say a prayer or cross your fingers that this is the lady we're looking for."

"What do you think I've been doing during this whole ride?"

"I'm afraid, Jack. This is the right thing to do, isn't it? What if Mrs. Brown doesn't think . . . What if she takes a shotgun to us . . . Don't go so fast, slow down. For some reason, I don't think many people come out here. She might be anxious with visitors. Maybe we should call out or something."

"Kristine, we're going up on that porch and knock on the door. Do you have all the folders?"

"I have everything. I probably have more than I need."

"What about the basket?"

"The basket's in the backseat. We agreed to wait on that."

It was a plain little white house with a small front porch and two rocking chairs. Window boxes sat under the windows and were chock-full of colorful petunias. An ageless dairy crock held luscious deep pink geraniums. There wasn't a yellow leaf to be seen among the emerald green leaves, nor was there a speck of dust on the old fiber carpet or rocking chairs. The windowpanes shimmered. Kristine clenched her fist and knocked on the door.

A spry little lady with a topknot and wire-rim glasses opened the front door, a smile on her face. "Good morning," she said pleasantly.

"Mrs. Brown? Mrs. Lela Mae Brown?"

"I was this morning when I woke up," the little lady quipped. "Now, how can I help you?"

"We need to talk to you, Mrs. Brown. May we come in?

My name is Kristine Summers, and this is Jackson Valarian. Some of your ancestors once worked for my family. Is that introduction acceptable?''

"Mercy, that was a long time ago. Come in, come in. Would you like some coffee?''

"We had some earlier, but thank you anyway.''

"Please, come into the parlor and sit down. I'm sorry my son isn't here. I imagine he's the one you want to speak with. His name is Jonah.''

Kristine opened the top folder in her hands. "No, Mrs. Brown, it isn't Jonah. We want to talk to you. Do you remember your parents or your grandparents talking about those long-ago days?''

"Do you mean when they were *slaves?*''

Kristine and Jackson both flinched at the word. "Yes, ma'am,'' Kristine said.

"Life was hard for them. It brings sorrow to my heart to talk about it. Are you sure you don't want to talk to Jonah?''

"We can come back and talk to him if you want us to. You see, Mrs. Brown, we . . . I . . . my family didn't know . . . we thought . . . We want to make it right in any way we can. Didn't you get the letters we sent you?''

"Yes. Jonah said it was some kind of scheme. He threw them away. Were they important?''

"In a manner of speaking. It's all right, though. What Mrs. Summers is trying to say is the Summers and Kelly families want to make restitution. Do you have a family Bible, Mrs. Brown?''

"Yes, sir, I certainly do. My family came from the Summers farm. My grandmama said her family was treated real good. Mr. Summers gave each man a small parcel of land when he married and had children. My own mama told me stories about the manor lady making sure the doctor visited and made certain everyone went to services on Sunday. The children were taught to read and write and didn't have to work in the fields. There was always a gift at Christmastime for each worker and one for each child. As each boy child grew and then married, a second patch of land was given. Today it might not seem fair, but back then it was. I'm not sure what it is you want to do."

The relief washing through Kristine left her feeling faint. "I thought . . . the records show that children were taken from their families and . . . and . . . sold. That was so barbaric I have trouble trying to comprehend it. We want to find those families and try to make it right. Do you know any of them?"

Lela Mae Brown sat up stiffly. Her lips thinned to a tight line. "I know one family."

"You do! That's wonderful! Tell us where they live. Please, Mrs. Brown. We want to help. This isn't some cocka-mamie thing we're doing here. We have tons of files and letters and those . . . awful . . . *lists*. We can help. I know we can. Where does the family live?"

"Right here in Richmond. Mima's people came from the Kelly farm. She has her own family now. She had five uncles and two aunts that were taken away. Mima's mama was the only one who got to stay on. She said her grand-mama just laid down and died when that happened. But before that, her grandmama did something no one knew about. Her and Joisa, her husband, made a deep gash that resembled a cross on the sole of each child's foot so it would leave a scar. For identification purposes later on. Later on never came. How can you make that right?"

Jack leaped from the chair he was sitting on. Kristine watched in awe as he danced around the room. She thought that at any given moment she'd have to peel him off the ceiling. "What is it, Jack?"

"We have four of them, Kristine! Four people re-sponded saying one of their ancestors had a cross scar on their foot. Four out of six, Kristine!"

"Yes, I remember now. Thank God. We've been send-ing out letters, Mrs. Brown, for the past few years, and one of the questions was, did any member of your family have any noticeable scars, marks, or anything that would help for identification purposes. Four letters came back with what you just said, a large cross on the ball of the foot. Three men and one woman.''

Kristine burst into tears.

Lela Mae Brown dabbed at her eyes with the hem of a pristine white apron. "I think I'll make fresh coffee now. What will you do for Mima?"

"Whatever she wants," Kristine said. "We'll send her grandchildren to college and their children also. We'll buy them land for their own houses if they don't already have it."

"Mima needs a new wash machine. She could use an e-lectric icebox. She's too old to be toting ice like she does."

"We can do that today or tomorrow. Does she have a big family?"

"Big as mine. I have nine children and twenty-six grandchildren. Mima needs to have some eye surgery for her cataracts. Can you take care of that, too?"

"Yes, ma'am, we can," Jackson said.

Kristine felt a head rush. "Can we see your Bible, Mrs. Brown?"

Lela Mae dried her hands on her apron. Her fingers were knotted with arthritis, Kristine saw. Her touch was reverent when she accepted the worn, tattered Bible. Jackson crowded next to her, almost swooning at the written words in the front. "May I please copy this down, Mrs. Brown."

"Don't you be fixing to try and take my Bible, young man. It goes to my firstborn son when I pass over."

"I would never do such a thing, Mrs. Brown. I feel privileged that you're even letting me look at it. I just want to copy the names and the dates. What a help this is going to be."

"What can you do now, Miz Summers?"

"I can send all your grandchildren to college for free, Mrs. Brown. When they marry and have children of their own, there will be a fund for them to go to college. As for your nine children, a piece of land, a house, an annuity.

We'll work it out. Is there anything you want? Isn't it lonely living way out here by yourself?"

"Do you mean like a fairy wish?"

Kristine smiled. "Yes, like a fairy wish."

"Well, a new truck for Jonah would be nice. He's my youngest. He drives across the states. He takes care of me and helps out his brothers and sisters. It has to be one of those trucks that has eighteen wheels. He'd be married by now, but he has too many obligations. He's a good boy."

"I can do that," Kristine said happily. "Will the weekend be soon enough?"

"Mercy, yes."

Lela Mae poured coffee. "Why are you doing this, Miz Summers? That's going to be the first thing Jonah is going to ask."

Kristine told her the story, sparing nothing. "It was wrong. People need to know where their family rests. I want to be able to sleep at night. I want to be able to look in the mirror. All I can do is apologize for my husband's family and what they did. In the scheme of things, an apology means nothing. In Las Vegas there is a saying— money talks and losers walk. I have the money, so it's up to me to do the right thing. Somewhere along the way, I may run out of money, but I want you to know I will work until every last single person is accounted for and taken care of. If it takes me a hundred years, then it will be up to my children to carry on what I started. I want you to believe me, Mrs. Brown."

"I think you can call me Lela Mae."

"Will you call me Kristine?"

"Yes I will!" Lela Mae said smartly.

"I got it all, Kristine," Jack chortled.

"I'm going to leave my card with you, Lela Mae. When your son comes home, tell him to call me. The only other thing we need is Mima's address."

At the door, Lela Mae put her thin arms around Kristine. "God bless you, child."

"He already did. He brought me here. Thanks for the

coffee. If you wait just a minute, I want to go to the car. I brought something for you. It's something I want to give you from my heart." Kristine returned in minutes with a Yorkie pup named Missy. She held it out, her eyes pleading with the old woman to accept it. "She has impressive papers. She will love you unconditionally, Lela Mae."

"Mercy, mercy, mercy." The old gnarled hands reached for the tiny pup, who immediately started to lick at her face. "I think she likes me."

"I suspect she does. Here are her papers. There's enough dog food here to last for two months. She's up-to-date with her shots and in perfect health. This is her favorite blanket and toy. Just take good care of her."

"I always wanted an animal that was my own. Thank you."

"It was my pleasure, Lela Mae."

"Drive with the angels now, you hear. I always say that to Jonah when he starts out," Lela Mae said as she nuzzled the little dog against her neck, a look of pure rapture on her face.

Kristine smiled as she patted Lela Mae's shoulder. "My guardian angel sits right here all the time," she said, patting her own shoulder. "She watches over me. If I didn't believe that, I wouldn't be here. We'll talk again, Lela Mae."

"I don't know about you, Kristine," Jack said when they were driving down the dusty road, "but I think I could walk on water right now."

"I was just thinking the exact same thing, Jack. Next stop, Mima Posy's house."

It was midafternoon when Jackson stopped the car on another country road similar to the one Lela Mae lived on. It was a pretty lot, Kristine thought, with old oak trees that dripped Spanish moss. The lawn was green and well tended with flower beds chock-full of Gerber daisies every color of the rainbow. A small vegetable garden, as neat and well tended as the flower beds, could be seen on the side of the small clapboard house.

A giant of a woman stood on the front steps, her hands clasped in front of her. In a voice that rang clear out to the car, she called, "Don't come any farther unless you have business here."

"We have business with you, Mrs. Posy. Lela Mae Brown gave us your address. We need to talk to you. May we come up on the porch?"

The woman moved to the side to allow Kristine and Jackson to climb the steps. "Sit!"

Mima Posy remained standing. "And you are?"

"I'm Kristine Summers, and this is Jackson Valarian. We need to talk to you."

"I'm listening, Kristine Summers."

In a halting voice that hinted at tears, Kristine went through her story a second time. She ended with, "What my husband's family did was wrong. I can't undo that. What I can do is provide for you, your family, and your grandchildren, and if you know of any other families, please tell us. We have something to give you, but we don't have it with us. Please listen while Jackson explains it to you."

Kristine watched the old woman's eyes fill with tears as her shoulders started to shake. "Are you saying you found three of my great-great-uncles and one aunt? How?"

"It was an exhausting job and it took us four years. Yes, Mrs. Posy, that's what we're saying. That's what I meant when I said I didn't have the letters with me."

"Let me show you something." The regal giant lifted her bare foot to reveal a scar in the shape of a cross. "Our families have done this, it seems like forever. After those infamous days, others did the same thing, I'm told. My clan did the cross. Others did the X and some did the circle with the line through it or a smaller circle inside the larger circle. The stories told to us down through the years were that all vowed to find one another. Our resources were so limited, it was impossible. Tell me, what is the next step?"

"More letters, more phone calls. For you, right now,

Mrs. Posy, a new washing machine and a new refrigerator, college educations for your grandchildren, plots of land. As soon as we can, Jackson and I are going to arrange a meeting with everyone we can find. I'd like to have it here in Richmond or even at my home in Leesburg. Whichever place is the easiest to get to. Jackson is going to handle that end of it. When we get home, we'll get the files out, and I'll call you and send you the names of the people we found who had crosses on the bottoms of their feet. I don't know if that will give you any comfort or not. Right now, it's all that we have. Our job isn't done yet.''

"I need to know why, so I can tell my children and my grandchildren,'' Mima said.

"Because it was wrong. Because you have the right to know where your family rests. Because I can't sleep at night knowing these things.''

"Then my family will accept.''

Kristine blinked. It had never occurred to her that the tall, regal woman wouldn't accept what she was offering. "There is one other thing. Mrs. Brown told us you require cataract surgery. With your permission, we could arrange it for you.''

"You would do that for me?''

"In a heartbeat,'' Kristine said. "Shall I make arrangements?''

"Yes. Yes, I accept.''

"Do you have a family Bible?'' Jackson asked.

"Yes, young man, I do. Why do you ask?''

"Because I need to copy down everything that's written in the front of it. With your permission, of course.''

"Come inside then. Would you like some lemonade?''

"Yes, I would, Mrs. Posy,'' Kristine said.

"Tell me about your family, Mrs. Summers. You already seem to know about mine.''

Kristine talked then as though Mima Posy was her oldest and dearest friend. She talked about her drinking problem, about Logan and his family, Woodie, and finally her children and grandchildren. "Aside from giving birth to my children, Mrs. Posy, working on this project is the single most rewarding thing I've ever done in my life. It's like Logan no longer matters. He's just someone I used to know. I'm slowly earning my children's respect and love. It's all going to come out right in the end. Now, tell me, what color would you like for your refrigerator and washer?"

"Just white. I like things to look clean and fresh. White is pure if you know what I mean."

"I do know. Is there anything else you want to ask me?"

"Are you really going to send all my grandchildren to college?"

"Every last one of them. Graduate school, too, if they want to go."

"That's a barrelful of money right there," Mrs. Posy said in awe.

"Right now the barrel is full. I expect at some point it might run out. If that happens, I'll find a way to fill it. My children will carry on when I can't do it anymore. Just the other day I was thinking about life, nothing in particular, and I realized that each of us is put on this earth for a reason. For a long time I thought my reason was to be Logan Kelly's wife. I still more or less think that because only through what happened am I able to do this. Does that make sense?"

"Yes, ma'am, it does make sense. My husband is never going to believe this. Things like this just don't happen. I'm grateful to you, Mrs. Summers. If I seemed standoffish a while ago, it was because my sight isn't good and I didn't know what you were all about."

"I'm sorry about so many things, too. I wish you didn't have that scar on your foot."

Mima leaned across the table. "You shush now. I carry the scar proudly, as do all my children and my grandchildren. We chose to make the mark on our feet. Sad as it may sound, it is our tradition. Those dark days of our ancestors are gone. The scars remind us to never allow it to happen again."

Jack gulped his lemonade in two long swigs. It was Kristine's signal to get ready to leave.

"We'll be in touch, Mrs. Posy. Thank you for talking with us."

She turned to Jack. "We might need measurements for the washer and refrigerator."

"Standard size is acceptable. I have plenty of room."

"Will tomorrow be okay for the delivery on the appliances?" Kristine asked.

"Tomorrow will be fine."

"Then we'll say good-bye. But first, I brought something for you from my farm. I'll be back in a minute." When Kristine returned with a second pup, she handed it to the old lady and cupped her hands in her own. "She's a pretty little thing, all gold and black at the moment. Her color will turn slowly, and her name is Honey. There's enough food for a few months. Her papers are up-to-date. She's had all her shots and is in perfect health. She will just love you to death. I hope . . . you like animals, don't you?"

"More than I like some people, Mrs. Summers. She feels so soft and warm. How big will she get?"

"Her top weight will be about five pounds. She's what we call a Teacup Yorkie. I breed them, as I told you earlier. She's my personal gift to you. If for any reason you can't keep her, call me, and I'll come and get her."

"She seems to like me. She likes to be held, doesn't she?"

"Yes, ma'am, being held is her favorite thing. She has a special little blanket and fuzzy toy. She sleeps with them."

"It was a pleasure to meet you, Mrs. Summers. I admire your perseverance because you have prevailed. Thank you for stopping by. And thank you for this wonderful present."

In the car, Jackson turned to Kristine. "She didn't warm up to us the way Lela Mae did."

"No, she didn't. That's okay, Jack. She has every right in the world to be suspicious of us. The proof will be when things start to happen. She was a little more open in the end when we gave her the dog. Perhaps her sight has something to do with it. All I know is that little dog put a smile on her face. I don't know why I brought the two of them. First I was only going to bring one. Then I said, no, take two. I'm so glad I did. When will we run out of money, Jack? I'm going to start worrying about that."

"Then stop. All those kids aren't going to be going to college at the same time. Some are probably finished by now. The money is going to grow and earn interest. Woodie invested it wisely. But, to answer your question, not for a very long time. We have it covered."

"I'm starting to feel real good about all of this. Four long years we worked on this. We're finally making it happen. I want to thank you for coming into my life, Jack. If you hadn't come down my road that day, none of this would be happening. You will work on some kind of meeting or party or something, won't you?"

"Count on it, Kristine."

Kristine nodded. "Right now we need to find an appliance store, then I want to go home."

"You got it."

She roll-called these last years as she sipped at her coffee. If she had it all to do over again, she knew she would do the exact same things. She'd put her personal life on hold these last four years. While she had regrets, she knew in her heart she would do that again, too. With the exception of Cala's and Mike's weddings, she'd rarely taken a day off, and when she did, she spent the night poring over the papers that were now in neat piles so she wouldn't get behind.

With the holidays a few short weeks away, she had to make a plan, stack the files and folders, and devise a concrete course of action for the new year.

And then there was her birthday that also loomed on the horizon. She was going to reach the half century mark a few days after the new year. Just the thought of turning fifty was mind-boggling. More than half her life was over and as far as she could tell the only thing she had done of any importance was giving birth to three children, children she loved with all her heart.

They were all happy and settled and no longer needed her, if they had ever needed her at all. Cala was happily married to Pete and lived in a small white house in town. They were also half owners of the business and they were proud parents to two little girls: Emily and Ellie.

The picture of the two little tykes tussling with Gracie and Slick on the front lawn brought a smile to Kristine's tired face.

This year, Christmas was going to be an event. Mike was coming home with his new wife and baby and Tyler managed to wrangle leave and had sent word he would arrive Christmas Eve with the stern admonition, "Don't do anything till I get there." Kristine smiled again, but the smile left her face when her gaze traveled to the picture of Woodie. Would he come for the holidays? She crossed her fingers, her eyes burning. God, how she missed him. A lump started to form in her throat when she recalled the last time she'd seen him and the bitter words he'd flung at her.

Kristine shivered even though her back was to the fireplace. It had been a warm, sunny day without a cloud in the sky. She'd been holding Gracie and Slick because she needed something to do with her hands. Until the moment Woodie stepped around the car she had been certain he wouldn't leave. . . .

"Woodie, wait. Please don't leave like this. I'm sure we can work something out. Why can't you understand? I have to do this. I have to make it right. If I don't, my whole family's life was and still is a lie."

"Kristine, I can handle all of that. I applaud you for what you want to do. What I cannot accept is your broken promise to file for a divorce. I want to marry you. I want us to live together. I offered to help with this mission because I think two heads are better than one, but I wanted us to do it as man and wife. I can't live like this. I *won't* live like this."

"Woodie, please. I'll do it. I'll go into town tomorrow and get things under way. I promise."

Woodie shook his head. "No, Kristine, that won't work. You have to do it because it's what you want to do, not what I want. I guess I can't understand why you don't want to do it. The fact that you don't tells me Logan is still in your thoughts and your heart. Three's a crowd, Kristine."

"No, it's not like that. You're right and you're wrong. I swear on my children. I'll do it tomorrow. Please, Woodie, don't leave." She was so close to him she could smell his aftershave. She wanted to reach out, but the dogs were snuggled in both hands against her chest. Slick growled deep in his throat while Gracie whimpered. Tears trickled down Kristine's cheeks.

Woodie kissed her, the sweetest kiss she'd ever gotten in her life. "If you ever need me, Kristine, leave word at the bank."

"Aren't you going to write or call?"

"No."

"Woodie, please. You can't just walk away. Damn you, that's what Logan did," she screamed.

"I'm not Logan, Kristine. I told you like it is, right up front. From day one," Woodie said as he settled himself behind the wheel. He reached out to tweak both little dogs' whiskers. Slick snapped at his fingers. Gracie continued to whimper against Kristine's chest.

"Where are you going? Can't you at least tell me that?"

"I don't know. I'm going to do that pin in the map thing. I'm going to get myself a man's dog, and it will be him and me or her and me. I need a friend right now. Someone who will understand me and love unconditionally. I wanted that person to be you but sometimes . . . It's not important. Good-bye, Kristine."

"Damn you to hell, Aaron Dunwoodie!" Kristine screamed at the top of her lungs. "You are so like Logan.

You're birds of a feather. Two peas in a pod," she hiccuped as she sat down on the steps leading to the front porch.

Kristine cuddled the little dogs. "How can he do this to me? How? He's just like Logan. No, he's worse. What he's done is hateful and ugly. He said it all right to my face. I told him I'd do it. Did he care? No, he did not. His mind was made up. Oh, God, he's gone. He's really gone."

Kristine ran into the house and up the steps. In her bedroom she flung herself on the bed, hard-driving sobs rocking her body. When the antique grandfather clock in the living room chimed the noon hour, she tottered into the bathroom to bathe her swollen eyes. She stared at her reflection. Woodie was right about everything, and she'd let him go off with her screams ringing in his ears. That's how he would remember her, a screaming shrew who had accused him of being like her husband. Tears filled her eyes again as she soaked a washcloth under the cold-water stream. "I'm so sorry, Woodie, so very sorry. What am I going to do without you?"

No bolt of lightning signaling a flash of impending insight struck the room.

"So go, see if I give a good rat's ass," Kristine snarled, mouthing her husband's favorite expression. "Who needs you? I'm doing just fine."

Well, if you're doing just fine, then why have you written a kazillion *letters you didn't bother to mail and why did you write the last one inviting him for Christmas?* a niggling voice queried.

"Because I was stupid. I admit I am the stupidest woman walking the face of the earth. I can't do anything right according to the men in my life. Well, we'll fix that right now." She ran to the dresser and yanked open the bottom drawer. Neat bundles of letters next to her wool socks stared up at her. Cut them up? Flush them? Burn them? Reread them? "None of the above," she murmured as she kicked the drawer shut. She'd gotten such comfort late at night when she wrote them. They were better than writing in a diary.

She recognized her pattern then as she stared at the

closed drawer. She'd written hundreds and hundreds of letters to Logan, pouring out her heart. Letters that she mailed, letters that came back marked ADDRESSEE UNKNOWN. Unknown. How could someone be unknown when you were married to him all your adult life? The next step, if she stayed true to her pattern, was to hit the bottle.

"It ain't gonna happen!" The words blasted from Kristine's mouth like icy bullets. "Come on, Gracie, hop up," she said as she bent down so the little dog could jump into her arms. Slick chased his stubby tail and then beelined for the hall and the long stairway leading down to the kitchen.

The phone rang just as Kristine opened the refrigerator for a soft drink. "Cala, where are you?"

"Down at the barn. Mom, can you baby-sit tonight? Pete and I want to do some Christmas shopping. They're forecasting bad weather for the rest of the week. Everything here is solid, so it's okay from this end. Pete wants to make a day of it, shopping, dinner, and a movie. I brought the girls with me on the off chance you would agree. If you have other plans, we can wait until next week."

"I'd be happy to baby-sit. Why don't you leave the girls here for the night? We'll have a pajama party, just the three of us. I'm going to pack up all my files and papers and put my mission aside until after the first of the year. My calendar is free."

"Mom, are you sure you don't mind?"

"Cala, I do not mind. I love spending time with the girls. We'll start on our Christmas cookies and maybe do a little decorating. Will it be all right to take them out in the snow this afternoon?"

"Mom, you're in charge. You know the girls like to be entertained. They love staying with you."

Kristine's heart soared. "Thank you for saying that, Cala. I was going to take a ride over to the Kelly farm today to check the house for the last time before the sale goes through. There's a little hill in the back and I thought the girls could sled ride a little. My old sled was in the attic. I cleaned it up and polished the runners a few weeks ago."

"They'll love it, Mom. I'll send the girls up to the house. Send Gracie and Slick down to make sure they get all the way up. Ellie likes to roll in the snow. All you have to do, Mom, is feed the dogs at six o'clock. I'll see you in the morning then."

"Sleep in, Cala. Make a short holiday of it. I can see to the dogs in the morning. The girls will help me. It's not like I have a busy schedule."

"Pete is going to be delirious. Thanks, Mom. See you tomorrow."

Kristine opened the kitchen door. "Go on, Gracie, bring the girls up. Go with Gracie, Slick."

Ten minutes later, the children barreled through the door, the two little dogs barking and yapping as the children squealed and whooped their pleasure.

They looked like Christmas cherubs with their golden curls, rosy cheeks and bright red snowsuits. They were so beautiful, Kristine's breath caught in her throat. *My very own grandchildren,* she thought.

"What we do, Granny?" Emily asked as she struggled to get out of her snowsuit.

"Cookies," Ellie muttered as she kicked her boots across the room.

"First you're going to give me a big kiss and hug. Then I'm going to make a list of things to do and wait for your approval."

They were warm and soft and smelled like children should, clean and fresh with a light powdery scent. The obligatory kiss and hug turned into a roll-on-the-floor tussling match with Gracie and Slick yapping as they, too, tried to wiggle into Kristine's arms.

This, Kristine thought as the girls settled on her lap, is what it's all about. The rest of the stuff is pure bullshit. *Thank you, God, for giving me this second chance with my family.* She wasn't sure, but she thought she heard someone say,

You're welcome. She laughed aloud. The girls giggled. The dogs yipped.

"This is what we're going to do. Now, listen up." The little girls tilted their heads and listened attentively. "We are going to make Christmas cookies. I even have aprons for both of you. But, we aren't going to do that till later. We're going to go over to the Kelly farm and do some sled riding. When we get back, we'll have some lunch and we'll all take a nap. When you wake up, we'll make some decorations for Mommie to hang on your windows at home. How does that sound?"

"Santy Claus," Emily chortled.

"Cookies," Ellie said.

"Everybody go to the bathroom! You know where it is. Emily, help your sister."

"Okay, Granny."

Twenty minutes later, they were tooling down the road with the sled on top of the car and singing, "Rudolph the Red Nosed Reindeer" at the top of their lungs.

Kristine eyed the long expanse of driveway that led to the ramshackle Kelly house. The 4-by-4 had no trouble plowing through the snow as she expertly guided the vehicle to the circular drive that led to the front porch.

"I want you to hold my hands and not wander off. Stay with Gracie and Slick. Do you hear me, girls?" Two little heads bobbed up and down as Kristine unhooked their seat belts just as the dogs scrambled over their laps to leap to the ground.

Inside the cavernous house, their breath circling them like Indian smoke signals, Kristine walked from room to room. Everything had been cleared out the previous month so now not even the rickety straight-backed chairs were in the kitchen. She had no clue as to what the new owners would do with the property. Would they demolish the house and build a new one or would they try to restore it? Whatever their decision, she hoped they had a lot of money. Six hundred thousand dollars was a lot of money to pay for this property. When the Realtor had first approached her, he'd said they would be lucky to get a hundred thousand.

She'd put the property on the market a year ago, the same day she'd finally gone to the lawyers to have Logan declared legally dead. Then, a contrary streak in her reversed her original plan and she'd filed for divorce first. When it was final, she'd started the paperwork to declare Logan dead. Now the children could inherit. Until that day the three of them had refused even to discuss any monies that might result from the sale of their father's property. Two hundred thousand dollars each would allow them to pay off their mortgages, put some money aside for the children's college education, possibly take a vacation and sock whatever was left into a nice mutual fund where it would grow nicely for their retirement.

Even Tyler had agreed and said now he could buy himself a little house on the beach somewhere so when he had leave he would have someplace to go home to. She'd expected strong opposition from Mike, but he'd agreed once he saw the papers for the divorce and the death certificate.

"Do you want to come upstairs or do you want to wait down here?" Kristine asked the girls. Silly question; both of them were halfway up the long staircase, Gracie and Slick waiting at the top. Kristine stifled a giggle as Ellie, padded to the nines, had to use her hands on each step to help her get to the top.

On the second floor, Kristine walked from room to room as the children and the dogs ran up and down the hallway, hollering and shrieking. Everything looked to be in order. Jackson Valarian had carted all the old trunks and records out of the attic years ago. Nothing remained except cobwebs.

Kristine had one bad moment when she opened the door to the room that had once been her husband's. Her eyes felt hot and gritty as she stared at the faded wallpaper and the rotten wood around the windows. What did Logan do in this room besides sleep? Did he sit by the window and daydream about her? Did he study here or at the kitchen table? Did he bring friends to his room where they played games or told secrets? Did he hide under the covers at night to read with a flashlight the way she had? She should know these things, but she didn't. She realized now that she had never known the real Logan Kelly at all.

"Time to go, girls! Gracie! Slick! Where are you?" Kristine singsonged as she closed the door behind her.

"You have to find us, Granny," a small voice near the attic steps shouted.

"Where can my little girls be?" Kristine said, playing the game. "Oh, I found you! Come on, you have to come out. What's that?"

Gracie backed up and growled. Slick did his circle dance, which he always performed when he was upset.

"A magic wand!" Emily said. "It's a secret place. It's dark!"

"Let me see!" Kristine said, dropping to her haunches as the girls scampered out of the small dark, hidey-hole.

Kristine clawed and waved her hands about as she pulled and tugged. She sneezed when she pulled out old blankets, a flashlight, a pile of books, and something dark that felt like fur. She dragged the contents to the window at the second-floor landing.

"What's this? What's this?" Emily babbled as she picked up the flashlight and some old, cracked dishes.

Kristine shook out the cape, her gaze going to what Emily called the magic wand and the piles of old *National Geographic* magazines. Her eyes started to burn again. "I think this might be . . . someone's secret." Why couldn't she say, your grandfather's secret? Because the man who was the grandfather to these two little girls didn't deserve the recognition. "I think we'll just put this stuff in the back of the truck and take it home. Careful going down the steps."

Kristine's hands trembled as she rolled the old blankets into a tight ball. Tonight when the children were asleep, she'd go through these things. Why, she didn't know.

Kristine lowered the back window of the Blazer, tossed in the rolled blankets, and withdrew the sled from the top of the truck. "Okay, ladies, pile on. Emily, you hold Gracie, and Ellie, you hold Slick. Do not pinch him, Ellie. If you do, he'll nip your nose. Be gentle."

"Okay, Granny."

The next two hours passed in a weary blur as Kristine pulled the tykes up and down the small hill on the Flexible Flyer. She whooped and shouted until she was hoarse as they tumbled in the snow after each ride.

When the first fat snowflakes began to fall, Kristine herded her charges into the car for the short ride home, but not before she scooped up the two small soaking wet dogs and stuck them inside her down jacket.

They sang "Jingle Bells" all the way back to the farm, the children's voices high and sweet, Kristine's weary and off-key. The dogs snoozed contentedly against Kristine's warm body inside her jacket.

The production of removing boots, wet mittens, wool caps, and the bright red snowsuits took fifteen minutes. Kristine used up another five minutes wrapping Gracie and Slick in bright blue towels. They were asleep as soon as she placed them in their beds.

"How does hot chocolate and peanut butter and jelly sound? Then a nice nap."

"Me have Gummi Bears," Ellie said wistfully.

"Marshmallows, Granny," Emily said hopefully.

"Gummi Bears when you wake up and absolutely there will be marshmallows in the hot chocolate. Wash your hands and go to the bathroom. Emily, help your sister."

By one-thirty the girls were sound asleep. Kristine was interrupted twice by the phone as she cleared the kitchen and then started to pack all the files and papers in the dining room for pending action after the holidays. The first call was from Jackson Valarian.

Kristine smiled at the bantering voice on the other end of the wire. "I know you are chomping at the bit, Jack, but it is just a few more weeks, and we can make our decision then. Yes, I know you've written the story in your sleep one hundred times. I'm weary too. Four years is a long time to wait for anything. You need to get married and have a family so you can think of other things. By the way, I went over to the Kelly farm this morning to walk through the house one last time. I found some odd things. To me they're odd. A faux ermine cape, a bunch of blankets and old towels, a flashlight and piles of *National Geographic*s. Actually, Emily found them in a kind of hidey-hole under the attic stairs, I brought the stuff home. I don't know why I'm telling you this since it doesn't have anything to do with anything. I'll see you on the second of January. If you like, Jack, you can come for dinner Christmas Eve and spend the night. My children will be here, and I know you got along well with Mike. You'll like Tyler, too. Okay, it's a date then.''

"Kristine?''

"Yes.''

"I just want to say again how sorry I am that we couldn't find any information on your husband. I'm grateful that you went through with your end of the bargain. If this is none of my business just say so, but I've been wondering if you've heard from Mr. Dunwoodie? *Him* we could probably find if you want us to.''

Kristine tried to remember at what point she'd become Kristine to the young reporter. When a date refused to come to mind she shrugged it off. It was strange, though, that Woodie had always been Mr. Dunwoodie to Jack. "I sent a letter a little while ago asking him to come for Christmas Eve. I haven't had a response.''

"Does he know you got a divorce and had your husband declared legally dead? Or is that something I shouldn't be asking.''

Oftentimes, when they worked late at night and both were tired, she would share a cup of coffee with the reporter and let her hair down. As a friend, Jack had every right to ask the questions he was asking. "It's okay to ask, Jack. I didn't tell him. I suppose it's possible he could know from someone in town. It is what it is, Jack. Life is going to go on no matter who comes to dinner Christmas Eve and no matter if I'm divorced or not. I guess I'm more a widow than a divorcée, but then I filed for divorce first. I should know the answer to that, but I don't," Kristine said fretfully.

"I don't think it matters in the scheme of things, Kristine. So, how's the Christmas shopping going. I know how to put doll buggies together and all that girl stuff. My sister has three girls, and I always have to do it."

Kristine laughed. "I'll remember that. I think I have it covered. When the girls wake up we're going to start to decorate the house. It's snowing. That means any minute now I expect to be riddled with Christmas spirit."

"Good for you. It's snowing here in Washington, too. The city is about to shut down. I'll see you Christmas Eve, Kristine."

"You're sure your family won't mind?"

"Not at all. They're going to Oklahoma to spend the holidays with my sister who just had a new baby. The first boy, so it's a big deal. I'm going for New Year's."

After Kristine hung up, she checked on her sleeping grandchildren and the dogs before she dressed for the outdoors in a heavy jacket and fur-lined boots. It was time to gather the evergreens to decorate the house. Time to bring the stuff from the Kelly farm inside so she could try to figure out what it all meant. Time to put something in the Crock-Pot for dinner before the girls woke from their naps.

It was midafternoon when Kristine sat down by the kitchen fire to sip at a cup of freshly brewed coffee. The dogs stirred but remained in their cocoon, warm and content. The pungent smell of evergreens on the newspapers by the back door was more heady than the expensive perfume on her dresser. She inhaled deeply as she stared through the window at the falling snow. In another hour or so it would look like a winter wonderland outdoors. Perhaps if the girls were up to it, they would go outside and make Christmas angels in the snow. She'd done that with her own mother when she was little, but she'd never done it with her own children.

"The past is prologue, Kristine. Don't look back. You can't unring the bell," she murmured as she got up to refill her coffee cup.

Her world was almost perfect. If it was a perfect world, would she be bouncing off the ceiling with happiness? If everything was perfect, where would the challenge be? What would there be to look forward to?

Kristine eyed the beige wall phone, willing it to ring. It did. She bounded out of the chair to catch it on the second ring so it wouldn't wake the children. "Hello," she said breathlessly.

"Mom?"

"Cala, what's wrong?"

"Nothing's wrong, Mom. Pete says we should stay in town. The roads are bad. Is that okay with you? How are the kids?"

"Pete's right. It's snowing pretty hard. The girls are fine. We went sled riding. They had a wonderful time. They ate all their lunch and should be waking up soon. We're going to make snow angels down by the barn when it's time to feed the dogs. We're making decorations when they wake up, then it's cookie-baking time after dinner. You and Pete enjoy yourselves."

"Do they miss us?" Cala asked wistfully.

Kristine blinked. "They jabbered about you all morning long," she fibbed.

"Snow angels, huh?"

Kristine blinked again. "Yes."

"I don't think we ever did that, did we, Mom?"

"No, Cala, we didn't. When you were younger, we lived in warm climates with no snow. When you were older, you were . . . I was too busy. I used to do it with my mother. If you don't think it's a good idea, we won't do it."

"No, no. The girls love snow. I promised to make a snowman with them."

"I know," Kristine fibbed again. "There will be plenty of snow to do that tomorrow, trust me."

"I do, Mom. Trust you, I mean."

"I know, Cala."

"Pete's giving me the evil eye. He wants to buy everything he sees for the girls."

"That's because he's a doting father. Jackson Valarian called a little while ago. I invited him for Christmas Eve. He said he's an expert at putting doll buggies and girl stuff together. I snapped him up."

"That's good, Mom, because Pete is all thumbs, and I can't follow directions worth a darn. If I tell him, he'll want to buy more. Make sure Ellie eats."

"Okay. Go on now, hang up and be careful driving home tomorrow."

"Bye, Mom. Love you."

The sweetest words in the whole world. "Love you, too," Kristine said happily.

Almost perfect.

Aaron Dunwoodie stood on the balcony of his rented condo to stare out at what the locals called the Pacific Jewel.

Hawaii, land of sunshine, luscious palm trees, gentle breezes, and sun-kissed beaches. His gaze was intent as he stared down at the honeymooners and the families with small children as they frolicked in the bright blue water.

Been there, done that. He had the deep bronze tan to prove it. He shifted his feet to lean on the railing. He was bored out of his mind. He'd read just about every book in the library plus all the local newspapers. He'd played endless games of solitaire until he'd worn out the cards, refusing to buy another deck. He'd watched inane television shows until he no longer bothered turning on the monster set in the living room. He'd long ago given up on the radio because he couldn't bear to listen to what he called mushy love songs. He'd actually screwed up his courage, driven to the North Shore, and surfed the Banzai Pipeline. He'd washed out, but that was okay. He'd done it and would have gone back a second time until he heard a bunch of brash kids refer to him as 'that old duffer on the boogie board.' *Shit, I am an old duffer.* An old duffer who still had all his hair and teeth and a solid waistline. An old duffer who could still get it up when and if the occasion warranted. He'd sold his surfboard the second day for a quarter of what he paid for it originally. His dreams of being the Big Kahuna were shot down by a bunch of pimply, smart-ass kids.

I feel fucking old.

Kristine said she loved Hawaii. Did she love the islands for what they were or did she love Hawaii because she'd come here with Logan and her children? He had to admit he didn't know.

From off in the distance he heard the afternoon bell signaling the mail was in along with his copy of the *New York Times* and *USA Today.*

Who in the goddamn hell spent Christmas in Hawaii? He needed to get out of here. He needed to go someplace where it was cold so he could shiver and think about what he was going to do with the rest of his life.

He'd made a mistake where Kristine was concerned. He never should have left that day. He never should have given her an ultimatum. Ultimatums never worked for either party. All you had in the end were regrets. And he sure as hell had a bushelful of those.

Pride had to be the most serious sin of all.

If he wanted to, he could be out of here in a heartbeat. For the past three months he'd lived in bathing trunks. Hell, he hadn't even bothered to unpack his winter clothes. All he had to do was gather up his shaving gear, throw his summer shorts, trunks, and sandals in a duffel, call the maid to clean out the fridge, and he was on his way.

If he wanted to.

"Shit!" he said succinctly.

He was a man with a purpose as he headed for the

elevator that would take him to the ground floor for his mail and papers.

Woodie carried the packet back to his apartment and dumped it on the dining room table. He popped a Budweiser and carried the papers to the small deck off the living room. He sighed. He'd always been conscientious to a fault. He trotted back to the dining room, ripped at the clasp on the bank envelope, and unceremoniously dumped the contents onto the glass-topped table with its elaborate silk flower arrangement. Bank statements, a pile of Christmas cards. He recognized his ex-wife's handwriting on one of the cards. Then he saw it, the familiar handwriting, the long white envelope with the return address of Summers Farm in the left-hand corner. His hands trembled so badly he could barely pick it up, and when he did, it dropped to the floor.

Woodie tortured himself for several minutes before he could pick it up a second time. Then he brought it close to his nose to see if it carried his love's scent. It did. For one brief moment he thought he was going to black out.

Kristine.

13

She was restless. *Antsy*, as Cala would say, and she didn't know why. Was she nervous because Mike and his family would arrive tomorrow and Tyler the next day? No, she decided. Maybe it was all the caffeine she'd been drinking these past two days. Unlikely. Three more days till Christmas. She was ready, had been ready for days now. The house was decorated from top to bottom. It smelled heavenly. The tree was up and decorated, the gifts wrapped in shiny silver paper with huge red-velvet bows. She'd been forced to pile them high around the tree and into the corners for the overflow. She'd even bought a red-velvet Santa Claus suit for Jack, who promised to play the great man Christmas morning.

Kristine shook her head to clear her thoughts. If what she was feeling had nothing to do with all of the above, what was wrong with her? There was no doubt in her mind that she was wired. Even though it was near midnight, she knew she'd never be able to sleep if she went to bed. The miniature colored lights on the twelve-foot Christmas tree were not having the tranquilizing effect she thought they would have when she sat down with the dogs for her last cup of coffee of the night.

She hadn't heard from Woodie. That was the bottom line. Woodie was her problem. She'd hoped and even prayed that he would call or send a card. Obviously, he wasn't going to forgive her. Where was he? What was he doing? Did he think of her?

Christmas was such a special time of year. Christmas was supposed to be a time of miracles, although she had yet to experience one. Wasn't she worthy of one? Surely she'd done something good in her life to warrant a small miracle. Just one.

Kristine looked at her watch. Almost midnight. Did she want to drive over to Woodie's house and sit outside like a lovesick fool? She'd done it hundreds of times over these past years and always felt like a fool when she got home. Still, she found it comforting to sit in his driveway, staring at his dark house. Once or twice she'd actually gotten out of the car, walked up to the door, and rung the bell, a rehearsed speech ready to roll off her tongue in case Woodie was home and opened the door.

The dogs, sensing her restlessness, whimpered softly. "It's snowing out," Kristine said. "We're going to have a white Christmas. The kids will love it. It's going to be so nice to see Mike's new baby. I hope he doesn't mind that I brought down my old cradle from the attic. Cala said he wouldn't mind. I'm not sure about that. Young people today want bright new things, not old antiques." Both dogs lifted their heads to listen to their mistress's sad voice. Gracie whimpered as Slick nipped her nose before he snuggled into the corner of the sofa where Kristine had been sitting. They watched her, their eyes alert, as she stared out at the falling snow.

"I'm going over to Woodie's house. You guys stay here where it's nice and warm. Be sure to guard all those presents under the tree. No chewing the ribbons, Slick," she said as she left the room.

"This is so stupid, it's beyond belief," Kristine muttered as she slipped the car into gear. "I never acted this stupid when I was sixteen and in love with Logan."

Kristine shivered as she waited for the 4-by-4 to heat up. She turned on the radio. Bing Crosby's mellow voice was crooning "I'll Be Home for Christmas." Hot tears flooded her eyes as she struggled to see through the swirling snow. The windshield wipers clicked back and forth with furious intensity. She turned the radio off.

Twenty minutes later, Kristine pulled into Woodie's driveway. "This is a stupid, dumb, asinine thing I'm doing. No one in their right mind would come out here at midnight during heavy snow to sit in the dark and stare at an empty house. No one. Absolutely no one." Yet, here she was. And she didn't feel one bit better. "I need to go home where I belong," she cried as she blew her nose lustily. She turned the radio back on to hear the old crooner still singing. It must be Bing Crosby night. Sentimental music for insomniacs.

It was toasty in the car, and she had a package of cigarettes. If she cracked the window a bit she could sit here and smoke for a little while. *My life*, she thought bitterly as she fished for a cigarette in her purse.

Woodie rolled over, his eyes going to the red numerals on the bedside clock. He groaned. Twelve-thirty! "Shit!" He'd always been a good sleeper. Regardless of the time, the minute his head hit the pillow he was out until six the following morning. *I don't have to go to the bathroom, I feel fine, the house is quiet, so what the hell woke me up?*

He'd rolled in at nine-thirty, dumped his bags in the kitchen, stashed the few groceries he'd bought at a Quick Check for morning, showered, and hit the sack at ten-thirty after he listened to the news. So what woke him up? Snow was quiet. It wasn't that windy outdoors. Some wild animal was probably prancing around on his roof. For some reason the raccoons loved his roof. Yeah, that must be it. He was about to roll over and go back to sleep when he realized he could see light from his bedroom window. "What the hell!" he muttered as he jumped out of bed to run to the window.

Woodie's heart leaped in his chest when he saw what looked like a utility vehicle sitting in his driveway with the lights on. Living way out here in the middle of nowhere, as he put it, he always knew one day he'd be the target of a burglar. "We'll just see about that." He was dressed in two minutes. He used up another five minutes getting his double-barreled shotgun out of the closet. He liked the comforting sound of the shells sliding home.

Woodie didn't bother turning on any lights as he made his way down the steps to the first floor and then out to the kitchen. *If I'm quiet, I can sneak around the back of the truck, creep up to the passenger side of the door, grab it, open it, and shove the shotgun in the motherfucker's face. Yeah, yeah, that's what I'll do.* His heart pumping, he followed his own instructions. He had one bad moment when his left hand reached out for the door handle. Maybe he needed to scream or yell like those Ninja people did when they were about to attack. The yell and the surprise element would give him time to get his right arm up with the shotgun.

He had a head rush then as his hand grappled with the door handle. Shit, what if the robber locked it? He removed his hand from the door handle and stepped back into midleg-high snow. *Think, think,* he told himself. His heart thundering in his chest, he advanced three steps and reached for the door handle with his left hand, his right hand and arm cradling the shotgun. He did a leap in the air, landing with his feet spread apart, yelling at the top of his lungs, "Yoweee! Move, and your brains are on the roof." He gave the door a vicious yank, yelling, "Yowee!" a second time at the top of his lungs as a cloud of smoke swirled about him and the most bloodcurdling scream he'd ever heard in his life shattered his eardrums. "Get your sorry ass out of that truck right now before I blow your fucking head right off your shoulders! Move! Move!" he shouted, snow and cigarette smoke blinding him. "The police are on the way!" he yelled. *Yeah, like they would really come all the way out here.* On the other hand, did this crook know the phone was disconnected? How long had they cased the place before making the decision to rob it? What the hell kind of burglar screamed bloody murder? "I told you to fucking move!"

"Woodie! Oh my God, Woodie, is it you!"

"Kristine! Kristine, is it you? Jesus, I almost blew your head off."

"I know. Why do you want to kill me? My God, Woodie, I can't believe it's you."

"Guess what, I can't believe it's you either. I just got home a couple of hours ago. How did you know?"

"I didn't know. I come out here sometimes and sit in front of your house. I cry and wail and smoke cigarettes, then I go home and sometimes I can sleep and sometimes I can't."

"I got your letter. That's why I came home. I almost killed you. If I had sneezed, I would have. This thing has a hair trigger."

"You didn't. That's all that's important. I'm so glad you came home. I love you, Woodie. I really and truly love you. If you still want to marry me, I'm yours."

"Listen, can we talk about this inside? I'm freezing my ass off."

"I'd love to go into your house. I missed you, Woodie."

"Not half as much as I missed you."

"Can we get married?" Kristine asked tearfully. "Where were you, Woodie? Why didn't you call or write?"

"Is tomorrow soon enough? I didn't think you wanted me to call or write. Kristine, do you look at me as an old duffer?"

Kristine backed up a step. "No way," she gurgled. "Why?"

"No reason. Want some coffee or something?"

"Or something. I want you!"

"Do you want to go for it right here or should we head up the steps?"

Kristine pretended to think. "I'll race you to the second floor!"

"In the old days you could have taken me," Woodie said, panting from the top of the stairs.

"In the old days I wasn't a grandmother," Kristine gasped.

"You're a grandmother!"

"Does that change things?" Kristine asked as she peeled off her heavy sweater and turtleneck tee shirt.

"It's probably right up there with being called an old duffer," Woodie said as he dropped his pants to the floor.

"Are those . . . ?"

"Never mind, Kristine."

"They are. They really are yellow Calvins!" Kristine hooted with laughter.

In spite of himself, Woodie laughed with her. "You ain't seen nothin' till you see me in my blue Speedo. I wore it to go surfing, and these wise-ass kids called me an old duffer. I could model it for you."

Kristine wiped at her eyes, still laughing. "I would like to have seen that."

"It wasn't pretty. I don't think I ever made love to a grandmother wearing long underwear."

"You learn any new tricks while you were away?" Kristine asked as she unbuttoned her long johns.

"Why do you want to know?" Woodie asked slyly.

"Because I'm four years worth of horny, that's why."

"Nah. Same old same old."

"That's good enough for me. I was just testing you."

"What about you, did you learn any?"

"A few. Cala tells me . . . things. Young people today are so . . . *limber*. They go by a *manual*."

"A manual?" Woodie said, perspiration dotting his brow.

"Uh-huh. Cala made photocopies of some of the more . . . interesting pages."

"Why are we even talking about this? It's obvious you don't have the pages with you."

"Oh but I do. They're in my purse."

"Oh."

"I don't see any point in getting dressed and going out to the car, do you? Let's just do what we always did."

"Get in this bed, Kristine. Now!"

"I love you, Woodie. I told you that, didn't I?"

"Yes. And I love you, too, even if you are a grandmother. Later, I want you to tell me how that happened. Come here, Kristine."

"I thought you would never ask," Kristine said, pulling the comforter over both of them. "Oh, God, I left the lights on in the truck. The battery is going to die."

"Who cares?"

"Not me." Kristine sighed as she rolled over on top of Woodie. "Now, just shut up so I can show you what I learned."

"But you said . . ."

"I lied."

"That was one of the best breakfasts I ever ate, Woodie. Lately, all I've been eating is a bran muffin and coffee for breakfast. You have to eat stuff like that when you're about to hit the half century mark. Are we going to get married today?"

"I'm for whatever you want. Wouldn't it be a good idea to do it the first day of the new year? You said the kids will be home for a week. You want them there, don't you?"

"Of course. We could do it twice. I don't want to let you out of my sight. We lost four whole years because of my stupidity. I don't want to lose another day. If we wait till New Year's Day, will you swear never to leave my sight?"

"I swear," Woodie said solemnly.

"You were golfing buddies with Judge Harmon, weren't you? Will you ask him to come to the house and marry us there?"

"Sure."

"I want you to come out to the house and stay with us. You'll have to start off in the spare bedroom, though. I have grandchildren now and I can't . . . won't . . . you know, plus the kids will be sleeping in the house. We'll figure something out. The worst-case scenario is we can go to the barn. It's heated, and there's all that lovely warm straw. That goes under the heading of experimental."

"I wouldn't have it any other way. Are you sure my staying at the house will be okay with the kids?"

"They aren't kids anymore, Woodie. They're young adults. They'll be fine with it."

"I want to hear everything. Let's take our coffee into the living room by the fire. I want to hear every single thing that went on while I was gone."

"Will you tell me every single thing you did?"

"Absolutely. This is going to be a marriage based on trust and truth. No secrets. Okay?"

"It's wonderful, isn't it, Woodie? How many people do you know who get a second crack at happiness?"

"Not many. The truth is I don't know anyone unless you count my ex-wife, and she married for money because she thinks all that wealth will make her happy. For her it might work, but I wouldn't bet the rent on it. I don't know if that counts. Probably not. Start talking, Kristine."

It was midafternoon when Woodie wound down from his adventures in Hawaii.

"I should call home."

"Yes, you should. Say hello for me."

"It's still snowing. This is so nice and cozy. I want to stay here forever. As much as I hate to, I have to go home."

"Why?"

"Why?"

"Yes, why? You said Cala lives in town. Pete and Cala run the business and the boarding kennel, so what's waiting for you? You said you packed up all your paperwork until after the holidays."

"When it snows like this, Pete and Cala stay in the old apartment over the garage. The girls love spending the night and when that happens, I usually make soup or stew and we all eat together. I have a real family now, Woodie. I want you to be part of it. You are going to love the girls. Smart as whips. They're into everything, and they are so good with the dogs. It's amazing how gentle they are around the animals. We all cry when a pup goes off to a new home. I could make stew, fresh bread, and a big garden salad if I need to tempt you. I might even make a pie.''

"Real homemade bread?"

"Yep. Cala bought me a bread machine for Mother's Day last year. I actually use it two or three times a week. Emily loves warm bread with butter and strawberry jam. Ellie just licks the jelly. Come with me, Woodie. Pack your things, and we'll play in the snow.''

"Okay. We need to jump your battery first, though.''

"I know. If all else fails, we can walk across the fields, or, better yet, you can carry me.''

"This old duffer?"

"Hey, I'll settle for an old duffer any time, any place. I think last night was one of the best times of my life. Pack while I call home.''

"Yes, ma'am,'' Woodie said, snapping off a salute. "I love you, Kristine Kelly.''

"It's Kristine Summers, Woodie. I took back my maiden name.''

"I love that Kristine, too.'' Woodie grinned.

Kristine dialed the barn. Pete picked up on the second ring. "Is everything okay, Pete?''

"Everything's fine. I had to turn away six people who wanted to board their dogs for the holidays. Business couldn't be better. It was a great idea to build that other barn. Cala loves the dogs. The kids can't wait to get here in the morning. Emily says she isn't going to preschool unless they have dogs on the playground. Cala is getting itchy over that. By the way, she's on her way to the airport to pick up Mike and Carol. They called around six this morning to say they got an earlier flight.''

"Oh, Pete, why didn't you call me?"

"I would have, Kristine, but I didn't know where you were. By the way, where are you?''

"Pete, you are never going to believe this. I'm at Woodie's house. He came home last night. We're getting married New Year's Day! In my entire life, Pete, I've never been this happy. Do you hear me, Pete, I'm in love?''

"I hear you, Kristine. And you were worried about having a dull Christmas. This must go under the heading of some kind of miracle. I am so happy for you. Cala will be, too, when she hears. Congratulations! Who's going to stand up for you?"

"I didn't get that far in my thinking but now that you asked, how about you and Cala? I know Woodie would love to have the two of you stand up for us."

"Then we accept, and it's a done deal. What about Mike and Tyler?"

"This is my wedding, so if we want to have three best men, then I say we go for it. Did Cala take the girls with her?"

"Yes. She couldn't wait to show them off to her brother. It's that twin stuff."

Kristine laughed. "I'll be home soon. If Mike and Carol are going to be home today, I'd like you all to stay for dinner. It will be so nice to have all of us together. I wish Tyler could make it home today. The roads look bad. There's a lot of snow out there. You are going to stay the night, aren't you?"

"Yep. Cala dusted up the apartment and changed the sheets. I lugged firewood in when I got up. Everything is fine here, Kristine. Jeez, I can't wait to see old Woodie."

"Do me a favor," Kristine whispered. "Somehow, someway, work into the conversation that you think he's an old duffer."

"For you, Kristine, anything. I'm not even going to ask why. He won't take a poke at me will he?"

"No, of course not. It's an inside joke."

"I get it. Like those yellow Calvins and the blue Speedo."

"Exactly."

"See you when you get here, boss."

Dinner was a rousing affair, and if eyes were misty from time to time, no one seemed to notice.

"This is so great," Woodie said. "I haven't sat around a dinner table with a family in twenty years. I hope we can do this often. Listen up, all of you. Your mother and I have an announcement to make. We're getting married New Year's Day. We'd both like your blessing. We want you— Mike, Tyler, and Pete—to be my best men. Cala and Carol will be your mom's matrons of honor. If it isn't correct wedding protocol, we don't care. That's the way it is. Your mother wants the ceremony here at the house in the living room by the fire."

Kristine beamed as she jiggled her newest grandchild on her lap, and her children shouted and clapped. Mike let loose with an earsplitting whistle of approval.

"What that means, everybody, is we get to buy some new duds for the affair. This is going to be the best Christmas ever," Cala said happily.

"It sure is. I like what you did with the house, Mom. The first day we got here and saw the condition of things was a day I'll never forget. You know what, it feels like home. It really does, Mom."

All eyes turned to Kristine. She flushed. To cover how overwhelmed she felt at her son's words, she brought the sweet-smelling baby close to her face so she could smother the little boy with kisses. Her eyes felt hot and prickly.

"Remember that Christmas Eve dinner? We chucked it, Woodie, and had hot dogs and Jell-O. That was a bad time, but we're past all that now. This family is growing by leaps and bounds. Before you know it, we'll fill up this long table. How many kids do you think Tyler will have?" Cala asked.

"Zero kids," Mike said. "He's a career officer, and children and marriage are not in his near future. Maybe he'll change his mind when he sees our kids, but I don't think so. I can't believe he made captain. It's been four years since I've seen old Ty. We write, but it isn't the same. How about you, Mom?"

"He was home two and a half years ago for two days. He spent most of his time playing with the dogs, eating, and sleeping. He's happy. That's the important thing. Cala is so right, this is going to be the most wonderful Christmas we ever had. I don't know where we're going to put all the presents you guys dropped off. We're out into the hallway as it is, and Woodie hasn't brought his in yet,'' she said slyly.

"Is that a hint for me to do my shopping quickly? Didn't anyone tell you the best buys come two days before Christmas? It's on my agenda for tomorrow. By evening, the overflow in the hall will fall into the dining room. Who wants some of your mother's blackberry pie?''

"Gummi Bears,'' Ellie said.

"Pie or nothing. No pie, and it's bedtime,'' Cala said firmly.

"Okay, Mommie.''

"I knew you'd see it my way, honey.''

"Ellie must have Pete's disposition. You never gave in.'' Mike hooted.

"She and Emily are a perfect mix of us both. How did you end up with Dillon? He's such a good baby. Does he ever cry?''

"Only when he's hungry.''

"He sure doesn't take after you. You had a hair-trigger temper. You still do,'' Cala shot back.

"They're going to go all out,'' Woodie said sotto voce. "Let's clean up, Kristine. I need some advice on my Christmas list.''

Kristine handed the baby over to Carol. She was struck again, as she always was, when she saw the girl her son had married. She was plain, with warm, brown eyes that continuously sparkled. Her short bob was maintenance free and complemented the dusting of freckles that rode high on her cheeks and then built a bridge across her nose. She had one of the most beautiful smiles Kristine had ever seen. Carol was smiling now as she accepted her child with outstretched arms. "I love this baby so much,'' she said quietly.

"I can tell." Kristine smiled. "Anyone for more coffee before Woodie clears the table?"

Mike and Pete held up their cups.

"If I'm going to clear the table, what are you going to do, Kristine?"

"I'm going to watch you," Kristine said smartly. "I cooked, so that means you clean up."

"Whose rule is that?" Woodie demanded.

"Mine."

"Oh," Woodie said.

"Guess that means you fit in, big guy," Pete whispered.

"Is that what it means?" Woodie asked in awe.

"That's what it means. I'd hustle if I were you. Your lady doesn't like to be kept waiting. She meant it when she said she's going to watch you."

"I love this family. I really do."

The kitchen cleaned, Woodie removed his apron. His voice was anxious when he said, "How'd I do, honey?"

"I don't think I ever saw this kitchen so clean. You did a marvelous job."

"That's not what I meant, Kristine. I meant with the kids."

"It's like Pete said, you belong. Mike, Tyler, and Cala always liked you. You know that. Emily and Ellie love you. It's like you were always a part of our lives. In one short dinner hour, you interacted more with my children than their own father did in years. Mealtimes were always more or less silent unless Logan had something to say. We ate, cleaned up, and left the room."

"How did you stand it?"

"I didn't know any better. I was stupid. Silence was golden. Take your pick. Want to go down to the barn to check on the dogs?"

"I'd love to go down to the barn to check on the dogs. Kristine, is that old sleigh still in that ramshackle barn?"

"Yes, why?"

"How about if I clean it up tomorrow and ask John Hollister if he'll lend us a few of his horses for Christmas Eve. A sleigh ride for the whole family. What do you think?"

"I knew I liked you for a reason. It's a great idea. The girls will love it. What about your Christmas shopping?"

"I was teasing before. I'm done. All I have to do is go into town to pick it all up. It's all been gift-wrapped."

"That's a sneaky way of doing things. You're supposed to pick out just the right paper for just the right present, then you're supposed to make just the right bow for just that present. You're cheating, but I don't care."

"That's good, because I'm not wrapping and tieing bows on anything. How do you wrap a scooter?"

"You buy a colorful bicycle bag and tie it with a bow. It's okay, I didn't know that either until last year. Each day I learn something new, Woodie. It's wonderful. I think I finally found that thing people call inner peace. I'm okay with everything in my life. Right now there is nothing I want to change."

"That says it all, Kristine. For the first time in my life, I feel the same way. Let's take that sleigh ride to midnight mass."

"That's a great idea. The kids will love it. We can carol on the way."

"C'mon, pretty lady, let's go see those dogs. How many do you have?"

"Pups or the kennel?"

"Both."

"We have twenty-two pups, and I think Pete said we're boarding thirty-six dogs. We have a full house. I need to give some thought to expanding the barns. It's a very profitable business. I was hoping, and don't say anything, that maybe Mike and Carol would want to come back and go into business with us. It's a great place to bring up children. I worry about California and earthquakes. Children need room to run and romp, and they need to see snow and play in mud puddles. I'm almost afraid to ask him, though."

"Do you want me to ask him?"

"No. It's something I'll have to do when the time is right. You might enlist his aid tomorrow when you're working on the sleigh. Sort of feel him out. Early on, Mike drew his line in the sand, and I don't want to step over it."

"He seems pretty mellow to me. It's been eight years, Kristine. He's a man now. Men think differently than hot-headed boys."

"What else are we going to do after we check on the dogs?" Kristine asked bluntly.

"I'm going to do wild, unimaginable things to you."

"An old duffer like you! I could get that book. You know the one."

"If you feel *you* need it, by all means. I certainly don't need it!" Woodie said as he beelined out the door, Kristine in hot pursuit, yelling her head off.

Mike motioned to Cala to join him at the window. "I never saw Mom run. I never saw Mom laugh like that. She seems so . . . *young.*"

"She's not the same anymore, Mike. Today she's the person we always wanted her to be. Cut her some slack. You need to be more forgiving. All that bad stuff is behind us."

"I'm past it too, Cala. I have a bad feeling, and I can't explain it. Carol says I'm overreacting to the trip home. That's not what it is. This is all just too good for words."

"I know what you mean. I've been having the same feelings. If you hadn't said something, I would have kept quiet. Pete says I just look for trouble. It's true, though. Everything is almost too perfect. It will be perfect when Tyler gets here. Mom's great. She's finally happy and getting married to a sweet guy. She's done all the things . . . she never got to do when we were young. She's really worked at it, Mike. And please don't say, too much, too little, too late. It pains me to say this, but we are better people because of our past. We overcame it all. Look at us now. You have a wonderful wife and son, a great job, and you live in sunny California. I have Pete, the girls, and all those amazing animals. What more could either one of us want?"

"That's what Carol says. Two against one, and I'm not even holding out. I agree with everything you said."

"Mom sold the Kelly farm. She told you, didn't she?"

"Yeah."

"She's dividing the money among us. We can pay off our mortgages, put some away for the kids' college fund, and sock the rest into a good mutual fund. Those are Mom's suggestions, not mine, but I agree with them. I probably wouldn't be able to accept if Mom hadn't had *him* declared legally dead. Dead I can handle. How about you?"

"I agree. The money will certainly make life easier."

"Mike, why don't you come back here to live. The farm is great for the kids. Mom has been talking about expanding. You get along with Pete, and I adore Carol. It would be so good for all of us. We could even use some of the money for the expansion and we can do a lot of the work ourselves. Will you think about it?"

"Did Mom put you up to this?"

"No, and don't say I even mentioned it. You need to start thinking about earthquakes and all that smog. What kind of place is that to bring up kids? Not to mention the perverts. I know there are perverts everywhere, but my one encounter happened there and I'm not likely to forget it."

"I'll think about it. What do you think they're doing down there?"

"Playing with the pups. Mom often goes down when she can't sleep. I used to find her curled up in the straw with six or seven of them all cuddled against her. Our Mom is an okay lady, Mike. And if she's doing something else, so what!"

Mike laughed. "You're right, Cala, so what! God, it's good to see you. It's even better to be home. This is home. It really is."

"I know. I had a hard time saying the words at first. Then they just started rolling off my lips."

"Home. It has a sweet, comforting sound to it. Home."

"We go home, Mommie?" Ellie asked sleepily.

"No, honey. We're staying here in my home tonight."

"Oh, goodie." A moment later she was asleep in her father's arms.

Home.

The most wonderful word in the English language.

14

Logan literally tripped down the street, his face buried in the wool scarf around his neck. His world was right side up, and he was going home to his loving, devoted wife. His hold on his briefcase that held his laptop was fierce. The laptop was something he could not afford to lose. It was as necessary to his life as were his heart and lungs. He should have given some thought to getting one of those gizmos to shackle it to his wrist. As long as his hold was secure, the case was safe. He needed coffee. Lots and lots of coffee. Perhaps a pastry or two.

His steps were brisk in the crunchy snow. Aside from the fact that he was freezing his ass off, he felt wonderful. His financial affairs were in order. His medical examination was golden, and he was going back to the States. *The prodigal returns,* he thought gleefully.

Wind and sleet spit in his face as he continued his walk. He needed to get out of the cold. His blood had thinned with his years in Africa, and he hated the cold. He wondered if it was snowing back in Virginia.

A young woman as bundled up as he was, jostled him, her arms full of Christmas packages. She smiled as she muttered an apology. Logan nodded curtly. He smelled the rich pastries before he saw the shop. He sucked in the heady aroma and his step quickened.

The small shop was full, which meant he would have to lean up against the counter to wolf down the pastries and guzzle his three or four coffees. That was okay. Sooner or later, someone would get up from the row of stools. Nothing was going to sour this day.

Logan loosened the heavy wool scarf and unbuttoned his overcoat, mindful of the approving glances he was getting from the shopgirls on their midmorning break. He preened. In the last three weeks he'd dropped twelve pounds, had his hair lightened and trimmed, and managed to keep his deep tan with the help of a tanning bed in the hotel. His blue eyes were brighter than Paul Newman's along with thanks to a good optometrist and contact lenses. He looked good, and he knew it. He smiled at the shopgirls, who were flirting openly with him. He knew he could have any one of them by simply starting up a conversation on something as mundane as the weather. Unfortunately, today was the wrong day for fun and games. Today was the day he was leaving Zurich for the States. Today was the day he was heading home to his family. Back to his wife with all that glorious money. Back to his children, who probably hated his guts. Back to his next game plan.

Home for Christmas. Just the way he'd promised. Eight years late. So what! He'd never said what *year* he was going to return. He'd always been a man of his word. He hoped he would remember to put his wedding ring on once he got settled on the plane. That would be the first thing Kristine would look for.

Logan stared through the steamed-up window. It was snowing lightly. He had three hours to kill until it was time to leave for the airport. All he had to do was check out of the hotel, pay his bill, and grab a bite of lunch. By this time tomorrow he would be on American soil.

A frown built on Logan's forehead as all of the "what ifs" surfaced in his mind. He gave himself a mental kick. He should have run some kind of check on his wife and family so he knew ahead of time what he was walking into. He'd never been one to do anything on impulse. When you did things spontaneously, they always backfired. He'd learned early on to be precise, to map things out, go by the book. The book was always on target. A worm of fear crawled around his belly. It disappeared the moment one of the shopgirls smiled, and said, "Merry Christmas." He acknowledged the greeting with a wide grin. Nineteen if she was a day. Her eyes looked older and wiser than Danela's.

He'd been thinking of Danela a lot these past few weeks, wondering how she was doing and how many of the CPAs she'd fucked while on the safari. Was she in London now shopping? She'd land on her feet. The Danelas of the world always landed on their feet.

The pastry shop cleared suddenly. A blast of cold air whipped through the small shop, and Logan shivered as he moved to the last stool along the counter to get away from the arctic air. He held out his coffee cup for a refill and pointed to the strudel under the glass dome. He was uncertain as to why he was reluctant to leave the warm, fragrant shop.

For the first time in his life, Logan Kelly felt uncertain about what he was about to do. His thoughts turned to Danela. Was it even remotely possible that he had underestimated the voluptuous woman? He started to shake inside his heavy wool coat as he racked his brain for a mistake he'd made along the way. He needed both hands to hold the heavy coffee mug, the briefcase with his laptop clutched between his knees. What *was* she doing?

Danela peeled off her khaki jumpsuit, dropping it on the bedroom floor. All she wanted was a hot shower and to wash her hair. Afterward, she wanted a hot gardenia-scented bath with a glass of wine. Perhaps two glasses, maybe even the whole damn bottle, after which she would dress in a skintight minidress for the drive to the airport with her safari group. "Logan, are you here!" she yelled at the top of her lungs. Where the hell was he? "Logan," she called a second time. Where were the servants? Why was it so quiet? Her naked shoulders stiffened when she saw the empty vanity. Then her eyes narrowed until they resembled gun slits.

Naked, she ran back to the bedroom, where she opened drawers and closets. She knew to an item what should be where. Underwear, socks, tee shirts, and the winter clothing kept in garment bags were gone. She raced through the rest of the house, shouting and cursing, her heavy breasts bouncing against her rib cage.

In the kitchen she opened the refrigerator. Empty. The room was spotless. There was no mail on the kitchen counter. She picked up the phone to find it was disconnected. Not caring if anyone saw her or not, she went out to the car in the garage to use her cell phone. She dialed the office and waited, her bare foot kicking at the tires of her car. "Answer the phone, Logan," she hissed. "Damn you! Damn you to hell!" she spit. Then she heard Logan's recorded message. *"Jambo!* Due to circumstances beyond our control, Eberhart Safaris is now officially closed. Danela and I want to thank all our loyal customers for eight wonderful years. *Kwaheri!"*

"You son of a bitch!" Danela screamed as she stomped her way back to the bathroom, where she showered and washed her hair. Thirty minutes later, dressed in a khaki sundress, her wet hair piled into a knot on top of her head, she drove to the offices of Eberhart Safaris. She sucked in her breath when she saw that Logan's laptop was gone. The bottom desk drawer that was always locked was open but empty—the drawer where Logan kept things he didn't want her to see, things she'd always wondered about but had been afraid to tamper with.

Danela sat down with a thump in Logan's customized swivel chair. Everything Logan owned was either one of a kind or custom-made. She picked up the phone and listened for the dial tone. She called the bank, rattled off the number of her checking account. She held her breath while she listened to the response. She had $25,010 in her account. Her airline ticket to London stared up at her from the desk blotter. She cried then. Eight years gone.

Her five million dollars was gone. All she had to show for her time with Logan Kilpatrick was $25,010, an airline ticket, and the clothes in her closet. "You fucking son of a bitch!" she screamed. "How could you do this to me? How?"

She needed to get hold of herself. She still had one thing left to do. In the bathroom off the main office, Danela washed her face with cool water, soaking her eyes with a cool cloth so the CPAs wouldn't see she had been crying. If nothing else, she had some pride left. She was never going to see them again once she dropped them off at the airport. Like Logan said, who gives a good rat's ass! She plastered on makeup and spritzed perfume all over her body.

She needed a stiff drink. Her gaze went to the portable bar with the crystal decanters. An inch of scotch remained in one decanter. Not bothering to use a glass, Danela swigged from the ornate bottle until her eyes watered. "You stinking, lousy, prick! If I ever find you, I swear to God, I will personally carve off your balls!" she screamed to the empty room. She proceeded to rant and rave until she was too tired to open her mouth.

When the phone rang, Danela thought twice before she picked it up. Her voice was husky-sounding from all the crying she'd done. "*Jambo,*" she said.

"Danela, this is Stephen Douglas. We're ready to leave for the airport. Not that we want to leave, but duty calls. That safari, thanks to you, is something none of us will ever forget. You sound funny, is anything wrong?"

"Everything you can possibly imagine is wrong. My partner skipped out on me and left me holding the bag while we were gone. It's not your problem, Stephen. Give me twenty minutes, and I'll be there. Be sure all your baggage is properly tagged and have your airport tax money ready. I'm going to leave now, but I have to stop for gas."

Danela wiped at her tears. It was going to be so hard to say good-bye to all the accountants. They'd all been gentlemen and while they had flirted with her openly, none had crossed the line, and for that she was grateful. Now they were going to return to their homes and pick up their lives while she did what? How long was twenty-five thousand dollars going to last her? Should she stay here, hire on to one of the other companies, or leave Africa completely? At her age, her party-girl skills wouldn't be much of an asset to her. If she went to England, would she get a job as a shopgirl and live in a mean little flat with no hot water? Tears burned her eyes. "If I ever find you, Logan, I swear, I will kill you and then hack your body to pieces."

"Merry Christmas, Danela," she whispered.

Thirty minutes later, Danela slowed the safari bus to a smooth stop. She could see that the men were chattering like magpies. They were probably discussing her and feeling sorry for her.

Her head high, a forced smile on her lips, Danela climbed from the bus, the soft khaki dress swirling about her ankles as she walked around to the back of the bus to open the door. She tried for a cheerful tone when she said, "Pile in, gentlemen." They did as instructed, now strangely quiet.

"Danela, can we talk to you a minute?"

Still working on her light tone, she queried, "Okay, which one of you forgot your souvenirs?"

"That's not it. We want to delay our return for a day or so. If we pay the difference in our tickets, can it be arranged? A bribe . . ." Douglas let his words hang in the air.

"I suppose it can be arranged. What is it you want to do?"

"Help you."

"That's very kind of you, but it isn't necessary. I'll be all right."

"Do you have any money? Do you own anything? You said you're from Italy but hold dual citizenship. Do you have family there, here or in the States?"

"No to everything. I had five million dollars once. My partner managed to lose it all in the business."

"That's what we're talking about. We're number crunchers. It's what we do for a living. You must have a set of books. We want to go through them. Let us help you. It's the least we can do. You've given us a memory for a lifetime. We talked it over, and we're all in agreement. There's twenty-four of us. That means twenty-four sets of eyes. Let us do this for you."

"I'll manage. I'm not afraid to work. *Penye nai ipo nija.* That's Swahili for where there's a will there is a way. Seriously, you don't need to do this. I appreciate your offer, and I know your hearts are in the right place. Logan's gone, and so is the money. We'll never find him. He did it once before, but I was too stupid at the time to figure it out until it was too late. I loved him, so I wanted to believe in him. I had a premonition this was going to happen."

Douglas ignored her words. "We can camp out in your offices and leave tomorrow or the next day. You handle the plane reservations and all of us will go through your partner's books. There are books, aren't there?"

"Of a sort. Logan kept everything on the computer. I'm sure he wiped out the hard drive and has it all on disk. His laptop is gone. He never went anywhere without that damn thing. That should have been my first clue."

"Sometimes people think they're too smart for their own good. They *think* if they erase their files they're gone. There are ways to get them back, and Brian here is just the guy to go after them. He did a stint with the FBI for four years before going out on his own. If there are files to be found, he'll find them."

For the first time since returning to find Logan gone, Danela felt a sense of hope. Stephen was a nice man, the leader of the pack so to speak. All the others, young as well as the middle-aged accountants, seemed to defer to him. He was soft-spoken, with dark brown eyes and sandy hair. He was one of those rare people who looked better in glasses than without. He settled his safari hat more firmly on his head. "So, do we give it a go or what?"

Danela shrugged. "Logan is clever. He set this all up before we even left. I guess he had been planning it for a while. I would like to get my money back if that's possible. I'd settle for half. Okay, let's go for it."

"Let's get one thing straight. You never settle for half when you can get it all. Just so you know, we aren't a bunch of *schmucks*. We do the taxes for just about every important government official inside the Beltway. All of us are at a point in our business careers where we aren't taking on any new clients. You are the exception. We aren't even going to charge you." He laughed, and Danela grinned.

"Get in the bus! I'll show you where everything is and then I'll get us some food and drinks. It might be better if I go to the airport to change your reservations, so I'll need your tickets and passports."

Stephen looked at her closely. "Do you still love that guy?"

"I haven't loved him for a long time. Why do you ask?"

"I just like to have the whole picture. Your situation is going to be important when we find the money. Make no mistake. We will find it. However," he said, holding up a warning hand, "finding it doesn't mean you'll be able to get to it. At that point we'll switch to Plan B. Don't ask me what that is at this moment, because I don't know."

Danela blushed when Stephen winked at her. She couldn't remember ever blushing in her entire life. "All right, here we are. I'll show you where everything is, and I'll leave you to do whatever you have to do. It's been a long time since anyone has done anything for me. If I don't seem grateful, forgive me. I have to be honest with you. When Logan told me I had to go on safari with your group, I fought him. I didn't want to go. I think even then, in my heart, I knew he was planning this. For whatever it's worth, I just wanted you to know that."

"You were kind of cranky the first day out," Stephen

grinned. "From here on in, it's slow and steady wins the race. How do you say that in Swahili?"

Danela laughed so hard she doubled over, tears streaming down her cheeks. *"Pole pole ndio mwendo."*

"Pretty pricey digs you have here."

"Don't be impressed. They aren't paid for. They'll probably repossess everything in the next week or so. Same thing goes for the house and cars. Everything was on paper."

"And you never questioned it?"

"I did, but it didn't do me any good. I'm in a third-world country with no money. I had no choice once the money was gone."

The next hour was spent setting up shop and rearranging furniture. Old dusty ledgers and boxes of bills and receipts were pulled from a storage closet. Yellow legal pads and sharpened pencils found their way to the center of Logan's desk. The two computers were turned on. From that point on Danela became invisible to the accountants. She backed quietly out of the office. No one noticed.

In the van she had a bad moment when she thought about the twenty-five thousand dollars and the airline ticket. Should she have confessed? Of course she should have, but she didn't, so she would live with it. What would they find, if anything? And what good would it do her? Logan was gone. Banks in Switzerland didn't give out information. She should know, she'd tried often enough. She wasn't going to get her hopes up. These men, nice as they were, were no match for Logan. In all these years, Kristine had never been able to find him. In the end she would be no different. Still, it was nice to know there were some good people in the world, people willing to help others.

Tears dripped down Danela's cheeks as she drove along. She needed to go to the airport to see about changing the plane reservations. When that was done she would go to the grocer's so she could prepare food. While it was cooking she would ransack the house to look for clues. In her heart she knew she wouldn't find any. Logan was too smart to leave clues. There wouldn't be so much as a matchstick lying around. She suddenly felt sorry for the faceless Kristine.

So many lies.

It was past sundown when Danela loaded the safari bus with all the food she'd prepared. The beer was an extravagance, but she didn't care. Her personal checking account now carried a zero balance. She didn't care. She still had the $25,010 in her savings account. Plus she had the water jug full of quarters. She'd been surprised that Logan hadn't emptied it. Silver was heavy, and Logan liked to travel light.

"He should have left me a note," Danela muttered as she shifted gears in the bus. "What goes around comes around, Logan," she continued to mutter.

No one paid the slightest attention to her as she set up the folding table with the food. They continued to ignore her when she said, "You need to eat this while it's warm." She filled her own plate and walked outside with it to sit on a bench in the cool evening air. With nothing else to occupy her, she thought about her life and how she'd ended up here in this third-world country with a man who'd robbed her blind. A man she'd been a fool to trust. *Love is blind,* she told herself. *Especially one-sided love.* She'd known in her heart that Logan didn't love her the way she'd loved him. She'd been stupid and naive to think she had enough love for the both of them. Love just didn't work that way.

In the beginning it had just been sexual romps. Logan's sexual appetites were as insatiable as her own. The day he found out about her five million dollars, things changed. He'd dogged her then, buying her flowers, candy, taking her to dinner and concerts and always the lovemaking afterward. The wild lust had tamed to sweet, gentle lovemaking. He'd started to talk about marriage and going into business. Partners for life, he'd said. Togetherness twenty-four hours a day. She'd been so delirious she didn't think twice about handing over her money. The only thing she'd truly homed in on were the words, partners for life.

It was everything Logan said it would be for the first few years. It had soured gradually, so gradually, she hadn't been able to pinpoint the time or the place when she knew it was all going bad. She would have gotten out then, but they were so far in debt, according to Logan, she couldn't bail out. Third-world countries weren't fond of people who didn't live up to their promises. He'd scared the wits out of her when he spoke about African prisons and what they did to white women. He'd never said what they did to white American men, and she hadn't asked. Stupid, stupid, stupid.

And yet she'd been willing to marry Logan. Of course it was a lie. Had she seen through it? Did she just want to believe it so the rest would be more palatable? It was Logan's way of getting her to go on the safari so he could pack up and leave. The twenty-five thousand dollars was the kiss-off, an expression Logan had used when he left Kristine. Now she felt even more empathy for the faceless Kristine.

The watch on Danela's wrist chirped. She looked down. Eleven o'clock. She debated about going back indoors to hand out the airline tickets and passports. She looked through the window to see the accountants working industriously. Maybe she should just curl up into a ball and go to sleep. When and if they finished, they would wake her. Or, she could sit here, smoke, and plot Logan's death a hundred different ways, each more painful than the last.

Danela fumbled in the dark for her package of cigarettes. Smoking was relatively new for her and a nasty habit at that. She'd taken up the habit when the stress Logan caused her became unbearable. She blew a luscious smoke ring. "Kiss me off with twenty-five grand, will you? Somehow, some way, I'm going to see your ass fry in hell, Logan. It might take me a while, but I'm going to do it," she mumbled.

The door behind her opened. "Danela, could you come inside for a minute? By the way, thanks for all the food. It was delicious. We need to ask you some questions."

"I need to talk to you, too. Logan left me twenty-five thousand dollars. I guess it was my kiss-off present. I should have told you that earlier. I guess I was so rattled with what went on it slipped my mind. I suppose it's Logan's contribution to my old-age fund." There, she'd confessed, and she felt better already.

"I know about that. In this day and age it won't take you very far. Who set up all these ledgers?"

"I did. I didn't know anything about computers back then, and Logan didn't want to teach me. I tried to be as accurate as possible. I even set up folders with receipts and filed them by date."

"The safari business is very lucrative, according to your files."

"It's a five-million-dollar-a-year business. But it's only as good as the people you have working for you. You also need to pay your bills. Your reputation is paramount. It was really good in the beginning. Money came in faster than we could count it."

"Where is it? Do you have any idea?"

"Switzerland at the moment. The only monies are from your safari. Logan didn't trust the banks here. He was banking in Zurich when I met him. He could wire money in and out in minutes. He had everthing set up on his computer. As far as I know he never called the banks directly from the offices or the house. I handled the phone bills and would have seen the toll calls. He did everything by computer. He was a wizard when it came to things like that."

"If he didn't want you to know your true financial situation, why did he allow you to keep books?"

"To give me something to do. I liked seeing how well we were doing. We made back our investment at the end of the second year. As you said, the safari business was very lucrative."

"It started to go sour in the fourth year. What happened?"

"Logan got cocky. He started acting like a drill sergeant and a five-star general. He wanted longer hours from our workers with no extra compensation. He was neither kind nor gentle. We lost all our good people. He started cutting corners, shortchanging the clients. Word of mouth was half our business. Twice he canceled tours at the eleventh hour. Our safari cruisers started breaking down. It was everything all at once. Logan didn't seem to care. He was fed up with Africa. He used to talk a lot about how this had always been his dream to live here and run a lucrative business. Then he started calling it a nightmare. We managed to hang on for a while and keep our heads above water, but we owed everybody. Logan didn't care. He left it to me to make all the empty promises. When your travel agent called, Logan was beside himself. He kept saying it was our chance to get back on top. I was so stupid, I went along with it. He just wasn't the man I thought he was," she said sadly.

"Do you mind me asking where your five million dollars came from?"

"A friend. Actually, Maurice was the only true friend I ever had. He was much older than me. He treated me like a daughter at first, then over the years it became a more intimate relationship. I was very fond of him, and he was fond of me. We had a very good life together. He passed away shortly before I met Logan. I lost a wonderful friend when Maurice died. I was trying to decide what to do with my life when a lawyer sought me out and said the family wanted to give me some money so that I would never cause a scandal. I never would have done something like that. I accepted the money. I banked it, got a job as a hostess in an upscale restaurant. That's where I met Logan. He swept me off my feet. It was a rebound kind of thing. It's my own stupid fault. I thought he loved me. I thought we were building a life together. I really don't want to talk about this anymore, Stephen. Tell me what it is you need to know."

"Well, Brian is a hair away from retrieving all the records that Logan deleted. If he's successful, we're going to need his password. Do you have any idea what it might be?"

"None. I'm the last person he would tell something like that to."

"Am I right that Logan put eight million dollars into the business?"

"Yes. I put in five, and we borrowed another six or seven from the banks."

"So, we're literally talking twenty-one million dollars."

"More or less," Danela said, an edge in her voice. "If you're trying to find some nice way to tell me it's gone, I know that."

"It's not gone. It's sitting in a bank somewhere. My guess would be a numbered account in Switzerland. That's if your books are accurate."

"They are painstakingly accurate. I made sure of that. I even listed a postage stamp if I bought it. I might be a fool when it comes to men, but I'm not stupid. Dumb yes, but not stupid. Okay, okay, so I was stupid, too. I told you, I believed in him, loved him back then."

"You realize you're liable for the bank loans, don't you?"

"Logan pointed that out to me on a monthly basis. Are you saying I have to give the banks the twenty-five thousand dollars?"

"No, I'm not saying that at all. What I need from you is anything at all you can remember about Logan. Any small detail, no matter how insignificant you might think it is. Brian is one of the best computer hackers I've ever come across. If there's a way to find your partner, he's the man who can do it. You've got two state-of-the-art computer systems, so that will make his work easier. Let's sit down and talk. You talk and I'll listen."

Danela poured herself a cup of cold coffee before she

settled herself in Logan's chair. When the sun could be seen creeping over the horizon, she got up, stretched and looked down at Stephen Douglas to see what impact her words had on him. "I don't think I left anything out. Did any of it help?"

"I wish I was a private detective. I'm sure there are things you said that are definite clues, but I don't know what they are. Probably everything he told you was a direct lie. It's the little things along the way that give a person away. We know he was married with children. It's iffy if he's divorced. He was a career military man. A full bird colonel. He has a very noticeable scar on his lower abdomen that he says was an appendectomy but is suspect in your opinion. He never spoke about his wife or children. He kept no personal papers or files either at the office or at home. We have to assume he had a safety deposit box somewhere. You say nothing of any importance ever came in the mail for him. His explanation for the eight million dollars was an inheritance from his family. We know he's American but where he actually lived and grew up is uncertain. You believe the name Kilpatrick is an alias but that Logan is his real first name. Does that about cover it?"

Danela felt like crying. She nodded. "Sad, isn't it?"

"Did he ever talk about his parents or siblings? Did you ever have a sense of him living on the East Coast as opposed to the Midwest?"

"Once he said his parents always liked to go to the nation's capital to see the cherry blossoms. I think there was a festival or a parade or something in the spring. He said they went every year. He said he never understood the attraction. Once you saw the blossoms they were the same every year. When he got older, his parents left him behind and he didn't have to, as he put it, trudge alongside of them as they ooohed and aaahed over the trees."

"That might narrow things a little. A trip every year would lead you to believe the family didn't live too far from the capital. That would place him on the East Coast or the tip of one of the Southern states."

"He was a farm boy with chores. He hated chores. That's why I believed him when he said Kristine lived in the Midwest."

"Did he have any hobbies? There are farms in Virginia and the Carolinas."

"Only if you count reading. He loved to read. Sometimes he would stay up all night reading. We got fifteen or twenty magazines a month. He read them all from cover to cover. He read newspapers the same way. He was very knowledgeable."

"Friends?"

"None that I know of."

"By the way, I almost forgot, how did you make out with our plane reservations?"

"You leave tonight at eleven o'clock. Switching up like this gives you two extra stops with only a fifty-dollar charge when you check in. It was the best I could do."

"That's good. We'll be done here long before that. We were talking among ourselves a little while ago, Danela. How would you like to return to the States with us?"

"Oh, I couldn't! What would I do there?"

"We'll find you a job and an apartment. I think the job market might be a little better in the States. You have a valid passport, don't you?"

"Yes. Why would you do this for me?" Going to the United States was something she'd always wanted to do. Logan had shot down that idea the moment she broached it by saying she'd last exactly one week because all Americans were crazy. Then he went on to tell her about the muggings, the knifings, the killings, and the carjackings that went on even in small cities.

"Just because we want to help you. Look, we were booked on one of your competitor's safaris and they canceled on us. The travel agent called everyone she could think of. No one would take us on. Yeah, we would have gotten our money back but even if we could find some other safari to take us, it would have been February at the earliest. But after New Year's, the shit hits the fan and we don't have time to take a deep breath until April sixteenth. We eat on the run, sleep in snatches, and work our asses off. You gave us a hell of a once-in-a-lifetime memory. The fact that you were so nice and went that extra mile for us didn't hurt either. To you, because you've done it hundreds of times, it's old hat. We'll never do it again. We're all taking home a memory we'll never forget. What kind of people would we be if we left you here to flounder? That's just not who we are, Danela. If I were you, I'd take that twenty-five grand out of the bank before they confiscate it. So, what's your answer?"

"Oh, yes. Yes, I would love to go to the United States. What about"—she waved her hands about—"all of this?"

"You leave all of this to us. Pack your things, get your ticket, go to the bank and come back here. We need some more food and coffee, too."

Danela literally danced her way out to the safari bus. "Thank You, God. Thank You so much. I didn't mean it when I said I would kill Logan. Maybe I'll just cripple him."

When Danela returned to the office with lunch it was past one o'clock. The accountants were waiting for her, sprawled every which way in the cramped offices. She passed out thick sandwiches, potato fritters, pickles, and coffee. "Are you finished?" she asked hesitantly.

"We've done as much as we can do here. We photocopied everything from the ledgers. I can give you the short version and then the long one on the plane. Brian here is the brains of this outfit, so I think I'm going to let him explain what we've found out."

Brian Lucas ran his fingers through his hair, his eyes wild. "First things first. I want you at the airport when I start hacking this computer. What I'm going to do is very, as in very, illegal. It's imperative that you be nowhere around here while I'm doing this. You are going to need witnesses who can say you were at the airport. Leave the bus for us. You take a taxi or, if you have a car, use it and leave it at the airport. A taxi driver will log the time. Mention time, look at your watch. Stop for gas, again, look at your watch, mention time. This is your business and you're a full partner. Anything that goes down here will make you liable, but not if you aren't here. As soon as we get the information we need, I'll crash the hard drive. I'll overnight the disks from the airport just in case some overzealous cop gets called in by the Defense Department or the banking industry. I know diddly squat about how this country operates. I'm going to do it right before we leave for the airport. I've got everything all set up. Are you following me?''

"More or less. What exactly are you going to hack into?" Danela asked.

"The military's files. I'm going to find out who Logan Kilpatrick is. I can access his medical records as soon as I find out who he is exactly. I'm doing it by sections of the country. If he was a full bird, that cuts down my work. If I can figure out his password, I can crack his bank account and get an address for him. That's where you come in, Danela. You need to give me words, phrases, things that might be helpful. Without his password all we can find out is his military background and where his ex-wife and children live. We won't find him. Now, start thinking.''

Danela's voice was full of awe. "You can do all that?"

"And more," Brian said proudly. "Hell, kids hack into the DOD all the time. *Anything* is possible in this computer age. You just don't want to get caught. Okay," he said, flexing his fingers, "start talking.''

"It could be a word in Swahili. Try Kristine. That was his wife's name. I never knew the names of his children. Try dream. Coming to Africa was a dream of his since he was a boy. Maybe it's bird or colonel. Lord, I don't know. Sex. Scotch. Trust no one.''

Two hours later, Brian called a break. "We're trying too hard. Usually it's a word that is common. Something obvious. You knew the man, Danela, think.''

"I am thinking. Jasmine. He loved the scent of it. He liked gardenia, too. He hated snow but he loved to walk in the rain. He loved the rainy season here. Reading, books. Magazines. Print."

At four-thirty, frustrated with her inability to contribute what was needed, Danela, said, "*National Geographic.* Logan loved that magazine. He said he used to snitch them from the library at school. Try school or library."

"Bingo! That's it! We are in, ladies and gentlemen! Lookee here!" Brian chortled.

The accountants and Danela crowded around the computer. "Here's your money, Danela. I say we move it out right now."

"Nah. Let's let it sit for a while. We don't want to tip our hand. If he's the kind of guy I think he is, he's going to be checking that account on a daily basis. We need to get Danela set up somewhere safe first. Twenty-two million dollars is a hell of a lot of money," Stephen said happily. "I wonder who it *really* belongs to."

"Not him, that's for sure," Danela said. "I can't believe you found my money. Merciful God, how can I ever thank you? What was the word, library or school?"

"Neither. It was NatGeo, for *National Geographic.* I told you this guy could do it!" Stephen said, giving Brian a high five. "It's a hell of a Christmas present, Danela. Once we get to the States and wire that money out, you are going to need one first-class estate planner, and we know the best."

Danela started to cry. "I'm sorry, I'm just overwhelmed. I never thought I'd see that money ever again."

"We're going to deduct the interest, too. So, it's more than five million." Brian chortled. "I wish I could see that bastard's face when he pulls up his account only to find it five mil short. This, ladies and gentlemen, goes under the heading of a good day's work."

"Hear, hear!"

"Okay, Danela, head for the airport and remember what I told you. We'll see you in a few hours."

Danela walked around the room kissing each of the accountants, effusive thanks bubbling from her lips. When she got to Stephen, she said, "You are a very kind man, Stephen. Perhaps someday I can do something just as wonderful for you. Merry Christmas, everyone."

They watched her leave, broad smiles on their faces. "I don't know why or how I know this, but that guy is headed Stateside. Trust me on this," Brian said.

"I say we clean out the prick's entire account except for $25,010. Let him see how it feels. All in favor, say aye!" one of the accountants said.

"It's a thought."

"We could go to jail for this, not to mention losing our licenses," Stephen said quietly.

"That's true, Oh Mighty Leader," Brian said. "Who is your money on, him or us? Somebody on the run like the colonel ain't going to squawk too loud, especially if he's on the run. All we're doing is looking for an address, a way to track him down. We'll deal with the bank and Danela's money when we know more. He's probably already figuring his next angle. As sure as I'm sitting here, I know he's heading Stateside. By the time we get on that plane tonight, his future is in our very capable hands. You interested in Danela, Stephen?"

"Shut up and take a nap," Stephen said. *I could be,* was his last conscious thought before drifting into an uneasy sleep.

15

❦

Logan signed the Hyatt's registration form with a flourish: Justin Eberhart. He looked around the gaily decorated lobby trying to remember if this grand hotel was on Capitol Hill the last time he was Stateside. He rather thought it wasn't. He smiled at the desk clerk as he reached for the card keys to his room.

"How long will you be staying with us, Mr. Eberhart?" the pretty clerk asked, an interested look in her eyes.

"My business should take me a month. Right now I need to do some last-minute Christmas shopping."

"We have some excellent shops in the hotel, sir. The gift wrapping is exquisite. Enjoy your stay."

Logan tipped the bellboy generously before he closed and locked the door to his suite of rooms. First things first. He withdrew the small folder with the extra card key and the key to the safe that stood alongside the portable bar. The computer disks with all his banking information were nestled inside a padded manila envelope. His touch was just short of reverent when he placed the envelope inside the safe, locked it, and pocketed the key. It would never do to keep the disks at the farmhouse, and taking the room for a whole month was something he'd planned on the long flight. Not only was it essential to his plan, but he might want some privacy at some point along the way. Kristine had a bad habit of smothering him, wanting to be at his side twenty-four hours of the day. There was no reason to believe her habits had changed over the years.

If anything, with his return, she would be even more affectionate, more cloying, more suffocating.

For now all he wanted was a nice hot shower, some food, and a short nap. After that he would peruse the shops in the hotel, make arrangements for limo service out to the farm for tomorrow, and *voilà!* life would start all over again. His way.

An hour later, Logan pushed the luncheon cart through the door to the hallway. While it didn't clutter up the suite of rooms, it didn't fit the decor. He liked things neat and tidy. He double-locked the door, removed the terry robe the hotel provided, and slid naked between the crisp clean sheets. He took a moment to warn himself to sleep no more than two hours. From long years of habit and training, he would wake precisely on time. As he drifted into sleep he tried to remember what Kristine looked like. All he could see was Danela's flaming red hair and deep green eyes. His right eye started to twitch. Danela was no passive Kristine. Danela was piss and vinegar, fire and flames, whereas Kristine was shy and quiet, eager to please and not the least bit experimental. A total wet blanket.

A long time later, Logan rolled over, his long tanned legs thrashing the bedcovers. Even in his sleep he knew his eyes were twitching, a sign that things weren't going the way he wanted them to go. He groaned in his sleep as he strutted up and down the parade grounds clad in his dress uniform, the stars on his shoulders gleaming in the noonday sun. In his gloved hands was the book he lived by, the book the others on the parade grounds tried to ignore.

"You're out of sync," he roared.

"So who gives a good rat's ass," Mike roared back.

"I care. That's all you need to know. You are not performing up to expectation."

Mike broke ranks. "I'm outta here. Stuff this drill, and, while you're at it, shove that book!"

"Get your ass back in line, Mike," Logan roared again.

Cala and Tyler followed Mike off the parade grounds while Kristine stood at attention. She snapped off a brisk salute. "I can always count on you, can't I, Kristine?"

"Yes, Logan, you can always count on me. Who is that redhead sitting in the stands waving the flag?"

"For God's sake, Kristine, do I have to do your thinking for you? Don't you have a mind of your own? It's Rita Hayworth."

"Rita Hayworth is dead, Logan. She died a long time ago. Why are you saying she's sitting in the stands? Why are you lying to me? Do you know that woman?"

"Of course I know her. Don't ever call me a liar, Kristine."

"I'm sorry, Logan. Do you like her better than you like me?"

"What was that, Kristine?"

"Nothing. Why is she watching us?"

"Because I want her to. Any other questions?"

"Is she your lover?"

"She was. I decided you are my one true love. That's why I came home. Do you forgive me, Kristine?"

"Of course. I love you, Logan."

"I thought you did. I came back because I knew you needed me. I'm glad you aren't independent like Danela."

"I thought you said it was Rita Hayworth."

"I said she looks like Rita Hayworth. You are so stupid, Kristine. I don't know how we're ever going to make this work again. Maybe it was a mistake for me to come back."

"Oh, no, Logan, it wasn't a mistake. Please don't leave again. I need you. I'll do whatever you want."

The woman in the stands ran down the steps to the ground, the flag waving in the brisk breeze. "Steal my money will you, you son of a bitch! He's a thief. He stole your money, too, and you forgave him! You must be the stupidest female on the face of the earth. All he wants is the rest of your money. He lies and cheats and steals. You can't trust him. Don't trust him, Kristine! He robbed me of all my money, so I was stuck with him. Run, Kristine, run to your children. Run! You have to get away. If you don't go now, you will be lost forever.''

Danela raced up to Logan, she whipped the flag through the air, and ran around him, totally wrapping him in the flag, immobilizing him.

"Run, Kristine, run!" she screamed.

Logan beat at the covers, pushing the pillows to the side as he gasped for air. He was drenched with his own body sweat, the sheets soaking wet. He swung his legs over the side of the bed as he struggled with a pounding headache.

His head dropped to his hands. *I never get headaches. I never dream either. Is this a harbinger of things to come?*

Danela was going to be a problem, he thought as he stepped under the shower once more. It wasn't just the dream. He knew in his gut he'd underestimated his former lover. Danela was no Kristine. He needed to give some serious thought to her. A phone call would not be out of order. He needed a sense of what she was going through. He could handle her anger, but her deviousness was something else. Something he should have paid more attention to. Twenty-five thousand dollars wouldn't buy him a scintilla of loyalty where she was concerned. He was definitely not running on all his cylinders. How the hell had he managed to screw that one up? Greed. Pure and simple.

What he needed right now was a couple of stiff belts in the bar and some lively conversation before he took on the dreary task of Christmas shopping for his ungrateful children and adoring wife.

Logan eyed the stunning blonde with admiration. He'd seen her earlier in the lobby and then again in the bar. Their eyes had met in the lobby; hers were as approving as his were at the time. He tried to ignore the old man in the wheelchair with the portable oxygen tank. His eyes bored into the back of the blonde's head, willing her to turn around. She did, and smiled. He nodded, a smile working at the corners of his mouth. He signaled for the waitress and ordered a bottle of Dom Pérignon to be sent to her table.

Father and daughter?

Ridiculous.

Rich old man and young woman? Rich old dying man and middle-aged woman who still looked good and was a nurse?

A possibility.

Husband and wife?

Too stupid a thought even to consider.

The woman turned and smiled in thanks for the wine. Logan nodded. He waited, sensing her indecision. Finally she crooked her finger for him to join them.

"Justin Eberhart," he said, using his alias. He held out his hand to the man in the wheelchair, who seemed oblivious to his outstretched hand.

"Maureen and Stedman Clovis. My husband's eyesight isn't the best, Mr. Eberhart. He elected not to have surgery to remove the cataracts. He knows you're here, though. It was very kind of you to send over the Dom. It's my favorite."

"Call it a Christmas present."

"I love Christmas," Maureen said. "So does Stedman."

"The venture capitalist? That Stedman Clovis?"

Maureen smiled. "The one and only. And you are Justin Eberhart."

"From Africa," Logan said without missing a beat. "I operate a safari business. I'm here half on holiday and half on business. It's a little lonely when you don't know anyone. Do you live inside the Beltway?"

"We live all over the world. Stedman wanted to come back here for the holidays." Maureen lowered her voice to a hushed whisper. "He loves the music, the decorations, and the hustle and bustle of the holidays. He especially likes the tree in the lobby. He could sit and stare at it for hours."

"And you? Do you like the holidays, too?"

"Love them to death," Maureen gushed. "Stedman wants me to buy out the stores. I willingly oblige."

Logan leaned over to inspect the shine on his shoes. He whispered, "Does he talk at all? I feel like we're ignoring him."

"Stedman has emphysema, and it's difficult for him to talk. He prefers to sit and watch what's going on around him. It's almost time for me to take him upstairs for his medicine. I usually read to him from one of the daily newspapers until he falls asleep. His nurse takes over from there."

"He must be grateful for your devotion."

"I'm the grateful one, Mr. Eberhart." Maureen's voice rose slightly. "My years with Stedman have been the happiest of my life. No one could want or ask for more," she said as she brought Stedman's bony, clawlike hand to her lips. She kissed it as she massaged it, the diamonds on her hand winking under the recessed lighting.

Logan felt disgust at the sight. He wondered just how rich the venture capitalist was. All he had to do was call the reference desk at any library and he could find out in ten minutes. That's what he would do first thing in the morning. Christmas Eve or not.

"That's wonderful," Logan said as he slipped his card key onto her lap. He sucked in his breath as he waited for her response. Either she'd let the card drop to the floor or she'd slip it up the sleeve of her dress. She did neither, letting the small piece of plastic lie on her thigh.

"Tell Stedman and me about Africa. It's one of the few places we haven't been. Perhaps when Stedman is more robust," she said vaguely, her gaze sweeping the room to come to rest on Logan. "Safaris sound so interesting. All those lovely wild animals."

Logan was like a wound-up toy as he talked, careful to address his dissertation to Stedman Clovis, who stared at him with unblinking intensity.

"It sounds wonderful, doesn't it, Stedman?" Maureen said.

"I think it's time for me to call it a day," Logan said. "It was nice meeting and talking with you both. Perhaps we'll see one another again before I leave to return to Africa. It's been a long thirty-six hours, and I'm not as young as I used to be. Jet lag," he said as an afterthought. He waited an extra moment to see if the card key would be returned. It stayed right where it was, on the lovely Maureen's luscious thigh.

"Look, Stedman, it's snowing again. I could go up and get your muffler and shawl and we could go outside for a bit. Mr. Eberhart can keep you company. Would you like that?"

Stedman Clovis turned to look out the window. Maureen took that moment to hike her skirt a little higher so she could slip the card into the top of her stocking.

Garter belt. Logan smirked. He did love garter belts.

The old man turned to face his wife. His skeletal head bobbed from side to side on his stem of a neck. Maureen sighed. "Then I guess we'll say good night, too, Mr. Eberhart. It was nice meeting you. Merry Christmas."

"The same to you," Logan said.

Upstairs in his suite, Logan looked at his watch. It was eight-thirty. Ms. Maureen Clovis would be here by ten at the latest. He was so sure of it, his fist shot upward. He still had it. He'd never had to do more than snap his fingers and women were his for the taking.

Logan picked up the phone to call for room service. He ordered two bottles of Dom Pérignon, caviar, fresh strawberries and cream. "Send them up at nine-forty-five," he said.

With nothing to occupy his time, Logan picked up the Virginia telephone directory. His hands trembled slightly when he flipped to the K's. There it was, K. Kelly and the number. He read the instructions on the phone before he pressed a 1 then an 8 and finally the number. A chill ran up his spine when he heard his wife's cheerful voice. He hung up immediately. He looked down at his arms to see goose bumps dotting his flesh. He started to shake then and didn't know why. Kristine had no right to sound so damn cheerful. No right at all. His hand snaked out to reach for the phone. He drew it back just as quickly. No point in tipping his hand. This feeling, whatever it was, would pass. It was just the shock of hearing his wife's voice and the excitement of seeing Maureen Clovis naked in his bed.

Logan sprawled on the king-size bed. His thoughts weren't on his wife or the lovely Maureen; they were on Danela. Where was she, what was she doing? He reached for the phone, then remembered he'd had the house phone disconnected. She certainly wouldn't be in the offices at four-thirty in the morning. She was probably in England blowing the twenty-five grand with no thought for what the future held for her.

Christ Almighty, am I getting soft in my old age? What is the fascination with Danela all of a sudden? Did he care for her more than he would admit to himself? Or, was it something else? More like fear. He shivered. Danela was like a smoking gun. Maybe she wasn't going to go quietly. Maybe he made a mistake in kissing her off so nastily. He wondered just how pissed off she was. Why was Danela bothering him like this? He was half a world away. What in the damn hell could she do to him?

Fear was a terrible thing.

Fear was something he'd never really experienced before.

He felt it now.

The spandex dress was so tight, Logan wondered how she moved. He risked a glance at his watch: 9:57. Right on schedule. He wondered why the thought didn't please him. "I wasn't sure you'd come. You didn't seem interested."

"You're very brazen. I like that. I love taking risks. It makes it so much more exciting. I love excitement."

"You remind me of a sleek alley cat," Logan said.

"You remind me of a tomcat on the prowl. I hope you're worth it," Maureen said as she started to remove her jewelry.

"What if your husband wakes up? Will anyone come looking for you?"

"Hardly. That's why we have a nurse. Stedman won't wake until eight tomorrow morning. I will make sure I am in my bed at that time. I don't get up until he's been made ready for the day. It's a depressing business."

"I bet it is," Logan said as he yanked off his Rolex. "Do you do this often?" he asked.

"Every chance I get, which isn't often enough. You do have protection, don't you? One can't be too careful these days."

"Of course." Like he really wanted to pick up some horrible venereal disease or, worse yet, AIDS.

"Then let's get to it. I have until seven tomorrow morning."

Logan wasn't sure why he felt put off by her words. His face must have given something away. Maureen was half-crouched over, undoing the buckle on one of her spike-heeled shoes. "Having second thoughts?"

"No. Most women aren't so . . . blunt."

"I'm not most women as you will find out. I came here to have sex with you. You gave me your card key because you wanted to have sex with me. You're here, I'm here, so let's get to it."

The erection Logan had moments earlier was a spongy mess in his shorts. "Let's have some champagne first."

"Is that your way of saying you can't get it up, and I'm going to have to work for it? If that's the case, it might be better if I leave right now."

"That is not the case. I will admit to one thing. I haven't been with a woman in a while. I had a seduction planned. It's that simple. There's more to sex than in and out. That's what rabbits do. Obviously, you aren't too choosy about your bed partners, while I—on the other hand—am choosy. Show me what you have going for you while I pour the wine."

"If we're going to do show-and-tell, I'd like to see your merchandise. We can take it from there. That whipped cream really isn't for the strawberries, is it?"

"No, it isn't."

"That's an awful lot of whipped cream," Maureen said.

"Yes, it is."

She looked every bit as good as he thought she would. Her breasts were high and firm, her waist tiny, her thighs hard and muscular. His dick shot straight in the air.

"Bravo!" Maureen said, clapping her hands. "Lick me all over," she said, grabbing a handful of the whipped cream to rub on her breasts and belly.

"Save some for me," Logan managed to croak.

"What's your feeling on blueberry syrup?" She giggled.

"Pretty sticky mess if you want my opinion," Logan gasped.

"The best is lick-off chocolate cream. I order it by the case."

"Jesus."

"Next time we'll use it," Maureen said.

Logan, his face mashed between Maureen's breasts, managed to say, "Is there going to be a next time?"

"You said you were going to be in town for a month. So are we." She moaned as Logan's tongue worked its way downward. Logan managed to reach for one of the luscious strawberries and jammed it in her mouth. She spit it out. "I'd rather suck other things."

"Then do it!"

She did.

Maureen pulled the spandex dress over her head and smoothed it down over her hips. "You were real good, lover. So, shall we do it again?"

"I'll call you. It's not like I'm going to be here in this hotel twenty-four hours a day. I told you, I'm here on business. That means I have to entertain and be entertained. I've got the whole state of Virginia to cover. At last count there were over a thousand travel agencies to meet with," he lied smoothly. "There's voice mail here, so leave me a message and I'll get back to you."

"You're making this sound like an . . . *arrangement,*" Maureen said.

"That's exactly what it is. You're married," Logan said, virtue ringing in his voice. "Just how sick is your husband?"

"He was supposed to be dead three years ago," Maureen snapped. "Not long, to answer your question."

"Then what will you do?" Logan asked. "Are you sure you're going to be provided for when the end comes."

"That's all been taken care of. We settled things before we got married. I get everything. Why do you ask?" Maureen snapped again.

"I'd hate to think you were screwing me for my money."

"Fat chance. I'll probably inherit more money than you could earn in your safari business in ten lifetimes. Maybe fifty lifetimes."

"Inherit, Maureen. That's the keyword. Your husband could hang on for another five years."

"So?"

"So nothing. I just protect my interests. Just don't be so sure you have more money than I do. That's all I'm trying to say. I like things out in the open from the git-go."

"Consider it out in the open. If you call me and leave a message, say you're Harry Winston the jeweler. Stedman never answers the phone, but the nurse does, and she tells him everything. It was a great night. Have a Merry Christmas."

"You too."

Logan waited until the door closed before he got up to engage the security lock. He needed a few hours of uninterrupted sleep before he was ready to return to his wife and children.

* * *

Right on schedule, Logan rolled off the bed onto the floor. He snapped to wakefulness as he eyed the messy room.

Lust was a terrible thing.

Ninety minutes later, the room was tidy, the cart with the remainder of the flat champagne, the wilted strawberries, and the empty container of whipped cream was in the hallway. He was showered, shaved, dressed, reading the day's edition of *USA Today* and sipping strong black coffee. Later he would go downstairs for a full breakfast. For the moment he was content to relax with his coffee and paper and plan his trip to the farm.

Logan's mind drifted over the financial section of the paper until he remembered he was going to call the library to see what he could find out about Stedman Clovis. When he hung up the phone his eyes glittered. One woman with all that money. It was almost impossible to comprehend.

Because the phone was still in his hand, Logan pressed the numbers to Maureen's suite. He held his breath as her voice came over the wire. "I just wanted to thank you for a memorable night. I thought about sending you flowers but decided that might be suspect. I've been working on my schedule for the week after Christmas. If you're amenable, I'd like to take you to dinner and perhaps a little dancing. I'm a romantic, what can I say."

"I'd love to see the bracelet. Perhaps we can arrange something between Christmas and New Year's. I'll speak to Stedman. You know I never buy anything without his approval. I'm sure we can work out a convenient time. If you're willing to come to the hotel, that's even better. This way Stedman can be with us. Perhaps luncheon. Thank you so much for calling. I look forward to meeting with you."

"I do too, baby."

The smirk stayed on Logan's face until he finished

reading the paper from front to back. He even read his horoscope: *You are in the catbird seat today.*

He really was.

Logan opened the drapes to a world that was so white it was blinding. What was this going to do to his trip to Leesburg? Damn, he should have thought about the snow. He did his best to peer out the sides of the window to try and gauge the amount of snow on the ground. A lot. No limo driver would chance this. *Where in the hell am I going to get a four-wheel drive on Christmas Eve? Goddamn it, why didn't I turn on the television?*

A minute later he had the phone book in his hand and open to the yellow pages. His voice was frantic even to his own ears when he dialed one car dealer after another. He blurted out his needs for the fifth time before he sighed with relief. Yes, a Ford Bronco could be delivered within three hours. Tuned, gassed, and ready to go.

Logan hung up the phone. *I guess this is part of being in the catbird seat,* he thought smugly. *Oh, yeah.*

Locking in some, if not all of Maureen's money for his next venture did bear thinking about. A billion-dollar luxury resort on an island, maybe Peter Island, a fantasy resort for wealthy people like Stedman Clovis, who wanted the finest life had to offer. He knew if he hired the right people he could be the finest hotelier in the world. Ocean frontage, golf course, pools, waterfalls, Frett Sheets, linen draperies, a five-star chef. He could do it. All he needed was bushels of money. Kristine had money. He had money but not the kind of money needed for such a grand plan. Maureen Clovis would have the kind of money he needed.

Logan wrinkled his brow. The lovely lady wasn't as young as he'd first thought. He'd seen the fine lines, the even finer scars that makeup camouflaged. Traveling all over the world, as she'd done, would allow for some of the best plastic surgeons in their field. Now that he thought about it, he put her age at roughly somewhere near his own. Hands and feet were a dead giveaway when it came to telling one's age. The next go-round of surgery would take its toll. He'd seen it before on some of the generals' wives. Maureen would be one of those women who would go down fighting. She was the type who would have no qualms about going under the knife right up to the time they wheeled her into the mortuary. Vanity would always win out.

Last night he'd given her a run for her money, and she wanted more. Just the way Kristine and Danela wanted more. Too bad he couldn't remember the names of all the other women who had wanted more. Not that it mattered. He needed to map out a strategy where she was concerned. That was okay, too. He knew how to be devious and insidious. He might even hold a degree in both departments. He would have to be careful, though. Maureen Clovis was shrewd. She might even be as insidious and devious as he was. He felt sorry for the old fool who had married her.

He was definitely one lucky son of a bitch. He'd just stepped into this one by pure chance.

She ordered lick-off chocolate cream by the case.

He *loved* chocolate cream.

16

~~

Kristine woke slowly to savor the warmth of the down comforter. Christmas Eve. The only things missing in her little world right now were Woodie and Tyler. She cracked one eyelid to squint at the clock: 5:30. Time to get up and get her day under way. Breakfast was only an hour away. Pancakes, sausages, bacon, eggs, mountains of toast, warm butter, and syrup, everything her children and Woodie liked. After the cleanup she would start cooking the big Christmas Eve dinner with Woodie's help. It was all so wonderful, this new life of hers.

"What have we here?" Kristine laughed as Gracie and Slick poked their little heads out from under the covers. She cuddled with them as they licked her face with their tiny pink tongues. "It's too cold to get up, but we have to. Listen to me, Gracie, do not, I repeat, do not, go off the porch. The snow is too deep. Stay on the porch and do your business on the paper. Slick, mind Gracie. Okay, go."

Gracie stared with adoring eyes at her mistress and the stern words she was hearing. "I mean it, Gracie." The little dog yipped as she leaped off the bed to follow Slick down the steps. Kristine headed for the shower.

She sang under the shower, something she only did when she was happy. She was in the middle of "Jingle Bells" when she remembered her son sleeping down the hall. He probably wouldn't appreciate her good mood at five-thirty in the morning. She hoped she hadn't wakened the baby.

Dressed in a warm fleece-lined sweat suit, Kristine headed downstairs to start her new day. The house started to fill almost immediately. Her granddaughters ran to her, each of them clutching one of her legs as she flipped bacon. Everyone liked extra crisp bacon. She needed to give some thought to getting a microwave oven. She could cook *pounds* in minutes.

Kristine froze when she heard Pete's footsteps on the back porch. "Kristine, Cala, hurry, we have to get the pups up here. The heat went out."

"What about the kennel?"

"It's out, too. We have to bring the dogs here and to the apartment. Call Woodie. Wake up Mike. Everyone get dressed. This is damn scary, Kristine. We could lose all those pups. I have no idea how long the heat's been off."

"It was on at two-thirty when I came up to the house. Cala, get Mike down here. I'll call Woodie."

"What the hell is going on? I'm awake, I'm here. What's wrong?" Mike demanded.

"The heat went off in the barn. We have to bring the pups to the house. We have thirty-six dogs in the kennel. Get dressed. Ask Carol if she'll stay with the girls," Cala said, shrugging into her heavy jacket.

"Woodie's on his way. If worse comes to worst, we can use his house. He said he'd crank up the heat before he leaves. We just had that heater serviced a month ago. Did you call Reynolds, Pete?" Kristine asked anxiously.

"I didn't have time. Get all the blankets and towels you can carry and fetch them to the barn."

Kristine raced upstairs, her finger punching out the telephone number of the Reynolds Propane company as she pulled towels and blankets from the linen closet. She dragged the piles to the top of the kitchen stairway and tossed them down. "What do you mean you're closed? This is an emergency. I have over sixty dogs here with no heat. You listen to me, Mr. Reynolds, I don't give a good rat's ass if this is Christmas Eve or not. You get someone out here right now. Obviously you didn't fix the heater when you were here last month. You damn well took my money, though. I'll call the police, the governor, the mayor. I won't stop there either, I'll call the ... White House. How's that going to look in the papers? I'll give the newspeople that shitty picture of you on your yearly calendar. It will show up real good on the six o'clock news. You just bring every spare part you have in your shop. I don't want to hear any bullshit that you don't have parts or you have to go back for more. Furthermore, I will sue your fucking ass off if even one of my dogs gets sick. Did you hear me?''

Mike, bug-eyed, stared at his mother from the bottom of the steps. "I probably couldn't have done that one bit better. Way to go, Mom!" A second later he was out the door with the towels and blankets.

"What can I do, Kristine?" Carol asked

"Stay with the girls. Give them breakfast. Say a prayer and cross your fingers. Turn the heat up as high as it will go. Light all the fireplaces. Drag all the blankets and comforters off the beds. We need to keep the dogs warm. The temperature dropped during the night. It's nine degrees.''

"I'll take care of things. The girls will help me. Go, Kristine, they need you."

Razor-sharp wind and bone-chilling cold ripped through Kristine as she trudged down to the barn. She was on her third trip to the house with two poodles wrapped in a blanket when she heard the blast of Woodie's horn. She wanted to cry her relief when he hopped out of his Rover, two portable heaters in his hands. "Hurry, Woodie, some of the dogs are almost frozen. Two and a half hours, Woodie. The heat was on when we left the barn. I think they're going to be okay. Hurry. Please."

"Get those dogs in the house, Kristine. We can talk about this later." She did as instructed. Carol reached for the poodles the moment the door opened. "Everything is okay here."

Kristine raced back to the barn. She stopped for brief

seconds as she listened to her son Mike issue orders that were followed immediately. She knew in that one instant that things would proceed like a well-orchestrated drill. She took another second to recognize, and wondered if her son did, too, that Logan was responsible for the detail and thoroughness Mike was using to get the evacuation under way.

At ten-thirty, all the animals were in the house and apartment over the garage. Frightened out of their wits, the dogs were docile, grateful for the warmth of the old house and the tidbits of bacon Ellie and Emily were feeding them. Tears streamed down Kristine's face as she watched three-year-old Emily walk among the frightened animals singing in her sweet, childish voice, "Hush little baby, don't you cry, Emily is here to pat your belly." She turned to see Mike wiping at his eyes.

"Now what, Mom?"

"We have to watch them all very carefully. Thank God the pups are okay. They were all snuggled up to their mothers. We need to thank God for that. They still have to be watched. How many dogs does Cala have in the apartment?"

"She took the big dogs, the two shepherds, the beagle, three collies and the springer. It's a hell of a Christmas, Mom. You really know how to throw a party and make a guy feel welcome. This might not be the time to mention it, but Cala asked me if I would be interested in coming back here. Carol and I talked about it last night, and she's all for it. Me too. This will be a great place for Dillon to grow up."

"Oh, Mike, that's wonderful. You're right, this is a hell of a party."

Mike's voice was anxious when he said, "They're going to be okay, aren't they, Mom?"

"I think so. One more hour and . . . I'm just glad Pete got up in time. He'll be so happy to hear you're coming. The business has been growing, and it's too much for him.

Cala can only do so much, with the girls and all. We did it, we pulled together, and it worked.''

"Mom?"

"Yes."

"Everything I did, everything I said, that was Dad talking. Not me. What's that mean?"

"It means it worked. That's all it means, Mike. We all knew we had to pull together. This was an emergency of the first order. It was basic common sense. All you did was put it into words. Don't torment yourself. Now, if you really want to be helpful to your old mother, get the pooper scooper and start scooping. That's something we have to stay on top of. Remember, boy dogs lift their legs and girl dogs squat. We need lots of newspapers. The girls will help you."

Mike nudged his mother. "Look at that."

Kristine smiled from ear to ear. "Children are very trusting. So are animals. From the first day they all took to Emily. Look, she's using two hands knowing she has to cover all the dogs. She whispers to them, sings songs, rubs their bellies, and gives out treats like an adult. Pete says it's because she's low to the ground and the animals don't have to look up so high. Personally, I don't care what it is. It works. I thought it would be sheer bedlam. Even allowing for the fright. I need some coffee. Mike, welcome home, honey."

"Thanks, Mom. It's good to be here."

"You know what they say," Kristine twinkled. "There's no place like home. Start scooping, there's no free ride at the Summers farm."

"You got it!"

In the kitchen, Kristine reached for the coffee cup Carol handed her. She finished it in three gulps and held it out for a refill. "I didn't think we'd make it there for a while. Mike told me you're okay with moving here."

"I can't wait. I love this family, I really do. Mike has just been itching for a reason to come. He felt . . . what I mean is . . ."

"I know. This is wonderful, isn't it? I mean, Christmas Eve and all. I don't exactly think this is a miracle, but it's pretty darn close. What do you think we should do about Christmas Eve dinner? I was planning on cooking all day."

"Mom, why don't we do what we did that first Christmas?" Mike said, coming into the kitchen.

"Hot dogs and Jell-O?"

"Yeah. Do you have any in the freezer?"

"I keep a hearty supply for the girls. Cala doesn't care about the nitrates. We could toast them in the fireplace on long sticks. Emily loves doing that. We even have marshmallows. I say we do it. Woodie loves hot dogs with sauerkraut and relish. I like onions and chili. I have some canned chili and sauerkraut. I love it when a plan comes together. You're sure now?"

"I'm sure. I don't think the others will care. We're all together with sixty some dogs, and it's Christmas Eve. What sound-thinking person would want or expect more."

"That's why I love this guy." Carol grinned. "He's really good in bed, too." She continued to grin.

"Carol!" Mike said in outrage. "This is my mother."

This is my mother. How wonderful it sounded. She laughed. "I think I knew that. He takes after his ... mother." She watched as her son flushed and stammered. "I'm going down to the barn to see how Mr. Reynolds is progressing."

Even though she was on the back porch, she could hear her son say, "Man, you should have heard my mother on the phone. She told that guy off up one side and down the other. She's one person you don't want to mess with. This is a hell of a Christmas, isn't it, Carol?"

"The best, Mike. I wouldn't have missed this for the world."

"Me either."

Kristine felt warm all over despite the arctic air as she trudged down the steps and out to the barn. "Thank You, God, thank You for everything. Thank You especially for my family and for helping us keep these animals safe and warm.

"What's the story?" she asked as she slammed the barn door.

"It's not good, Kristine. You need a whole new unit. The bottom line is it just fritzed out. It's no one's fault. The unit is seven years old. It's been doing double duty with those extra lines we ran to the other barn. I told you to get a second one, but you said money was tight. If you don't want to go through this again, you need to order two units. It will take at least a week to get a new one," Reynolds said

"A week!" Kristine gasped. "Can't you jury-rig something?"

"I don't think so, honey. We're in for a solid week of freezing temperatures. Don't take a chance on it. Remember the fire your parents had years ago," Woodie said.

"God! Yes, I do remember. Okay, Mr. Reynolds, order new heaters and put a rush on them. In the meantime, the dogs stay at the house."

"I can take some to my house," Woodie volunteered.

"We have it covered. If we stay on top of it, it will work out. The kids are really working at this like a project. It is so under control it's amazing. I imagine dinnertime will be a little hectic. By the way, our dinner menu has changed. We're toasting weenies and marshmallows. Jell-O for dessert. Carol is making the Jell-O. I love her, Woodie. They're going to move here. I think we're making enough money to pay Mike a decent salary. We're going to need another barn, though. I have this feeling you are going to have to support me. Once I settle all that other business after New Year's, I'll probably be broke. A pauper. Are you sure you want to marry a pauper?"

"I'm damn sure. Weenies and marshmallows. Sauerkraut?"

"You bet. With real caraway seeds."

"You are too good to me."

"That's because I love you."

"Ahem!"

"Yes, Mr. Reynolds."

"I'll go back to the office and try to place your order today. If I'm not successful today, then I'll do it the day after Christmas. I'm sorry this happened. Tell me, would you really have called the news station?"

"Yes, sir, I would have. My animals are just as precious to me as my children are. From now on, I want you to service the units once a month. I don't ever want this to happen again."

"I'll be on my way then. Merry Christmas."

"The same to you, Mr. Reynolds."

"Is this a blizzard, Woodie?"

"I'd say so."

"That means we're going to be snowed in together with sixty dogs and my kids," Kristine chortled.

Woodie laughed. "Listen, I have to go back home to get my gifts. I'll be back late this afternoon. I have some phone calls I need to make and a few things to take care of. Are you sure things are under control?"

"More than sure. Our freezer is full, we have plenty of dog food, everyone is here but Tyler and Jack. We just have to stay on top of it. Are you sure you don't want something to eat?"

"I had a banana before. I'm okay. I love you, Kristine Summers. I'm counting the days and the hours till the first of January. I can't wait till I get to the point where I'm counting *seconds*."

"Me too, Woodie. I just want you to know I've never been this happy in my entire life. I had no idea I could feel like this. I love you so much I ache. Go on now before my mind starts to do strange things."

Woodie kissed her long and hard.

"I liked that. Do it again. This time with more gusto."

"No, no. I know what you're thinking. I'm not pulling my pants off in this subzero barn for anyone. I want all my parts in working order when the time comes to use them."

"Scaredy cat," Kristine teased.

"You got that right. Oh, oh, I hear a car. Actually there are two cars."

"Oooh, maybe it's Tyler and Jack."

"You're on the money," Woodie said, closing and locking the barn door. "I'll say hello and head on home. What time is dinner?"

"Dinner is whenever you get here. Drive carefully, Woodie."

"If you need me sooner, call."

Kristine was ahead of him, running to her son, her arms outstretched. "Tyler! Oh, it's so good to see you! Welcome home, honey, and Merry Christmas. Everyone is here. Wait till you see Dillon and the girls! Jack, it's good to see you. Listen, we had a bit of a problem a while ago. This is going to be a very unusual holiday for all of us. I hope you can get into the spirit of things and pitch in."

"Man, I almost didn't make it. Those roads are bad," Tyler said, his arm about his mother's shoulder. "What kind of problem?"

Kristine looked up at her son. Something clutched at her heart when she saw how each year he resembled his father more and more. "The heaters went out. We have sixty dogs in the house. Well, maybe not sixty, seven of them are in the apartment over the garage. We've got things under control, though. I think it's kind of wonderful, all of us home together with the animals. By the way, Woodie and I are getting married the first of January. You can stay, can't you, Tyler?"

"No kidding. You bet I'll stay."

"Me too," chirped Jack.

"You have to do your share, Jack. I know you're a cat man, but these are extenuating circumstances. Are you up to the challenge?" Kristine teased.

"I'm yours if you feed me. What are we having, turkey, ham, or prime rib?"

Kristine doubled over laughing. "Actually, Jack, we're following a tradition we started years ago. We're toasting weenies, marshmallows, and Jell-O for dessert. Woodie and Mike cleaned up the old sleigh and we plan to take it out after dinner. We might have to do it in shifts, but we're going to do it. A real old-fashioned Christmas."

"Huh?" the reporter said.

"No kidding! I haven't had a hot dog in years. Good going, Mom," Tyler said.

It was all perfect. So perfect it was downright scary. *Thank You, God. I know I said that before, but I need to say it again.*

Kristine opened the kitchen door. "Hey, everyone, look who the storm blew in." She stood back to witness the robust greeting Tyler received from his siblings. She continued to watch as he oohed and aahed over baby Dillon and then scooped Ellie up on his shoulders. When he sat her down on Cala's lap he turned to Emily.

"Hello, Uncle Tyler. Merry Christmas. I need some help with the animals," she said in her serious grown-up voice.

"Then I'm your man. Tell me what you want me to do. Be explicit. I know how to follow orders."

"I do, too. You watch me and do what I do. I only have two hands, and there are a lot of bellies. They're scared like when the lights go out. You have to talk slow and quiet like when Dillon is going to go to sleep. Can you do it, Uncle Tyler?"

"I'm going to watch you first so I don't make a mistake. Are you in charge of all this?"

"Yes. All the dogs in the living room are my friends. They trust me. Daddy says they know they can trust me. Get down low. They like little people."

"Yes, ma'am," Tyler said, raising his eyebrows to his family, who were watching him with interest. "This is a piece of cake. I can handle this," he called over his shoulder.

Mike guffawed.

Kristine smiled.

Cala laughed and laughed. "He just might learn a trick

or two. Sometimes, Mom, Emily is scary. She acts like a little old lady. Where does she get that?''

"From me," Pete said, like the proud father he was.

"I don't know about the rest of you, but I need something to eat," Kristine said. "We need to shovel paths so we can walk the dogs by late afternoon. If we all work at it, it won't take too long."

"There are sandwiches on the table, and I cut up some fruit," Carol said. "Fresh coffee is perking. Is dinner tonight dress up?"

"I hope not," Kristine said, biting into her sandwich.

"Mike and I already ate, so we'll start shoveling. Looks like Tyler is busy so that leaves you, Jack. If you want to partake of this family's food and generosity, get dressed and grab a shovel," Pete said.

"You guys need a snowblower," Jack grumbled good-naturedly.

"That's what you can get us next year for Christmas. Mark that down." Mike grinned.

"Duly noted," Jack said, zipping up his jacket.

Kristine munched on her sandwich, her gaze going to the calendar. A long time ago, she'd sat here at this same table, drinking wine and staring at the Reynolds Propane calendar. It seemed like a lifetime ago.

"Is something wrong, Kristine?" Carol asked.

"Not really. I was thinking about the year we all came back here. It was such an awful time. I'm sure Mike told you about it. I get a little sentimental at this time of year. I just wanted to have some kind of closure. I never got that. The kids needed it, too. If I live to be a hundred, I will never understand how a man could do what Logan did to this family. I guess we'll never know. That was a very tasty sandwich, Carol. Thanks for pitching in."

"Ellie helped me make the sandwiches. I hope I have a little girl one of these days."

"I hope you do, too. By the way, where is Ellie?"

"She took the wood out of the wood basket, spread a towel inside, scooped up Gracie and Slick, and they're all sound asleep." Kristine laughed. "I can go out and shovel if you'd rather stay inside."

"No, I need the exercise. For some reason I have this very . . . I don't know what to call it, tense feeling. It has nothing to do with the animals since we have that all under control. It's like, all of this is too perfect and something is going to go awry. I've never been happier in my life and yet this feeling keeps popping up. Maybe shoveling will work out the kinks to whatever it is."

Outside the wind howled and shrieked as snow swirled in what seemed like angry circles.

"I don't know, Mom. This seems like a losing battle," Mike said.

"I know but we have to do it. Shovel close to the house where it isn't so deep. The overhang will break the snow a little. The big dogs won't mind. It's the little ones who will be afraid of the snow when they sink into it. We could use the porch for the smallest ones. I keep newspapers spread for Gracie and Slick. They know the drill," Kristine shouted to be heard over the storm.

An hour later, Kristine called a halt. "I think we should start bringing the dogs out two at a time. We'll feed them early, take them out one more time, and that will be it for the night. Cala, how are the dogs in the apartment?"

"They're doing just fine. It's warm and cozy. I was just going to take them downstairs into the garage and let them do their business in there. I spread papers a while ago. The really remarkable thing is they're getting along. Each one staked out a spot and no one else ventures near it. I think they sense something serious is going on. We did good, Mom, real good. When we aren't so tired, we need to celebrate."

"When do you think that will be, Cala?" Kristine chuckled.

"Next year," Jack piped up.

"He's right. We're going to be doing this until next year," Pete said.

"I'll start bringing the dogs out. Mike, you take the

first two, and Jack, you take the second two. Cala, are you going to the garage? Come straight back here and follow your footsteps.''

"Yes, Mom.''

"Pay attention, Cala. If you get turned around and lose your bearings, we'd never be able to find you much less hear you shout. Follow the footsteps,'' Pete warned.

"Yes, Pete,'' Cala said mockingly.

"Your husband is serious, Cala, and so am I. Pay attention,'' Kristine said.

"All right, Mom. Let's not beat this to death.''

"Give her exactly fifteen minutes, Pete,'' Kristine said. "Mike, get ready for the dogs. They're going to be a little schizy at first. Most of them have been boarded here before, so they know us. We've never had weather conditions like this before, though.''

"We'll handle it, Mom. Go get the dogs.''

"I wish Woodie was here,'' Kristine muttered to herself as she trudged up the steps and into the house.

Logan Kelly looked at the new Ford Bronco sitting in the driveway under the overhang of the Hyatt Hotel. It was covered with snow. It occurred to him to wonder what color it was. Not that color was important in the scheme of things.

"It's gassed and ready to go,'' Don Mitchell said. "I have to warn you, Mr. Eberhart, the roads are treacherous. Merry Christmas. By the way, how far are you going?''

"Leesburg. It's not that far. I'm a good driver,'' Logan said coolly.

"Good drivers, bad drivers, it doesn't make a difference in this kind of weather. The snow is drifting badly. Visibility is about five feet. Be very cautious. I threw in some flares just to be on the safe side. They're on the floor of the backseat. Ford also includes a first-aid kit, flashlight, and road map. Merry Christmas, Mr. Eberhart.''

"The same to you.''

Twenty minutes into the bumper-to-bumper traffic, Logan knew he'd made a mistake. He should have stayed in the hotel and waited for the storm to subside. Oh, no, he had to make his grand entrance on Christmas Eve. He was lucky if he'd gone a mile. The salesman was right; visibility was almost nil. He bit down on his lower lip, cursing under his breath, mindful of the red taillights in front of him.

If he didn't watch it, he would start to lose control, and that never worked for him. A good soldier was always in control. It was just a lousy fucking snowstorm. He'd been through snowstorms before. The only thing that made this one different was he was finally going home to his family. He never should have set a timetable for himself. Too many things could go wrong with timetables. Like snowstorms.

Damn, the wiper blades were icing up, and the red lights in front of him were barely visible. He had no clue as to where he was. If memory served him right there were twenty-one miles on the truck when the salesman dropped it off. He'd gone a mile and a half, perhaps a little more. Closer to two miles. At this rate, he'd be lucky to make Leesburg by midnight.

He needed to shift his mind into the neutral zone and think about other things. Things that were pleasant, things that were good. Unbidden, Danela's face surfaced in front of him. His nemesis. Thinking about her the way he had these past few days had to mean something. Gut instinct, intuition. Something. Logan cursed again. Danela no longer had a place in his life. She belonged to the past, and if there was one thing he never did, it was look back. He needed to start thinking about Maureen Clovis and how she could help him once he split this place.

Instinctively, Logan steered into the slide he was experiencing. Sweat dripped down his face before he had the four-wheel drive back on track. *Pay attention to the road,* he warned himself. Eyes dead center on the whiteness beyond the windshield, Logan hunched over the wheel as he strained to see the pinkish lights in the distance.

Logan sat that way for over three hours as he crawled along the interstate. At some point, he turned off 270 and passed the sign for Broad Run Farms. He was alone on the road now, no red taillights to guide him. He brought the Bronco to a full stop when the wipers failed completely. Hunching into his wool jacket, he stepped outside to try and break the ice free from the wipers. His fingers were numb and cold, and it was impossible to tell if the ice was breaking off or not. In frustration, he gave them a vicious whack and felt rather than saw chunks of ice sail in all directions. He strained to see off in the distance. All his headlights showed him was swirling snow. He had no idea if he was on a road or not. He bent down to run his numb hands over the snow, hoping to find tire indentations. There were none. He realized for the first time that he could very well die out here. When would his body be found? When would the hotel open the safe in his hotel room? Would the bank disks be turned over to Kristine and the kids? Probably not, since he'd registered as Justin Eberhart. Would the authorities track him back to Africa? If so, Danela would be the one to take control of all his funds. Danela would get the last laugh. "Like hell," he muttered as he climbed back into the Bronco.

Logan continued to drive, stopping every fifteen minutes to break the ice from the overworked wipers. The digital clock on the dashboard read 8:20 when he climbed out of the car once again to attack the wipers. He saw the oversize sign then, swinging in the wind. The sign that said, SUMMERS KENNELS.

He was home.

Logan drove slowly down the long driveway that led to the farm and the main house. He sighed wearily when he saw the lights of the house. As he drew closer, he saw the colored Christmas lights strung across the wide front porch. There were lights everywhere, spotlights, lights on the outbuildings, but it was the lights from the big farmhouse that drew his attention. He thought he could see a twinkling Christmas tree through the swirling snow. He frowned, deep grooves etching his forehead. Five vehicles. Four too many. The frown deepened. Company? Who? The kids? Who else? He could feel his heart rate speed up. What did it matter who was inside? Kristine would throw herself at him, and that would be that. Everything else would fall into place.

Presents. The diamond bracelet he'd bought for Kristine was in his coat pocket. The top-of-the-line skis for the kids were in the back with bright red bows. If he struggled, he should be able to carry all three pairs up the steps to the back porch. He had a moment of indecision when he couldn't make up his mind if he should knock or just walk in. As the newly appointed head of the household, he would open the door and walk in. A husband and father belonged. There was no formality to adhere to.

Logan was on the back porch, shifting the skis from one shoulder to the other when he froze as the most bloodcurdling sound struck him dumb in his tracks. He had a clear view of the kitchen through the window. Animals came from everywhere, big ones, small ones, medium-sized ones, their teeth bared as they slammed into the back door. He backed up, his heart thundering in his chest. What the hell was going on here? He saw small children, strangers, and Kristine holding hot dogs on sticks, their eyes glued to the kitchen door and the wild animals.

He listened to the panicked voices shouting that someone was at the door while other voices tried to calm the dogs. He hated dogs. Always had and always would. He waited, the cold air searing his lungs as he fought to take deep, even breaths to calm his nerves.

And then there was total, thundering silence. Logan felt himself flinch. He watched as Kristine walked, as though in slow motion, to the back door, the stick with the hot dog still in her hand, Mike and Tyler on each side of her. The door opened slightly and then the wild wind blew it against the side of the door.

"Logan!"

"Dad," the boys said in unison, disbelief registering on their faces.

"Oh, shit," Woodie muttered to Pete, who was standing next to him, his mouth hanging open.

"Aren't you eight years too late?" Cala said bitterly.

"Whozat?" Emily and Ellie squealed.

The dogs reared up again, teeth bared, tails between their legs.

"Logan," Kristine said a second time.

"Merry Christmas, everyone!" Logan said jovially.

17

Kristine stared at the man in the open doorway. In the blink of an eye, the last eight years of her life flashed before her. This couldn't be Logan. He couldn't just appear and say, "Merry Christmas," like nothing happened, eight years late. No, this wasn't real. This was a bad dream she was having after the exhaustion and the trauma of the day. She poked the stick holding the hot dog against her leg. She felt the pain. It was no dream. It really was Logan, and he was standing in her kitchen. She needed to say something, and she needed to say it quickly.

"Close the door, Logan," she said with barely a catch in her voice. She watched as her ex-husband's eyes narrowed to slits. In the old days it would have been a warning for her to shut up and do whatever it was he wanted. The old days were long gone. "What do you want, Logan? Why are you here?"

"I wanted to come home. I wanted to see my family. Do you mind if I take off my coat?"

"Yes, I do mind. I think we all mind. You don't belong here. You deserted us. I don't owe you anything, and my children don't owe you anything."

Logan ignored Kristine's words. He advanced into the kitchen and removed his jacket. *This is not going according to plan,* he thought uneasily. *This isn't the Kristine I remember. Not the Kristine I could bamboozle just by looking at her.* His stomach tightened into a hard knot when he turned to see the hate-filled eyes of his children. He addressed his wife. "I think you need to tell me what's going on here. What are all these animals doing here? Don't I deserve to be introduced to these strange people in my kitchen?"

"No."

"No?" Logan moved around, offering his hand, which no one reached for. "I'm Logan Kelly. Kristine's husband."

"I had you declared legally dead, Logan. After I divorced you. This is my house, not yours. I'd like you to leave. You spoiled too many holidays for us, and I won't allow you to spoil this one."

Of all the things in the world Kristine could have said, this was the most unexpected. He could see his plans falling apart. "Obviously, you were premature, Kristine. I'm here. I'm alive. What you did will be invalid." *Fall back and regroup,* his mind shrieked. *Plan B is just as good as Plan A.* The only problem was he hadn't gotten around to forming Plan B. Bluff it out. He'd always been good at that.

"It will hold up in any court of law. I made sure of that. Where's my money, Logan?"

"Right here, honey. I didn't touch it." Carefully, so the animals didn't spring in his direction, Logan carefully withdrew an envelope from his inside jacket pocket. "Your eight million dollars plus interest and your personal-checking-account monies. There's a long story behind it we can discuss another time."

"Keep it and leave."

This was definitely not going according to plan. Who in her right mind would turn down money like this? Certainly no one he knew or would care to know. When Kristine refused to touch the envelope, he laid it on the kitchen table. "You didn't answer my question, Kristine, what are these animals doing in the house?" Of course she didn't need the money, she had bushels of it now, thanks to her inheritance. "I'm rather tired. Which room is mine? You really fixed up this rattrap. I didn't think it was possible to salvage it."

"All our rooms are filled. The apartment over the

garage is full of animals. There's no heat in the barns, but there is lots of straw. There are no extra blankets or quilts. If you don't like the idea of the barn, you can sleep leaning up against the wall. I want you out of here as soon as it gets light."

"I'm not going anywhere."

"See that corner of the wall by the fireplace? That's your spot. The dogs won't allow you to move. Get it through your head, Logan. You don't belong to this family anymore. Take it or leave it."

In the blink of an eye, Jack Valarian had Logan by the shoulders and propelled him to the designated wall. A hundred-and-thirty-pound black Lab named Sugar followed them, her teeth gleaming pearl white in the kitchen light.

"Good going, big guy," Pete hissed in Jack's ear. "I didn't think you had it in you."

"I hate that son of a bitch," Jack hissed back.

Shaken to her soul, Kristine looked around at her family. "All right, let's finish our weenies and marshmallows and retire to the living room, where we will sing our carols, drink our eggnog, and open our presents. It's Christmas Eve, and we're going to . . . to celebrate." Out of the corner of her eye she saw total disbelief and hatred on her ex-husband's face. *So there, Logan. So there.* She wondered if anyone noticed how badly she was shaking.

"Are we just going to pretend he isn't here?" Cala asked.

"Yes, unless you can come up with something better," Kristine whispered in return. "We'll talk about it in the living room. I think I'm in shock. No, that's not true, I *know* I'm in shock."

"Mom, what about Woodie? His eyes are glazed. Now, that's shock," Tyler said.

"Oh, God."

"Yeah, oh, God."

"I have an idea," Carol said. "Jack and I will do the weenies and bring them into the living room. Pete can bring in the little tables with the Jell-O and eggnog. You guys organize the dogs and the presents. It won't take long, the fire's really hot."

"Bless your heart, Carol. It's a great idea." Anything to get away from Logan's penetrating eyes.

"Come on, kids, we have to fix the dogs' beds and get ready to sing 'Jingle Bells!' "

"I love 'Jingle Bells,' " Ellie said, as Woodie scooped her up and onto his shoulders. Mike grabbed a giggling Emily and did the same thing.

The dogs voiced their disapproval as the little people suddenly turned to giants. Suddenly every dog in the house was chasing after one another. They leaped over furniture, stomped on presents, lifted their legs, squatted, howled, and barked.

The moment Mike set Emily on the floor, the house grew quiet. "Everybody lie down," the little girl said, clapping her hands. "I need more treats, Grandma," she said.

Treats meant she had to go back to the kitchen, something she didn't want to do.

"I have an idea, Emily. Since this is Christmas Eve, why don't we cut up some of these nice hot dogs Aunt Carol made and share them with our friends."

"Oh, goody," Emily said.

"Woodie, please don't look at me like that. Say something. Please."

"I don't know what to say, Kristine. In a million years I never thought this would happen. I guess I want to know what you think and feel. Your kids are in a state of shock. Hell, I'm in a state of shock myself."

"I know. Like you said, in a million years I never thought this would happen. He's here, and he brought the money. It must mean something. I knew it was all too perfect. For weeks now I've been waiting for the other shoe to drop. I know that sounds crazy. Right now I feel like I should be carted off to the mental ward."

"I'll tell you what I think it means. I think he came back for the rest of it. For all you know, the checks could bounce. I'm just assuming they are checks. What are you going to do, Kristine?''

"I'm not going to do anything. You know that old saying. When you don't know what to do, do nothing. We're divorced, Woodie. I guess the part about me having him declared dead is going to be a problem. The way I see it, it's his problem. What should I do about the kids?''

"Nothing. They aren't kids anymore. Mike and Cala have families of their own. Tyler will have a family someday. However they choose to deal with it, accept it. I imagine right now they're wondering how and what you're going to do. I think they're waiting to take their cue from you. A word of warning, go slow, think things through, and don't make mistakes that will come back to haunt you.''

"The amazing thing is he looks the same. A little older but the same. How is that possible? He's got a perfect tan, he has all his hair, he's dressed well. He waltzes in here like the eight years never happened. With presents yet. Did you get a look at those skis? Very pricey. Wherever he was, life must have been good.''

"Hot dogs! Jell-O! Pickles! Potato chips! Gummi Bears! Come and get it!'' Pete shouted from the doorway.

"Oh, Daddy, you have to make more. We need treats for the dogs. It's Christmas Eve, and we have to share.''

"It's not a problem, honey,'' Carol said, holding her tray aloft. "We have enough for everyone.''

"What's *he* doing, Carol?'' Mike asked through clenched teeth.

"He *was* leaning on the wall. Now he's kind of squatting on his haunches. He's afraid of Sugar. If he wiggles, she shows her fangs. I gave him a hot dog, but Sugar snatched it and ate it. What does all this mean, Mike?''

"It means if he stays, we go.''

"Oh.''

"He's not staying,'' Kristine said quietly. "It's Christmas Eve. There's a wicked storm going on outside. Tomorrow is another day. When he sees he isn't welcome, he'll leave of his own accord.''

"Don't count on it," Mike said, biting into his hot dog.

"He brought skis," Tyler said. "Top of the line. He didn't acknowledge any of us. Did you notice that?"

"We aren't deaf, dumb, and blind, Ty. He really thought he could prance in here like nothing happened. I'm home! You did good, Mom. You okay?" Cala asked.

"I'm okay. I'm just as shocked as you all were. And he brought the money. I can't wait to hear the reasoning behind that."

"Life must have been real good. Did you see that tan? New hairstyle. Expensive threads. Yes, I'd say life has been real good to our old man. Before he leaves, I think we should all recite chapter and verse about how hard our lives were for a little while. I think he really thought we were all going to smile and welcome him with open arms," Mike said.

"Boy these hot dogs are good. They're almost as good as that Christmas eight years ago," Cala said.

"Nah, those were the best," Tyler said. "He wants something."

"Time to sing the carols, then it's off to bed for you guys," Pete said to his daughters. "Remember, Santa doesn't come until everyone is asleep."

"How many presents, Daddy?" Emily asked as she snuggled with a fat little dog named Josephine.

"One. Pick the biggest one with the prettiest red bow."

"Is it a wagon?"

"You have to open the bag to see what it is. Tomorrow morning when you wake up you'll see what Santa put under the tree for you."

"Will the dogs scare Santa?"

"Nope. He likes dogs. I bet he even brings them some presents."

"Oh goody," Ellie said as she snuggled sleepily against her mother's chest.

Once during the robust caroling, Kristine thought she heard Logan shout, "Kristine, get this damn dog off me." If the others heard him, they gave no sign. She ignored the sound, too, her brain whirling so fast the words to the carol she was trying to sing coming out garbled beyond description. No one paid any attention to that, either.

Later, when Cala returned to the living room after putting the girls to bed and Mike checked on Dillon, the family sat around in a circle on the floor with the dogs. There were no happy smiles, only tense faces and jerky movements. It was Pete who turned on the stereo to drown out whatever they were going to say to one another.

"As much as we say it isn't spoiled, it is. It's like someone zapped every bit of Christmas spirit I had," Cala said. Her siblings nodded.

"Would you guys rather I went to bed?" Jack asked.

"No, Jack. You know the story. You held my hand for a long time. It's okay. We're just in shock. I don't think any one of us knows what we should do or say," Kristine said in a choked voice.

"What's to decide? Tomorrow you boot his ass out of here just like you said. I want this right up front, Mom. Either he goes, or I go," Mike said vehemently.

"That goes for me, too," Cala said.

"I feel the way Mike and Cala feel," Tyler said.

"Don't any of you want to hear what he has to say?" Kristine asked.

"Hell no, I don't. I can't believe you'd even ask that," Mike said.

"What could he possibly say that would interest me?" Cala demanded.

"Why are you all looking at me like that?" Tyler demanded. "If it was up to me, I'd boot his ass out right now, storm or no storm."

"Mom?" the three said in unison.

"I agree, but I want to hear what he has to say. I for one need that one last little bit before the final closure. I know you don't understand that. I just want to know. I think I have a right to know."

"Then go out there now and ask him. Let's get this over with once and for all. I don't want him hanging over my head. I want him out of my life. I mean it, Mom, Carol and I are outta here if he stays," Mike said.

"So are we," Cala said. "Pete's a good vet. He can get a job anywhere."

"That goes for me, too," Tyler said.

Kristine's heart fluttered in her chest. It was all falling apart right in front of her eyes. All because of Logan. She couldn't bring herself to look at Woodie. He wasn't understanding any of this. If she didn't do what her children wanted, she was in danger of losing them all over again. They would take her grandchildren away from her. *Damn you, Logan. Damn you to hell.*

"Listen, I think I'll go home," Woodie said. "This is a family matter, and I'm not family . . . yet."

"Woodie, please don't go. It's Christmas Eve. We should be all together."

"There's one too many people here, honey. I'm not comfortable with the situation, and I don't want to say something I might regret later on. Do you want me to take any of the dogs with me?"

Kristine shook her head. Her face was miserable. Of course he was right. Woodie was always right.

"If you don't mind, I'll go out the front door."

"Your jacket is in the kitchen," Kristine mumbled.

"You know what, Kristine? I'd rather freeze than go back in there for it."

"I'll get it," Pete said. He was back in a moment with the shearling jacket. He held it while Woodie slipped his arms into it.

"Merry Christmas, everyone," Woodie said as he was about to close the door behind him. Kristine stood rooted to the floor, her eyes filling.

"We're going to bed," Mike said. Tyler, Cala, and Pete were on their feet in seconds.

"But what about the presents. I thought . . . Never mind, go to bed. We'll open them in the morning with the girls. Sleep . . . sleep well."

Kristine wiped at her eyes with the hem of the sweatshirt. "God, I need a drink." She turned to see Jack behind her.

"No, you don't need a drink. A drink is the last thing you need. What you need is a ton of guts. You got them—haul them out and use them. You got through eight of the worst years of your life. Your horizon is full and rich. I know I'm not family even though sometimes I feel like I am. The best is yet to come for you. Woodie is a hell of a guy. Your kids love him. Jesus, you love him, too. This . . . this, whatever this little visit is, is nothing more than a setback. Look it in the face, deal with it, and go on. You're tough enough to do that. You're an okay lady in my book. Please don't screw it all up now. That's all I have to say. I think I'll go to bed. Merry Christmas, Kristine. If you need me for the dogs during the night, just come and get me."

"Okay, Jack. Thanks for that little pep talk."

"My pleasure."

Kristine gathered up the glasses, napkins, and leftover trash to pile on the trays. She carried it out to the kitchen. She stared at Logan for a full five minutes before she called Sugar to her side. "You can sit at the table, Logan. Would you like a cup of coffee? I see that there is some left in the pot."

"I'd rather have a drink."

"I don't keep alcohol in the house. I turned into an alcoholic when you didn't come back. With the help of a dear friend, I overcame it. I'm still an alcoholic," she said, pouring coffee she knew was going to be black and bitter.

"You aren't . . . I expected . . ."

"I know what you expected, Logan. You thought I sat here pining away for you and that when you returned, I would throw myself into your arms. There was a point when I would have done that. That was a long time ago. All I want from you now is to tell me why you're here and what it is you want. Tomorrow, I want you out of here. I don't ever want to see you again. I think I speak for the kids as well."

"You poisoned them against me, didn't you?"

"I didn't have to. You did that yourself. They turned on me, too, for allowing you to ruin their lives. It's taken all this time to convince them I'm a worthwhile person, a mother who loves them deeply. They didn't trust me any more than they trusted you. At best, our relationship is still fragile. I will not allow you to invade our lives and inflict harm on any one of us."

Kristine fumbled in her pocket for a cigarette. She lit it, and then blew a luscious smoke ring that moved up until it circled Logan's head like a halo.

"You don't smoke. When did you take up that filthy habit?"

"That's pretty funny coming from you, Logan. You smoked like a chimney. But, to answer your question, I took it up around the same time I started to hit the bottle. You still haven't answered my question. Do it soon, Logan, or I'll boot your ass right out the kitchen door. I will get great pleasure from doing that."

"I'm trying to find the right words, Kristine. This is very hard for me."

"Just tell me why you took my money? Tell me why you deserted us. That's all I want to know. By the way, I sold the Kelly farm. I'm giving the money to the kids."

"You can't do that. That was my parents' farm."

"You should have thought about that before you deserted us and stole my money. My patience is wearing thin, Logan."

"I didn't spend it, Kristine. It's all there in the envelope. At first I thought I was going to need it. I left you and the kids because . . . I'm dying. I didn't want to put you through that torture. I knew you wouldn't be able to handle my deterioration on a daily basis. I guess I thought . . . I had this cockamamie idea that I could buy a new kidney. To do that I needed a lot of money. Treatments were expensive. That's the best excuse I can offer. The two specialists I consulted had different opinions. One gave me eighteen months, the other said with proper treatment and dialysis,

I might last three years until a donor could be found. As the years went on, I didn't get any worse, but I didn't get any better either. There were a lot of really black days. Until a few months ago, when my condition worsened. My days are numbered. I wanted to come back, to try and make things right. I guess I want to die on American soil. I want to die with my family around me. I see now that kind of thinking was a mistake on my part. I don't know why it didn't occur to me that you would all be so hateful and bitter. I understand it, though. I don't care about the farm. I'm surprised you got anything at all for it.''

Kristine tried to absorb what she'd just been told. She fired up another cigarette. "I'm sorry to hear that, Logan.'' Logan dying. She could feel hot tears prick her eyelids. Something stirred in her, something she hadn't felt for a very long time.

"Not half as sorry as I am. This is a last-ditch effort on my part. There's a kidney specialist at George Washington who I was referred to. I've seen him twice. The best he can do is prolong things for a little while. I'll leave in the morning if that's what you want. I can stay in a hotel in DC. In fact, that might be better. I'll be closer to the hospital. I really wasn't going to come out here today. Then I started hearing the Christmas music, seeing the holiday shows on television, and I got sentimental. Yeah, hard as that is to believe, I really did feel it. So, the way I look at it is this. We're square. I gave you back the money, I apologized for leaving with what I thought at the time was a good reason. Look at you, Kristine. You look beautiful. You're healthy, you have your family, grandchildren, and a business. Talk to me, Kris. Tell me about your life these past eight years. Tell me how I can make things right before I . . . go.''

Her whole body trembling, Kristine got up from the chair to stand by the sink. She filled the sink with hot, soapy water to have something to do. "I told you, I turned into a drunk. I overcame it, started the business, and it's thriving. It was hard on the kids. We just had enough money to get by. They worked all during college and during vacations. They hated me for a long time. I never saw them until they graduated. I never knew you beat them, Logan. I will never forgive you for that. Never! They don't just detest you, they hate you. And they blamed me for it all. I allowed it to happen. How could you do that? How? They flat out told me in the living room that if I allowed you to stay, they would leave.''

"I guess I wasn't a very nice person back then. You're making me sound like some sadist.''

"I saw the scars, Logan. Good little soldiers don't cry or tell tales. You were insidious.''

"It was the drugs I was on. I just learned that a few years ago. There were days I used to look in the mirror and wonder who it was I was seeing there. I knew I couldn't get off the medication. I didn't want to burden you. I hated myself for turning into that hateful person. If I explain, will they listen?''

"I doubt it.''

"I need to try. I don't want to go to my Maker with that on my soul. Just let me talk to them once. After that, I'll leave. I want to know I tried, that I gave it my best shot.''

"You're looking for absolution, Logan, and we're fresh out. You know that old saying, too much, too little, too late.''

"When you're dying it's never too late. I thought I could stay here, help out, do whatever is needed until I get to the point where I have to go to the hospital for the last time. I'd like us to have another shot at our marriage. We were happy once. We could be that way again. I always loved you, Kris. We were so good together. Those wonderful memories are what kept me going these last eight years.''

"Stop it, Logan. I don't want to hear all this. I divorced you. I had you declared dead. You aren't in my life, and that was by your choice. I would have taken care of you. I believed in the vow, in sickness and health, till death do us part. I would have honored that. Why couldn't you trust me?"

"I was trying to spare you and the kids. The end isn't going to be pretty. When I did my disappearing act, I thought I only had *months* to live, a year at the most, unless a miracle was found along the way. Eight years later I'm still looking for that miracle. I wanted you to be my miracle, Kris. I really did. Tomorrow before I leave, try and get the kids to talk to me so I can explain things. I don't want them to carry around hatred for me all their lives. By the way, I want to be cremated."

"Shut up, Logan. Just shut up."

"Would you mind getting me a glass of water, Kris. I need to take my pills. I'm a few hours late in taking them. That dog wouldn't let me move."

Kristine felt a rush of guilt. She filled a water glass and handed it to Logan. She watched as he pulled six different pill bottles from his heavy jacket. He lined them up with precision before he popped the lids to shake them out.

"What are they?" she asked.

Logan shrugged. "They all have names that are difficult to pronounce. They're keeping me alive. One of these days they won't work anymore."

"I'm sorry to hear that," Kristine said. "I'm going to bed. You can sleep on the couch."

"Wait a minute, Kristine. I want to give you something. I didn't come empty-handed."

Kristine watched as Logan withdrew a jeweler's box from the inside pocket of his heavy jacket. He slid it across the table toward her. In spite of herself, she picked it up. She gasped. "It's beautiful, but you need to take it back. I don't move in the circles where I would wear something like this. I work with the animals all day. Return it and get your money back." She slid the velvet box across the table. Hot tears pricked her eyelids again. She needed to get away from this man and into the privacy of her room, where she could think and allow herself to feel all the emotions she was trying to stifle.

"I thought you would like it. Each stone is flawless. A half carat each. One for each year of our married life, even the last eight. I guess I can't do anything right. I'm sorry if I made a poor choice."

"I do like it. It's gorgeous. However, it's not practical for someone like me."

"Why are you working so hard? Didn't you come into a hefty inheritance? Why are you doing all this? There must be a hundred dogs here. This can't be sanitary."

"Sixty dogs. The heat went out. Yes, the inheritance came through, but it's going right back out. It's a long story, and I'm too tired to go into it. I have to work. I have to make this business into something that will provide security for our children and grandchildren."

"But the inheritance, I don't understand."

"It's simple. Your ancestors and my ancestors were the worst kind of slave traders. What they did to their workers was a sin. For the past four years Mr. Valarian and I have been working to try to track down descendants of those families so we can make things right. I don't want that kind of money on my conscience. Nor do my kids. We're giving it back."

"That doesn't make any sense, Kristine," Logan sputtered. "I resent your implying my ancestors had anything to do with something like that."

"I have the records, Logan. There are *slave lists.* The words are so ugly I find myself getting sick each time I say them out loud. I spent four years of my life following up leads, writing letters, going all over the country trying to find families our families tore apart. It was an ugly, hateful, disgusting thing to have happened, and if I can do something about it, I will. You believe what you want to believe, and I'll believe what I know I can prove."

Logan sighed. "You always were a do-gooder. I guess that was one of the reasons I loved you. I still do, Kristine. Can you ever forgive me, Kris? I know you still care for me. I can see it in your eyes."

"Come along. I'll walk you to the couch. It's warm in the house, so you won't need any covers. Stay on the couch and don't get off, or the dogs will go after you. You're new to them, and I can't vouch for your safety. They've been through one trauma today. We'll talk in the morning."

"Kristine?"

"What?"

"Merry Christmas."

Kristine nodded. She didn't trust herself to speak.

In her room with the door closed, Kristine started to pace. From time to time she knuckled her eyes. Logan was dying. She needed to deal with that. Could she turn her back on him? Did she dare risk losing her children's love and respect for a man like Logan? What kind of person would she be if she turned her back on a dying man? No better than some of her ancestors. A divorce decree was a piece of paper. She'd borne the man downstairs on the couch three children. How did you turn your back on family? On the father of your children? What would six months or a year be out of her life?

What about Woodie? She should call him. To try and explain. He'd looked so miserable and sad when he left. Woodie would never understand if she allowed Logan to stay and die at the farm. As broad-minded and as understanding as Woodie was, his mind would be closed to anything other than Logan leaving. Maybe she could let him stay in the apartment over the garage. If he didn't make his presence known and felt, perhaps the kids would tolerate him. Did she dare go to Pete and Carol and hope they had enough influence over their mates to . . . what? All she was doing was passing the buck so she wouldn't have to face down her own children.

Kristine sat down in the rocking chair. Soft little mewling sounds escaped her lips. It wasn't fair. As Woodie said, life was never fair. You deal with it, then you move on. She eyed the phone. She knew if she called Woodie, he would pick up the phone on the first ring. If she called him, what would she say? What would he say?

The hot tears stinging her eyelids finally rolled down her cheeks. She crept from the rocker to drop to her knees. "Please, God, tell me what to do. Help me do the right thing for everyone."

18

With the one remaining thin quilt from her bed, Kristine wrapped herself for warmth. She curled up on the window seat to stare out at the cold, snowy night. Her index finger idly scratched at the frost on the drafty windows before she stuck her hands down into the quilt. If she sat there long enough, maybe she would freeze to death and then she wouldn't have to deal with Logan's return.

Why now? Why this particular Christmas? Is this some terrible game he is playing? Do people ever lie about dying? Would Logan lie about something as serious as dying? Once she would have disavowed any such thinking. *He looks well, tanned, healthy. When will he start to deteriorate? He says he loves me, and yet he abandoned me. To spare me anguish. And then the bracelet and the expensive skis. What does that mean? Is everything he says suspect? He returned my money along with interest. He said. I never looked at the contents of the envelope. If the money is coming back to me, it is honest money, money from my parents that Logan had invested. It would be the kids' to keep, to do whatever they wanted. It would certainly make life a whole lot easier. We could build a new barn, demolish the old one and possibly even build a larger kennel. With the way the business was growing, it would be the way to go. Mike and his family would be part of it. Tyler's share would be carved out for him.*

Maybe I'll take a vacation with my eight thousand dollars. I'll go far away, maybe some third-world country where no one knows me. Or, maybe I'll go to some lush, exotic paradise, where people will wait on me hand and foot, or until my money runs out.

If only I lived in a perfect world.

Kristine crept off the window seat and dropped to her knees. She needed to pray, something she didn't do on a regular basis. "Oh, Holy Father . . ."

She heard the snick the doorknob made when the door opened. She turned to see her three children outlined in the dim hall light. She stumbled over to the fireplace and watched as Mike, his face grim, added more logs to the dying embers. They sat, Indian fashion, in a tight little circle. They were waiting for her to say something.

"I've been praying. I know what you all want me to do. I want to do it, too. However, after you all came upstairs, I went into the kitchen and spoke with your father, who by the way is sleeping on the sofa. He won't move till morning."

"What could he possibly have to say, Mom, that would even make you *think* about allowing him to stay?" Mike asked.

"He's dying."

"Yeah, right," Cala said.

"I don't remember Dad every telling outright lies," Tyler said. "He was always right up front, in your face. He used to beat our asses if he even *thought* we were lying. Do you believe him, Mom?"

"He brought back our money. I can't imagine someone lying about dying. I suppose there is that possibility. He said he wants to die here. He's going to a specialist in Washington. He said he was on a donor list, but that he was far down on the list. He said when he left us he was told by one of his doctors that he only had a few months, and he was trying to spare us."

"Eight years ago!" Mike said, disbelief on his face. "Now it doesn't bother him to come home to die? What am I missing?"

"I don't think you're missing anything, Mike. He wants to be around his family when his . . . time comes. He wants to talk to all of you in the morning. It's up to you if you want to listen. I don't want any of you to have any regrets later on. He said if we didn't want him here, he would take a hotel room in Washington. Christmas is supposed to be a time of miracles. I think he's viewing us taking him back, as a miracle."

"What about Woodie, Mom?" Cala asked.

"I don't know, Cala. I have to think about all that. I can only deal with one thing at a time. What did Pete and Carol say? They do have a say, you know."

"Pete said . . . what he said was . . . he can't, he won't desert you. He said if I want to stay in town that's okay. I don't know how I feel about that."

"Carol wants to stay. She's Miss Peacemaker herself. She loves it here. She did say the decision was up to me," Mike said.

"Tyler?"

"This is something for the rest of you to decide. I'm going to be leaving. Death is final. I think we've all read articles, seen shows, heard people say that they wished they had done this or done that before a loved one died. Mom's right. I don't think any of us wants regrets later on. My vote is to allow him to stay and die here in peace. How hard is it to be civil? I'm not talking about love. He destroyed that. Even if Dad doesn't think so, we turned out to be decent human beings. I'm not a parent, but I would think your kids have the right to know their grandparent. When they get older they're going to ask questions. Do you want to lie to them? Kids have a way of looking at things differently than adults. That's all I have to say. Oh yeah, I say we throw those shitty skis he brought us in the old barn."

"Your father brought me a diamond bracelet with a half-carat diamond for every year we've been married," Kristine said in a strangled-sounding voice. "I gave it back. It's on the kitchen table with the envelope. That's our money. We can do whatever we want with it. That doesn't go into the . . . fund."

"Do you want him to stay, Mom?" Mike asked.

"God, no! However, it is the right thing to do. He was my husband. I loved him with all my heart at one point in time. He's your father. You can never change the part of you that is his flesh and blood. If we don't do the right thing today, none of us will ever truly enjoy another Christmas. That much I do believe."

"Mom's right. Pete said almost the exact same thing, but in a different way. Pete's staying."

"So did Carol. Okay, Mom. Just don't expect me to hold his hand. I can be civil and polite. That's as far as I'm willing to go," Mike said.

"I knew I looked up to you for a reason," Tyler said, clapping his hand on his brother's back.

"Where has he been, Mom?" Cala asked.

"I don't know. I didn't want to know. I'm not handling this any better than you are. I admit it, I don't know what to think or do. He seemed sincere." She hated her shaking voice, hated the way her body was trembling.

Cala was bending, Kristine could see it in the set of her shoulders and the expression in her eyes. Why was it so easy for women to forgive and forget?

"If he stays," Mike asked, "where . . . *exactly* will he be staying?"

Kristine cringed as three sets of eyes bored into her. Where indeed? "The apartment over the garage is empty. Of course the stairs might become a problem at some point. We could clean out the storage room. It's quite large. A portable heater or two, and it would serve the purpose. The bathroom is right next door to it and the kitchen is right here. That would probably be the best choice for . . . for later on. For now, if you all agree, the apartment will do nicely. If you're wondering if he's going to be making any trips to the second floor, get that idea right out of your heads. We are divorced." She wasn't sure, but she thought she heard three sighs of relief.

"Woodie?" Cala ventured again. "What about your wedding? It's only a week away."

"Under the circumstances . . ." Kristine let whatever she was about to say hang in the air.

"I want to make sure I understand something. Dad left us because some doctor told him he was going to die. Within a short period of time. Let's say a year. It is now eight years later, and he's still alive and looks as good as the last time I saw him. Yet he says he's still dying only this time it's for sure. You know, definite. Unless he gets a kidney transplant, which seems unlikely if he hasn't gotten one in eight years. Speaking strictly for myself, I think the whole thing is a crock," Mike said.

"Medical conditions sometimes go into remission. For years. Other times, they worsen very quickly. Medication can only do so much. Your father mentioned dialysis. He seems to have taken care of everything in regard to . . . to . . . his condition. It seems he's been in DC for over a week meeting with a specialist who was recommended to him. He did say if we didn't want him here, he would go to Washington and get a hotel . . ."

"You sound so forgiving, Mom. I guess I'm trying to figure out why," Mike said.

"Because I let it all go. I'm happy now. I have all of you, the little ones, Woodie and Pete and Carol. The business is doing so well it's downright scary. What more could I possibly want? What does your father have? No family, no career, no home, and he's dying."

Bitterness rang in Mike's voice. "By his own choice."

"We all make bad choices at one time or another. I've certainly made my share. I learned from mine. Some people are not that fortunate. I'm not sure if your father is one of those people or not. Time will tell us which way it's going to be."

"What time is it?" Tyler asked.

Cala looked at her watch. "Four-thirty. We might as well get dressed and go downstairs. The dogs will be ready to go out soon. The girls will be getting up around six-thirty, if not sooner. Then there's breakfast."

"We have to do some more shoveling. It's been snowing

steadily since we came upstairs. Do we do breakfast before we do the gift opening? What do you think is best?" Kristine asked fretfully. "I'm sorry, I can't seem to think clearly right now."

"I say we wing it. Let's get the shoveling out of the way first. I'll wake Pete and Jack. Will you ask Carol if she'll keep her ears open for the girls in case they wake up?"

"Sure. I'll meet you downstairs in thirty minutes," Mike said.

"I'll be the guy at the bottom of the steps," Tyler said.

"Mom, I need to ask you something. What did you feel when Dad walked through the door?" Cala asked.

"Rage, hate, dying love. I think I ran the whole gamut. Part of me wanted to pound him to a bloody pulp with my bare hands. Another part of me wanted to run to him, to hug him. Only because he was alive and finally we knew it for a fact. Right now I don't feel anything. Possibly sadness because our lives will go on, and his won't. I want you all to think about something. Look at all of us and then look at what your father is facing. We survived these past eight years on our own. We are better people for it, too. We're healthy, we're happy, our business is thriving, and we have many, many tomorrows to look forward to. We'll be able to watch the children grow up here. We are blessed. Sometimes we just don't take the time to think about things like that. I want you all to think about that while you're out there shoveling."

Cala turned and came back to her mother. "You're right about everything. Maybe some good will come out of this, Mom. None of us likes the situation, but it's in front of us and we have to deal with it and we will. I'm sure we'll stumble and fall, and I'm also sure there will be harsh words, but we'll survive. It's Christmas morning. You should call Woodie. Merry Christmas, Mom."

Kristine didn't trust herself to speak. She could feel her eyes start to fill. When the door closed behind her children, she sat down on the edge of the bed and let the tears flow.

Sniffling, she made her way to the bathroom. She'd call Woodie after she showered and dressed.

Dressed in a bright red fleece-lined sweat suit with a large Santa on the front, Kristine picked up the phone. Her knuckles turned white as she brought the receiver to her ear. Woodie picked up on the first ring. But then she knew he'd been sitting in his easy chair, the portable phone in his lap, just waiting for her call.

"Let me talk, Woodie. I need to say all this at one time. When I'm done you can talk. Okay?"

The words tumbled from Kristine's mouth in short, jittery phrases. When she finally wound down, her shoulders slumped. "I don't see any other way, Woodie. I have to be able to live with myself. None of us likes the situation, but it's here, and we have to handle it. When it comes right down to it, we really don't have a choice. Now you can talk, Woodie."

"What do you want me to say, Kristine? I understand. I truly do. I applaud you and the kids for your generosity of spirit. Are we getting married or not?"

There it was, the words she knew were coming. The words she didn't want to hear because to hear them demanded she give a response. "Yes, but not now. After . . . later on. When . . . when it's appropriate."

"Kristine, you are divorced. What does getting married have to do with Logan staying in the apartment over the garage? We can still get married and live at my house."

"Everything and nothing. I couldn't . . . can't . . . I need you to understand."

"I understand that you want me to wait around until Logan dies."

"No . . . yes . . . it's not like that, Woodie. Look, I don't like this situation any better than you or the kids do. It's something I have to do. I can't turn my back on someone who is dying and needs me. What kind of person would that make me? I can't subject you to what I know I'm going to be going through. I love you too much to do that to you. This is my problem, and I'll deal with it."

"Where does that leave me, Kristine? Are you going to tell him about us?"

"At some point. I don't know if it will be today or not. We have our hands full as you know. Today is Christmas. What time are you coming over? I thought we'd take the sleigh out at some point this afternoon."

"Kristine, I'm not coming over. Maybe you can handle this, but I can't."

"But . . ."

Kristine started to cry. "All we seem to do is argue and separate. It always seems to be my fault. Why is that, Woodie?"

"I don't know. No one likes to be second-best. I don't, and I don't think your ex-husband does either. I guess it just wasn't meant to be. Merry Christmas, Kristine."

Kristine stared at the pinging phone in her hand. She hurled the phone across the room, watched it hit the edge of the dresser, ricochet upward to land in the fire. Her face murderous, she stomped from the room and down the steps.

"I'd like to go to the bathroom, Kristine," Logan said when she reached the foot of the stairs.

"So go," Kristine shot back. "I want to go on record right now, right this minute, as saying I hate your fucking guts, Logan Kelly."

"Can't say that I blame you, old girl. Is there hot water for a shower? Do you think someone could get my bag out of the back of the truck?"

"You brought it, you get it. I have things to do. Don't use all the hot water, either."

"Why are you being so nasty? I told you I would leave. Christmas breakfast would be nice."

"Yes it would. Why don't you make it for everyone. I have to shovel and take these dogs out."

"What would you like me to make?"

"Whatever you can find. No one around here is fussy."

"Kristine, do you think, just for today, that we could

pretend to be a family again? I'd like to carry some kind of memory away with me."

Kristine turned. The sharp retort on her lips went unuttered when she saw Logan's eyes fill with tears. "I think we can do that, Logan. Don't expect more."

"See, that's why I love you. Your heart is big and full. Do you think anyone will mind if I wear the same clothes today?"

"In the scheme of things, I doubt it. The bathroom is off the kitchen. There are towels in the linen closet," Kristine said.

Dressed in stocking cap, whose tail served as a muffler, and a heavy jacket, Kristine opened the kitchen door to a blast of frigid air. It was just getting light. Thank God the snow had stopped. She looked in disbelief at the eight-foot-high drifts leading to the barns. In the dim morning light, she searched for Logan's truck. It was almost buried, the drifts almost to the top of the windows. She slogged her way over to the utility vehicle, doing her best to sweep at the snow with the broom in her hand. The car was new, the sticker price still on the window. Later she would ask why a dying man needed a brand-new thirty-thousand-dollar vehicle. For now, she opened the door and crawled inside to heft two duffels to the floor from the cargo area. Struggling through the snow, she carried them into the house, cursing herself every step of the way. This was something the old Kristine would do, not something the new Kristine would do.

"Logan, your bags are in the kitchen," Kristine shouted.

"Thanks, hon."

Thanks, hon. Kristine shivered in the warm kitchen. That was how Logan had always responded to her in the old days when she did something nice for him. Just those few words would leave her smiling for hours. A plethora of emotions swept through her. Once a fool, always a fool.

"Howzit going?" Kristine shouted to her children.

"You can start walking the dogs," Pete shouted. "More

to the point, how's it going with you? Did you call Woodie, Kristine?''

The shoveling stopped at Pete's words. All eyes focused on Kristine. "Yes, a little while ago. He won't be coming for Christmas dinner. He said he understands completely but that doesn't mean he has to accept the situation. I'd rather not talk about it if you don't mind.''

"Where's the old man?'' Mike asked.

"Don't refer to your father in that manner, *Michael*. To answer your question, he was taking a shower. I imagine he's toasting by the fire now. He offered to make breakfast for everyone.''

The use of his full name meant his mother was in no mood for anything other than the matter at hand. "Whatever you say, Mom.''

It was full light when Kristine led the last dog into the house. All she had to do now was clean up the papers from the back porch, lay down clean ones, and make a final check of the living room.

"Merry Christmas, Kristine,'' she muttered.

Logan looked down at the economy-size package of bacon sitting on the counter. He hated cooking even though he did it well. Cooking was women's work. Kristine had always been a good cook, able to improvise at the last second and put a full-course dinner on the table when he brought home unexpected company. Same old Kristine for all her bluster. She'd brought in his bags. For all her professed independence, she was still Colonel Kelly's wife. Divorce or not. A stupid piece of paper. *That* he had not expected. Still, it wasn't an insurmountable problem. He'd always been able to wrap Kristine around his little finger. The kids had performed as expected. He discounted them from the git-go. All three of them were hotheads. He'd had all night to think on the matter. Everything was workable or as the young people said today, doable, if you worked at it.

A strip of bacon spit at him. He turned it over just as Emily padded into the kitchen, her sister following her, trailing a tattered blanket that was dingy and gray. Cala had the same kind of blanket when she was little, he remembered. He tried to feel something for the little ones staring up at him. He'd never much liked kids, his own or anyone else's for that matter.

"What's your name?" Emily asked.

"Logan Kelly. What's yours?"

"Emily. This is my sister Ellie. Did Santa Claus come last night? I looked out the window, but I didn't see any reindeer tracks?"

Logan turned off the stove. "Come here," he said, motioning to his lap. "Let me explain what happened. Last night it snowed a lot. It was hard for Santa to see so he had to fly really high."

"Didn't Rudolph light the way?"

Who the hell is Rudolph? "Of course he did. It was still hard to see because the snow was coming down really hard. As soon as he landed on the roof the tracks filled up. I saw one by the chimney when I got up."

"Didja see the tracks, didja see the tracks?" Ellie squealed.

"You shouda woke us up, Mister," Emily said. "Did he drink the milk and eat the cookies we left him?"

Mister? Something gouged at Logan's gut.

"I left Santa some reindeer treats. Did he take them?" Ellie queried around the thumb in her mouth.

"I'm sure he did. Santa doesn't like it when the children wake up. The reindeer get scared if they see little children."

"Did Mrs. Santa Claus help Santa with all the toys, Mister?"

Mister. "No, not this year. She had to stay home to make supper for the elves."

"Wha'd she cook, Mister?"

"Do you think you could call me Logan or ... Grandpa?"

"Why?" Emily asked.

"That's my name. You should call people by name."

"My grandpa's name is Fred," Emily said.

"Didn't anyone tell you that you can have two grandpas?"

Ellie started to cry. "Don't want two grandpas."

"Okay. How about if you call me Logan."

"I can call you Logan," Emily said seriously. "I'm hungry."

"I thought I heard you girls in here. Oh, Mr. Kelly, are they bothering you?"

"No, not at all. We were having a discussion on Santa Claus. Is this your son?"

"Yes. He's ten months old."

Logan felt like a fool when he asked, "Are you Mike's or Tyler's wife?"

Carol flushed. "I'm Carol, Mike's wife. Tyler isn't married. Last night was . . . unexpected. Would you mind holding Dillon while I heat his bottle? I'll make the girls breakfast as soon as I feed the baby."

"I started breakfast, but these little rascals wanted a discussion on reindeer tracks. By the way, did you see the two tracks on the roof before the snow covered them?"

"Oh, my yes. Big tracks. The whole roof was full of them. Then the wind blew snow in the tracks," Carol said, her eyes wide for the girls' benefit.

"Rudolph?" Logan said, his brow furrowed in frustration. Like it or not, he was holding the sweet-smelling baby. Again, something churned in his guts as one chubby fist wrapped itself around his index finger.

"You know, 'Rudolph with his nose so bright . . .' "

It was all Greek to Logan. He nodded as though he understood perfectly. He stared at Carol as she bustled about the kitchen. She reminded him of Kristine when she was younger. He said so.

"That's a very nice compliment, Mr. Kelly. I like and admire Kristine. Mike is very fortunate to have a mother like her."

"Yes, he is. Kristine was a wonderful wife." He wasn't going to touch the motherhood thing. Noway, nohow.

Carol handed Logan the bottle. "Your choice, feed him and I cook, or I feed him and you cook."

Logan surprised himself by agreeing to feed the baby. He watched with interest as the baby guzzled the bottle, his chubby cheeks blowing in and out. He looked just like Mike and Cala at the same age. "Does he eat food?"

"Baby food. He only has four teeth. It's amazing that he has a full head of hair, though. And curly, too. I think if I had a choice, I'd want more teeth and less hair. It would make feeding time a lot easier."

Logan threw back his head and laughed. Dillon let loose with a robust burp that sent the girls, Logan, and Carol into peals of laughter just as Kristine and the others stomped their way into the kitchen. Logan watched as her eyes narrowed to slits. "Wash up, everybody, and give me your breakfast order. I set the playpen up in the dining room. You can put him in there, Logan. He'll play with his toys. Crank up the mobile for him, and he'll be good for hours."

"When are we going to open our presents, Mommie?" Emily asked. "Do I have two grandpas?"

"Yes, you have two grandpas."

Kristine felt the urge to smash something. Preferably over Logan's head. Instead, she poured herself a cup of coffee.

"Would you mind getting me one, hon?"

"Not at all, Logan," Kristine said sweetly. "I forget, how do you take it these days?"

"Hot, black, and strong."

Kristine poured the coffee. This was Christmas, she reminded herself. Just as she was about to set the cup down on the table, Gracie and Slick ran between her legs to get to Emily. The rubber soles of her boots stubbed the hardwood floor and the coffee spilled into Logan's lap. He reared up and out of his chair, muffled curses exploding from his mouth.

Kristine clucked her tongue. "Oh, my, look what I did. Clumsy me. It's these darn boots. Shame on you, Logan. We do not curse around the children. There's some ointment in the medicine cabinet. The first cup is always the hottest. I've never been able to figure out why that is."

"You did that on purpose, Kristine," Logan hissed as he passed her on his way to the bathroom.

Kristine looked around. Suddenly everyone was looking somewhere else.

"So, ladies, did Santa come last night?" Jack asked to cover the tricky moment.

"Yes," Emily said solemnly.

"Let's go see what he brought," Cala said. "You're sure you were good this year."

"I was very good," Emily said.

"Ellie?"

"Me too, me too."

"Okay, then let's go. Pete, do you have the camera? I guess Jack dressing up as Santa is not going to work this morning. Ah, well, next year, you're doing it, Jack."

"All set to go."

"What about breakfast?" Carol asked.

"We can eat later, Carol," Kristine said as she poured herself another cup of coffee. "Did anyone call while I was outside?"

"No, Kristine."

"Am I invited or should I stay out here like the pariah I am?" Logan asked.

"Suit yourself. You were never interested in memories. Christmas is always a memory. I remember each and every one of ours."

"So do I, Kristine. Anytime you like, I will match you memory for memory."

"I have some real shitty memories, too, Logan."

"Yes, I guess you do. That was then, this is now."

"So it is."

"Truce. At least for today. When do you want me to leave?"

"We'll discuss it later after the kids open their presents."

Kristine burst out laughing as she entered the living room in time to see Emily load up her new wagon with the smallest dogs. Ellie covered them with her blanket.

"They aren't interested in the other things," Cala wailed. "We spent so much time picking and choosing and wrapping everything. Who would have thought a red wagon was so important?"

"Oh, oh, we're switching up here," Pete whispered. "The doll buggy is in play. How many dogs do you think Ellie can fit in there?"

"At least three. She put the spaniel in the cradle five minutes ago. This sure is a doggone good Christmas." Tyler hooted. "Start clicking that camera, Pete, and I want a complete set of prints. The guys at the base ain't never gonna believe this family. That's a compliment, Mom," he added hastily.

"I knew that," Kristine said smartly.

Two hours later, all the gifts were opened, and a mountain of colored paper littered the living room.

It was time.

"You guys go ahead. Pete, Jack, and I will clean up here," Carol said.

The Kelly family trooped out to the kitchen where they took their seats around the old round table. Kristine set out cups, cream, and sugar before she poured from the fresh pot of coffee. She took her seat, looked from her children to Logan. "It's time for you to tell your children why you're here. They have a voice in everything we do around here."

Logan looked around the table. There were no smiling faces. Kristine looked grim. He cleared his throat to go through his practiced spiel. There was no doubt in his mind that he could pull this off.

"For starters, I want to thank all of you for giving me the chance to at least talk to you this one last time. I just want you to know, this isn't easy for me. I'm taking my lumps, and I'm not complaining."

"Let's get to it, Dad," Tyler said not unkindly.

"Okay."

19

The headache hammering away at the base of Kristine's skull raced upward to pound away behind her eyes. She felt nauseous as she watched Logan take the seat at the head of the table. Her eyes spewed sparks. What right did he have to sit at the head of *her* table? No right at all. She could rectify it in a second if she wanted to. All she had to do was tell him to move. But did it really make a difference where he sat? Yes, according to the looks on her children's faces. Give Logan an inch and he'd steal a whole yard.

"I think it will be better if you sit here, Logan," Kristine said, pointing.

"It's all right, hon. This is comfortable for me."

"It's not comfortable for me, Logan. That's my chair you're sitting on."

"Oh." Logan shrugged but got up immediately. "This is rather like a meeting, isn't it?" he said.

Kristine sipped at her coffee willing him to get on with it so she could run upstairs and gulp down four aspirins.

"It's also a bit disconcerting," Logan said. The faces around the table remained blank.

"Can we get on with it, Logan?" Once she had hung on every word, every utterance that came out of her husband's mouth. *What are you doing right now, this minute, Woodie? Are you going to change your mind and come out to the house? Are you just going to let me flounder here by myself?*

Logan cleared his throat not once but twice before he

spoke. "I guess your mother told you about our conversation last evening. I understand your feelings. Now, I would like you to understand mine. I want all three of you to close your eyes and imagine, if you can, some doctor telling you that your life is coming to an end in mere months. If you have trouble imagining yourself being on the receiving end of such news, try imagining you are hearing it about your spouse or one of your children. The first emotion you experience is total, blind panic, then disbelief. You ask yourself how it can be? You feel fine, you look fine, but you're going to die. You'll never see the sun come up again. You'll never feel wind in your face, rain droplets on your head or walk through snow or smell burning leaves. I imagine other people think different things. I'm telling you what went through my mind. I wasn't going to be able to send the three of you off to college, watch you graduate and get married, walk the hospital floors while you waited for your child to be delivered.

"Your mother can verify that I was on some very strong medication. For most of my life I've taken medication for my kidneys. In my case it had an adverse effect on me. I'm sorry to say I took it out on the three of you. For whatever it's worth, I apologize. I wasn't myself. I've always loved you. I guess I didn't show it the way you wanted me to. As for your mother, she's always been the wind beneath my wings.

"Cutting to the chase here, I got this cockamamie idea that just maybe I could buy myself a kidney somewhere. I knew it would take a lot of money. The costs of the treatments were outrageous. Yes, I took the money. I took it for two reasons. One to see if I could heal myself and the other to make my death a little easier. I didn't want to be a burden to any of you, especially your mother. It did not work. That's the bottom line. The money is intact, plus interest. I apologize for that also. All I did those eight years was go from country to country, from specialist to specialist. I didn't get any better, and I didn't get any worse. In the end all I could do was wait for my time."

Kristine stared at the hanging fern over the sink. She mentally charted all the tiny leaves that were on the verge of turning yellow from the drafty old window. She wanted to feel something for the man sitting across the table from her but couldn't conjure up anything at all where he was concerned. She brought her gaze back to Logan, who was lighting a cigarette.

"Not too long ago I went for another checkup. The news this time was deadly. Three specialists confirmed the first doctor's opinion. They recommended a kidney specialist in Washington. I've seen him twice now. Dialysis is all I have going for me. I'm on a donor list, but so far down it isn't the least bit hopeful. That's pretty much my story.

"I asked your mother if I could come back here to spend my last days. She pretty much laughed in my face. I can't say that I blame her. I thought with what little time I had left, I could try and make amends, help out a little. I have no intention of getting in anyone's way or interfering in your lives. I realize you all made new lives for yourselves. Eight years is a long time. In my case, almost an eternity. I guess it simply never occurred to me that you wouldn't want me. I do understand, though. So, now that I've said my piece, I guess I'll shovel out my truck and be on my way. It really was nice seeing you all again. You know, you look like a jury sitting there. You're judging me. I guess you're entitled to do that. I would like to leave you with a thought. Until you walk in shoes like mine, don't ever be judgmental."

Logan rose from the table and buckled slightly; the knuckles of his hand grasping the table edge turned white. Tyler grabbed for him. "Sorry about that. I can't sit for long periods of time. Kristine, do you know where my jacket is?"

"No, I don't know, Logan. Maybe Carol hung it in the closet. I'll ask her."

"Don't bother, Mom. We decided Dad can stay," Mike said. "I'm going to help Cala bring the dogs in the apartment over here. We'll clean it up and get it ready. You can move in this afternoon.''

"You don't want me in the house, is that what you're saying?"

"No, Logan, that's not what they're saying. It's what I'm saying. I would never turn you away. That doesn't mean I owe you anything other than civility and common decency. You can take your meals here. Everything you need is in the apartment. You can do your own cooking if you want to. I'm a health-food nut and I know you are a meat and potatoes man.''

Logan sighed. "Not anymore, Kristine. Is there anything I can do for any of you before I settle in over there?''

Kristine stared at her children, aware that a blowup was about to happen. Mike stood up as did Tyler. When both boys were eyeball-to-eyeball with their father, Kristine saw him flinch. She saw something in Logan's eyes she'd never seen before and couldn't put a name to it. These were no longer little boys. Today Mike and Tyler were grown men with responsibilities much like Logan himself had been when he was their age.

What she was seeing on her ex-husband's face was fear. Fear of dying or fear of his sons? The latter she decided. The realization shocked her.

They were whispering but she couldn't hear what they were saying. Obviously, Cala couldn't hear either. She rolled her eyes in her mother's direction. Kristine nodded, the headache still pounding inside her head. *I wish you were here, Woodie. It's not right that you're alone on Christmas. I want to be with you. I need to be with you, but I can't turn my back on a dying man—a man I once loved who happens to be the father of my children, no matter what he's done. I just can't do that, Woodie.*

"You have one of those headaches, don't you, Mom?" Cala said.

"A little one. I was going to go upstairs and take some aspirin.''

"We can manage here. Go ahead, Mom. While you're

up there, call Woodie. I bet that will make your headache go away," Cala whispered.

"I might try that as a last resort," Kristine said wanly.

"Hon?"

"Please don't call me that, Logan. What?"

"I want to thank you for . . . intervening with the kids. I won't get in your way." Kristine nodded curtly before she left the room.

Outside the kitchen, life appeared to be normal. Emily was still pulling the dogs around in the red wagon, Ellie was pushing Gracie and Slick in her doll buggy, while Carol was struggling with a jigsaw puzzle. Jack was reading what looked like a two-pound book of instructions for a VCR while Pete rolled on the floor with a golden retriever named Goliath bent on chewing at his ear. Kristine waved halfheartedly as she made her way up the steps.

In the safety of her room, with the door locked, she blew her nose with gusto before picking up the phone to call Woodie. This time he didn't answer on the first ring. She was about to hang up when finally she heard his voice.

"Woodie. I miss you. This . . . I didn't think anything could be worse than that first Christmas, but I was wrong. I need you, Woodie. I need you to tell me this is all right. Please. I don't know if I have the stamina to handle this. The kids . . . the kids said he could stay. It is so bizarre, so unreal. I keep thinking I'm dreaming, and I know I'm not. I want it to be a nightmare so bad I can taste the feeling."

"Did you tell him about us, Kristine?"

"No, Woodie, I didn't. It wasn't the right time. I will tell him, though."

"When it comes to Logan, Kristine, it is never the right time for anything. We've been through this twice already, and I don't intend to go through it again. You need to take a stand. We can still get married. We can live at my house. You can drive to the farm every day to take care of business. You can certainly hire nurses to take care of your ex-husband when and if that becomes necessary. I really hate to ask this, but what are you and Jack going to do after New Year's? Are you still going to go through with your plans?"

"Woodie, I don't know. Would you please put yourself in my place for just a little while. If the situation were reversed and it was your ex-wife in the same circumstances as Logan, I wouldn't say a word."

"Kristine, you threw a fancy fit when you thought I was seeing her that day in the parking lot. You were ready to cut me out of your life without even giving me a chance to explain."

"I was jealous. I wasn't in a good place at the time, Woodie."

"This might surprise you, Kristine, but I'm not in a good place right now. We're just dogging this to death. You're trenching in, and so am I. One of us has to bend, and it isn't going to be me."

"Is that an ultimatum, Woodie? You did that to me once before, and we wasted four years of our lives."

"It's whatever you want it to be, Kristine. I asked you to marry me. You accepted. Now you're telling me you want to postpone the wedding. Eight years, Kristine. Don't you find that a little strange?"

"Of course I do."

"Logan could live ten more years. They're making tremendous medical strides every day. For his sake, I hope he does live ten more years, but not at my expense."

"Are you saying we're finished, that you're dumping me?"

"I guess I am saying that unless you change your mind. You aren't going to do that, so I think I'll say good-bye."

"Woodie, please don't . . . Woodie!"

Kristine crawled into bed. She was too tired, too drained to shed another tear. "It is what it is," she whimpered as she clutched at her pillow. A moment later she was sound asleep.

* * *

Logan looked around the small apartment that was now neat and tidy. He could handle this. While the furnishings were old and shabby, they were clean and comfortable. There was even a thirteen-inch color television set perched on a small table in the living room. A fire burned steadily in the fieldstone fireplace.

Logan opened the old-fashioned refrigerator. A bottle of wine, a brick of cheese, and three apples along with soft drinks filled the shelves on the door. He looked for a telephone, but there was none in sight. There was a small radio alarm clock in the bedroom but no sign of a telephone jack anywhere to be seen. That was okay, he had his cell phone. The only problem was, he had no one to call.

A nap would be good since he'd barely closed his eyes during the night.

Logan bounced on the bed. It was comfortable. He propped up the down pillows and laced his hands behind his head. He'd pulled it off, he thought smugly. Maybe he hadn't *totally* pulled it off. Mike's eyes were suspicious, and the hissing words he'd whispered in his ear had turned his blood cold. Tyler's eyes had been cold, but he was giving the old man the benefit of the doubt. What was it his son had said to him? Like he would forget something so ominous. "We're doing this because Mom said it's the decent thing to do. I, for one, am not buying your bullshit. Fuck with us one more time, and I won't think twice about pounding you to a pulp, and there isn't a jury in the land that will convict me. I'm not speaking for Mom, but I am speaking for the three of us."

Well, that certainly narrowed the field. He would just have to work his magic with Kristine. Once she fell into line, the rest of them would follow suit. Or would they? Whatever. He would have to be more diligent and work fast. How the hell hard could it be to seduce his wife? He knew which buttons to press, knew exactly how hard to jerk her chain. He'd start first thing tomorrow. For now he was going to take a nice long nap, and when he woke up he'd drink the wine and eat the cheese from the refrigerator. He made a silent bet with himself before he nodded off that, come six o'clock, either Kristine or one of the kids would trudge over to the apartment with a piping hot dinner. Oh yeah.

As his eyes closed, Logan shifted his thoughts to Peter Island and his next endeavor.

Woodie was like a caged, angry cat as he paced the long family room. Once he stopped to throw a monster log in the fire, stepping back when sparks shot upward and outward in every direction like a Fourth of July fireworks display. Like he really gave a damn if the whole place went up in smoke. *Son of a fucking bitch! She did it to me again. And it always comes back to Logan.*

Now what the hell am I supposed to do? Sit here and suck my thumb while I wait for Logan Kelly to die? Am I supposed to cut and run? And go where? Two days ago, just forty-eight hours ago, he'd been the happiest man on the face of the earth. Today he was the most miserable. On top of that it was Christmas Day.

Maybe he needed to get drunk. Maybe he needed to drown his sorrows. Or, maybe he should open his mail? Or, he could go into his little office and start getting his tax records together. If he decided to leave, he would have to have things ready to hand over to the accounting firm in Washington. Good old Steve. He wondered what his old college buddy was doing these days. Probably getting ready to do battle with the IRS over one thing or another. The only thought that appealed to him was the one about getting drunk, but, if he was going to do that, he needed to eat first. And it certainly wouldn't hurt if he prepared something ahead of time for his hangover tomorrow.

Woodie stomped his way into the kitchen, where he yanked open his kitchen cabinets. Kraft macaroni and cheese, Lipton noodle soup, baked beans, Spam, tuna, canned vegetables, canned juices. A Duncan Hines cake mix. Hell, he hadn't baked a cake in years. Maybe he should give that a shot. A casserole would be good. He could just dump everything in it and hope for the best. It occurred to him to wonder how old the stuff was. Maybe it would kill him, and his worries would be over. He wondered if Kristine would shed more tears over his death or Logan's.

The phone rang. Woodie stared at it. Kristine wouldn't call a second time. So, who was it? Someone calling to wish him a happy holiday. He picked it up on the sixth ring and barked a greeting.

"My goodness, Aaron, is that any way to answer the phone. This is Maureen, sweetie. How are you? I called to wish you a Merry Christmas. You are having a merry time of it, aren't you?" Maureen trilled.

"The merriest there is. Where are you, Maureen?"

"In Washington at the Hyatt. Stedman wanted to come back for the holidays. I wanted to stay in St. Tropez but in the end I always do what Stedman wants."

"What makes you think I'm interested in your whereabouts or your itinerary, Maureen?" Woodie all but snarled.

"Sweetie, we were married once. That means we'll have a bond of sorts all our lives. I'm really very fond of you. If you'd had more money, I would have stayed with you. I would even have lived in that awful tree house of yours."

"I'm not exactly poor."

"No, sweetie, but you are stingy. Do you want to know what Stedman gave me for Christmas?"

Woodie clenched his teeth. "I can't say it will make my day complete. More to the point, what did you give old Stedman? By the way, how is he?"

"The poor darling has good days and bad days. We have round-the-clock nurses for him. He sleeps quite a bit these days, which gives me loads of free time. I thought when the weather cleared, I'd drive out to see you. To answer your question, though, I gave Stedman a cashmere, monogrammed muffler. He loves mufflers. He gave me a

French villa and a diamond belt. Did you ever in your life hear of anything more outrageous? Each stone is a full carat. They're perfectly matched. I know you aren't up on fashion, so I'll tell you: it's one of those belts you wear when you're naked.''

Woodie choked on the smoke from his cigarette, then he laughed.

"When I come out to visit, sweetie, I'll show you how it looks. Are you still dating, goodness, isn't that word archaic, that farm woman?"

"No," Woodie barked.

"Oh, sweetie, did things go sour?"

"You could say that," Woodie barked again.

"Do you want me to call before I come out or should I just pop in? I won't come empty-handed. I bought you a lovely gift, and I wrapped it myself. I love to give presents. Stedman gets such joy out of seeing me shop. We have so many houses I've lost track. Life couldn't be better.''

"If it's so goddamn wonderful, why are you calling me?"

"To stay in touch. Just like the telephone people tell you to do. It's also very boring here today. There is so much snow, there's nothing going on in the hotel, and Stedman is napping." Maureen laughed. "I'm reaching out to touch someone.''

"Well, touch someone else. I'm busy right now. Merry Christmas, Maureen, and Happy New Year. That's my greeting for the new year, too, so you won't have to call me again.''

"You're such an old grouch, Aaron. I don't know why I bother with you.''

"Good-bye, Maureen.''

"Diamond belts to wear when you're naked. Now I've heard everything," Woodie snapped as he flipped open his cabinets in search of liquor. His old housekeeper must have replenished his liquor when he called to tell her to get the house ready. The stuff in the cabinets must be fresh, too. What to choose? Scotch, gin, vodka, rum, or cognac? What the hell, he'd sample all of them while he cooked his Christmas dinner.

It was five minutes of four when Woodie staggered over to the kitchen counter to survey his culinary masterpieces. He was as drunk as the proverbial skunk, knew it, and didn't care. He was going to get even drunker if he didn't pass out first.

Woodie splashed Bacardi rum into a glass. He gulped at it. The fiery liquid popped his eyeballs to attention just as he heard a high-pitched whine outside the house. In his drunken state he couldn't make out the direction of the earsplitting shrieking noise. Probably another damn burglar. Well, his shotgun was ready and loaded. All he had to do was find it.

"Aha! Okay, I'm ready for you!" Woodie said, leaning up against the refrigerator, the barrel of the gun pointed in the middle of the kitchen door. It was quiet. Too quiet! The bastard was probably going to come in through the front door. Was it locked? What difference did that make? Burglars knew how to break and enter. The first sound he heard at the door and he'd start blasting. For one crazy moment he wondered if it was Maureen in her diamond belt. God, what if he killed her dead and all she was wearing was a diamond belt? How would he explain that to the banking industry? He *used* to be a pillar of the banking industry. Now he was nothing. Kristine didn't want him because she had to wait for old Logan to kick the bucket. Maureen didn't want him because he wasn't rich enough. Even his housekeeper didn't want him anymore because she said there was nothing for her to do in his house. Damn, he couldn't make anyone happy.

"Shit!"

The kitchen door opened and closed. Woodie stumbled his way through the dining room and out to the kitchen. "You take one more fucking step, and you'll be picking these shotgun shells out of your teeth," he roared.

"Woodie, it's me, Pete! Put that damn gun down before you shoot someone. Is it loaded?"

"Yeah, it's loaded. D'ya think I'm stupid?"

"Hell, yes, I think you're stupid. I don't like guns, and I particularly don't like drunks with guns," Pete said in a jittery voice, his feet rooted to the floor.

"Then what the hell are you doing here?" Woodie said, leaning the gun in the corner.

"Don't you have to do something to that gun? Put a safety on it or uncock it or something?" Pete asked, his face full of worry.

"I already did that. I told you I wasn't stupid. Kristine thinks I'm stupid, but I'm not."

"Kristine doesn't think any such thing. She's miserable. As miserable as you look. What's all this stuff?" Pete asked, waving his arm about.

"This is liquor. This is macaroni and cheese. This pot has noodle soup in it. This is tuna fish with little green things in it. This plate is full of Spam. I don't know what to do with it. This is baked beans, the kind that has a cube of something white in it. And this is . . . hell, I don't know what it is. It's my Christmas dinner."

"I think it's succotash. I hate succotash," Pete said.

"I hate succotash, too," Woodie said, his head bobbing up and down. "Want a drink? Christmas holidays and all. How'd you get here?"

"On one of the snowmobiles you bought for Kristine for Christmas. Don't you remember? They came yesterday morning before all hell broke loose. I hid them in the old barn."

"Yeah, yeah. So, do you want the drink or not? We need to toast old Logan and his return."

"I'll take the drink, but I'm not making a toast to Logan or anyone else. You need to stop torturing yourself. It's not Kristine's fault her husband came back. She wanted to kick him out. So did the kids. However, when someone is dying, that's kind of hard to do. Even though you're drunk, you should understand that."

"Well, I don't. She won't marry me. She put me on hold. Do you got that? Me, she put on hold. Maybe later

I'll be good enough to marry, but not now because Logan has to come first. That should tell you something, Pete Calloway.''

"It tells me Kristine has emotions and decency. She's trying to do the right thing so that when . . . when the end comes, she can hold up her head and know she did the right thing.''

"She can still do the right thing and marry me. We could live here. She could go to the farm every day. I don't begrudge her taking care of her ex-husband. I don't, Pete. I'm not good enough to marry. I'm an . . . interference. Are you going to eat this crap or not?''

"No.''

"Then why'd I cook it?'' Woodie grumbled.

"To have something to do while you were drinking, I guess,'' Pete said.

"Maureen called me. Guess what old Stedman gave her for Christmas besides the French villa?''

"I don't have a clue,'' Pete said.

Woodie leaned over the table, his eyes popping from his head. "He gave her a diamond belt. Ya wear it when you're *nakid!* Whad'ya think of that?''

"I'm impressed.'' Pete grinned.

"Me too. She's coming out here to model it for me. Whad'ya think of that?''

"I'm really impressed. Are you going to wear the yellow Calvins or the blue Speedo?''

"Smart-ass. You sound like Kristine. I don't like her today.''

"Yeah, I know. I just came out to see if you were okay.''

"I'm okay.''

"What are you going to do, Woodie?''

"I'm-going-to-Tibet!''

"No shit!''

"Yep. I might get a cat, too.''

"That's pretty far. Tibet isn't around the corner. You gonna seek out the Dalai Lama?''

"Maybe. Maybe I'll ask Maureen if I can stay in her

French villa. She said a part of her will always love me. Kristine never said that."

"That's because the whole of her loves you, not just a part of her. I have to get back to the farm. It's almost time to take the dogs out. You need some coffee and a nap. How about if I make you some coffee and tuck you in?"

"The best man won, Pete," Woodie said as he flopped down on one of the kitchen chairs.

"That's not true, Woodie. You're the best man. Listen. This is just a temporary setback. Look, I'm going to come back here tomorrow when you're sober and talk sense to you. We can work this out. I don't want to see you or Kristine throw away something you'll both regret."

"Call first. I might have company."

"No one comes out to this godforsaken place."

"Maureen will. She knows where it is. You can tell Kristine that, too."

"Okay, big guy, the coffee is perking. I'm putting all this liquor back in the cabinet. Promise me you won't drink any more."

"No, no. When I make a promise, I keep it. I might want to drink some more later. After I eat this feast. What are those green things in the tuna?"

"It looks like leaves from the plant over the sink. Parsley?"

"Yeah, maybe it's parsley. Are you going to tell Kristine I love her?"

"Do you want me to?"

"Nah. Are you going to tell her I'm going to Tibet?"

"Do you want me to?"

"Nah. How about Maureen?"

"Yeah, I'm gonna tell her about the belt."

"You are!" Woodie reared up in his chair. "Why?"

"It's important." Pete grinned.

"Yeah, yeah. I didn't know they made things like that."

"I didn't either. Isn't it great the way we learn something new every day? Okay, here's your coffee. Come on,

I'll help you into the living room and put the television on for you. Are you going to be okay, Woodie?"

"Maybe yes, maybe no."

"I'll come back later. Now drink that coffee."

Woodie took one swallow before he set the cup on the end table. He leaned his head back into the softness of the sofa cushions. Moments later he started to snore.

Pete went up to the second floor for a blanket. He removed Woodie's shoes, straightened out the lanky form, covered it, then turned off the television. He checked the fire and adjusted the fire screen.

In the kitchen, he unplugged the coffeepot and threw dish towels over the array of food on the table and counter. He felt like crying when he went outside in the cold air. Sometimes life just got in the way of life.

Pete arrived back at the farm just in time to help with the dogs.

"I was wondering where you were," Kristine said.

"You know me. I couldn't wait to try out *your* new snowmobile. I gotta tell you, Kristine, it was a blast."

"Where did you go?"

"I went over to check on Woodie. He's drunk. I made him some coffee and put him to bed on the couch. He's going to have a hell of a hangover tomorrow."

"Did he say anything?"

"Actually he said a lot. You know drunks. They talk a lot. I didn't mean . . ."

"No offense taken. What did he say, Pete?"

"If I tell you, you won't like it."

"Try me," Kristine said.

"His ex-wife is in Washington and she called to wish him a Merry Christmas. It seems her husband gave her a diamond belt for Christmas, the kind ya wear when you're *nakid*. She's coming out to model it for him. If you're planning on going over there, call first. That's what he told me to do."

Kristine stomped into the house, her face murderous.

"It was my best shot, Woodie," Pete murmured as he followed Kristine into the house.

"It was a great dinner, Mom," Tyler said.

"I'll help clear up, but first I want to put the kids to bed. Both of them are out on their feet," Cala said.

"Take your time; Mike and I will clean up," Carol said.

"I'm going to fix a plate for your father," Kristine said with an edge in her voice. She waited to see what her children would say to that. They ignored her comment and went about their business.

"I can take it over if you want me to," Jack said.

"It's okay, Jack. I need to talk to Logan to straighten out a few things."

Pete poured fresh coffee into his cup. "All things considered, it's been a great Christmas, Kristine. It's amazing how the animals adapted. My biggest worry is when their owners pick up their pets after the new year that they're going to want to be pulled around in a red wagon. How are we going to explain that?"

Kristine smiled. "Look at it this way, it's a service we provide. They can bring them back anytime and I'm sure Emily and Ellie will oblige. For a fee of course."

"Now why didn't I think of that?"

"Because Mom's the brains," Cala said, tossing him a dish towel. "Are you coming up to say good night, Pete?"

"As soon as I finish my coffee."

Kristine arranged everything on Logan's plate in neat little sections. Pete watched her with clinical interest. "That's rather tidy, Kristine."

Kristine looked down at the plate. "It's the way Logan always ate. Nothing touched anything else. If it did, he would toss it out." She ripped off a piece of tin foil when she saw Pete's jaw drop.

"You fixed his plate?"

Kristine clenched her teeth. "Yes."

"Cala would boot my butt out the door if I asked her to do that. What did you do if he tossed out a plate?"

Kristine unlocked her jaw. "Made another one."

"Uh-huh," Pete said.

"You don't understand," Kristine said lamely.

"You're right. I don't. Please don't explain it to me either, okay?"

Kristine yanked at the aluminum foil and dumped the contents of the plate into the trash. A minute later she tossed food onto the same plate any old way. She slopped gravy onto the mess, dusted it all with salt and pepper before she crunched the same foil around the plate. "Satisfied?"

"Hey, this is none of my business. I have to say good night to my kids," Pete said, heading up the back stairway.

Jack Valarian's pitying look almost drove Kristine to tears. Carol refused to meet her gaze. Tyler bent over to tie his shoelace, and Mike shook out a clean trash bag as he danced around Gracie and Slick.

"I'll be back in a few minutes."

Outside in the cold air, Kristine followed the shoveled path. She must be crazy to be doing this. She'd always been crazy where Logan was concerned. She needed her wits about her.

She didn't bother to knock, but kicked at the door with one foot to announce her arrival, then opened the door. "I brought you some dinner. You better eat it now before it gets cold."

"That was nice of you, Kristine. What is it?"

"Prime rib, mashed potatoes, gravy, vegetables, salad, and plum pudding."

Logan folded back the aluminum foil. "Did you fall on your way over?"

"No. Why?"

"It's all messed up. I can't eat this."

"That's a shame. That's right, you like little spaces between your food. How could I have forgotten something so important?" She watched as Logan set the plate aside.

He picked up a chunk of cheese and nibbled at it. She shrugged. "Your loss, Logan, it was a good dinner."

"Sit down, Kristine. Do you want to talk?"

"Actually, Logan, no, I do not want to talk. By that I mean I don't want us to have a conversation. I volunteered to bring dinner over to you because I wanted to tell you something. I plan . . . planned on getting married New Year's Day. Now that you're here, I will postpone it until . . . a more . . . later when it's warm. I thought you should know."

"You're getting married!" Kristine smiled at the shock on her ex-husband's face. "How can you do that? Are you saying you've been having an *affair*? Who is it? Kristine, I cannot believe you would do that to me. You've been carrying on with someone behind my back?"

Kristine stared in awe at Logan. If he wasn't so serious, so shocked, she wouldn't have laughed. She doubled over, howling with mirth. "You are absolutely unbelievable. You really are."

Logan found his voice. "Who is it, Kristine? I think I have a right to know that."

"You have no rights where I'm concerned, Logan. However, I don't mind telling you. It's Aaron Dunwoodie."

"Woodie. He was always a stuffed shirt. I bet he has a paunch and is half-bald. Woodie!"

Kristine laughed. "Wrong. He's taller than you, full head of hair, all his own teeth, one-eighty without an ounce of fat, and he's so virile he makes my head spin. Eat your dinner, Logan. I'll see you tomorrow."

"No, no, it doesn't work that way, Kristine. You stay right here and explain all of this to me. I can't believe you turned into a slut!"

Kristine whirled around so fast Logan stepped backward but not in time to ward off the resounding slap she centered on his puffing cheek. "If you ever make a remark like that about me or to me again, I will personally slice off your prick while you're sleeping. Are we clear on that, Logan? You aren't answering me. Are we clear on that?"

"You struck me! Jesus Christ, Kristine, what's gotten into you. I don't know you anymore."

"That's true, Logan, you don't know me anymore. You never knew me. And, pay attention to this, you aren't going to get to know me now at this point in time. Good night, Logan. Sleep well."

"Kristine, wait. I'm sorry. You can't just throw something like that at me and expect me to . . . to say congratulations. You shocked the hell out of me. I need to know more. I need to digest what you said."

"No, you don't. It's my business, not yours. You can digest and dissect this all night long after I leave. You really should eat your dinner, Logan. It was very good. I'd heat it in the oven, though. It must be cold by now."

"Kristine, wait."

"I can't, Logan. My family is waiting for me."

Kristine zipped up her down jacket. It was clear and cold, the sky star-spangled. She drew the drawstring on the hood tight as she trudged around to the front of the house. Christmas was almost over. She sat down on the front steps, her hands jammed into her pockets.

How could Logan talk to her like that? Was she supposed to make allowances for him because he was dying. Had he always been that inconsiderate, that cruel? Of course he had, and she'd put up with it. Tonight she'd shown her backbone, though.

Too much too little too late.

20

"The daffodils are about to bloom. I guess we can count on spring arriving a little early this year," Pete said, his gaze sweeping around the backyard.

"It's about time," Kristine said. "This past winter was a horror. We survived, though. I'm very excited that Mike and Carol will be here by Easter. Dillon should be walking by now. Actually, he is toddling around, Carol said. And he's into everything. Business is great. They're going to start on the new barns as soon as the ground warms up. By summer we'll be up to speed. I'm up to four pages on my waiting list. It warms my heart. I heard in town a few weeks ago that Taylor's toy store had a run on red wagons. Mr. Taylor personally thanked me," Kristine's voice was so flat-sounding that Pete blinked.

"We're dancing around this, Kristine. Talk to me about Woodie and Logan. I don't like the way you're acting. It's almost as though you're a robot just going through the motions."

"There's nothing to say, Pete. I heard in town that Woodie is doing some consulting work at the bank. He hasn't called. I've called him, but I always get the machine. I leave messages, but he doesn't return them. Maybe he's seeing his ex-wife. Before you can ask, of course I miss him, and, yes, I still love him. I've come to the conclusion that if it's meant to be, it will be. As for Logan, we are civil. I inquire about his treatments. He's helped me a little with the books. He clears up after dinner. One evening we even sat on the back porch and talked. We didn't discuss anything important. Mostly it was the weather, what kind of summer we'll have, putting a new roof on, things like that. He was quite pleasant. He's never said another word about Woodie.''

''Jack Valarian?''

''I think Jack is about ready to give up on me. Logan has been looking at the records and he found stuff Jack and I missed. You're going to find this hard to believe but it was Logan's ancestors who were the big slave traders, not mine. Somehow Jack mixed up some of the records. In the end it doesn't really matter which side of the family did it. We're going to make it right. Logan is agreeable to it all. He said he didn't want to go to his Maker with that on his conscience. So, some good has come of all this— by *this,* I mean his return. He even volunteered to input all the records and files into a computer. He ordered one last week. It should be set up today or tomorrow. He also hired a handyman to clear out the storage room so he can move into it. He's having trouble with the stairs. He said he doesn't sleep well at night, so he might as well work at the computer to keep himself busy. I hesitate to say this, but he isn't the same old Logan I used to know.''

''I saw you going for a walk the other day,'' Pete said sourly.

''I went for a walk. I go for a walk every day. That particular day, Logan tagged along. He didn't get far. I went ahead and picked him up on the way back. If you have something to say, Pete, then say it.''

''I just did. I'm sorry, Kristine, but I don't like your ex-husband. I never did, and I don't see any point in pretending I do. I stayed on here because of you.''

''I know that, Pete, and I'm grateful. Cala talks to him, and she should, because he's her father. Emily and Ellie are polite, but they don't seem to like him much. Children instinctively know who they can run up to and hug. The dogs leave Logan alone, too.''

"Guess what, Kristine. The animals hate him. Kids and animals are astute judges of character."

"I know that, Pete. Just let things take their natural course."

"Fine, I'll do that. I want to make sure you aren't blinded by what you see on the surface. You already screwed things up with Woodie." Pete's voice was so sour-sounding that Kristine wanted to swat him.

"I resent that, Pete."

"Too bad. When something is true, it's true."

"Is Woodie seeing someone, Pete?"

"How would I know something like that?"

"Forget I mentioned it. If he is, I don't blame him. So, what would you like for lunch, tuna salad or egg salad?"

"Surprise me," Pete said, heading for the barn.

Kristine stood at the bottom of the stairs leading up to the back porch. She looked up to see Logan sitting on the folding chair with Gracie and Slick in his lap. He was tickling their ears. "Get down!" Kristine shouted. When the dogs stayed where they were, she raised her voice a second time. Slick leaped to the ground. Gracie stayed on Logan's lap.

"Why didn't we ever get a dog?"

"Because you hated animals," Kristine snapped as she snatched Gracie from Logan's lap. She swatted the little dog on her rear end. "When I call you, you come," she said, wagging her finger under the little dog's nose.

"What do you want for lunch, egg salad or tuna?"

"Egg salad will be fine."

"We're having tuna," Kristine said as she opened the screen door.

"Tuna's fine, too. Do you want me to do anything? I cleaned up the kitchen earlier. You are a messy cook, Kristine."

"What time is your appointment today?"

"Two o'clock. I'll be home by five. In case you're interested, the doctors say I'm doing better than expected. Don't worry, I'm sure I'll die right on schedule, and you can marry Aaron Dunwoodie. That certainly is a strange relationship. Do you ever *see* him? I'm beginning to think that confession you made to me on Christmas Day was all a figment of your imagination. You just said it to get a rise out of me, and I fell for it."

"Think what you want, Logan. My relationship with Woodie is none of your damn business. If you want to talk about infidelities, why don't we discuss some of yours. I know you carried on affairs while we were married. Don't bother to deny it, Logan. I might have cared then, but I don't care now."

"Yes you do. I can see it in your eyes when you look at me. You remember all the good times we had. We loved each other. I'll never believe you stopped loving me."

"In your dreams, Logan. This is not something I care to discuss. Not now, not ever. I'm warning you now, when you move into the storage room, that's where you will stay. You do not step foot on the second floor."

"You're afraid of me, aren't you?" Logan teased.

"No, I'm not afraid of you."

"Then you're afraid of yourself."

Kristine wondered if it was true. "Make yourself useful, Logan," she said too quickly. "Chop the onions and celery for the tuna. I have to go down to the barn for something."

"Why didn't you just tell me to make the sandwiches, Kristine? I don't mind. If I can make things easier for you, I'll feel like I'm earning my keep."

Kristine washed her hands. When she turned away from the sink she stepped right into Logan's arms. She gasped as his lips clamped down on hers. She struggled briefly and then gave in to the moment—the moment she'd dreamed about for so many years. The moment when Logan returned, to sweep her into his arms and promise undying love. It was a sweet, gentle kiss that spoke of things to come.

At that precise second, she wanted those other things yet to come.

The sound of steps on the back porch brought her back

to reality. Logan released her, a little smile tugging at the corners of his mouth. "I've wanted to do that since the night I came home. Do you know what I want to do to you right now?"

Out of the corner of her eye, Kristine saw Pete take the steps off the porch two at a time. Her stomach immediately tied itself into a big, hard knot.

"Don't do that again, Logan."

"I'm sorry. I liked it. You responded. To me that means you liked it, too. It seemed natural. I always used to kiss you when you were standing by the sink. Don't you remember? One time we went for it right there with the kids out on the back porch playing Monopoly. Do you remember that?"

"No," Kristine croaked.

"Liar," Logan said in the same light, teasing voice.

Flustered, Kristine opened the door for the dogs. She followed them to the barn, dreading the look she would see on Pete's face. She wondered if Pete would tell Cala what he'd seen. If he did, Cala would then call Mike, who would in turn call Tyler. *And all through no fault of mine*, she thought. *Of course it was your fault, Kristine. You even liked it there for a minute, and you wanted more. Admit it,* a voice inside her head argued with her.

"Woodie is the better kisser. I love Woodie. God, how I love Woodie," she muttered.

If you loved him, you wouldn't be standing here trying to figure out what you're going to say to Pete. He's never going to believe you weren't a willing partner in that kiss, the voice continued to argue.

What I do or don't do in my personal life is none of Pete's business. It's not my children's business, either.

That sounds like a pretty lame excuse to me, the voice grumbled.

"Stuff it," Kristine mumbled as she made her way to the small office where Pete was poring over AKC records. He looked up, a scowl on his face. Kristine reacted.

"Look, Pete, it isn't what you think. I don't owe you any explanations. That's all I'm going to say on the matter."

"That's fine with me. Don't fix any lunch for me. I lost my appetite."

"Isn't that kind of childish?"

"Is that what you think?"

"I told you, it isn't . . . wasn't what you think. I'm in love with Woodie. I will go to my grave loving that man."

"It might be nice if you told him so."

"He knows it, Pete. I'm doing what I feel is right. Woodie and I differ on what we think is right. If this is going to be a problem between you and me, spit it out now."

"Your life is your life, Kristine. I'm still not hungry."

"Fine," Kristine snapped as she gathered up the papers she wanted. "Mrs. Danziger called this morning. She wants a companion for Mitzi. I told her all the pups were promised, but she could have her pick from the first summer litter. I told her you would call her."

"Kristine, the woman already has four dogs. She's sixty-six. Are you sure you want to give her another pup?"

"She's got live-in help around the clock. Those dogs are her greatest enjoyment in life. She called, I promised, and that's the end of it."

"Yes, ma'am," Pete said smartly.

"I have to go into town. I'll be back by three. Do you need anything?"

"No," Pete said curtly.

"Then I'm going up to the house to eat my lunch."

Kristine felt Pete's eyes boring into her back as she walked up the path to the house.

"It's all ready, hon," Logan said as he took his place at the table across from Kristine.

Kristine looked down at the plate. The sandwich was toasted to perfection, the carrot curls and thin slices of cucumber looked delicious. The napkins were folded just right, the apple juice properly chilled. "Too bad you never did this when we were married, Logan. If you had, I wouldn't have had so much stress in my life."

"Ah, Kristine, we can't unring the bell. That was then, this is now. I wish I could do more for you. If I'm not too drained when I get back, let's go out to dinner. Or you could drive in and meet me. We could grab a fast bite in town and take in a movie. I haven't had Chinese in a long time. You love Chinese, and there are two good restaurants in town. Come on, you don't do anything here at night but wait for the phone to ring. Three hours tops. Come on, say yes."

"Yes."

"Yes. You mean it? It will be like old times with no strings."

"Yes, like old times with no strings," Kristine said.

"I'll meet you in town at five o'clock."

"Five o'clock is fine. Where do you want to meet me?"

"At the Golden Dragon."

"I'm going to leave now. Do you mind clearing up, Logan?"

"Yes, I do mind, but I'll do it."

"Never mind, I'll do it. I suppose it's fair since you made lunch. You need to leave now so you won't be late," Kristine said.

"I'll make lunch all this week. I'll clean up, too. You're a sweetheart, Kris."

"Just go, Logan."

Fool, fool, fool, Kristine's mind shrieked.

When the kitchen was all cleaned up, Kristine poured herself a second cup of coffee. As she sipped at it, she realized she had absolutely nothing to do. If she went down to the barn, she would only be in Pete's way. Cala would be out soon with the girls. She couldn't take Cala's job away from her or the little chores Emily and Ellie loved doing. The house was clean, the laundry all caught up. The paperwork was still in piles in the dining room waiting for Logan's final input. As much as she hated to admit it, he was right about a lot of things. In just a few days things would be ready to be put into motion. It had been Logan's idea to form the Summers Kelly Foundation that would

disburse the monies to those family members they had
documented and had been able to locate. Even Jack Valarian had agreed with Logan, which for some reason
excited him, so much so Kristine found herself being jealous when Jack deferred to Logan over her.

She needed to think about that kiss by the kitchen sink.
She had felt something, and she would be a liar if she
denied it. It was a physical thing, not a head and heart
thing like she felt for Woodie, she finally decided.

Kristine checked the kitchen clock. She had three hours
to kill until it was time to head to town to meet Logan. If
she waited until the last minute, she could go to the drive-
through teller at the bank so as not to run into Woodie.
If she had time to spare, she could go to the candy shop
and get the candies and chicks for Emily's and Ellie's Easter
baskets.

The long afternoon stretched ahead of her. What
should she do? She supposed she could settle down with
a good book or do some needlepoint. Neither thought
appealed to her, so she headed upstairs to take a bubble
bath. If she was going to the bank, she needed to look her
best. Just in case. She wondered if she had anything fetch-
ing in her closet besides jeans and sweat suits. She couldn't
remember the last time she'd bought anything new. Years
probably. She wanted something bright and colorful, something that said, "Here I am." The flip side of that particular
thought was Logan would think she got dressed up for
him. He was so cocky, so arrogant, so . . . so Logan.

"Wow!" Cala said at four o'clock when Kristine entered
the kitchen. "Do you have a date with Woodie?"

"I wish. I'm going to the bank."

"Mom, the bank closes at four."

"The drive-through is open till six."

"You did your hair, put on makeup, dolled yourself up
in a slick-looking linen dress and are wearing high heels
and perfume to go to the drive-through teller at the bank!"

"You get money for ice cream, Granny?" Ellie asked.

"You bet," Kristine said, hugging the little girl.

"You know, I might see . . . Woodie might recognize my car and come out, any number of scenarios could happen."

"Mom, why don't you just walk into the bank and ask for him? That's what I would do," Cala said.

"I'm not you. Woodie gave me an ultimatum. I can't seem like . . . this is best."

"Where's Dad?"

"He went for his treatment. I'm going to meet him for Chinese and a movie."

"Oh."

"Oh. That's it, oh."

"Mom, you're all grown-up. Whatever you do with your life is your business. Next time don't try to snow me by saying you got all duded up to go through the drive-through at the bank. Either tell me an outright lie or don't tell me anything. Come on, girls, let's go help Daddy."

Kristine would have cried except she knew her mascara would run.

As she backed her car out of the driveway she could see Cala and her little family staring at the car from the barn door. She almost rolled the window down to shout, "I'm telling you the truth, why don't you believe me?"

When she sailed through the drive-through at the bank, she tried to appear nonchalant as she looked around for Woodie's truck. It was nowhere in sight. She accepted her deposit ticket and didn't bother to check it. Instead, she leaned out the window and said, "Has Mr. Dunwoodie left for the day?"

"You just missed him, Ms. Summers. He left about ten minutes ago."

"Thank you." So much for getting dressed up and dousing herself with sinful perfume that was now going to be wasted on Logan Kelly.

* * *

"So, how's it going, Steve?" Woodie asked as he slid into a booth at the Golden Dragon.

"Busy as hell. I can't wait for tax season to be over. I'm going to sleep for a week."

"It was nice of you to bring my returns out here. I would have come in to pick them up."

"No problem. I wanted to get away from the office anyway. You know how wild it gets at this time of year. I thought we could eat, have a few drinks, and, if you didn't mind, I'd bunk with you and head back to town at the crack of dawn."

"Great idea. I'm loose these days. How about you? Sorry we couldn't get together over the holidays."

"This is the first I've seen you in, what is it, over four years? Postcards don't quite cut it. Mailed receipts and IRS forms don't cut it either, buddy. Weren't you supposed to get married?"

"Yeah, but it didn't quite work out. Like I said, I'm loose. How is it you're still a bachelor?"

"By choice. Always remember that. I did meet someone while we were on safari in Africa. Man, you missed one hell of a trip. It was like being a kid again. We didn't have to shower, we wore the same clothes, didn't shave. We had this great tour guide. I'm telling you, Woodie, it was the experience of a lifetime. We even managed to get a little intrigue into the end of the trip. We brought the tour guide home with us. We got her a job, an apartment, and she's happy. The intrigue concerns her."

"Her? Is the her the someone you met? Such good English," Woodie laughed.

"Yeah. I don't know if anything will come of it or not. At the moment, we're good friends. You need to take things slow at first. I'm not in a rush. I like being a bachelor, I like not having to share. I have a great life."

"Kids?"

"I don't know. I think fifty is a little late to start having kids. When I'm seventy I might regret it, but not now."

"How old is the lady in question?" Woodie asked.

"I'm not sure. Probably past the childbearing stage. She just came out of a bad relationship so she's in no hurry to start up something she isn't ready for. Friendship is great. Sex complicates things. How about you?"

"You're right about that, Steve. Her ex showed up out of the blue. We were supposed to get married the first of the year, but she put it on hold because he's dying and . . ."

"Yeah, and what?" Steve asked, biting into a crusty egg roll.

Woodie dunked his egg roll in duck sauce. He watched the sauce drip to his plate before he answered. "She feels she has to be there for him, to take care of him. I guess I'm stupid because I don't get it. He dumped her, swindled her and her kids out of all their money, and now he wants everyone to make nice so he can . . . go in peace. I guess I'm just a cold-hearted bastard. It's not a question of money. Round-the-clock nurses would be no problem. The kicker is, this guy looks as healthy as a horse. I hate to say this aloud for fear God will strike me dead, but the guy . . . I don't know, I think he's lying. It's just a suspicion. I didn't voice my opinions, either. She's done this to me twice before. That's why I took off after I retired. This guy is ruining my life, and hers, too and she doesn't see it. Why is it women are such suckers where men are concerned?"

"You're asking the wrong person, Woodie. I guess that's why I'm still a bachelor. Funny, though, the same thing kind of happened to Danela. The rat took off with all her money, too. D'ya think it's because I deal in numbers all day long and you dealt with money and investments all your life? Are we obsessed with money?"

"No. We respect what money can and cannot do, and we are responsible people. People depend on you the way they depended on me. We are not in the majority, Steve, we're in the minority."

"Are you just going to sit around and . . . and . . . ?"

"You can say it. Am I going to sit around and wait for him to die? No. I'm doing some consulting work for the bank. Hell, I'm turning work away. I fish once in a while. I take people out to dinner. I spend a lot of time reading and watching television. I've seen the world, so I have no desire now to do any traveling."

"What happens when the time . . . when he finally buys it? What will you do if she wants you then? Are we talking true love here?"

"I was. I thought she was, too. She said if she didn't take care of him she would regret it all her life. Maybe because I don't have children, I don't understand the bond between people who do have them. Like I said, maybe I'm just stupid. I told her it was him or me, and she picked him. I don't want to be second-best. Would you?"

"That's a tough one. No one wants to be second-best. I don't think I'll ever get married. I'll play ball with someone else's kids."

"Do you smell that?" Woodie asked.

Steve Douglas sniffed. "Yeah. I've bought enough perfume in my time to know good stuff when I smell it. I'm one of those guys who likes to sniff. Heady stuff. So, what are we ordering? Do you want to do the mix and match or one of those flaming platters? It all looks damn good. I suppose we could try a little of everything. Man, I haven't had lichee nuts since the last time I was out here to see you, and that must be over four years. I'm going to get some to go when we leave."

"Shut up, Steve. It's *her.* Look at her, she's all spruced up, and she's the one with the perfume. I gave her that perfume, and she's with *him!* Son of a bitch! Don't look now. They're two booths ahead of us. Look into the mirror and you can see him."

"I thought you said he was dying. What the hell is he doing eating in a Chinese restaurant? Now, that's a good-looking woman, Woodie. He looks familiar."

"I went to school with him, for God's sake. Logan Kelly.

Don't you remember my telling you how jealous some of my classmates were when he went to West Point?''

"Did you say Logan Kelly?'' Steve asked.

"Yeah. Does he look like his days are numbered to you?''

Steve leaned over the table. "We need to get the fuck out of here right now, Woodie. Do not ask me any questions and do not look at that table again. Can we get out of here without being seen?''

"What are you talking about? We just got here. Okay, okay,'' Woodie said, pulling money out of his wallet.

"I'll tell you, but not here. Scratch those drinks and bunking at your house. We're going to my house with one stop on the way. Listen, you drive, Woodie. I'll come back with you and pick up my car tomorrow. I'm going to be making phone calls all the way in. You're sure that's Logan Kelly? I'll kind of inch my way out of here. Don't stop to chitchat, okay.''

Woodie snorted. The last person he wanted to chitchat with was Kristine and Logan Kelly. "This better be good, Steve.''

"This is so damn good you are going to owe me your life. You aren't even going to choke when you see your tax bill *and* my bill. I'll meet you outside.''

"Go already,'' Woodie said as he sniffed Kristine's perfume, which wafted toward his table each time she moved. So far she hadn't seen him. He wished he knew what all the cloak-and-dagger stuff was about.

The moment Steve was out the door, Woodie was on his feet and heading for the buffet bar where the metal canopy hid the upper part of his body. He sighed with relief when the warm spring air rushed at him.

"Never mind the damn cell phone. Tell me what's going on.''

"Woodie, you are never in your life going to believe this. C'mon, put the pedal to the metal and I'll fill you in. I'm telling you, you are never going to believe this.''

"Stop saying that and tell me what's going on.''

"Mr. Logan Kelly, aka, Colonel Logan Kelly, aka, Logan Kilpatrick, aka, Justin Eberhart of Eberhart Safaris in Africa is sitting at the table with your ladylove. He is not dying. He's a scam artist. He scammed Danela, that tour guide I told you about. He made off with her five million dollars and a lot of money from some banks. He left her holding the bag. When we got back from the safari, everything was cleaned out. She lived with him for eight years. We didn't know his real name was Kelly; Danela didn't know either. Brian hacked into the military files and that's when we found out. He also, are you ready for this, hacked into his numbered Swiss bank accounts. Man, we could lift that money at the drop of a hat. We've been sort of biding our time trying to get through tax season, then we were going to close in on him. You just handed him to us."

"Just tell me one thing. Is the guy dying or not?"

"Hell, no, he's not dying. We have his medical records. Chew on all that while I start making my phone calls."

Woodie listened in awe as Steve made one call after another, his voice going from jubilant to ecstatic to reverent. His first call was to his private secretary. "Marian, I hate to do this to you, but you need to go into the office now and work through the night. File for extensions on all the returns that aren't finished. I won't be in for the rest of the week, maybe next week. Call the clients and apprise them of the situation. Of course it's a family matter. Why else would I be doing this? I'll stay in touch. Of course there's a bonus in it for you.

"I kind of feel like God right now." Steve chortled.

The next call was to Brian Lucas. "Hey, buddy, close up shop and head for my house. File for extensions. You're going to be busy for the next week. Call the guys to meet at my house. Key's under the flowerpot. Yeah, yeah. I found the son of a bitch! He was in a Chinese restaurant here in Leesburg. You were right, Brian, he headed home. He's pulling another scam. Bring all the disks. See you."

The third call was to Danela. "It's me, honey. Listen up. We found Logan. He's right here in town. I want you to go over to my house. The guys will probably get there first, but just in case, the key is under the flowerpot. We saw him chowing down at a Chinese restaurant. He's not going anywhere. If you want the first crack at him, he's yours. I think there's going to be a long line ahead of you, though. Everyone I know wants a shot at this guy. Yes, he's with his wife. Excuse me, ex-wife.''

"You got any questions, Woodie?" Steve asked as he pressed the power button on his cell phone. "I've seen that guy somewhere and just recently. Can't place it, though."

"He said he was getting treatments at George Washington. Have you been there lately? Maybe visiting someone or maybe you saw him in the parking lot. Kristine said he goes in twice a week for dialysis."

"No, it was more of a social scene. For some reason I don't think it was recently. I did see him though. I remember thinking he had a super suntan."

"That was back around Christmas time. That's when he arrived here. Kristine said he had been in DC for a week or so before he went out to the farm on Christmas Eve. Maybe you saw him around town."

"I went to half a dozen cocktail and Christmas parties around then. Two were at the Ritz Carlton, one at the Ambassador. That was pretty stuffy. There were a couple at the Hyatt on Capitol Hill. Yes! It was at the Hyatt. He was sitting with a guy who had a portable oxygen tank and a . . . Jesus, it was with your ex-wife Maureen."

"Tell me you made that up. How in the hell could he know Maureen? She called to wish me a Merry Christmas and she didn't say anything about meeting him."

"Think about it, Woodie, why would she tell you something like that? You're divorced. They were just sitting there drinking. I remember thinking they were probably together, and the old guy with the oxygen was one of their parents. Talk about a small world."

"Mr. Clovis is my ex-wife's husband," Woodie said.

"At the risk of repeating myself, it really is a small world. Listen, Woodie, let's stop by the hospital and make some inquiries about Mr. Kelly. By the way, how can we get in touch with Maureen? We need to nail this stuff down. No point in going off half-cocked and blowing the whole thing.''

"I have no idea. She said Stedman wanted to come back for the holidays. I think they travel all the time. She said she was going to come out to the house, but she never did. She never called again, either. I don't feel right about this, Steve.''

"I'm trying to save your ass, buddy. What the hell does that mean, you don't feel right about this?''

"I don't want to be the one to jam all this into Kristine's face. It should be something she does on her own. She made her choice.''

"Are you saying you want me to drop all this? The guy's a fucking crook. We have the means to nail his ass to the wall. He ripped Danela off for five mil. He stole his wife's money. He's probably going to do it again. On top of that, the guy is a consummate liar. We've got him by the short hairs. If you need a clincher, how about this one? He's into some African banks for close to ten million dollars. It's all sitting in that numbered Swiss account.''

"That's not my problem.''

"The hell it isn't. It's my business, too. He's ripping off the IRS. He hasn't filed returns in over eight years. Are you condoning that, along with ripping off those banks and my friend Danela?''

"No.''

"Then what the hell are you saying, Woodie?''

"I don't know what I'm saying other than my instincts were right about Logan Kelly.''

"Are we going to the hospital or not?''

"I'm okay with that part of it. It will probably just confirm that Logan isn't dying. However, I don't think hospitals give out that kind of information.''

"All we're asking is if he's an outpatient.''

"I still don't think they'll tell us anything," Woodie said.

"Then Brian will hack into their system. We'll find out. I don't get it, Woodie, you want to know all the information but you don't want to do anything about it. It doesn't make sense."

"Kristine has to see all this for herself. I understand how she feels. She was married to Logan for a long time. They had three children. She thinks he's dying, and she wants to do the right thing. It's me that can't accept the situation. Let's just play this by ear and see how it goes, okay?"

"It's your life, buddy," Steve said, slumping down in the seat.

"Yeah, it's my life," Woodie muttered.

The rest of the long drive into the city was made in silence.

"Okay, we're here," Woodie said, pulling into a parking space. "I think this is a waste of time, but let's go for it."

"Let's try Admitting first," Steve said. "If we don't find out anything there, we can try the business office. If you offer to pay someone's bill, they rear up and listen."

"I never would have thought of something like that," Woodie said, his voice full of awe. "I'll catch up with you. I want to stop at the men's room."

Woodie was reading the overhead signs and trying to decipher the colored zones on the wall when he felt someone tap his arm. He turned. "Maureen! What are you doing here?"

"Stedman is here," she said wearily. "We never left after the holidays. This is the third time he's been admitted since Christmas. He doesn't have long, Aaron. A week, maybe two, but that's it. I really don't understand what I'm feeling. Part of me wants him to live forever. He's been so good to me, so kind, so gentle. He's a wonderful man. I never once heard him complain. I don't know what to do."

"Let's go in the coffee shop and have some coffee. We can talk there. First I have to go to the business office to tell my friend where I'll be. Are you okay?"

"Look at me, Aaron. Do I look okay to you?"

Woodie really looked at her then. Her hair was disheveled, she wasn't wearing makeup, and she looked like she'd slept in her clothes.

"I've seen you look better. That's not to say you look bad. You're under stress right now."

"I stay here all day and night. Stedman is in ICU, and they only allow me to see him ten minutes on the hour. I brought changes of clothes with me. Do you want me to order you some coffee?"

"Sure and maybe an egg salad sandwich. Hospital coffee shops always serve the best egg salad. I don't know why that is."

Maureen smiled wanly. "That's what Stedman said. He can't eat now. He's hooked up to an IV gizmo. Most times he doesn't even know me."

"Get the coffee. I won't be long."

Woodie loped down the long hallway, one eye on the colored zones and the arrows and his other eye on the small protruding signs that announced each office. When he met up with Steve Douglas, Douglas winked at him, and said, "I'm getting something. I just don't know what it is."

"Listen, Steve, I ran into Maureen outside the coffee shop. Her husband is in Intensive Care. He's dying. Right now she's in need of a friend. Here's the car keys. I'm going to stay with her for a while, and I'll take a taxi to your house."

"Okay, but don't forget to ask her about Kelly."

"Get off it, Steve. I'm not asking her any such thing."

"Then get her damn phone number, and I'll call her. I'll see you at the house. Christ, I hate hospitals. People *die* here."

"Yeah," Woodie said, walking away.

"It's nice to see you again, Aaron," Maureen said as he slid into a chair beside her. "Not under these circumstances, though. I really meant to drive out to see you after Christmas, but Stedman took a turn for the worse. I know you didn't really want to see me. I don't know why I need the . . . security of knowing I can call you from time to time. It's not like we were married forever. I do like you, Aaron. I always will."

"I'm flattered. Is there anything I can do for you? Does your sister still live in the area?"

"No. She moved to Argentina when she married that soccer player. I haven't heard from her in years. I don't make friends easily. When the . . . when the time comes, will you help me?"

"Of course. Why don't you go home, Maureen, and get some rest. If you want, I'll sit with your husband."

"You can't. Visiting is only ten minutes on the hour for the immediate family. I am all the immediate family Stedman has. Besides, I promised I would stay here. I've never, ever broken a promise to Stedman."

"Do you just . . . sit?"

"I read a little. I knit."

"You knit!"

"Surprise, surprise! I made Stedman argyle socks, a sweater, and a couple of mufflers. It keeps my fingers limber. I'm not a bimbo, Aaron."

"I never said you were."

"You thought it, though. I admit to . . . having a few . . . trysts. Stedman knows, but we don't talk about it. He trusts me to be discreet and I am. I was just as good to Stedman as he was to me. It's important to me that you believe me."

Woodie reached across the table for Maureen's hand. "I do, Maureen."

"How will I get over it when Stedman . . . goes?"

"Time will take care of everything. Do you know anything about your husband's business? Could you step in and work at something? I know work will interfere with getting your hair and nails done, but it is good therapy."

Maureen shrugged. "I haven't had my hair or nails done in over a month. You know what, Aaron, it doesn't matter. I think maybe I grew up a little these past few months. It is funny, though, that you mention working. Stedman has been trying for the past few years to get me to take an interest in things. We more or less committed to a project just recently. We're going to build a resort on Peter Island. The Brits own it. Stedman handed over a chunk of money sometime in February, a couple of hundred million. He wants me to oversee it. It's really a grand project. There won't be anything like it anywhere. Really, really pricey. It's about set to go. Starting date is sometime in May, I think. Do you think I'd look good in a hard hat? Stedman says I will. He's counting on me. I think that's what really pushed me over the edge. He trusts me to do it and to finish it even though he won't be here. I know diddly-squat about things like that."

"Then what you have to do is hire people who can be trusted to do what you can't do. Then you ride their asses twenty-four hours a day. You stay on top of it all the way. I think you can do it, Maureen."

"Do you really, or are you just saying that to make me feel good?"

"I never lied to you."

"No, Aaron, you never did. When this is all over, will you be my banker?"

"No. I'm retired. I just do a little consulting these days to keep my hand in. I can, however, turn you over to some people you can trust."

"Okay. I appreciate your taking the time to talk to me tonight. I have to get back upstairs. I hope we can be friends forever and ever."

Woodie nodded. "Hey, Maureen, did you ever wear that belt your husband gave you for Christmas?"

"Once or twice. It itches. See you around, Aaron."

"Call if you need me."

"Count on it."

Woodie walked out of the hospital into the spring night. It was cool now, chilly, actually. He wondered where Kristine was and what she was doing. Was she sitting in front of the fire with that lying bastard who was once her husband? Were the dogs curled up on their laps? What were they talking about?

Woodie hailed a cab that was sliding to the curb. Whatever they were doing, it was none of his business, even though Stephen Douglas thought it was.

None of his business at all.

"I'll say good night, Logan. It's been a long day and I'm tired."

"It was nice, though, wasn't it? Remember how we used to search out Chinese restaurants because they were your favorites? I thought it was like old times. Every man in the restaurant eyed you up and down. You smelled as delicious as you look. That's a great perfume. Is it new?"

"Yes," Kristine said carefully. "It was a gift."

"From Woodie?" Logan asked just as carefully.

"Yes. He gave it to me for my birthday."

"Do you still use gardenia bath salts?"

"Why are you asking me these questions, Logan?"

"I don't know. I guess to have something to say. I don't want the evening to end. Lately, more and more, I realize what I've been missing. I wish . . . oh, Kristine, I wish so many things. I wish we were still married. I wish you could forgive me. I wish the kids liked me. I wish I wasn't . . . I wish life would go on and we could be happy."

"Logan, did you ever love me?"

He took so long to respond that Kristine had to prod him for a reply.

"In the beginning I loved you with all my heart and soul. I wanted it to be that way forever. Things cooled a little for me when the kids came along. You got more and more dependent on me. At the time I didn't know if I liked that or not. You never argued with me. You never put up a fight, and you never said a cross word. After a while I started to feel suffocated. Sometimes I felt like I couldn't breathe around you. It seemed at the time, anyway, that there were no more challenges. I wanted and needed more excitement. I'm sorry now. I can't get those years back. Right now I would give anything if I could. I still love you, Kristine. I need you to believe me. If there's anything I can do or say to convince you, just tell me. I'll do it in a heartbeat.''

"I don't love you, Logan. All my feelings for you are gone.''

"That's not what that kiss said by the kitchen sink. Let's try, Kris.''

"No.''

"Don't be afraid of me, Kris.''

"I'm not afraid of you. Why can't you understand? I love Aaron Dunwoodie. My feelings for you died a long time ago. This situation we find ourselves in is not good; it was probably a mistake, but I couldn't turn you away. Please don't confuse my generosity with feelings of love.''

Logan refused to give up. "Woodie was a stand-in for me. You just refuse to admit it. I had a hard time with that at first, but I'm okay with it now. When I'm gone you're going to miss me. You'll never really know, will you, Kristine?'' He saw the blossoming doubt in her eyes. He hammered home his point. "Will you, Kristine?''

"Do you think my going to bed with you will make me realize you are the one and only love of my life? Is that what you believe, Logan? When I look back now I realize what we had was sex, not love. I was the one doing all the loving and giving. You just went through the motions. I think I even knew it then but refused to acknowledge it. I was afraid you'd leave me. I thought I needed you to make my life complete. My God, I even allowed myself to turn into an alcoholic because I thought if you weren't in my life, I would curl up and die.''

Logan felt shaken by Kristine's words. "Okay, if that's how you want to delude yourself, be my guest. I accept that you love Woodie. I also accept the fact that you refuse to acknowledge your feelings for me. I guess I'll say good night. Oh, what have we here? You didn't tell me they hooked up the new computer.''

"They must have done it after I left. I guess Pete let them in."

"Who cleaned out the storage room?"

"I did some of it this afternoon before I left to meet you. I guess Pete did the rest while they were installing the computer. You need to thank him."

"I will, first thing in the morning."

"I have to check the dogs," Kristine said.

"I'll walk with you. I always loved the way old barns smell. I wonder why that is. Remember how we used to make out in the straw in the loft?"

"No, I don't remember that," Kristine said.

"Liar," Logan said softly. "Remember how we used to fool around under that old peach tree?"

"No, I don't remember that."

"Liar," Logan whispered.

"Logan, before we sold your parents' house, Emily found some stuff under the attic steps. It was in the storage room. I was going to throw it out, but in the end, I didn't. There was a cape, a flashlight, some pillows, blankets and piles of *National Geographic*s. They were so well read and tattered I had to wonder if they meant something special to you."

Logan's heart skipped a beat. "Just a place to hide so I wouldn't have to do chores. You know how kids are. I forgot all about that until you mentioned it just now. That was a long time ago. It looks like all the dogs are okay. Everyone is sleeping. Let's roll around in the hay. Just for fun, Kristine."

"You never did anything for fun in your life, Logan. The answer is no. I'm going up to bed."

Before she knew what was happening, Logan had her in his arms. He carried her over to one of the empty stalls that held fresh straw. "I'm going to make love to you, Kristine, whether you like it or not."

"No you aren't, Logan. Don't make me fight you. I'm telling you no. Damn you, Logan, no means no!"

Logan's response was to rip at her dress. The sound of

tearing fabric was like thunder in Kristine's ears. She felt the clasp of her bra open and Logan's sweaty hands on her breasts.

"Damn you, Logan, let me go. Don't do this. Please don't do this, Logan."

"Shut up, Kristine, and lie back and enjoy your husband making love to you."

"You aren't my husband. This is rape, Logan. Get off me. Get off me right now."

"Shhh, Kristine."

21

Logan zipped up his pants as he watched Kristine run out of the barn and out to the field. Where the hell did she think she was going at this time of night? He gave a moment's thought to running after her but negated the thought almost immediately. She was all grown-up. If she wanted to act like a silly teenager, that was her problem.

Anger rivered through him as he walked toward the house. In the whole of his life this was the first time a woman had fought him off. A woman who didn't want anything to do with him. A woman who said she hated his fucking guts. "You're going to pay for that one, Kristine. Big-time," Logan muttered.

When he sat down at the brand-new computer, he had a bad moment. What if Kristine returned with Woodie? Woodie would want to lay him out cold if Kristine gave a blow-by-blow description of what happened. Still, it was her word against his. Sometimes sex got a little rough. Sometimes clothes got torn or discarded in the excitement of passion.

He needed to give some serious thought to moving up his departure date.

Logan's fingers tapped the keys furiously. He'd promised to input all the files from the attic, and he was going to keep his word. As his fingers flew across the keyboard, he mentally calculated the money he had stashed in his Swiss account. The numbers had swelled since Stedman Clovis's check cleared. Once he cleaned out the Summers account, he would be so golden he would glow. With Clovis dying, Maureen wouldn't be in any hurry to ask for an accounting. He would make arrangements to meet her somewhere after the big event. Christ, he hated widow's weeds. She'd go the whole nine yards, too. The grieving widow decked out in designer black from head to toe. She'd probably even wear one of those black veils. He wondered if he was underestimating the soon-to-be-widow just the way he'd underestimated his ex-wife. Was it possible he was losing his charm? Was he giving off some bad vibes that women picked up on?

Logan smiled when a parade of numbers marched across the seventeen-inch computer screen. He did love electronic banking. Even Kristine was impressed with it, once he showed her how it was done on his laptop.

Logan shoved a disk into the hard drive to transfer the files he'd done previously on his laptop. He worked steadily until the sun came up. He stopped, made coffee, showered, and sat back down at the computer. Two more hours and his work would be done and his promise kept. Kristine would thank him profusely when she returned. It would make her life a lot simpler.

At ten o'clock, when there was still no sign of Kristine, Logan turned off the computer and pocketed the disks. He scribbled a breezy little note to leave on the kitchen table. It was time for a trip into Washington to visit Stedman Clovis and to see how Maureen was holding up.

Logan turned his Bronco around and headed out to the main road. He looked into the rearview mirror to see if anyone exited the barn. Everything was quiet, even the dogs. He wondered what it meant.

Kristine watched her ex-husband from her crouched position behind the old John Deere riding mower in the garage. When she was certain Logan was out of sight, she finally moved, looking first to the right and to the left to see if Pete was anywhere nearby. Satisfied, she clutched her ripped dress and ran around to the front of the house.

Inside, she drew a deep breath and ran up the steps to the second floor, where she locked herself in her room.

She stripped down and then wadded her clothes into a tight ball that she tossed into the fireplace. The match flickered and then caught the edge of the fabric. Her chest heaving, Kristine watched until the clothes were nothing more than ashes. Satisfied that there were no signs left of her encounter, she marched to the bathroom where she showered until the water ran cold. That night was something she was never, ever going to think about or talk about again.

Never, ever.

"Where's Mom, Pete?" Cala asked as she jumped out of the car.

"I guess she's in the house. Is something wrong?"

"No. I just wondered where she was. I saw Woodie in town when I stopped at the automatic teller. He asked how she was. I thought she might want to know."

"What did you tell him?"

"I told him she was miserable. She is, you know. He didn't ask about Dad at all. He said to say hello. He looks as miserable as Mom does."

"It's not our business, Cala."

"Yes, it is. Pete, why can't I feel anything for my father? We wave to one another. I don't think we've said ten words in three months. Should I be doing something? You know, make overtures or something?"

"I think you should do whatever feels right to you. One of us needs to go on the Internet to search out information on your father's condition. I'm the first to admit I know nothing about dialysis, but I thought, and I don't know where the thought came from, that a person on dialysis was pretty debilitated and couldn't do things most people do. Your father is driving a car, going into the city, working around the house. To me he looks as good as he did the night he arrived. Is this something that hits you all at one time or is it a slow process? We should know that, Cala. Does your mom know?"

"I don't know, Pete. We aren't hooked up to the Internet."

"There is now a state-of-the-art computer system in your storage room. Get us hooked up."

"Sure, honey. I had a terrible dream last night."

"So did I. I don't want to talk about bad dreams. We're living one. Do you want me to pick the girls up from preschool?"

"Sure, if you don't mind. They just hate it. Tell me again why we're making them do something they don't want to do?" Cala said.

"They need to learn how to get along with other children. It's going to broaden their horizons. They learn to share with others."

"That's a crock, and you know it. How can it be that beneficial when they refuse to cooperate? They stay by themselves and suck their thumbs. Mrs. Ainsely is about to boot both of them out of her preschool."

"Okay, okay, I'll give notice when I pick them up."

"As of tomorrow. I can't take the crying and the wailing every day. I think they're starting to hate us for making them go there. Today is the last day."

"Does this have something to do with your dream or your father, Cala?"

"Probably. I don't ever want them to feel the way I felt about my mom for a while or the way I feel about my father. Go get them now, Pete!"

"Right now?"

"Right now. Do I need to do anything here?"

"It's under control," Pete said. "What was the dream, Cala?"

"I followed up on the lawsuit Mike and I started years ago. Dad was served papers at the airport as he was leaving us. Again. Mom was standing on the tarmac crying her eyes out and begging him not to leave us."

A chill ran up Pete's arms. "That's a nightmare all right."

"I'm going up to the house. Are you sure you want me to sign up to go on-line?"

"Yeah."

Cala whistled for Gracie and Slick to follow her up to the house. Her mother's car was parked in front, but there was no sign of her. "Go get Mom, Gracie."

The little dogs ran to the kitchen steps.

Cala saw the note addressed to her mother. She knew she shouldn't read it. She walked away, opened the refrigerator, and took out a bottle of soda. If she didn't touch the letter, did that count as reading it? By stretching her neck she was able to decipher the scrawled note. She swore at that moment she could feel her blood start to run cold.

Sweetheart,

Thanks for last night. What a memory. It was so much like old times I found myself slipping back in time. How adventuresome you've become. I hope your dreams were as good as mine. I'm off to DC. The doctors want to talk to me today about some tests they ran yesterday. I may not be back this evening. If I stay in town, I'll be home tomorrow. Either way, I'll call you. By the way, all the files are loaded now. Just click on Summers Farm and it will come up right away. This is going to make your work a hundred times easier and faster. I was only too glad to do it for you, hon.

My love endures, my darling.

Logan

Cala carried her soft drink out to the back porch. What did the note mean? Had her mother lost her senses? Was the note some kind of trick? Where was her mother? Obviously she was still upstairs, and it was the middle of the afternoon. She felt her insides start to churn at the thought of her mother lying in bed dreaming about her father. "Damn."

Gracie whined at her feet. Cala bent down to pick her

up. "Couldn't find her, huh? Okay, let's go upstairs and see what's going on."

It was so quiet on the second floor, Cala shivered. Bright sunlight shone through the wavy glass of the old windows, casting rainbows on the walls. It looked so pretty, she traced one of the patterns with her finger. Gracie whined in her arms.

"Mom, are you up here? Gracie and Slick want in, Mom," Cala said, knocking on her mother's door. "Mom, are you all right?"

Kristine opened the door and reached for Gracie. "Is something wrong?"

"Nothing's wrong. I just wanted to tell you Pete and I agreed to take the girls out of preschool. Pete went to get them. Dad left a note on the table for you. You look awful, Mom. Do you have one of your headaches?"

"I didn't sleep well. Is there any coffee?"

"Not fresh. I can make some. I just got here a little while ago. Pete wants me to sign up to go on-line."

"That's interesting. I hear you can become addicted to it."

"I don't have time to get addicted. Are you coming downstairs?"

"Of course."

Cala followed her mother down the stairs. She watched as Kristine picked up the note to read it. She blinked when she saw the note being crunched into a ball and the way her mother's hands were trembling.

"What's wrong, Mom?"

"Nothing. Why do you ask? Oh, you read the note, is that it?"

"Yeah, Mom, I read it. I'm afraid to ask you what it means."

"Then don't ask," Kristine said as she rinsed out the coffeepot. "If you have some free time, I'd like you to help me with something."

Cala felt as though she'd been slapped. "Sure, Mom," she said flatly.

"I want you to help me pack up your father's things. We'll put them all on the front porch. I want the door to the apartment locked, and I know somewhere around here we have some keys to this house. I want our doors locked from now on."

"Mom, do you mind . . . ?"

"I mind. Either help me or go down to the barn."

Cala bit down on her lower lip. "In boxes or bags?"

"I don't think it matters."

"I'll start now, then," Cala said, ripping dark green leaf bags out of a box from under the sink. "Just tell me this. Are you kicking him out?"

"Yes," Kristine said curtly.

"Even though he's dying?"

"Yes."

Cala shrugged as she made her way over to the small apartment over the garage.

Kristine walked into the storage room. The brand-new computer stared at her like a giant evil eye. She moved like a robot as she took her seat on the hard kitchen chair. She waited until the screen came to life before she opened the file that stored the bank balances of all her accounts. She almost fainted with relief when she typed in her password and watched the balances spring to life. When she saw that all the accounts were still intact she was so dizzy with relief, she had to put her head between her legs. She initiated a new password. In a million years, Logan would never come up with it. She typed in the word BETRAYED and once again clicked on the file that would show her the bank balances. Satisfied, Kristine turned the computer off.

In the kitchen, she picked up the phone to call Jack Valarian. "I'm ready to go back to work, Jack. Is tomorrow too soon? Fine, I'll look for you around ten. Yes, this is a good thing we're doing. I'm fine. Everyone is fine. Drive carefully."

Kristine poured coffee. She watched as her daughter

dutifully trudged across the yard, two lawn bags in her hands.

"That's it, Mom."

"Two bags? That's all he had?"

"I guess when you're . . . I guess he travels light. Clothes, a few books, his shaving stuff. Everything looks so *new.*"

"What about his briefcase and his laptop?" Kristine asked coldly.

"They weren't there. Maybe he took them with him or maybe he keeps them in the car. He is kind of secretive, Mom. Are you sure you're all right?"

"I'm fine, Cala."

"If Dad is leaving, does that mean you and Woodie are back together?"

"No, Cala, that's not what it means. Jack is coming out in the morning, and we're going to start to disburse the monies. It's time. I'm sorry I didn't do it the first of the year the way I'd planned on doing. Still, the monies earned three months' more interest, so it isn't all that bad. When I'm finished, I think I'll take a trip. Would you and Pete mind watching Gracie and Slick?"

"Of course not, Mom. Where are you going?"

"I'm not sure yet. Someplace where I can get my head on straight. Maybe I'll go visit Sadie."

"What about Dad . . . how long are you going to be away?" Cala asked fearfully.

"I don't know to both questions. Did you lock the apartment?"

"Yes, Mom."

"I'm going to take the dogs for a walk. You said you wanted to use the computer, didn't you?"

"Yes. Do you want me to do anything else while I'm here?"

"I can't think of anything. Are you sure you're doing the right thing by taking the girls out of preschool?"

"I'm sure, Mom."

"Okay. If you have time, see if you can find the keys to the doors. I know they're somewhere in one of these drawers. Put the key under Gracie's dish on the porch if I'm not back before you leave.''

"Mom, I know something's wrong. Why won't you talk to me? I'm not a little kid anymore.''

Kristine smiled as she reached for her knapsack. "They get tired after the first thirty minutes and I have to carry them," she said, hooking the leashes on to the dogs' collars. "Look, Cala, I just have something I need to work out. Don't fret about me. I can handle this.''

"What is *this*?" Cala screamed.

"You read the note. Don't ever, for one minute, think that what your father implied actually happened. Your father is one sick man, mentally and physically.''

Cala wrapped her arms around her mother. "I love you, Mom.''

"And I love you. If you're gone when I get back, I'll see you tomorrow.''

Kristine waved jauntily as she set out with the two yipping, yapping dogs. She walked for hours, stopping every so often to light a cigarette. Gracie and Slick snoozed inside the knapsack. She walked for another hour before she realized she was bone tired. She sat down, lifted the dogs out of the sack, and fired up a fresh cigarette. Gracie yapped, her little paws digging at the ground. Slick growled, his hair standing on end. She watched in horror as the two dogs suddenly took off at a speed that boggled her mind. She gave chase, reared up short when she plowed through a thicket to see that she was in Woodie's backyard.

From her position in the thicket she could see Woodie stretched out in a chaise lounge on his back deck. "Get over here," she hissed to the dogs. "Gracie, get over here, or I'm going to fan your bottom." The little dog ignored her and ran to the deck. Slick followed. There was nothing for her to do but follow the dogs.

"What have we here?" Woodie exclaimed when Gracie jumped into his lap, Slick right behind her. Woodie looked around. "How are you, Kristine?"

"I'm sorry, Woodie. We were out walking. I didn't realize we'd come so far. I'm sorry they woke you."

"I wasn't sleeping. I was just sitting here thinking about you and here you are. Is everything okay?"

"I guess that depends on what you mean by okay. I don't think I'm in a good place right now. I've missed you."

"I've missed you, too. All I do is think about you and our time together."

"Me too. I packed up Logan's things. He'll be leaving in the morning. I tried to do the right thing for all the wrong reasons. Logan took advantage of the situation. We got us a brand-spanking-new state-of-the-art computer out at the house. It can do everything but make coffee. Jack's coming by in the morning and we're going to start disbursing the monies and setting up the scholarships. When we finish with that, I'm going away."

"What about . . ."

"There is no what about."

"Where are you going to go, Kristine?" Woodie asked gently.

"I don't know. Maybe one of those retreats somewhere where all you do is listen to flute music, think, and run under waterfalls. Maybe I'll go see Sadie. Maybe I'll hike the Appalachian Trail. It's kind of iffy in my mind at the moment. I didn't come here on purpose, Woodie, I've been walking for hours. Maybe subconsciously, I wanted to come here." Kristine shrugged.

"Want some coffee or a soft drink?"

"Coffee would be nice."

"Did something happen, Kristine? Do you want to talk about it? Is there anything I can do?"

"Be my friend," Kristine said in a choked voice.

"Always and forever."

Kristine started to cry.

"Come here." Woodie held out his arms. Kristine buried her face against the wall of his chest and Woodie crooned to her, stroking her hair. "Tell me what's wrong."

"I went to town and had dinner with Logan last night. It was pleasant enough but strained. I was starting to get cabin fever, that's why I agreed to go. When we got back, Logan . . . what he did was . . . I went down to the barn to check on the dogs and he . . . he tried to rape me. He ripped my clothes off me. I fought him. I kicked him, I bit him, I scratched him. He was like a maniac. I got away from him and ran across the fields. I was going to come here, but I lost my way in the dark, so I went back and stayed in the garage all night. I hid behind the old John Deere mower. I was afraid to go anywhere else for fear he'd find me. When he left this morning, I went to the house and found this," Kristine said, pulling Logan's wadded-up letter out of her pocket. "This sounds like we made love and that we're getting back together. Cala found it. I could tell by the look on her face that she believes it. He tried to kiss me in the kitchen and Pete walked in. God only knows what he thinks. Logan refuses to believe I don't love him. Cala packed his things, and that's the end of that."

"I'm sorry, Kristine."

"Don't be sorry. I changed the password on the computer for the bank accounts. Can you call the bank for me tomorrow and change the account numbers? I don't know why, but I think Logan is up to something. You know what else, Woodie? I don't think he's dying at all. He was too strong. He's all muscle. He smokes, he drinks, and he eats more than three people. All I did during the night was think. I thought my brain was going to explode."

"The bastard didn't hurt you, did he?" Woodie asked, his voice full of anguish.

"A few bruises and bumps. They'll go away. I need to know the why of all this."

"If I could *show* you the why of it all, would that make you happy?"

"I was so happy when you came back, Woodie. I thought my life was complete. Then Logan came back and ruined everything."

"No, Kristine. You allowed Logan to ruin it."

"You're right. I wanted to do the right thing. I thought I was doing what any woman would do. I guess I was wrong. No guessing. I was wrong. I'm sorry, Woodie."

"I saw you and Logan in the Golden Dragon last night. I was there with my accountant. I was so jealous I thought I was going to lose it right there in the restaurant. I smelled your perfume. I looked up and there you were. We left," Woodie said, his face miserable.

"I stopped by the bank yesterday before I met Logan. I was going to tell you what an awful mistake I made. The drive-through teller said I had just missed you. What did you mean when you said you could show me the why of it all?"

"If you want to know, if you think you can handle it, I'll take you into DC to Stephen's house. The explanations are there. Do you have to go back home tonight?"

"No. I will need to call Pete, though. What about Gracie and Slick?"

"They can stay here. We'll put some paper down by the back door. They'll be fine till we get back. You're sure you're up to this?"

"I think so. You're making it all sound so mysterious. Why can't you just tell me whatever it is?"

"This is something you need to see for yourself. I never would have told you, Kristine. Steve wanted me to, but I said no. I want to make sure you understand that."

"Let's go then. Where does this leave us, Woodie? My God, how many times have we said that to one another?"

"You know what they say, the path to true love is rocky at best."

"Did you make that up?"

"No. Erma Bombeck said it in one of her columns a long time ago."

"Oh. He didn't rape me, Woodie. I'd tell you if he did."

Woodie nodded. "I think we should be on our way, then. Call Pete, then I'll call Steve."

* * *

It was a beautiful old house on Connecticut Avenue. Kristine knew it would be as immaculate inside as it was outside. "Does your friend live in this big house all by himself?"

"Yes, and he uses all the rooms and all the bathrooms, too. He's got stuff spread everywhere. Some of the rooms aren't even furnished. This guy will be a bachelor forever. Steve, Brian, and I hung out together all through college. We'll probably be friends all our lives. I told you about them. Don't you remember?"

"I remember you saying you were going to introduce me to them, but you never did," Kristine teased lightly as Woodie rang the doorbell. "I'm not going to like whatever it is you plan on showing me, am I?"

"No, Kristine, you're not going to like it. You'll be able to live with it, though."

"Woodie, Woodie, two visits in two days. My life is full and wonderful. Introduce me to this lovely lady," Steve said happily.

"Kristine Summers, this is Stephen Douglas, the guy I speak about so lovingly. And this is Brian Lucas, the other guy I speak of so lovingly."

"This is our friend Danela, Kristine," Steve said, introducing a lovely redheaded woman.

Kristine smiled as she shook hands all around.

"Danela is from Africa, new to this country, although she has dual citizenship. Come in. How about some wine, beer, the hard stuff?"

"Coffee or a soft drink. I'm a recovering alcoholic," Kristine said.

"No problem. We have both," Stephen said.

"I'll get it," Danela said. "Cream or sugar?"

"Black will be fine. You have a lovely house, Stephen."

"It was my parents'. I'm afraid it looked a lot better when they lived here. I just pile stuff everywhere. Take a seat. Get comfortable. Woodie wants us to tell you something that is going to sound like it came out of a bad movie. You're going to need to be comfortable."

Kristine felt her shoulders stiffen.

"Okay, here goes," Stephen said as he leaned back on the chair facing the computer.

Kristine listened, her eyes going to Danela from time to time and then back to the narrator of the story. When she was finally able to speak she said, "Show me."

"Come here, Kristine. Take this seat. Brian put it all on one disk, so it would be easier reading for you."

Kristine dragged the mouse to the top of first one page and then the other. "This is how you found him?"

"Yes. Are you ready for the Swiss bank account?"

"Yes," Kristine said through clenched teeth. She gasped. "Where did all this money come from? Does it belong to Logan? That's such a stupid question I can't believe I even asked it?"

"I guess he's scamming someone else these days. Colonel Kelly still doesn't know we know about this account. With Danela's help we got the password. We can whisk this money out of there in the blink of an eye. We're just waiting for the right moment. Woodie tells me your husband, excuse me, your ex-husband, gave you back your children's money."

"Yes, he did. I think he was getting set to take it again along with some inheritance money. Are those medical records accurate?"

"Ma'am, they are on the money as of December 21," the redhead said. "There's no mistake. In all the years I've known Logan, he was never sick a day. As a matter of fact, he was robust. He led a very good life. I'm sorry to have caused you pain, Ms. Summers. I didn't know about you in the beginning. Then Logan said you were divorced. I believed him because I was in love with him at the time. He stole my money and left me with $25,010. Stephen and the others brought me here so the authorities wouldn't come after me for the bills Logan ran up. I did my best to pay what I could with the little money he allotted me.

I know this must be a terrible shock to you. I am truly sorry. If there's anything I can do, I will gladly do it."

Kristine shook her head. "Where would Logan get two hundred million dollars?"

Woodie frowned. "I just heard that number mentioned recently. I can't think where, though. I'm sure it has nothing to do with Logan. Is there anything you want to ask, Kristine?"

"If there's more, I don't think I want to hear it. Wait, there is one thing. The medication Logan has taken all these years, would it make him do . . . bizarre things like . . . beat his children for no reason?"

Stephen cleared his throat. "No."

"The only thing Logan ever took while we were in Africa was aspirin. In the beginning we had to take malaria pills, but that was it. Logan had an aversion to any kind of drugs," Danela said quietly.

"My God, he even lied about that," Kristine said. "If I were you, Danela, I would take your money now before he skips out again. My daughter packed up his things this afternoon. I don't know where he'll go or what he'll do. Just out of curiosity, what was his password?" Kristine wondered if she looked as ill as she felt.

"NatGeo. It was a fluke that I even thought of it at all. We were so desperate at the time, we were just throwing out words," Danela said softly.

"Steve, do you mind if I use your phone? I want to check something. I just might know where that two hundred million came from."

"Are you kidding? Go ahead, there's a phone in the kitchen."

Woodie dialed the information operator and asked for the number of George Washington Hospital. He scribbled the number on a pad on the counter before he dialed. He asked to be put through to the Intensive Care Unit, where he inquired about Stedman Clovis and asked how he could speak to Mrs. Clovis. His shoulders slumped when he was told Stedman Clovis had passed away earlier in the afternoon and that Mrs. Clovis was at the Hyatt. Did he dare call Maureen? Of course. She might need him. He dialed the information operator again. Minutes later he heard Maureen's tearful voice.

"I called the hospital and they told me. I'm sorry. Tell me, what can I do?" He listened as Maureen told him what needed to be done. "It's late now, Maureen. I'll come by first thing in the morning. Listen, do you know a man named Justin Eberhart? You do? Is he the one you're going to build the resort with? He is. Just curious. I heard his name in town today. Amazing. Drink some hot tea and go to bed. I'll take care of everything. Maureen, do you still have that account at our bank? The last time I looked it still had twenty dollars in it. You do. Good. I'll take care of everything in the morning. Try and get some sleep. You don't have to thank me. We're friends, right? Do you want to come to my wedding? See, I knew that would make you feel better. I'll see you in the morning."

Back in the living room, Woodie looked around at the glum faces staring at him. "I know where Logan got the two hundred million!"

"Where?" four voices asked in unison.

"My ex-wife. Her husband, who by the way, passed away this afternoon, gave it to Justin Eberhart to build a resort on Peter Island. Is this a small world or what? Guess what else? Maureen has a checking account at my bank that has twenty bucks in it. Clean the goddamn account out right now. Give Danela hers and transfer Maureen's into that checking account. Don't look at me like that. Get the damn account number from my old tax forms. When we were married we filed joint returns."

"My God, what if they put you in jail for this?" Kristine dithered.

"It ain't gonna happen," Brian said as he flexed his fingers. "The Swiss are a tight-lipped lot. We got the password, and that's all they care about. Give me your account number, Danela." She rattled it off. They crowded around the computer as Brian clicked away. "Here's the magic box. Are you guys ready? This works in seconds once I type in the password. Steve, you got the number for Maureen's account?''

"Right here, buddy. Go for it!''

"Did it work?'' Kristine asked in a shaky voice.

"Damn straight it worked. What should we do with the last ten million?''

"It belongs to the African bank. I have the account number right here,'' Danela said as she rummaged in her purse. "They'll confiscate it the minute it gets into the account. Please, leave $25,010 dollars in the Swiss account.''

"You got it. Okay, we are finished, ladies and gentlemen. Colonel Logan Kelly, alias Logan Kilpatrick, alias Justin Eberhart is now a poor man and will have to work for a living. I'm crashing all the files and the hard drive now. I want everyone's word that we will never, ever speak of this aloud.''

Four heads bobbed up and down.

"Steve, will you take Kristine home? I'm going to stay in town tonight. I told Maureen I'd do what's necessary for her. She's in no shape to do anything.''

"No problem,'' Steve said.

Woodie squeezed Kristine's hand. "I'll talk to you soon.''

Kristine cried all the way home. Stephen reached over from time to time to pat her arm.

"Are you sure you won't get into trouble over this?'' Kristine asked when he brought the car to a stop by her back door.

"Brian is an absolute wizard. What your ex-husband has been doing is illegal. We just one-upped him. You will probably never see him or hear from him again. He's never going to figure out how it happened. If we had left the $25,010 in the account, he could have traced it to Danela. We only left sixty-nine dollars in it. He'll get the message. Don't tell Danela.''

"I won't,'' Kristine said.

"My buddy is a great guy, Kristine."

"I know that."

"Just so you know."

"I've known it from the first day I met him."

"Isn't that funny? That's what he said about you."

Kristine laughed. "Thanks for everything."

"You need your taxes done, I'm your man."

"I'll remember that."

"Good night, Kristine."

"Good night, Steve. I'm glad I finally got to meet you. Danela seems like a real nice lady."

"She is. See you around."

Kristine slept deeply and dreamlessly. She didn't waken until she heard Jackson Valarian shout her name from the bottom of the steps.

"Put the coffee on, Jack. I'll be down in twenty minutes."

Two days later, Kristine signed the last check. "This is a good thing we're doing, Jack. I don't think you're going to get a Pulitzer for it, though."

"That was just bullshit talk, Kristine. When and if it's my time, I'll get one. You've done a wonderful thing for all those families. The scholarships will go a long way on a lot of families' budgets. You know what else? I'm not writing this story, either. This is a private, family matter. When you do good things you don't have to tell the world. All those families you're helping know it, your family knows it, I know it, and that's all that's important."

"You're an okay guy, Jack. What are you going to work on next?"

"The Swiss banking industry. I got a few hot tips. And, the paper is sending me to Switzerland. How lucky can a guy get!"

Kristine laughed until her sides hurt. "Go for it, Jack, and if you get stuck, call me. I just might be able to help you or at least put you in touch with the right people."

"Yeah, that's right, Woodie's a banker. I almost forgot about that. What's next for you?"

"Well, Mike is coming home this weekend. I'm leaving for a while. I have a lot of things to discuss with my kids. That's pretty much it."

"Woodie?"

"Woodie is the stuff dreams are made of. Right now he's helping his ex-wife. Her husband died yesterday. Woodie is . . . you can always count on Woodie."

"You sound sad, Kristine."

"A little. I thought . . . never mind. See you around, Jackson. Don't forget to send me a postcard."

"I want to say good-bye to Pete and Cala."

"Go to it. I'm going to pack. Don't let those Swiss bankers intimidate you."

"Never happen, Kristine. I won you over, didn't I?"

"So you did, Jack, so you did."

"Mom, you really need to tell us where you're going. What if we need to get in touch with you? The house could burn down; the kids could get sick; Tyler might come home. You can't just up and go away like this," Cala said.

"Why not? I'm leaving things in good hands. You're the best of the best. Emily, Ellie, make sure you take care of Gracie and Slick until I get back. I want your promise. I'll call when I land somewhere. I really will."

"Look after my family, Pete." Kristine choked up as her son-in-law gave her a crushing bear hug.

"I'll do my best, Kristine. Call, okay."

"I will but probably not for a while."

"What about Woodie, Mom?" Mike asked her as he gave her one last hug.

"I'll stop and say good-bye."

Tears rolled down Kristine's cheeks as she drove away. She was doing the right thing. Probably the first right thing she'd done in a long time. It was going to be so hard to say good-bye to Woodie. She crossed her fingers that he wouldn't be home. Then she uncrossed them because she wanted to see him one last time.

She heard the music the moment she stopped the car in front of Woodie's house. It seemed to be coming from the back deck. Maybe Woodie was sunning himself. She picked her way carefully through the fallen pinecones and then she burst into laughter. Woodie was standing on the deck with a flute in his hands, the garden hose looped over the railing. Water cascaded down the sides. "I'm not really playing this thing. That music you hear is from one of those massage tapes. This is my version of a waterfall. We can run through it together. I'm packed and ready to go, or we can stay here and do other things."

Kristine stepped up to the waterfall. "It's no fun doing it by yourself. Get down here, Woodie, and tell me what you mean by other things. Be explicit."

Woodie leaped over the railing.

"That wasn't bad for an old duffer." Kristine laughed.

"Wait till you see what this old duffer can do under a waterfall."

"Show me."

"Are you going to marry me or not, Kristine? I'm not showing you anything until you agree."

"Let's go get the license right now."

"We're soaking wet."

"I don't care. Do you care?"

"Not me. I'll drive. You're too damn slow."

"I love you, Aaron Dunwoodie."

"And I love you, Kristine Summers."

"Are we going to live happily ever after?"

"Damn right. Now get in the car."

"Bring the flute. We're going to need some music."

"Just shut up, Kristine, and get in the damn car."

Logan listened to the evening news, his thoughts on Maureen Clovis and the few minutes he'd spent with her earlier in the afternoon. Her husband had died three days ago. She'd looked so drawn and haggard he wasn't sure he knew the woman wailing and carrying on like a truly bereaved widow. His skin crawled when he thought about the rich old man she was grieving for and his emaciated body. What the hell was there to grieve over? He was dead, and that was the end of that. She'd have him cremated, lug his ashes around for a few years, then dump them somewhere and get on with the business of spending her husband's money. She'd travel around the world, have her little affairs, and think about him once in a while. Was Maureen trying to convince him she had really loved her husband? Like he cared. At least she hadn't asked him to help with the final details. She hadn't said a word about the two hundred million dollars, and neither had he. Maybe this would be a good time to split. Maureen would play the bereaved widow for at least another week. He could be on another continent in one day, setting up shop.

Logan looked down at his Rolex watch. He didn't have to go back to the farm. He'd outstayed his welcome there. He already had Maureen's money, so what was the point in hanging around? Where to go was the big question. Hong Kong with its millions of people, Singapore, Bora Bora?

Logan turned off the television, opened the small safe, and took out a stack of passports. Who should he be today? A wealthy industrialist, a Wall Street tycoon, head of a global law office? Maybe he should just be Joe Schmuck with a winning lottery ticket. He flipped open the different passports, looking for the one with the most flattering picture of himself. The wealthy industrialist won out. He could get lost in Hong Kong the minute he arrived. He called the airport to make his reservation, charging it to an American Express card in the name of Caleb Quasar. "Of course I want first-class," he barked. He copied down the confirmation number and agreed to pick up his ticket in an hour.

Because he was a greedy man, Logan unzipped his

laptop for one last look at his accounts. *I might as well transfer Kristine's monies now.* There was such security in high numbers. He tapped in Summers Farm and waited. He typed in the old password, DOGS, and waited. ACCESS DENIED. What the hell? He typed in the password a second time. Access was still being denied. Kristine wasn't smart enough to transfer the code. He must have made a mistake. Maybe *dogs* wasn't plural. He typed the word dog. He typed every word, every combination of words he could think of. Access to the account was still denied. Think like Kristine. What would she use? Something with the kids or the grandchildren. Something about the dogs. Again he had no luck.

Logan blinked in horror when he used the mouse to scroll down the page. He frowned when he saw the word, MESSAGE. Maybe Kristine wasn't as dumb as he thought she was.

> *Dear Logan,*
> *Sorry, you bastard, but these funds are committed to something more important than your luxurious lifestyle. Remember that book you made us all live by? This message will serve as my final chapter. At this moment in time, you are just someone we used to know.*

The message was signed, Kristine Summers soon-to-be Dunwoodie.

Logan cursed, using words he hadn't used since leaving West Point. When he ran out of those words, he made up more as he went along. He'd never felt such fury. He looked down at his watch. He needed to get to the airport or he'd miss his flight to New York. His hands trembled as he snapped the lid of the laptop before he returned it to the canvas bag.

"Son of a fucking bitch!"

Two hours later, Logan settled himself in the first-class section of the plane on the first leg of his journey to Hong Kong. He waited until they were airborne and the elderly gentleman sitting next to him was asleep before he pulled out his laptop. He waited a moment to accept the scotch on the rocks the stewardess handed him before he turned on the laptop and plugged in to the phone jack on the seat back. So he lost Kristine's fortune. He was resilient. Two hundred million dollars would take him anywhere and allow him to do whatever he wanted with the rest of his life.

He typed in his password, NatGeo, and waited for the numbers to race across the small screen. Two numbers sat alone on the screen with a $ sign in front of them: $69. This was impossible. He turned off the laptop, waited ten minutes, and turned it on again. He typed in his password. The same two numbers stared up at him.

Logan gulped at the scotch in the glass, draining it.

Danela.

"You miserable, stinking, lousy bitch!" he cursed under his breath.

Logan thought he could hear Danela's tinkling laugh as the giant silver bird raced through the sky. Or was it Maureen's laughter he thought he was hearing. Then maybe it was Kristine's.

Logan held up his glass for a refill. He smiled at the stewardess. This was all just a bad dream, and he was going to wake up on the couch in the Hyatt any minute now. He'd had dreams like this before. Usually when he was under stress. In the meantime he would hit on the pretty stewardess in his dream and make plans for the layover in a few hours.

It was a hell of a scary dream, though.

Dillon in his arms, Mike could only stare at his sister, her words burning into his brain.

"Easy, big brother," Tyler said, taking Dillon from his arms.

"It's true. Mom told me. You guys were in town. She

said she was going to say it once and never mention it again.''

"Let me make sure I understand this. Our father was scamming us. Again. He's not really dying at all. He weaseled his way in here Christmas Eve with that story so he could . . . what?''

"My guess would be to get his hands on the rest of Mom's money. The money she committed to her project with Jack. And maybe take back that eight million he returned to Mom, our money. Our father's a dick. We've always known that. I don't think any of us believed his story for a minute. I know I didn't. Hell, I'm not sure Mom really believed it, either.''

"Every time I think of him touching Dillon I want to knock him through a wall,'' Mike said vehemently.

"I wanted to believe him,'' Cala whimpered. "Now we have to live with this!''

"Hey, he's gone. We're well rid of him. He'll never show his face around here again. With Mom giving up all that money, there's no reason for him ever to see any of us again. Christ, I hate his fucking guts,'' Mike snarled.

"No more than I do,'' Tyler snarled in return. "If any of you ever tell me again that I look like him, I'll lay you out cold.''

Cala reached for Dillon. "I always had this dream of being Daddy's little girl. That's never going to happen.''

"Look at the plus side, Cala,'' Mike said, putting his arm around her shoulder. "Your little girls will be their daddy's little girls. You'll get to see and experience that. That's really a plus in my book.''

"There's always winners and losers in everything, and we're the winners. You can take that to the bank. Dad is the loser, and he doesn't even know it or care. I say we drink a Virgin Mary toast to the prick and lay him to rest once and for all. Where's that bottle of Tabasco? Ah, here it is. Think about your toast very carefully now,'' Tyler said.

Mike clapped his brother on his back as he poured the

"spiked" tomato juice liquid into exquisite goblets. "To Dad, may he grow bald and get as fat as Fatty Arbuckle."

"To Dad, may his life be plagued with impotence and watered-down booze," Tyler said.

"To Dad, may all his dreams come true," Cala said.

Epilogue

❧

"What do you think, Mrs. Dunwoodie?" Woodie asked.

"I think, Mr. Dunwoodie, that in our lifetime, we will never see anything as wonderful as this celebration. We finally did it, all our little celebrations rolled into one. God, I'm tired. Celebrating is hard work, Woodie. There are hundreds of people in my backyard. All my kids are here, my grandchildren are here, and Jack is playing host. The animals are here. More important, you and I are here. We're married, we're happy, and life is wonderful."

"I can see Mima Posy from here, sporting her new shades, with her dog in a knapsack," Woodie said. "All those people around her are the nieces and nephews of her three uncles and aunt. I've never seen happier smiles. Lela Mae arrived in her son's eighteen-wheeler with her dog in tow. Everyone is getting along. It's almost as if all these people you helped have known each other all their lives."

"The best part is that Jack delayed his trip to Switzerland to host this celebration. The second-best part is Logan isn't here to foul things up and the third-best thing is this isn't a public show. We're the only ones who know about it." Kristine waved her hand toward the tents, where people were milling about. "They wanted it this way."

"Your kids are doing a great job circulating among our guests. I saw Emily take off her shoe a while ago. She wanted everyone to see the X on her bare foot that Pete made for her with a magic marker. She said she wanted to belong. Look, she's on Jonah's shoulders, and he's showing off his new rig. Leave it to the kids. I think we should partake of some of that food, Mrs. Dunwoodie. I still can't believe you, Cala, and Carol cooked it all.''

"I can believe it. It took us three days. We cheated on the biscuits and the coleslaw. We got it from Kentucky Fried Chicken. Do you think anyone will know?''

"Nah. My blisters have blisters from shucking all that corn. We need to circulate a little.''

"If I fall asleep on my feet, Woodie, pinch me. I don't think I've ever been this tired and this happy at the same time. We did good, didn't we?''

"Yes, we did. I'm so proud of you, Kristine, I could just bust. Your kids feel the same way.''

Embarrassed, Kristine slathered butter on an ear of corn. She was biting into it when she heard her name called from one of the band members.

"Speech!''

"Oh, Woodie, I can't do that! I can't get up in front of all those people. What in the world will I say?''

"Say whatever is in your heart. I'll hold your corn.''

"C'mon, Grandma, shake it!'' Emily called.

Kristine laughed as she made her way to the makeshift bandstand. She had to clear her throat twice before she could speak.

"I want to thank you all for coming. I . . . I'm not much of a speech person. I just want to say that this is the proudest day of my life. I know that there are some people missing who should be here. We tried our best to find them. We're not going to give up. We have a wonderful network now. With your help, I'm sure we can find those that are missing today. Any lead, any possibility, just call us. We'll do the rest. Uh . . . Thank you. Now, let's celebrate!''

"That was good, Grandma,'' Emily said. "They listened to you. When you talk soft, people listen so they don't miss any of the words.''

"Is that right?'' Kristine laughed.

"That's right, Grandma. That's my new friend Billie over there. He knows how to fish. Petey has four rabbits. Is it okay if I take them down to the barn and show them my seventy-seven dogs?"

"You bet it is."

"Mrs. Summers, I'd like to thank you for so many things," Mima Posy said, coming up to stand next to Kristine. "That's a fine-looking man standing next to you."

"The very finest. How's your eyesight, Mrs. Posy?"

"Couldn't be better. I'm going to teach your daughter to knit before I leave."

Kristine laughed. "I hope you have better luck than I did. Where's Honey?"

Mima reached behind her and yanked at her shoulder bag. "Right here. She's snoozing. Between my husband and me, this dog's feet hardly ever touch the ground. I need to be thanking you for that, too, Mrs. Summers."

Kristine wanted to tell her her name was now Dunwoodie, but she didn't. In the scheme of things, it hardly mattered. "I'll be saying my good-byes now. All these people want to shake your hand, and I'm taking up their space. I'd be real honored if you'd come to visit sometime."

"I'll do that, Mrs. Posy. Good luck with the knitting lesson."

He was as big as a tree and had the gentlest smile Kristine had ever seen. Standing next to him was Lela Mae, with Missy in her arms. The little dog woofed happily. Kristine tweaked his ears and laughed. "I bet you feed her table food, don't you?"

Lela Mae pursed her lips. "Only Sunday dinner," she said, unlocking her lips. "Jonah wants to thank you. He's bashful."

"Mama, I'm not bashful. Most times I don't have anything to say. Right now, though, I do. Men name ships when they go out to sea. I go all over the country and truck drivers name their rigs, too. Mine's called *The Big Kristine.* Eighteen wheels means the truck is big. I brought a bottle of wine so you could christen it. Will you do it?"

Kristine blinked. A truck named after her. *It doesn't get any better than this,* she thought. "I'd be honored, Jonah. Lead the way."

"Wait a minute, we need a drumroll," Woodie said.

The guests grew quiet as the band leader ordered the drumroll. Kristine marched up to the sleek, silver eighteen-wheeler, the wine bottle clenched firmly in both hands. She stared at the words, *The Big Kristine,* and swung the bottle. She bowed low to the applause.

"Here's your corn," Woodie said, holding out a paper plate.

"I'm too tired to eat, Woodie."

"Let's sit down under that tree over there and watch the celebration," Woodie said.

"That's a great idea."

Five minutes later, Mr. and Mrs. Aaron Dunwoodie were sound asleep. They were still sleeping when the blues band packed up to leave. They continued to sleep as the guests trotted by, one by one on their way to their cars.

Mima was the last to leave. "You take care of this family of yours, young woman," she said to Cala. "God didn't make anyone better than your family. If He did, He would have kept them for Himself."

"Thank you, Mrs. Posy."

"Drive with the angels," Kristine said sleepily as she snuggled into the crook of Woodie's arm.

The Kelly children stood on the front porch waving until the last car was out of sight.

"Too bad Dad wasn't here to see this day," Mike said.

"Yeah, too bad," Tyler laughed.

"What are you two laughing about?" Cala demanded.

"I just had this crazy mental picture of Dad driving down the road and seeing Jonah's rig with Mom's name on it."

"I wonder where he is?" Cala said.

"Probably on some South Sea island with his laptop scamming someone. His loss. Our gain," Tyler said.

"Mrs. Posy was right when she said family is the most

important thing in the world. Well, she didn't say those words exactly, but that's what she meant. We got the best, right guys?" Cala said.

"For once this sister of mine is right," Mike said.

"When you're right, you're right," Tyler said.

"Let's go out back and wake up Mom and Woodie. We need to drink a toast to this family," Cala said.

"Not without us," Pete said, pointing to Carol, Dillon, and the girls. "We belong to this family, too, you know."

"We're the best," Emily said.

"You got that right, kiddo," her father said, swinging her up on his shoulders.

The Kelly children looked around. As one, they said, "It doesn't get any better than this."

DON'T MISS FERN MICHAELS'S NEW PAPERBACK!

For generations, the Windsors have lived on the family's estate in Crestwood, South Carolina, as intertwined with local life as sweet tea and pecan pie. Now, on the anniversary of her daughter Emily's death, Sarabess Windsor believes she may be the last one to carry the family name—unless she can find her second daughter, Trinity, who disappeared fifteen years ago.

Trinity grew up as Trinity Henderson, adopted by the Windsor foreman and his wife. She ran away at fifteen and hasn't been seen in Crestwood since. But the town has never forgotten her . . . especially not handsome lawyer Jake Forrest.

Trinity swore never to return to Crestwood. But some ties—to a place, to a past, to the people we once were and dreams we once had—can never be fully broken. And as family secrets are revealed, and desires old and new come to light, Trinity may discover the one thing she never expected to find in Crestwood: a place to call home at last.

Turn the page for a special preview of
UP CLOSE AND PERSONAL by Fern Michaels,
a Zebra paperback on sale
in April 2009!

Prologue

The hour was late, the middle of the night to be precise, and the silence was so total it was ominous. The woman standing at the window stared out at the dark night. Here and there she could see tiny pinpricks of light, but she had no idea what they were. She could also see her reflection in the dark window as well as the entire room behind her.

The woman closed her eyes and wondered if she would ever sleep again. How long could a person go without sleeping? She should know the answer. Why didn't she know? When she opened her eyes she could see the reflection of a woman standing in the middle of the open doorway. She was still as a statue.

The woman knew that the figure in the open doorway wasn't going to speak until she was spoken to. Strange how she knew that and yet didn't know how long a person could go without sleep. "Did you do as I asked?"

The woman waited for a response. None came. "Grace, I'm speaking to you. Did you do what I asked you to do?"

Five seconds passed, then five more seconds before Grace said, "Yes."

The woman at the window turned. She peered at Grace, and said, "You sound unsure. You can't lie to me, Grace. I gave you enough money to put your four boys through Ivy League colleges. When you told me your husband had medical problems I gave you enough money to buy a small lake house so you could both retire. With the additional money you demanded, you can both live quite comfortably for the rest of your lives. Now, I am going to ask you again. Did you do what I asked you to do?"

The woman turned back to the window. She stiffened when she heard the single word, "Yes."

"Thank you, Grace. I'll be leaving in a few hours. Thanks to you, I'll be able to leave with a lighter heart. I don't ever want to see you again. I don't want our paths to cross again. It will be best if you never return to this state again. When you leave you will follow all my instructions to the letter. Do we understand each other, Grace?"

"Yes, ma'am, we understand each other."

The woman watched Grace Finnegan's reflection in the window as she left the room, closing the door behind her. Long ago she had committed Grace's face to memory; not that she had any intention of remembering her in the days to come. There was no need to say good-bye. After all, they weren't friends. Business associates, if you will. She banished the picture of Grace Finnegan from her mind as she continued to stare out at the tiny dots of light. Soon the sun would rise, and she'd walk away from this place and never look back.

1

It was a beautiful summer day, but the agitated woman pacing and kneading her hands barely noticed. Warm, golden sunshine flooded the sunroom where she was pacing, doing its best to warm the trembling woman. As hard as she tried, she couldn't avoid the gallery of pictures that lined one wall. She knew she shouldn't have come here this morning, of all days. Yet she'd carried her coffee cup in with the intention of sitting on one of the rattan chairs. Not to think. Never to think. She knew it was impossible, but she'd come anyway. The sunroom had been Emily's favorite room in the whole house.

Once this room had held a life-size giraffe, easels, paints, brushes, a blackboard and pastel chalks, a television, a pink polka-dotted sleeping bag with the name EMILY embroidered across the front in huge, white silky letters. An oversize toy box, also with the name EMILY stenciled on it, was stuffed with animals and assorted toys. Deep, comfortable furniture suitable for a sickly little girl had been covered in all the colors of the rainbow, just waiting for her to sit or lie down with her storybooks.

Once, a long time ago, a hundred years ago, a lifetime ago, this had been Emily's favorite room. Before she had become bedridden.

Tears puddled up in Sarabess Windsor's eyes. Why had she come in here? She looked around for her coffee cup. She reached for it and sipped the cold brew. Okay, she'd had some coffee. Now it was time to leave. But could she walk out of this room today? Of course she could. She had to.

Sarabess looked at herself in the mirror that hung on the back of the door leading into a small lavatory. She'd taken exceptional pains with her dress. She was wearing her grandmother's pearls, her mother's pearl earrings, and a mint-green linen dress that so far was unwrinkled. If she sat down, it would wrinkle. She wanted to look put together when Rifkin Forrest arrived, and part of that put-together look did not include tears. Every silky gray hair was in place. Her makeup was flawless; her unshed tears hadn't destroyed her mascara. Just because she was sixty didn't mean she had to *look* sixty. The last time he'd been to the house, Rif had told her she didn't look a day over fifty. Rif always said kind things. Rif said kind things because he'd loved her forever.

Sarabess turned around at the door, seeing the sunroom as it was. Other than the gallery of pictures, all traces of Emily were gone. Now the room held rattan furniture covered with a bright-colored fabric. Dozens of green plants and young trees could be seen through the wall-to-wall windows. Overhead, two paddle fans whirred softly. A wet bar sat in one corner. She was the only one who ever came into this room. Once a year on this date she unlocked the door, walked into the room, and allowed herself ten minutes to grieve. Most times she cried for the rest of the day. For weeks afterward she wasn't herself. Still, she put herself through it because she didn't want to forget. As if a mother could ever forget the death of her child.

Sarabess closed and locked the door. Maybe she would never go into the room again. Maybe she should think about moving away. But she did not see how she could. Emily was buried here in the family mausoleum. She could never leave her firstborn. Why did she even think it was a possibility? Then there was Mitzi Granger lurking on the fringe of her life. Even Rif couldn't do anything about *squirrelly* Mitzi. Something had to be done about Mitzi.

The Windsors had lived on Windsor Hill in Crestwood, South Carolina, for hundreds of years. She was the last of the Windsors, though only by marriage. Then again, maybe she wasn't the last of the Windsors. She would have to wait for time to give her an answer.

As the mistress of Windsor Hill walked down the hallway toward the heavy beveled-glass front door, she realized she'd left her coffee cup in the sunroom. Well, it would have to stay there for another year. Or, until she felt brave enough to unlock the door and enter the room that was simply too full of memories. At the end of the hallway, she opened the door and walked out onto the verandah. She looked around as though seeing it for the very first time. She was surprised to see that the gardener had hung the giant ferns, cleaned the wicker furniture, laid down new fiber rugs, and arranged the clay pots of colorful petunias and geraniums. Even the six paddle fans had been cleaned and waxed.

How was it possible she hadn't noticed? Because she was so wrapped up in herself, that was why. She tried to remember the last time she'd sat out here with a glass of lemonade. When she couldn't come up with any answer, she started to pace the long verandah, which wrapped around the entire house. Where was Rifkin? She looked down at her diamond-studded watch. He was ten minutes late. Rif was never late. Never. She wondered if his lateness was an omen of things to come.

For the first time since getting up, she was aware of the golden June day as she stared out at the Windsor grounds. Once the endless fields had produced cotton and tobacco. Now, they produced watermelons, pumpkins, and tomatoes that were shipped coast to coast. The acres of pecan trees went on as far as the eye could see. The pecans, too, were shipped all over the country. On the lowest plateau of the hill, cows grazed, hence the Windsor Dairy. Horses trotted in their paddock. There was a time when she'd been an accomplished horsewoman. Once there had been a pony named Beauty and a little red cart that carried Emily around the yard. Just like Emily, they were gone, too.

Sarabess heard the powerful engine then. She looked

down at her watch once more. Twenty-three minutes late. What would be Rif's excuse this fine Monday morning? Did it even matter? He was here now.

When the Mercedes stopped in front of the steps leading to the verandah, Sarabess waved a greeting before she rang the little bell on one of the tables next to a wicker chair—Martha's signal that she should serve coffee on the verandah. Sarabess walked back to the top of the steps to wait for Rif's light kiss on her cheek. She smiled when she realized there was to be no explanation as to why he was late. Rif hated to make explanations. It was the lawyer in him. She motioned to one of the chairs and sat down across from the attorney.

He was tall and tanned from the golf course. His hair was gun-metal gray. His eyes were sharp and summer blue and crinkled at the corners when he smiled. She loved it when he smiled at her. An intimate smile, she thought. Because he was semiretired, Rif felt no need for a three-piece suit on his days off. He was dressed in creased khakis and a bright yellow T-shirt. His only concession to his profession was the briefcase he was never without. He dropped it next to his chair before sitting down. His voice was deep and pleasant when he said, "You're looking particularly fine this morning, Sarabess."

"Why thank you, counselor. You look rather fit yourself this fine morning. Are you playing golf today?"

"Unless you have something important you need taken care of. You sounded . . . urgent when you called."

"It's time, Rif."

The attorney didn't bother to pretend he didn't know what she was talking about. He knew his old friend was waiting for him to say something, but he opted for silence. Sarabess raised an eyebrow in question. Instead, he reached for the cup of coffee the old housekeeper poured for him. He sipped appreciatively.

Sarabess set her own cup on the table. "I want you to hire someone to find her. It's time. And it's also time to do something about Mitzi. I . . . I want her taken care of once and for all. Do we understand each other, Rifkin?"

Rifkin. Using his full name meant Sarabess *was* serious.

Rifkin watched as a tiny brown bird flew into one of the ferns. He knew the little bird was preparing her nest. "Let it be, Sarabess. You need to stop obsessing about . . . about Mitzi. There's nothing I can do legally, and we both know it."

Sarabess leaned forward. "How can you say that to me?"

"I can say it because I'm your friend. Mitzi aside, you should have called me fifteen years ago to ask me to find her. I warned you this would happen. Now, it's too late."

Sarabess stood up. "It's never too late. You hounded me daily for years to do what I'm asking you to do now, and suddenly you're telling me it's too late! I don't believe that. If you won't do it, I'll find someone who will. Mitzi may have me on a short leash financially, but I am not without influence in this town. As you well know, Rifkin."

Suddenly he felt sick to his stomach. "You waited fifteen years too long. If you think for one minute that that girl is going to forgive you, you are wrong." Rif brought the coffee cup to his lips. He didn't think he'd ever tasted anything so bitter.

"She's my daughter. I'm her mother."

Rif sighed and closed his eyes. His voice was so low Sarabess had to strain to hear it. "You gave birth to her. You were never her mother. You were Emily's mother. As your attorney, I'm advising you to let matters rest. As your friend and lover, I'm asking you to let matters rest. Please, Sarabess, listen to me."

"I have no intention of following your advice, Rifkin. It's time."

"For you, perhaps. Not for Trinity. If she wanted to see you, she knows where you are. She could have come home anytime. The fact that she hasn't called or written in fifteen years means she doesn't have any interest in seeing you."

"She doesn't even know Harold died. She should know

that," Sarabess said coldly. "Mitzi knows. If you could just get inside that . . . that *squirrelly* head of hers, we could find Trinity in a heartbeat."

"Now, almost fifteen years after the fact, you think Trinity should know her father died! I can't believe I'm hearing what I'm hearing. I advise you to think seriously about what you are contemplating, Sarabess. You gave birth to Trinity so you could use her bone marrow so that Emily would live. Then you gave that child to your foreman and his wife to raise. You hauled her up here one day a year on Princess Emily's birthday. You had the Hendersons dress her up like a poor relation; then you sent her away after the party. Not to mention the humiliation of those countless other command performances—whenever Emily pitched a fit. You're delusional if you think Trinity will want to see you."

"I had no other choice. Emily would have died. Because of . . . of that . . . procedure, I had thirteen more years with my darling daughter. Thirteen years! I wouldn't trade those thirteen years for anything in the world. When . . . When I explain things to Trinity, I'm sure she will understand. She is my daughter, after all. She has only one mother. We all have only one mother." Despite Sarabess's efforts, her voice was colder than chipped ice, her eyes colder still.

Is he buying into my explanation? At first blush, it doesn't seem like it. Well, that will have to change quickly.

"I don't care how much it hurts, Sarabess, but you were never that girl's mother. You didn't sit with her at night when she was sick. You didn't take her to church, you never took her shopping. You never once looked at her report card, never went to a school meeting. You never read her a bedtime story or tucked her into bed. Half the time you couldn't remember what her name was. Emily didn't like her, either, thanks to you. Guilt is what took Harold to an early grave, and we both know it. I guess you're just a lot tougher.

"Trinity has never touched the trust fund your husband, her father, set up for her. I believe that Harold told her about it when she was quite young. I cannot even begin to imagine what that young girl thought at the time if, indeed, he did tell her. Maybe the knowledge of that monstrous trust fund was what made her run away. At least that's Mitzi's theory. If so, apparently Trinity didn't want any part of it, you, or Harold. Let it be."

Sarabess fingered the pearls at her neck. She felt choked up at her lover's words. "When did you get so ugly, Rifkin Forrest?"

"Ten minutes ago, when I saw what you were about this morning. Today of all days. Why didn't you make the decision a week ago, a month ago, yesterday? Today is the anniversary of Emily's death. In seven months Trinity will be thirty and will come into the trust," Rif said, his voice sounding ominous.

Sarabess didn't think Rif's voice could get any colder, but it did. She actually shivered in the humid June air.

"You went in that room, you looked at the pictures, you relived the thirteen years that Trinity gave your daughter. You probably cried, and then you decided maybe this was a good time to find your other daughter. The thought probably crossed your mind that you might have grandchildren somewhere. That's the part I want to believe.

"The other part, having to do with the trust fund that will revert to you if Trinity dies or isn't found in time to take possession of her trust, is not something I want to think about today. I'm sorry, but I have to leave. I have a tee time in thirty minutes."

Sarabess was speechless. "You're leaving?"

"Yes, I'm leaving. I don't want any part of upsetting that young woman's life for your own selfish desires."

Sarabess started to cry. "Please, Rif, don't leave. I . . . I'm not doing this for me. You may be right—it may too late— but I won't know if I don't try. I just want to find her. I won't invade her life if it looks like I . . . if . . . she isn't interested. I thought that Jake," she said, referring to Rif's son and law partner, "might do the search. He used to play with Trinity when they were little children. Emily used to watch them from the sunroom. She was so envious."

A linen handkerchief found its way to her eyes. It all sounded good to her ears. It should—she'd rehearsed this little speech for hours in front of the mirror.

Rifkin sighed wearily. "It always comes back to Emily, doesn't it?"

"Yes, it always comes back to Emily. You can't expect me to turn thirty years off and on like you'd turn off a light switch. I made a mistake. I want to try and make it right." *That sounds good, too,* Sarabess thought smugly.

"Jesus, Sarabess, you didn't just make a mistake, you made the Queen Mother of all mistakes. Now you want the child you threw away back. I'm sorry, it just doesn't work that way. On top of that, it's too late."

"Stop saying that. I didn't throw Trinity away. I . . . What I did was pay the Hendersons to take care of her. I couldn't do it. I was fighting for Emily's life. Trinity had a roof over her head, good food, adequate medical care. If she was neglected, as you say, it was only by me and my husband. I will concede the point that the child needed a mother, and that's where I failed her. If she . . . If I had brought her here to the big house, she would have been raised by servants. At least with the Hendersons she had a normal life. She wanted for nothing, and don't try to tell me otherwise."

Sarabess had said these words so often, they sounded truthful to her ears. She struggled to cry. She whipped the handkerchief past her eyelashes as she watched Rifkin carefully. She needed him.

"Too bad you couldn't pay the Hendersons to love her. When are you going to factor in Trinity's trust fund?"

"The fund has nothing to do with this. The Hendersons did love Trinity in their own way. They are plain, hardworking people. They're not demonstrative. That doesn't mean they didn't love Trinity. They raised her for fifteen years. There was feeling there. Even as sick as he was, and living with *that woman,* Harold told me they were heartbroken when Trinity ran away. Harold would never have lied about something like that."

Rifkin watched the little brown bird as she dived into the fern with a piece of string in her beak. Preparing her nest for her young. *That's how it's supposed to be,* he thought. *Even the birds know about motherhood.* "Were you broken-hearted, Sarabess? Did Trinity's running away affect you in any way?"

He was just saying words, words he'd said hundreds of times. It was a game, pure and simple.

Sarabess drew a deep breath as she fingered her pearls. "No. It barely registered. I was still mourning Emily. Nothing registered. Nothing." *Such a lie,* she thought.

"I have to leave now, or I'll miss my tee time."

"Well, a tee time is certainly important. Even I understand that. Run along, Rifkin. Enjoy your golf game," Sarabess said, in an icy voice.

Rifkin refused to be baited. He waved as he descended the steps. "Thanks for the coffee."

Sarabess wanted to tell him to go to hell, but she bit down on her bottom lip instead. Her eyes filled again. Everything Rif had said was true. Tomorrow she would think about everything he'd just said. Everything she'd been thinking about for the past fifteen years. Tomorrow. Then again, maybe she wouldn't.

Today was Emily's day. Today she had to go to the cemetery to talk to Emily.

Tomorrow was another day. Rif would come around; he always did.